Gil Addison show... for stripping.

If he'd undressed any slower, Bailey would've ripped the shirt off. But she had asked for this. All she could do was watch in torment.

With her training, Bailey could bring most men down. But Gil...Gil was the real deal. His body rippled with muscle.

"Cat got your tongue?" he taunted.

Her legs shaking, she curled her arm around the bedpost. "Just admiring the view." She touched his chest. "I want to please you."

"You do, in every way. I love your strength, your integrity. The way you treat my son."

"He's lucky to have you."

His finger on her lips silenced her. "I spend all my time being Cade's father. Tonight...tonight I'm just a man. A man who wants you."

* * *

Beneath the Stetson
is a Texas Cattleman's Club:
The Missing Mogul novel
Love and scandal meet in Royal, Texas!

BENEATH
THE STETSON

BY
JANICE MAYNARD

MILLS
BOON

Published in Great Britain 2014
by Mills & Boon, an imprint of Harlequin (UK) Limited,
Eton House, 18-24 Paradise Road, Richmond, Surrey, TW9 1SR

© 2014 Harlequin Books S.A.

Special thanks and acknowledgement to Janice Maynard for her contribution to the Texas Cattleman's Club: The Missing Mogul miniseries.

ISBN: 978 0 263 91453 5

51-0114

Harlequin (UK) Limited's policy is to use papers that are natural, renewable and recyclable products and made from wood grown in sustainable forests. The logging and manufacturing processes conform to the legal environmental regulations of the country of origin.

Printed and bound in Spain
by Blackprint CPI, Barcelona

Janice Maynard is a *USA TODAY* bestselling author who lives in beautiful east Tennessee with her husband. She holds a BA from Emory and Henry College and an MA from East Tennessee State University. In 2002 Janice left a fifteen-year career as an elementary school teacher to pursue writing full-time. Now her first love is creating sexy, character-driven, contemporary romance stories.

Janice loves to travel and enjoys using those experiences as settings for books. Hearing from readers is one of the best perks of the job! Visit her website, www.janicemaynard.com, and follow her on Facebook and Twitter.

For my wonderful Texas friends,
Karen, Rob, Elaine and Bob. Thank you for the fun,
the laughter and the "tall" tales of life in Texas.
I count you among my blessings!

One

Gil Addison didn't like Feds. Even when they came wrapped in pretty packages. Perhaps it was the trace of Comanche blood in his veins that kept an atavistic memory alive…all those years of government promises made and broken. Gil was a white man living in a white man's world, no doubt about it. Nothing much of his Native American heritage lingered except for his black hair, brown eyes and olive skin.

But the distrust remained.

He stood inside the house, hand on an edge of the curtain, and watched as a standard-issue dark sedan made its way down the long driveway. Technically, the woman for whom he waited wasn't a Fed. She was a state investigator. But she had been trained by Feds, and that was close enough.

"Who is it, Daddy?"

His four-year-old son, Cade, endlessly curious, wrapped

an arm around his father's leg. Gil glanced down at the boy, smiling in spite of his unsettled emotions. "A lady who wants to talk to me. Don't worry. It won't take long." He had promised Cade they would go riding today.

"Is she pretty?"

Gil raised an eyebrow. "Why would that matter?"

The child with the big, far-too-observant eyes grinned. "Well, if she is, you might want to date her and fall in love and then get married and—"

"This again?" Gil kept his hand over the boy's mouth in a mock insistence on changing the subject. He knelt and looked Cade in the eyes. "I have you. That's all I need." Single parenting was not for wimps. Sometimes it was the loneliest job in the world. And Gil wondered constantly if he was making irrevocable mistakes. He hugged his son before standing up again. "I think I've been letting you watch too much TV."

Cade pulled the curtains even farther aside and watched as the car rolled to a stop and parked. The car door opened and the woman stepped out. "She *is* pretty," Cade said, practically bouncing with the energy that never seemed to diminish.

Inwardly, Gil agreed with Cade's assessment, albeit reluctantly. Bailey Collins, despite the professional pantsuit that was as dark and unexceptional as her car, made an impression on a man. Only a few inches shy of Gil's six-one height, she carried herself with confidence. Wavy, shoulder-length brown hair glinted in the sun with red highlights. Her thick-lashed eyes were almost as dark as Gil's.

Though she was still too far away for Gil to witness those last two attributes, he had a good memory. Today was not his first encounter with Bailey Collins.

As she mounted his front steps, he opened the door, refusing to acknowledge that his heart beat faster than normal. The first time he met her, they had faced each other across a desk at Royal's police station. Even then he'd felt a potent mix of sexual hunger and resentment. But Bailey was on his turf now. He'd be calling the shots. She might think her credentials gave her power, but he was not prepared to accept them at face value.

Bailey caught her toe on the edge of the top step and stumbled, almost falling flat on her face. Fortunately, she regained her balance at the last second, because in the midst of her gyrations the door flew open, and a man she recognized all too well stood framed in the doorway.

Gil Addison.

Even as she acknowledged the jolt to her chest, she was taken aback by the presence of a second male. The man for whom she felt an unwelcome but visceral attraction was not alone. He held the hand of a small boy, most likely—according to Gil's dossier—his son. Even without written verification, she could have guessed the relationship. The young one was practically a carbon copy of his older counterpart.

The child broke free of his father's hold and stepped forward to beam at Bailey. "Welcome to the Straight Arrow," he said, holding out his hand with poignant maturity. His gap-toothed smile was infectious. "I'm Cade."

Bailey squatted, holding out her hand, as well, feeling the warmth of the small palm as it nestled briefly in hers. "Hello, Cade," she said. "I'm Bailey."

"Ms. Collins," Gil corrected with a slight frown. "I'm trying to teach him manners."

"It's not bad manners to use my first name if I offer the privilege," Bailey said evenly, rising to face the man who had already given her sleepless nights.

Cade looked back and forth between the two adults.

The thinly veiled antagonism between them was unfortunate, because Cade seemed first confused and then unhappy. The boy's chin wobbled. "I wanted my dad to like you," he whispered, staring up at Bailey with huge blue eyes that must have come from his mother.

Bailey's heart melted. "Your dad and I like each other just fine," she told Cade, daring Gil to disagree. "Sometimes grown-ups get frustrated about things, but that doesn't mean we're angry." Even as an adult of thirty-three, she remembered vague impressions of her parents arguing. Yelling. Saying wretched, bitter words that couldn't be unheard.

Bailey knew what it was like to be a child with no power to shape the course of events. It was because she *did* understand Cade's dismay, that she summoned an almost-genuine smile and aimed it in Gil's direction. "Thank you for seeing me today. If we can sit down for a few moments, I promise not to take up too much of your time."

With Cade standing squarely in between them, there was nothing for Gil to do but agree. He ruffled his son's hair, love for his child and wry capitulation in his gaze as he spoke. "Why don't you join us in the kitchen, Ms. Collins? Cade and I usually have lemonade and a snack right about now."

"You may as well call me Bailey, too," she muttered, not sure if he heard her or not. She followed the two of them back through the house to the historic but updated kitchen. Gil had taken over the property from his parents when they retired and settled in Austin. The senior Addisons had inherited the Straight Arrow from Gil's grandparents. The ranch, whose name ironically described its owner to a T, was an enormous operation.

Four years ago when Gil's wife committed suicide, Gil had hired an army of extra ranch hands and housekeepers, so he could be the primary caregiver for his toddler son. Bailey knew the facts of the situation because she had investigated the man …and admired him for his devotion. But that didn't make her any more forgiving of the way he had stonewalled her in their earlier interviews. Even though her file on Gil Addison was thorough and extensive, she was no closer to understanding the man himself.

Cade pulled out a chair for Bailey, sealing the deal. The kid was irresistible. Clearly Gil was not kidding when he mentioned teaching manners. Something about witnessing the boy's interaction with his father made Bailey's assessment of Gil shift and refocus. Surely a man who could be so caring and careful with a child was not all bad.

Bailey's own exposure to male parenting was more like a metaphorical slap up the side of the head. *Toe the line. Don't complain. Achieve. Be self-sufficient.* Even the most generous assessment of her father's motives left no room for seeing him as anything other than a bully and a tyrant—presumably the reason Bailey's mother had walked out, leaving her young daughter behind.

Bailey sat down somewhat self-consciously, and placed her cell phone on the table. While Gil busied himself retrieving glasses from the pine cabinets and slicing apples to go along with peanut butter, Cade grilled Bailey. "Do you have any good games on your phone?"

His hopeful expression made her grin. "A few."

"Angry Birds?"

"Yes. Are you any good at it?"

Cade shot a glance at his dad and lowered his voice. "He thinks that too much time with electronics will make me…um…" Clearly searching for the desired word, Cade trailed off, his brow furrowed.

"Brain dead." Gil set the glasses on the table and returned with the plate of apples. Taking a chair directly across from Bailey, he sat down and turned his son's hand over, palm up. The little fingers were grimy. "Go wash up, Cade. Ms. Collins and I will wait for you."

When Cade disappeared down the hall to the bathroom, Bailey smiled. "He's wonderful. And unexpectedly mature for a four-year-old."

"He'll be five soon. He didn't have too many opportunities to be around other children until I began bringing him to the daycare center at the club occasionally, so that accounts for the adult conversation. As much as I'll miss him, I think it will be good for him to start kindergarten this fall."

Bailey cocked her head. "I may have misjudged you, Gil Addison. I think you *do* have a heart."

"Don't confuse parental love for weakness, Ms. Collins. I won't be manipulated into helping you take down one of my friends."

The sudden attack startled her. Gil's classic features were set in grim lines, any trace of softness gone. "You really don't trust me at all, do you?" she asked, her voice husky with regret at this evidence of his animosity.

"I don't trust your kind," he clarified, his tone terse. "Alex Santiago was kidnapped, but now he's been found. Sooner or later he'll get his memory back and be able to tell us who took him. Why can't you people drop it and leave us here in Royal to clean up our own messes?"

Bailey glanced toward the hallway, realizing that Cade could return at any moment. "Surely you're not that naive," she said quietly. "Because Alex has no memory of what happened to him, trouble could strike again at any time. We have no choice but to track down his abductors. Surely you can see that."

"What I don't see is why you think anyone I know is responsible."

"Alex was well-liked in Royal, though obviously he had at least one enemy. *You* know a lot of people. Somewhere in the midst of all that I hope to find the truth. It's my job, Gil. And I'm good at it. All I need is your help."

Cade popped into the room, the front of his shirt damp from his ablutions. "I'm really hungry," he said. At a nod from his father, he scooped up two apple slices and started eating.

As Bailey watched, Gil offered her a piece and took one himself. His sharp white teeth bit into the fruit with a crunch. She tried to eat, but the food stuck in her throat. She needed Gil on her side. And she needed him to trust her. Perhaps that would require time.

Biting her lip, she put down her uneaten snack and tried the lemonade instead. As father and son chatted about mundane matters, she strove for composure. Usually it took a lot to rattle her. But for some reason, winning Gil's approval was important.

When his phone rang, he glanced at the number and grimaced. "Sorry, Ms. Collins. I need to take this in private. I won't be long."

Cade glanced up at his dad as Gil stood. "Don't worry, Daddy. I'll entertain her."

When Gil returned thirty minutes later, he felt a pinch of guilt for abandoning Bailey to his son's clutches. Not all women were good with children, and Bailey struck him as more of a focused career woman than a nurturer. When he crossed the threshold into the kitchen, he pulled up short. There at the table, right where he had left them, were Cade and Bailey. Only now, they were sitting side by side, their heads bent over Bailey's phone.

The lemonade glasses were empty, as was the plate that had held apples.

Bailey shook her head. "Remember the angles," she said. "Don't just fire it off willy-nilly."

When Gil's son gazed up at Bailey, Gil's heart fractured. Never had he seen a boy so starved for feminine attention. Despite Gil's best efforts at being a perfect parent, nothing could substitute for the love of a mother. If Gil were not careful, Cade would latch onto Bailey and create an embarrassing situation for all of them.

Gil cleared his throat. "Cade. If you'll give me half an hour to speak with Ms. Collins about some grown-up business, I promise you we'll leave for our ride immediately after that."

Cade never looked up from his game. "Sure, Dad. Let me just finish this one—"

Gil took the phone and handed it to Bailey. "You have permission to use the computer in my study. Now scram."

"Yes, sir." Cade gave Bailey a cheeky grin on his way out the door. "Will you say goodbye before you leave?"

Bailey rose to her feet and glanced at Gil.

Cade's father nodded. "I'll let you know when we're done."

In Cade's absence an uncomfortable silence reigned. The little boy's exuberant personality had served to soften the edges of Gil's aggressive displeasure.

Bailey hesitated, searching for a way to break the ice.

Gil did it for her. He held out an arm. "Since Cade is in my office, we might as well step onto the back porch. If that's okay with you," he added stiffly.

Bailey nodded. "Of course." The January weather was picture-perfect, and as was often the case during the winter, a bit erratic, as well. Last week Royal had endured storms and temperatures in the mid-fifties. Today the thermometer was forecast to hit eighty, almost a record.

As they stepped outside, Bailey had to smile. The

Straight Arrow was an enormous, thriving cattle operation. In addition to its efficiency and profitability, every aspect of the ranch's physical appearance was neat and aesthetically pleasing to the eye. It took money to carry out such attention to detail. But Gil had money. Lots of it. Which was a good thing, because his wealth meant he had the luxury of spending time with his son.

Watching and listening to Cade, Bailey understood how very well Gil had managed to give his son emotional security. The child was bright, friendly and well adjusted. Growing up without a mother was no picnic. But Gil's parenting had mitigated Cade's loss as much as was possible.

Gil remained standing, so Bailey followed suit. If she had made herself comfortable in one of the cushioned wicker chairs, he would have towered over her. She suspected he would like that.

Bailey, however, had a job to do. She wouldn't be cowed by Gil's fiercely masculine personality. She worked in a world where men still dominated the profession. Self-preservation demanded she be tough on the outside, even if she sometimes felt as if she was playing a part.

Gil fired the first shot. "I thought you went back to Dallas."

She shrugged. "Only for a week. The case is still open. After I finished the earlier interviews, my boss pulled me to work briefly on another project. But we're in a lull now, and they want me to do some more digging."

"You didn't do so well the last time," he mocked.

Bailey met his hot gaze with composure. "Investigations take time. And just so you know…I get it, Gil."

"Get what?"

"You were insulted to be on the suspect list. I impugned your honor, and you're pissed. Have I hit the nail on the head?" She challenged him deliberately, not willing to play the bad guy indefinitely.

His jaw was granite. "I'd think your time would be better spent questioning the criminal element instead of harassing upstanding members of the community."

Her lips twitched. Hurt masculine pride was a tricky thing. "I have extensive training in psychological evaluation. And you know very well that you were never a suspect. It was my job to speak to anyone and everyone who knew Alex…to look for clues, for any shred of information, no matter how minute, that might help solve the kidnapping."

"And yet you came up with nothing."

She tensed, tired of being under attack. "Alex is back in Royal," she pointed out.

"No thanks to you."

His mockery lit the fuse of her temper. She could take what he was dishing out, but she didn't have to like it. "You have no idea what goes on behind the scenes. And I don't have to justify myself to you. Can we please get back to the matter at hand?"

"And that would be?"

As they had exited the house, Gil had scooped up a well-worn Stetson and dropped it on his head with one smooth motion that bespoke the love of a cowboy for his hat. Now the brim shadowed his eyes.

Bailey was not immune to the picture he made. In well-washed denims that rode low on his hips and molded to his long, muscular legs, he was a walking, talking ad for testosterone. His chamois shirt must have been hand-tailored, because it managed to accommodate his broad shoulders nicely. Gil Addison was the real deal, right down to his expensive, though scuffed, leather boots.

Bailey felt the physical pull. Acknowledged it. Experienced a pang of regret for something that would never be. It had been a long time since she had met a man so appealing. But Gil didn't much like her, and her newest assignment was not going to improve matters.

With an inward sigh for her barren love life, she cut to the chase. "I need access to the membership files at the Texas Cattleman's Club."

"Absolutely not." He bowed up almost visibly.

Bailey leaned against the porch railing, her hands behind her. It was either that or fasten them around Gil's tanned neck and squeeze. The man was infuriating. "I have all the necessary warrants and paperwork," she said mildly. "But I'd prefer not to go in guns blazing. Why don't you be a gentleman for once and politely invite me to the club as your guest?"

The word he muttered made her wince. "I'm the *president* of the TCC," he pointed out…as if she didn't already know. His scowl was black. "People trust me with their secrets. How is it going to look if I turn all that over to an outsider?"

That last jab hurt, but Bailey held her ground. "You don't really have a choice…even if you do have a judge or two tucked away in your back pocket. These orders come down from on high. I'm going to comb through those files one way or another. You can either make my life miserable or you can cooperate. Your choice. But I *will* get the information I need."

Two

Gil ripped his hat from his head and ran a hand across his damp brow. It was January, damn it. No reason in the world the heat and humidity should be this bad.

Bailey, on the other hand, despite wearing an unflattering suit jacket, seemed cool and collected. She watched him warily, as if he were a dangerous rattlesnake about to bite.

What she didn't know was that he *had* fantasized about nibbling her…all the way from her delicate jawline to the vulnerable place where her throat disappeared inside that boring blouse. His body tightened. The woman probably had no idea that her no-nonsense clothing revved his engine. Instead of focusing on the government-employee quasi uniform, he imagined stripping it off her and baring that long, lean body to his gaze.

His sex thickened and lifted, making his jeans uncomfortably tight. With a silent curse, he stared out across the acres of land that belonged to him as far as the eye could see. Searching desperately for a diversion, he fell back on the universal topic of weather.

"Are you familiar with the Civil War general Philip Sheridan?" he asked, keeping his body half-turned to avoid embarrassing them both.

Bailey wrinkled her nose. "History wasn't my strong suit in school, but yes…I've heard of him."

"After the war, Sheridan was assigned to a post in south Texas. It's reported he said that if he owned Texas and hell, he would rent out Texas and live in hell."

"I'm surprised you would mention it. I thought it was heresy to insult the mother ship. All you native Texans are pretty arrogant."

"We have reason to be…despite the heat," he added ruefully, replacing his hat and wanting desperately to wrap this up before he pounced on her.

"So I'm to believe that everything in Texas is bigger and better?"

Shock immobilized him. Was Bailey flirting with him? Surely not. He glanced over his shoulder at her. As far as he could tell, nothing in her demeanor was the least bit sexual. Too bad. "Yes," he said curtly. "I thought you would know that, being from Dallas."

"I'm not *from* Dallas. My dad was in the army. We lived all over the world. Dallas is where I'm assigned at the moment."

"So where do you call home?"

Seconds passed. Two, maybe three. For a brief moment he saw bleak regret in her brown-eyed gaze. "Not anywhere, really."

Such rootlessness was hard for him to imagine. Texas was as much a part of his lifeblood as breathing. Sensing her unease with the topic, he turned to face her, at last somewhat in control of himself. "Well," he said laconically, "at least if you weren't born here, you came as soon as you could."

Bailey, arms wrapped around her waist, smiled. "I guess you could say that."

He pursed his lips. "Apparently, I have no choice about your interference. Is that what you're telling me?" The facts of the matter still stuck in his craw.

"You've got it." Though seeing him admit defeat must have pleased her, Bailey's expression remained neutral.

"Very well. Meet me at the club at ten in the morning. I'll show you where to get started."

"I'm a highly trained computer specialist, Gil. I shouldn't have to take up more than a week of your life."

Too bad. He glanced at his watch. "Come say goodbye to Cade."

In his office, he watched, perturbed, as once again his son lit up at seeing their visitor.

Gil's son beamed. "I unlocked three more levels, Bailey."

She nodded. "Good for you."

Cade looked at his dad. "Are you gonna call her *Bailey?*"

"I suppose I will," Gil admitted. "She's going to be around for a while."

Cade grinned charmingly. "That's good."

Gil pinched the boy's ear. "Behave, brat. I don't need your help finding women."

Bailey's face turned crimson, affording Gil a definite sense of satisfaction. It was fine by him if she felt uncomfortable. It was only fair. She was messing with his life from stem to stern in all sorts of ways. Not the least of which was his recalcitrant libido. The sooner she finished what she had to do and left town, the better.

* * *

Bailey arrived at the Texas Cattleman's Club fifteen minutes early the following morning. A heat wave still held the area in an unseasonable grip. Though by no means reaching the brutal temperatures of July and August, the day was plenty warm. Which meant that the winter clothing Bailey had brought with her was stifling.

Deciding she could maintain a professional demeanor *without* her blazer, she stripped it off and laid it carefully in the backseat of the car. Rolling up the sleeves of her white silk blouse, she breathed a sigh of relief as she immediately felt cooler.

In all honesty, part of her warmth stemmed from the prospect of facing Gil Addison again. Gil was in the clear as far as the investigation went, but she was going to have to work with him to some extent in order to do her job. The fact that she was attracted to him complicated things.

As she approached the club, she assessed the physical features automatically. Built around 1910, the large, rambling, single-story building was constructed of dark wood and stone with a tall slate roof. For over a century, it had been an entirely male enclave. In the past couple of years, however, a handful of women had finally been admitted as official members. During her stay in Royal, Bailey had heard rumblings of discontent. Not everyone thought change was a good idea.

Despite her early arrival, Gil was waiting for her in the lobby. Guests were admitted only in the company of a member. She wondered if Gil felt he was betraying his position by bringing Bailey into the mix.

She greeted him quietly and looked around. High ceilings gave a sense of spaciousness even as dark floors and big leather-upholstered furniture created a cozy, masculine space. "Nice," she said. "Is Cade with you?"

Gil pointed to the room just to the left of the entryway. "The old billiards room has been converted into the new day care center. I promised Cade if he behaved nicely for a couple of hours, he could join us for lunch."

"I'd like that," she said. "Your son is a pretty awesome kid."

"I happen to think so." He shoved his hands in his back pockets. Today, perhaps in deference to his position as president, he wore a tweed blazer over a white dress shirt. He hadn't given up his jeans, however. Although Gil hadn't worn his hat inside his own home, apparently within the walls of the club, a Stetson was de rigueur.

It wasn't fair, Bailey thought desperately. How was she supposed to be businesslike when everything about him made her weak in the knees? Well, *almost* everything, she amended mentally. His arrogance was hard to take. She had come up against Gil's bullheadedness in her initial interview with him. Pushing for answers had been like a futile military assault against well-fortified defenses.

Gil was a man accustomed to steering his own course. Though she didn't pick up any vibes that he scoffed at the idea of a woman working in law enforcement, nevertheless she suspected he didn't like having to cooperate.

As they walked down the hall toward Gil's TCC office, she asked the question that she should have asked the day before. "Have you been to see Alex since he's been found?"

Gil pulled a key from his pocket and unlocked the solid oak door. Ushering Bailey inside, he nodded. "I did…but since he's lost his memory, the visit was rather pointless. He had no clue who I was."

"Were you close before he disappeared?"

"Close enough. Not bosom buddies, but we knew each other pretty well."

"You probably should go see him again when you have

a chance," she said. "You never know when a face or voice might jog something loose."

"I'll think about it...."

She placed her purse and briefcase on a low table. She and Gil were standing in what appeared to be an outer reception area. More masculine leather furniture outfitted this small space. Someone had added a stuffy arrangement of artificial flowers, perhaps hoping to soften the ambience. But with various examples of taxidermy staring down from overhead, it was hard to imagine any woman feeling at home here.

Apparently, the office itself was through the closed door a few steps away. "I don't want to snarl up your day," she said. "If you don't mind writing down the user name and password...and giving me a quick rundown of the program you use to input information, I should be able to work on my own."

Gil smiled, genuine amusement on his face. That expression alone was enough to shock her. But the momentary appearance of an honest-to-God dimple in his tanned cheek took her aback. "Did I say something funny?"

He stepped past her to open the other door. "See for yourself."

Expecting to discover the customary computer and printer equipment inside, she drew up short at the sight facing her. A dozen wooden file cabinets, four drawers high, lined the opposite wall. By the window, a deep bookshelf housed a collection of thick leather ledgers. Dust motes danced in a sunbeam that played across a patterned linoleum floor. A battered rolltop desk sat just to the left, its only adornment a brass placard that said President.

She held up her hands in defeat. "You can't be serious."

Gil leaned in the doorway, his relaxed posture in direct opposition to her own state of mind. "There's something you need to understand, Bailey. The Texas Cattleman's Club is an institution, certainly as much a part of Royal's history as the churches and the mercantile or the feed store and the saloon. Men have come here for decades to get away from wives and girlfriends…to play poker and make business deals. Anyone who walks through the door as a full member has money and influence."

"And your point?"

"Heritage and tradition are etched into the walls. The guys around here don't like change."

"Which is why the child care center drew so much controversy."

"Yes. That, and the inclusion of women. So it shouldn't come as any surprise to see how we keep records. The good old boys may have their iPads and their internet, but when it comes to the TCC, the old ways are the only ways. At least so far."

"So there's hope for modernization?"

"Maybe. But I can't force it on them. It has to be a gradual process. If I'm lucky, and if I can spin it the right way, they'll think it was their idea to begin with."

"And it won't hurt matters if a few of the old guard ride off into the sunset in the meantime."

"You said it, not me. The TCC was here before I was born, and it will be here long after I'm gone. I'm under no illusions that being president gives me any real power. It's more of an honorary title, if you want to know the truth."

"I'm sure they think a great deal of you."

His eyebrows lifted. "Why, Ms. Collins. Was that a compliment?"

The teasing grin caught her off guard. Apparently, dumping her in a dusty room full of nothing but file folders sweetened his mood. "I doubt you need compliments of *any* kind, Mr. Addison. In fact, I'm surprised your head isn't already too big for that clichéd cowboy hat."

"Don't insult my hat," he said solemnly, though his eyes were dancing. "Since I'm stuck with you for the foreseeable future, we might as well drop the formality, don't you think?"

"Does that mean you trust me now?"

"Not for a minute," he said promptly. "But I figure it's my job to keep an eye on you…Bailey."

The way he said those two syllables made her stomach curl with something that felt a lot like desire. But such an emotion was doomed to wither on the vine. Despite her unwilling host's humor, she was not deceived. Her presence at the TCC was tolerated at best.

For a man who was innocent of any wrongdoing, Gil seemed curiously suspicious of authority. Was there something in his past that made him so? What did he have to fear from Bailey? Nothing that she could see. So perhaps it was government interference in general he hated. Not a particularly uncommon attitude, especially in this neck of the woods. But she felt the sting of his disapproval nevertheless.

Maybe in time she could prove to him that she was more than an outsider meddling in his business. She liked to think they could get to a place where he regarded her as something more than a nuisance. In a tiny corner of her heart, she wondered what it would be like if she and Gil were on the same side. If no walls between them existed. If they could be just a man and a woman. Exploring the sweet lure of attraction.

"I suppose I'd better get started," she said, trying not to let him see the way her hands trembled and her breathing quickened at the thought of actually being on friendly terms with the sexy rancher.

"Start where?"

"Are you genuinely interested, or is that another suspicious question?"

He shrugged, straightening and running a hand across the back of his neck. "A little of both, I guess."

She nodded, deciding not to take offense at his honesty. "My plan is to pull all the files of the people I interviewed in the initial investigation. I'll comb through them and see if anything stands out."

"In other words, you're looking for a needle in a haystack."

"Despite what television and movies would have you believe, law enforcement is seldom glamorous."

"Why did you choose this career path?" he asked, his gaze reflecting genuine interest.

Bailey hesitated.

"Sorry," he said quickly. "None of my business."

"No. It's okay. I suppose I was debating how to answer that. As a teenager I would have told you I wanted to serve my country."

"And that's not true?"

"It *is* true, but I'm not the starry-eyed idealist I was back then. And I'm a little more self-aware, I think. I've come to understand that I do what I do because I wanted to make my father proud of me."

"I'm sure he must be."

She grimaced. "Not really. He wanted me to go into the military. He's a career army guy. But that never seemed like the right fit for me, so state law enforcement was my compromise. I thought he would come around eventually, but he hasn't."

"Parents can be shortsighted. Do you regret your choice?"

No one had ever asked her that. Her job was fulfilling

and she was good at it. But she wasn't sure it was going to be her life's work. "To be honest, I wanted to be a musician. I'm pretty good on the guitar and the piano. I took advantage of almost all my electives when I was in college to sign up for music courses."

Gil stared at her. Hard. As if trying to see inside her head. "You're an interesting person, Bailey Collins."

She might not be the most experienced woman on the planet, but she knew when a man wanted her. The look in Gil's eyes was unmistakable. There was enough fire and passion in his dark eyes to make her body go liquid with longing. She had felt the spark the first time they met and doggedly ignored it because he was a potential suspect.

But Gil was innocent, and the feelings were still there. If she encouraged his interest, things might get very intense during her time in Royal. The truth was, she was afraid that getting involved with someone who played a role in her investigation was unprofessional at best. Keeping a clear line between business and pleasure was not going to be easy.

She met his gaze reluctantly. "So are you, Gil. So are you."

He jerked when she said his name. As if her utterance of that single syllable shocked him. Now the frown returned in full force. "I have things to do," he said gruffly. "Are you all set?"

If she hadn't known better, she would have thought he was ready to beat a hasty retreat. "I'm fine," she said. "How long do I have before we meet Cade for lunch?"

"A couple of hours. He gets a snack at the center, so I made a reservation in the dining room for twelve-thirty. Does that work for you?"

"Of course. And will I be able to come back this afternoon and pick up where I left off?"

"Yes. Feel free to leave everything out. I'll lock the door when we go to eat, and no one will bother your papers."

"You're being very accommodating all of a sudden."

"I've been pretty rough on you," he admitted, his neutral gaze hard to read. "I know you're merely doing your job. I don't like it, but I suppose there's no point in shooting the messenger."

She took a step in his direction just as he did the same. Suddenly they were nose to nose in the small office. Her hands fluttered at her sides. "Thank you, Gil. Your cooperation makes my life a lot easier." She heard the huskiness in her voice and winced inwardly. Her eyes were level with his throat. They stood so close to each other she could see the hint of a dark beard on his firm, sculpted chin.

Without warning, Gil slid his hands beneath her hair, thumbs stroking her neck. He tipped her face up to his, their lips mere centimeters apart. His beautiful eyes teemed with turbulent emotion "You're going to be trouble, aren't you, Bailey Collins?"

"Why would you say that?" she asked, knowing full well what he meant but wanting to hear him admit that the attraction wasn't one-sided.

His lips brushed hers in a caress that could barely even be called a kiss. She leaned into him, wanting more.

But straight-arrow Gil Addison was a tough man. "Women and government are always trouble. When you put both in the same package, there's likely to be hell to pay."

Three

Bailey leaned against the desk for a full three minutes after Gil left the room, her legs like spaghetti. She had wanted to know if he had felt it, too, the heated connection between them. Now she had irrevocable proof. It was a wonder the tiny room full of aging paper hadn't gone up in flames on the spot.

Fanning her hot face with one hand, she reached for her briefcase and pulled out her laptop and portable scanner. It was one thing to contemplate seducing the steely-eyed rancher, but another entirely to realize that all he had to do was touch her and she melted.

She was here to do a job. Before she contemplated any hanky-panky, she needed to get her priorities in order. Fortunately, she had made a plan already, so even though her concentration was shot, she was able to follow through with her agenda.

The method of attack was fairly simple. Using a list

of interviews from her earliest days in Royal, she pulled
file folders methodically, keeping them in alphabetical
order. Though she hadn't anticipated the complication of
not having anything digitized, she would cope. As long
as she didn't do something stupid like knocking a pile of
paper off the desk, she should be able to proceed with relative efficiency.

Thirty minutes later she had finished reading through
three folders and had developed a throbbing tension headache. She banged her fist against her forehead. Not only
was much of the information *not* typed or organized in
any discernible fashion, but the handwritten portions were
barely legible.

To call this mess *record-keeping* was generous. It was
impossible to compare one file with the next, because
every member's information was different. Other than an
initial sheet that documented simple details such as name,
address and date of initial membership, all the other pages
were a hodgepodge of business deals, sporting records and
family connections.

It took her another half hour, but she finally managed to
come up with a spreadsheet that allowed her to input the
pertinent items that might be of use in the investigation.
Her stomach growled more than once. She hadn't eaten
breakfast, too nervous about meeting Gil again to be very
interested in food.

She glanced at her watch and sighed. The minutes
crawled by. Perhaps she was bored with the job, or maybe
she was looking forward to lunch with Gil and his precocious son. Her distraction didn't bode well for the days
ahead....

Gil prowled the familiar halls of the club, pausing again
and again to greet and chat with men he had known for

years, many of them since he was a child at his father's side. He was comfortable within these walls, centered, content. The Texas Cattleman's Club had suffered a few growing pains lately, but it would survive and thrive.

Tradition and stability were important. Which was why Gil had passed the day-to-day running of his ranch over to other hands so he could concentrate on his son's well-being. One day, everything Gil owned would go to Cade. Cade would get married, settle down and hopefully have better luck in the romance department than his father had.

What really stuck in Gil's craw was the knowledge that the genesis of his unease sat not far away, her beautiful head bent over a stack of dull club papers, trying to find dirt on someone who might be Gil's friend. Perhaps the real problem wasn't that Gil didn't trust Bailey. Perhaps what bothered him the most was the notion that someone in Royal could have committed such a terrible crime.

Alex was back home, true. But a man with no memory was as vulnerable as a baby in the middle of a busy city street. How would Alex know if the perpetrators came at him again? How would anyone ever know what evil roamed the streets of Royal if Alex *never* remembered?

For years, Royal had been a great place to live, to raise a family. Occasionally the sheriff was forced to contend with cattle rustlers. And once in a while a two-bit drug dealer might try to set up shop. Of course, there were the usual domestic disturbances, or teenagers letting off steam on a Saturday night. But all in all, Royal was a pretty safe place.

At least it was until Alex Santiago had disappeared. The local and state authorities had crawled all over the town in the beginning. There were rumors of a potential drug war or maybe even bad blood between Alex and Chance Mc-Daniel, who had appeared interested in the same woman.

But since that time, everyone Gil knew intimately had been marked off the suspect list.

Which was all well and good except for the fact that *still* no one knew who the kidnappers were.

Maybe Gil should be more helpful to Bailey. He wanted his town back to normal, and Bailey wanted to close her case. So perhaps it was in Gil's best interest to help her. The sooner she was finished, the sooner she would leave town and go back to Dallas. That would be the smartest thing that could happen.

Gil didn't need the complication of an uncomfortable sexual attraction that was not likely to go anywhere. Already, Gil's son liked Bailey. Which meant that soon Cade would be weaving scenarios where Bailey became his new mom. Gil had seen it happen before. The boy's unwavering fixation on finding a mother meant that Gil no longer dated in Royal.

Not that he ever had dated much. When his physical needs became too demanding, he either dealt with them via a cold shower, or he met up with an old female friend in another town who was as uninterested in a serious relationship as Gil was. Those encounters left him feeling empty and oddly restless. But Gil had yet to find a woman who came even close to what he thought his son needed.

Bailey was a career woman whose job involved a lot of travel. Though Bailey and Cade had clicked at their first meeting, Bailey didn't strike Gil as the nurturing type. Cade had lost so much. If and when Gil ever remarried, it would be to a woman with traditional values, a woman who believed in the importance of being a full-time parent.

Gil had played that role for a very long time. And never once regretted his decision. Cade's sweet spirit and outgoing personality were proof that Gil had at least done something right. But Cade would soon be going to school full time. As much as Gil would miss his son, he was looking forward to once again taking an active role in the management of the Straight Arrow.

What he and Cade needed was a down-to-earth woman, one who would supervise the domestic staff, plan meals for the housekeeper to carry out and organize social events… tasks Gil had no interest in at all.

That paragon of a woman was out there somewhere. Gil had to believe she was, because the prospect of spending his entire life as a single parent and a single man sounded very lonely indeed.

At ten after twelve, he gave up the pretense of being busy and headed back to his office. Bailey didn't appear to have moved at all since he left her two hours ago. She was surrounded by stacks of paper. Her fingers flew with impressive speed over the keys of her laptop computer.

She didn't even notice when he came in.

He cleared his throat. Bailey's head snapped up as she glared at him. "It wouldn't hurt you to knock," she said. "You scared me to death."

"It's *my* office," he responded mildly. "You're only visiting." He grabbed a ladder-back chair and turned it around, straddling the seat. Bailey was behind his desk, so he now faced her across the cluttered surface. Her thick russet hair was drawn back into a ponytail at the nape of her neck. Tendrils waved around her face. Her work must have been frustrating, because the vibe he was getting from her was definitely harried. "Problems, Bailey?"

Her eyes narrowed. "You *knew* how impossible this was going to be, didn't you?"

He lifted a shoulder. "I have the utmost faith in your capabilities." He paused. "Any luck?" He didn't really want to get involved in what he considered a breach of privacy for the members of the club, but at the same time, he didn't want to be blindsided with any surprises.

She gnawed her lip, her gaze flitting back to the computer screen. "It's a little early to tell. But I do have some questions about this man." She shoved a folder toward Gil. "According to his file, he's been cited three separate times for fighting on club property. Do you know if he had any kind of grudge against Alex Santiago?"

Gil glanced at the name on the tab and shook his head, grinning. "Just a good ole boy who gets rowdy when he's had one too many beers. We keep track of such incidents, just in case, but our policy is to prevent members from doing damage to themselves or anyone else. Someone usually takes the offender home and keeps his keys until the following day. I know this guy, Bailey. He didn't kidnap Alex."

The slight frown between her brows deepened. She handed him a second file. "And this one? He filed a formal complaint when the club hired a Hispanic chef. His letter includes a number of racial slurs."

Gil flipped open the folder and shook his head. "You're grasping at straws. There are bigots everywhere. But that doesn't mean this guy had any reason to kidnap Alex." He touched her hand briefly, surprising himself when he felt a *zing* of something from the simple contact. "Have you considered the possibility that you might be stirring up unnecessary trouble?"

"What do you mean?"

She was so earnest, so dedicated to her work. And clearly able to take care of herself. Even so, Gil felt a distinct urge to protect her. Her white silk blouse was thin, thin enough for Gil to notice the outline of a lacy bra. Despite her extensive training and her credentials, she seemed vulnerable and surprisingly feminine even taking into consideration her deliberately bland and professional clothing.

Bailey's soft skin, gently rounded breasts, and graceful hands reminded Gil that beneath the outer shell of efficiency, she was a woman. He met her brown-eyed gaze with a calm he didn't feel. Some way, somehow, he had to convince her to back off this investigation. The feeling in his gut could be called premonition…or simply common sense. But he trusted that feeling…always.

"What you're doing is dangerous, Bailey. If word gets out that you're poking around in the TCC records, whoever kidnapped Alex may get spooked and try to harm you."

She sighed and closed her computer. "Is this genuine concern, or are you trying to get rid of me?"

"All of the above?" He asked it jokingly, but he sobered rapidly. "Alex escaped and made his way back home. Which means somebody out there is really pissed off and may try again. There's a good chance Alex is still in danger. By involving yourself in his situation, you court the same trouble."

Her chin lifted. "I'm doing my job. No more, no less."

"And if your job could get you killed?"

"I'm a paper pusher, Gil."

"You're a pain in the butt," he groused, realizing he wasn't going to win this round. But hearing her say his name was a small victory, nevertheless. He stood and held out his hand. "I'm starving, and Cade will be, too. Let's go find him."

The club dining room was packed. Bailey looked around with interest as the hostess led them across the floor. In a far corner at a table for two sat Rory and Shannon Fentress, still basking in the glow of being newlyweds. It was rumored that Rory had his eye on the governor's mansion.

Like Bailey, Shannon was not much of a girlie girl. She owned and managed a working ranch and dressed accordingly when she was in town on business. Judging by the way Rory looked at his new wife, he liked her just the way she was.

Gil had reserved a table by the window because Cade liked to watch the horses outside. Though of course the TCC had a parking lot, it wasn't at all unusual for someone to ride up, tie his mount to the wooden railings out front, and saunter inside for a bite of lunch.

Cade was his usually bubbly self. "I'm glad you're eating lunch with us, Miss Bailey." His form of address was the compromise Gil had allowed in his insistence that his son learn manners.

Bailey smiled at him. "Me, too. Did you enjoy yourself this morning?"

Cade nodded, already filling his mouth with crackers.

Without saying a word, Gil removed the basket from his son's reach. "I think a lot of the members have been surprised at how nice it is to be able to drop off a son or daughter or even a grandchild and to know that the kids are close by, happy and safe."

"Do you think the trouble is over?"

"I do. I really do. I still hear grumbling, of course. Particularly from the old guard."

"You mean like him?" Bailey cocked her head unobtrusively, not letting Cade see. A few tables away sat Paul Windsor, a charter member of the TCC.

Gil grimaced. "Yeah. He's one of the worst. But even so, I doubt he'd ever actually do anything to cause problems for the center."

Bailey shuddered inwardly. She had interviewed Paul during her initial investigation, and the man had given her the creeps. Divorced four times, Windsor considered himself a ladies' man. During the course of her questioning, Bailey had discovered without a doubt that Windsor was perhaps the most overt and obnoxious chauvinist she had ever met. He made no secret of his disdain for Bailey.

"I feel sorry for Cara," she said, "having such an overbearing father." Bailey knew what that was like far too well.

"I'll admit…Windsor can be a jerk. But he wields a lot of influence around here, so it would be a plus to stay on his good side if you want to make any progress with your investigation. If he were to raise a stink, he could convince others that you shouldn't be here in the club."

"But I have a legal warrant."

"Yes. And ultimately that would prevail. In the interim, though, things could get ugly."

"Is my presence going to cause big problems for you, Gil?" The thought troubled her.

He laughed, his dark eyes warm and teasing. "I can handle trouble, Bailey. Don't worry about me."

Cade, tired of being ignored, piped up, a sly smile on his face. "Do you know how to cook, Miss Bailey?"

Bailey raised her eyebrows. "Where did that come from?"

Cade took a bite of the hot dog their server had delivered moments ago. Pausing to chew and swallow, he fixed her with the blue eyes that helped make him such a cute kid. "I dunno," he said, the picture of innocence. "Dad says when I'm getting to know someone, it's nice to ask them questions…but not too personal," he added hastily, glancing at his father with a guilty expression.

"That's good advice," Bailey said. "So, in answer to your question, yes…I'm a pretty good cook. I started learning when I was not much bigger than you."

Cade nodded solemnly, his milk mustache adding to his charm. "And do you like little kids?"

Suddenly, she understood what was happening. She was being interviewed for a job. As Cade's mommy. *Dear Lord.* Fortunately for her peace of mind, the rest of their meal arrived, and in the hubbub of drink refills and the server's chatter, the moment passed.

Bailey had looked forward to an intimate lunch with the two Addison men, but unfortunately, this was not the venue. Gil could barely eat his meal because of repeated interruptions from club members happy to see him. What Bailey suddenly understood was that Gil had sacrificed an enormous amount in choosing intentionally to be the caregiver for his son.

Over the course of almost five years, Gil was wealthy enough to have hired the best nannies in the world. He could have gone about his business, running the ranch, hanging out at the TCC, meeting women, perhaps marrying again. Instead, he had made his son a priority. Fortunately, his current role as TCC president was more of an honorary position than a demanding job.

The enthusiasm with which club members greeted him during one short lunch indicated both that Gil was extremely popular and well-liked, and that he likely was not able to be present at the club as often as many of his cohorts.

Cade bore the intrusion of one table guest after another with equanimity. Several of the men addressed him personally. For a child not yet old enough for school, his composure and patience were commendable.

Not many boys of Bailey's acquaintance would be able to tolerate an extended meal in public without raising a ruckus. She sneaked him a couple of extra French fries off her plate while Gil was otherwise occupied. "Is it always like this?" she asked.

Cade nodded. "Yep. Everybody likes my dad." The words were matter-of-fact, but Bailey heard the pride behind them.

"So," she whispered conspiratorially, "do you think we get dessert?"

Cade wrinkled his nose. "If I eat most of my salad." He stared dolefully at the small bowl, clearly not a fan of spinach mix.

"I remember once when I was about your age, my mother made me eat black-eyed peas that I didn't like. I broke out in a rash all over my whole body, and I never had to eat them again."

"Can you teach me how to do that?" Cade's eyes widened with fascination.

"Unfortunately, I think the rash happened because I was so upset. But you could always try using a red marker to put dots all over your skin. I'm kidding," she said hastily, suddenly visualizing an awful scenario where Gil realized Bailey had been giving his son tips on how to bypass healthy eating.

"I know that." Cade rolled his eyes. "You're funny, Miss Bailey."

Bailey had been called a lot of things in her life... responsible, hardworking, dedicated. But no one had ever called her funny. She kind of liked it. And she very much liked Gil's precious son.

Gil stood and touched Bailey's shoulder. "If you two would excuse me for a few moments, I need to speak to a gentleman at that table in the corner. I won't be long, I promise."

"Your food will get cold," Cade said.

"I bet the chef will warm it up for me. Love you, son. Back in a minute." Gil kissed the top of Cade's head and strode away.

Four

Bailey looked for signs that Cade was leery of being left with a virtual stranger, but quite the contrary. With his dad out of the picture, Cade was free to resume his interrogation. "What *kinds* of things do you like to cook?" he asked, returning to the original topic.

"Well, let's see…" Bailey folded her fancy napkin and laid it beside her plate. The meal had been amazing. Tender beef medallions, fluffy mashed potatoes and sautéed asparagus. A hearty meal that men would enjoy. Not a ladies' tearoom menu with tiny bowls of soup and miniature sandwiches.

She grinned as Cade poked halfheartedly at his spinach. "I love to bake," she said. "So I suppose I'm good at bread and pies and cakes."

Her companion's eyes rounded. "Birthday cakes, too?"

"I suppose."

"My birthday is comin' up real soon, Miss Bailey. Do you think you could make me a birthday cake?"

She hesitated, positive she was negotiating some kind of hidden minefield. "I'll bet your dad wants to surprise you with a special cake."

Cade shook his head. "Our housekeeper will make it. But her cakes are awful and Dad says we can't hurt her feelings."

Just like that, Bailey fell in love with Cade Addison. How many years had she come home from school on her birthday, hoping against hope that her father had remembered to stop by the corner grocery and pick up a store-bought cake.

But he never did. Not once.

By the time she was nine, Bailey had quit expecting cakes. Two years later, she quit thinking about her birthday at all. It was just another day.

"I tell you what, Cade," she said, wondering if she were making a huge mistake. "If I'm still here when your birthday rolls around, and if your father doesn't mind, then yes...I'd be happy to make you a cake."

Cade whooped out loud and then clapped a hand over his mouth when several people turned around with curious looks. "Sorry," he mumbled.

"It's okay. This room is noisy anyway. Eat your salad, and when your dad gets back, we'll order dessert."

Cade managed four bites with some theatrical gagging, but when Bailey didn't react, he finished it all. "Done," he said triumphantly.

She high-fived him. "Now that wasn't so bad, was it?"

"I guess. But I'd rather have ice cream."

"Who wouldn't?"

They laughed together. She marveled at the connection she felt with this small, motherless child. On impulse, she leaned forward, lowering her voice, though it was doubtful she'd be overheard in the midst of the loud conversations all around them. Texas cowboys had a tendency to get heated when they discussed politics and religion and the price of feed. There was a lot of testosterone in this room.

"I want to tell you something, Cade."

He looked up at her trustingly. "Okay."

"I know you want a mother, but you are a very lucky little boy, because your dad loves you more than anything in the world. Do you know that?"

He seemed surprised she would ask. "Well, yeah. He tells me all the time."

"Not all dads are like that." Her throat closed up as unexpected emotion stung her eyes.

Cade stared at her, mute, as if sensing her struggle. "Are you talking about *your* daddy, Miss Bailey?"

She nodded, trying to swallow the lump. "My mom ran away and left us when I was about your age. And she never came back. So it was just me and my dad. But he wasn't like your father. He was…" She trailed off, not sure what adjective to use that an almost-five-year-old would understand.

Elbows on table, chin in hand, Cade surveyed her solemnly. "He was mean?"

Out of the mouths of babes. "Well, he didn't hurt me, if that's what you're thinking. But he didn't care about me. Not like your dad cares about you. Be patient, Cade. One day your father will find a woman he loves and he'll marry her and you'll have that mother you want. But in the meantime, be a kid, okay? And not a matchmaker."

Gil halted suddenly, shock rendering him immobile. Bailey Collins had just given his son the kind of advice Cade needed to hear. And she had done it lovingly and in a way he could understand at his young age. Gil was torn between gratitude for her interference and compassion for the personal pain she had revealed.

He backed up a step or two and approached the table again, this time more loudly. "You were right, Cade. I bet my lunch is cold. Sorry it took me so long. You ready for dessert?"

Bailey flushed from her throat to her hairline, her expression mortified. "How long have you been standing there?" she asked.

He kept his expression neutral. "I just walked across the room, Bailey. Why?"

"No reason," she mumbled, taking a gulp from her water glass.

Gil noticed the exchange of glances between his son and Bailey, a conspiratorial look that was oddly unsettling. Gil was accustomed to being his son's sounding board, his protector, his go-to guy. To see the boy so quickly accept and relate to Bailey made Gil worry. Perhaps he should keep the two of them apart.

When Bailey returned to Dallas, inevitably leaving a heartbroken Cade behind, Gil would have to pick up the pieces. On the other hand, would it be fair to deprive Cade of a relationship that provided him enjoyment in the meantime? Again, the frustration of being a single parent gave Gil heartburn. He was not the kind of man to unburden himself to anyone and everyone.

He had friends. Lots of them. But raising Cade couldn't be left up to a committee vote. Gil had to decide what was best for his son.

Over ice cream and pound cake, Cade grilled his father. "Are you and Miss Bailey going to do this every day?"

Gil lifted an eyebrow, looking to Bailey to answer that one.

"A week…ten days. I'm working as fast as I can, but it's slow going."

Cade grinned widely. "I like the child care center. They have a computer station and about a jillion Lego blocks, and my friends miss me when I don't come."

Gil rubbed a smear of ice cream from his son's chin. "Well, in that case, I'll set up some meetings with the executive committee for the next few days and get some club business out of the way."

When the meal was over they dropped off Cade and headed back to Gil's office. Walking in, he noticed the faint, pleasing scent of Bailey's perfume lingering in the air, something light and flowery. The scene that transpired in the dining room had affected him deeply. It was hard to mistrust a woman who treated his son with so much gentleness and compassion.

"Do you need any help?" he asked abruptly, wishing he had a reason to stay.

Bailey glanced at him, her gaze guarded. "No. But thanks."

He leaned a hip against his desk. "What do you do for fun, Bailey Collins?"

"Fun?" The question appeared to confuse her.

"I'm assuming you've heard of the word."

"I have fun," she said, her tone defensive.

"When?"

Her mouth opened and closed. "I like to read."

"So do I. In bed. At night. But what do you do in your leisure time?" He shouldn't have mentioned the word *bed*. His libido rushed ahead in the conversation and visualized the two of them entwined on soft sheets.

Bailey shrugged. "I work long hours. But in the evenings I like to walk around my neighborhood. It's a close-knit, established community with sidewalks and people who sit on front porches. I have several older friends I check on from time to time."

"Sounds nice."

"It is."

"And is there a man in your life?" Well, he'd done it now. There was no way she could interpret his question as anything other than what it was. He was attracted to her. And he wanted to know if he'd be stepping on any toes were he to follow up on those feelings.

Bailey glanced at her watch. "I need to get back to work."

"Does that mean, 'Back off, Gil'?"

"What? No. Not at all. But I…"

He waited. Silently.

"You don't even like me," she said, her expression troubled.

"Correction. I *tried* not to like you. That first day in the police station when you were grilling me like a seasoned pro, I found you wildly appealing, despite my disgruntlement. And since I am a man who believes in laying all the cards on the table, I think you should know."

"What changed?"

"Dogs and children are very good judges of character. My son adores you already."

"But that makes you uncomfortable."

The sadness lurking in her brown eyes shamed him. "It does. I don't want him to get too attached to you."

"Because I'll be leaving soon."

"Yes."

"I suppose I can understand that."

"It has nothing to do with you personally. But Cade has this unfortunate tendency to latch onto any woman who walks into my life, no matter how briefly."

"Why haven't you married again?"

He hadn't expected the blunt question. It caught him off guard, and for a moment, grief, regret and disappointment flooded his stomach. He shoved the negative feelings away. "There aren't too many women these days happy to be stuck out on a ranch in the middle of nowhere."

"Oh, please," Bailey said, giving him a reproving look. "You're rich, handsome and successful. I'm sure some poor soul in Royal would apply for the job."

Her mock scolding erased the momentary sting of allowing the past to intrude. "But not you?"

"I have a job."

"One that could get you killed." The realities of her position still disturbed him. Alex needed to get his memory back in a hurry. Before somebody else got hurt. Gil hadn't meant to change the subject, even if he was genuinely worried about her. "May I be honest with you, Bailey?"

"Please do."

"As angry as I was with you when we first met, I felt a definite *something*. In the weeks you've been here, I haven't stopped thinking about that feeling and wondering if it was one-sided."

She paled and wrapped her arms around her waist, clearly shocked by his candor. "It wasn't one-sided," she said quietly.

Exultation flooded his veins, despite the tiny voice inside his head that said he was making a mistake. "Good to know." The three words were gruff, but it was hard to speak when arousal made his entire body tense with need. "There's more," he said.

A tiny smile appeared and disappeared. "I'm bracing myself."

He stood up, no longer able to feign relaxation. "It's not easy for a single man my age to live in a place like Royal and do something as prosaic as dating. When Cade was almost three, I tried it for the first time."

"And?"

"It was terrible. Everyone tried to give me sympathy and child-rearing advice, or they offered to bake me casseroles."

"Not altogether bad things."

"Of course not, but I wanted to forget for a while that I was a single dad. I wanted companionship and…"

"Sex."

He saw no judgment in her gaze, but his cheeks reddened nevertheless. "Yeah," he sighed. "It would be easier if I lived in a big, anonymous city, but here in Royal everything I do is fodder for the gossip mill. I value my privacy, and I don't think my personal life needs to be front-page news."

"But you don't want to spend a lot of time out of town because of Cade."

"Exactly."

"You've given up a lot for him."

Gil frowned. "I haven't given up anything. He's my son. And I love him."

Bailey crossed the tiny distance between them. Putting a hand on his chest, she looked up at him. "You're a very nice man, Gil Addison." Her smile warmed him to a sobering degree.

He moved restlessly, fighting the urge to grab her. "It's not about being nice, damn it. It's what a parent does."

Some of the light left her eyes. "Not all of them."

He wanted to tell her that he had heard what she said to Cade, that his heart broke for a little girl with no mother and a surly dad. But her confidences had to be freely given or not at all. He wouldn't embarrass her that way. "Cade is the best thing that has ever happened to me. His childhood will pass quickly enough. I don't want to miss out on anything."

She went up on tiptoes and pressed a soft kiss on his lips. "If you're asking me to spend some…*time*…with you while I'm here, then the answer is yes. I understand the rules. You don't have to worry. And I will do my best not to let Cade get attached to me."

He winced. "God, you make me sound like an ass."

Her expression was wry. "Not at all. You're simply a straight arrow of a guy who doesn't hide behind platitudes. I respect that."

He gave in to temptation and stroked his thumb over her cheekbone. "You have the softest skin," he muttered. Slowly, he cupped her face in his palms and tipped her mouth toward his. "Have I told you how much your ugly suits turn me on?"

Bailey melted into him. "My suits are not ugly. They're professional." Her tongue mated lazily with his, hardening his sex to the point of pain. Of all the dumb ideas he'd ever had, this one ranked right up near the top. The door wasn't locked. Though no one was likely to disturb them, their current behavior was risky at best.

He kissed his way down her throat, toying with the buttons on her silky top. Bailey's eyes were closed, her lips parted. More than anything he wanted to bend her over his desk and take her hard and fast. Lust wrapped his brain in a red haze. His hands trembled as he found his way past her blouse to her breasts covered in lace.

Each soft mound was a full, perfect weight in his hand. He squeezed gently, shuddering when Bailey's low moan went straight to his gut and stoked the fire. He was rapidly reaching the point of no return. The problem with long bouts of celibacy was that a man tended to go a little insane when the woman he wanted was in touching distance.

"Tell me to stop," he pleaded.

Her hands tore at the lapels of his jacket. He helped her remove it and tossed it aside. He was burning up from the inside out.

"Touch my skin," she pleaded.

How could he say no? Each delicate nipple furled tightly as he stroked her with reverence. He lifted her onto the desk. Now he could reach her with his mouth. Shoving aside the gossamer cups of her bra, he first licked her, then suckled her, growing more and more hungry with every second that passed.

Her hands tangled in his hair, pulling him closer. "Bailey. Bailey…" He didn't even know what he wanted to say.

"Gil," her voice was little more than a whisper.

He inhaled sharply, close to begging. "What?"

"I think we have to stop. I don't want to, but we're at the club."

"At the club?" He could barely make sense of the words. He needed to be inside her more than he needed to breathe.

She shoved him, her two hands braced on his shoulders. "Stop, Gil. Please."

At last her protest penetrated the fog that bound him. He staggered backward, wiping his mouth with the back of his hand. It hurt to look at her. He leaned against the file cabinet, burying his face in his arm. Agony ripped through him. He had caged the tiger that was his lust for too long, and now the animal was free.

Seconds passed. Minutes. He sucked in great lungfuls of air, desperately trying to regain control. Behind him he heard rustling sounds as Bailey adjusted her clothing.

When her hand touched his back, he jerked. "Don't," he groaned. "Not if you want me to leave."

"I don't want you to go," she said quietly. "But for now, you have to. I'm sorry."

He whirled around. "Sorry for what?"

Her eyes were huge and dark. "I didn't mean for this to happen."

"Neither did I. At least not right now." He had never been as torn as he was at this moment. Everything inside him insisted he lock the door and make her his. But he dared not. Not for her sake, and not with his son in the same building. "We'll talk…tonight…when Cade is in bed. I'll call you and we'll make plans."

Her gaze searched his. "I'd like that very much."

Five

Gil didn't call that night. Bailey took his silence stoically, though deep inside her, a little kernel of excitement shriveled. Clearly, Gil's second thoughts about getting involved had trumped his momentary sexual need. She could understand his reluctance. He was not free to follow every whim or passing fancy.

In the cold light of reason, he had probably weighed the risks and benefits of getting involved with her and decided it was too risky. It hurt that he hadn't bothered to call and tell her straight up that he had changed his mind, but perhaps he'd been busy with Cade.

As much as it pained her to admit it, Gil's about-face was probably for the best. Bailey had her own doubts. She'd never been a rule-breaker, and though it wasn't technically illegal or even unethical for her to have a personal relationship with Gil, it was at the very least unwise.

She needed to be able to rely on him as a source of information in her investigation. If he ended up in a position of having to defend one of his friends against her accusations, the situation could get ugly fast. No matter how much she responded to Gil physically, it was better for everyone if she ignored the needs of her body and her heart and focused on doing her job.

The following morning, she and Gil met at the club as they had the day before. Only this time, Gil still had Cade in tow. Not by word or expression did Gil evidence any memory of the heated interlude in his office the afternoon before. Bailey didn't know whether to be relieved or insulted, but she guessed he didn't want to give anything away in front of his son.

Cade bounced up and down in his father's grasp, finally breaking free long enough to wrap his arms around Bailey's thighs in an exuberant hug. "Hey, Miss Bailey," he said. "Are you going to eat lunch with us again?"

Bailey glanced at Gil. The slight negative shake of his head let her know the answer. "I'd love to, Cade, but today I'll probably just snack at my desk. I have a lot of work to do."

The disappointment in his big blue eyes filled her with guilt. "I understand." His body language imploded, leaving him long-faced and dejected.

Gil's jaw tightened. He removed a key from his pocket and handed it to Bailey. "I have a full schedule today," he said, the words terse. "Be sure to lock the door whenever you have to step out. I'll stop by before you go home and retrieve this."

"Thank you," she said, her words as stilted as his. As she watched, Gil turned on his heel and led his son toward the entrance to the child care center. Cade looked over his shoulder at Bailey just before they disappeared. She gave him a little wave and smiled, hoping to cheer him up. Truthfully, she liked the little boy, almost as much as she liked his taciturn father.

Feeling unsettled and confused, she made her way to the office and got to work. Today went a little faster, since she had at last decided how to comb through the files in a way that was more organized and less haphazard.

Here and there names popped out at her. Slowly, she began to build a list of men she would like to interview. She wondered if Gil would stonewall her when she suggested it. Every man she flagged had been interviewed in the initial investigation, but with Alex still in the dark, it was imperative that she not miss any links to motive or opportunity.

Her stomach growled loudly midday. Fortunately, she had an apple, a bottle of water and a granola bar in her tote bag. No one was allowed to eat in the club dining room unless he or she was the guest of a member. And since Gil had made it clear that he wasn't interested in sharing lunch with Bailey, she was on her own.

She could have taken a break and headed over to the Royal Diner. The food was good and the ambiance cheerful, but she wasn't in the mood to talk to anyone, much less defend her reasons for spending time at the club. Often, her job made her as popular as an IRS agent.

The day crawled by, but at five o'clock, she was satisfied with the amount of work she had accomplished. She had shut down her laptop and was straightening the various stacks of files she was using when, after a brief knock, someone opened the door.

It wasn't too difficult to guess the intruder's identity. Bailey was very proud of her calm, friendly smile. "Hello, Gil. I was just finishing up." She fished in her pocket. "Here's the key."

When he took it from her, their fingers touched. His

were warm and slightly calloused. She almost jerked her hand away in reaction, but instead, turned to scoop up her tote bag and purse. "See you tomorrow." If her voice had been any brighter, she could have powered a lightbulb.

Gil touched her, curling his hand around her forearm. "Stay," he muttered. "For a minute."

Her stomach quivered at the unmistakably intimate tone. But she wouldn't be so easily won over. "No."

"Please." His dark eyes were contrite.

"You didn't call me last night," she said evenly. "That was rude and uncalled-for."

He nodded. "I know. I'm sorry."

"Why didn't you?" She was genuinely curious in the midst of her pique. Gil was standing so close, she could see the tiny flecks of amber that gave light and depth to his night-dark irises.

He stroked her arm, almost absently, with one fingertip. "I couldn't decide what I wanted to say. You confuse me." His breath was warm on her cheek.

"Is that good or bad?" To hear that he was as conflicted as she was calmed some of her indignation. Today, he wore a simple button-down oxford shirt in lemon-yellow. The color suited him. As did the neatly creased dress slacks whose precision fit came only from hand-tailoring.

Bailey wished she had worn something more appealing than her usual workaday attire, but an investigative agent on the job had to be prepared for any eventuality. Occasionally, despite the clerical nature of her customary assignments, she had to chase down a bad guy or crouch in a grimy location to do surveillance.

Feminine vanity was useless in her line of work. Unless, like Sandra Bullock, she was ever called upon to pose in a beauty pageant, her chances for wearing seductive clothing on the job were slim.

Gil ignored her pointed question. But judging from the way he looked at her, the answer was definitely *good*. "Have dinner with me tonight," he said abruptly. "Cade is spending the evening with my cousin and his wife. I don't have to pick him up until nine. I'll take you to Claire's."

Claire's was an upscale restaurant with white linen tablecloths and real silver cutlery, definitely a special-occasion place. Bailey's heart beat faster at the implications. And because it did, she was determined not to let him see that his invitation rattled her. "As long as I pay for my own meal to avoid any ethical considerations. And besides, are you sure you want to be seen with me in public?" Her tart question was a fair one given his ambivalence.

He winced. "I deserve that. I'll admit that I still don't like what you're up to…a witch hunt that may bring down one of my friends. But I find that my scruples are far less compelling than the taste of your lips."

Pulling her close, he kissed her gently, lazily. Where yesterday had been frantic and laced with desperation, this contact was infinitely sweet, deeply tender, endlessly erotic. She linked her arms around his neck, sighing when he aligned their bodies perfectly.

As a teenager, she had hated being taller than many of the boys in her class, but now, her height gave her an advantage. She felt the press of his belt buckle against her belly, inhaled the spicy scent of his aftershave. Beneath her fingertips, his hair was silky and smooth.

He held her confidently, like a man who knew his way around a woman's body. Despite his professed lack of opportunity, his technique was not rusty at all. Against her breast, she felt the steady thud of his heartbeat. Perhaps it was a bit ragged, who could tell? She only knew that this moment had been weeks in the making.

"You're very persuasive," she whispered. When his teeth nipped the ticklish spot below her ear, she laid her cheek on his chest.

"Is that a yes?"

"I'll have to go home and change. I could meet you back here in an hour." She was staying at McDaniel's Acres. Though she had no time to indulge in the dude ranch activities offered, her single room in the spacious ranch house was comfortable and more private than a B and B.

Gil tugged her ponytail. "I'll pick you up."

"It's not necessary."

He stepped back and cupped her face in his big hands. Searching eyes met her reluctant gaze and held it. For one instant, she felt a connection that was more than physical. "Don't fight me on this, honey," he said. "No matter how we both might twist and squirm in the wind, we're caught in this together. Let's see where it leads us."

"It won't lead anywhere," she said flatly, not sure why she had to remind him of that.

His half smile was laced with self-derision. "But we might have fun along the way, right?"

She wasn't armed against the charm of a man whose masculinity was as potent as hundred-proof whiskey. He had made an indelible impression on her the first time they met, and nothing had changed in that regard. "I suppose I have to wonder if you'll stand me up," she muttered. "Considering I waited by the phone last night like a silly schoolgirl."

With his thumb, he traced the curve of her ear, a newly discovered erogenous zone. "I'll make it up to you." Suddenly, he was kissing her again. Any sweetness that had lingered on their lips was instantly vaporized by a shot of pure fire. She felt it from her breasts to her pelvis, a tingling, sizzling vein of sensation.

His arm was hard across her back, his erection thrusting urgently against her lower body. The unapologetic passion he offered her was persuasive. She wanted to melt into him, feeling incredibly alive yet, at the same time, fearful of losing herself.

She pulled away, though it required great resolve. "I'm going now," she said, the words hushed.

Gil stood, head bowed, and pressed the heels of his hands against his eyes. "I'll be there at six-thirty. Don't make me wait."

He shuddered when the door closed behind her. Bailey had no idea how tenuous his control was around her. Perhaps she imagined that her drab clothing could disguise the appeal of her body, but she was wrong. When he held her, he felt the strength and softness of her frame. Neither skinny nor overweight, she was the epitome of a healthy young woman. Her required training regimen kept her fit. He liked that. A lot.

And though it only made his physical discomfort worse, he couldn't help imagining all that energy and flexibility at his disposal in bed. God help him.

When he could leave the room without embarrassing himself, he locked the office and went in search of his son.

Thirty minutes later he dropped Cade off in town and raced back out to the ranch to change clothes. Taking Bailey out tonight would spark gossip, but for once, he didn't care. Perhaps if word got around that the two of them were an item, no one would look too closely at Bailey's reasons for spending time at the club.

As he drove out toward Chance McDaniel's thriving operation, he contemplated the fact that Chance was about the only person he could think of who might have an ax to grind with Alex Santiago. Both men had shown interest in Cara Windsor, but it was Alex who had managed to put an engagement ring on her finger. Since Alex and Chance were very close friends, Chance might have seen the other man's actions as a betrayal of their friendship.

Gil wasn't sure what impact Alex's disappearance and subsequent memory loss had made on Alex's relationship with Cara, but it couldn't be easy for a woman to be with a man who didn't remember her.

As Gil pulled up in front of the impressive ranch house, Chance waved at him from across the corral. It occurred to him that Bailey must be seeing a lot of the handsome, blond cowboy. The lick of jealousy he felt was disconcerting. Chance was his friend. And since Bailey still had not ruled out Chance as a suspect, Alex was relatively sure that neither Bailey nor Chance would be inclined to get chummy. With Bailey suspicious and Chance on the defensive, they would likely keep their distance.

Gil's unsettling thoughts were derailed when Bailey stepped out onto the front porch. His first thought was "Hot damn." She had worn her hair loose, and it rippled around her shoulders in the evening breeze. Her gaze met his directly, but with a hint of reserve. She still wasn't sure of him.

The knowledge hurt. He'd been so busy with his self-righteous indignation at being questioned, he hadn't paused to consider how his truculence would affect Bailey.

He met her halfway up the stairs and held out his hand. "You look beautiful," he said, wishing there was another word for her vibrant appeal. The black knit, V-necked wrap dress she wore emphasized her narrow waist and curvy breasts. Cap sleeves revealed slender arms.

"Thank you."

Bailey's skirt ended several inches above her knees. For the first time since they met, Gil got a glimpse of her legs.

The vision was enough to hog-tie his voice. He decided then and there that it was a crime for such beauty to be covered up by an ugly pantsuit. But on the other hand, at least her mode of dress meant other men weren't ogling her.

Gil considered himself an evolved, twenty-first-century kind of guy. Yet when it came to Bailey, he was finding himself strangled by impulses that were decidedly Neanderthal. He had no right to be possessive, no right at all. But he couldn't deny what he was feeling.

Conversation languished on the ride into town. By the time they were seated at Claire's and looking over the menu, though, he recovered enough to make small talk. "Have you eaten here before?" he asked.

Bailey shook her head with a grin. "No. These prices are a little bit above my per diem meal allowance. But I can splurge occasionally."

Gil chuckled. "I can recommend the salmon and the beef bourguignonne."

He barely noticed what he ate. Bailey was enchanting…sweetly serious about her job, and yet she possessed a dry sense of humor that took him off guard at times. He knew they were being watched by curious diners, most of whom knew him well. But he couldn't bring himself to care. It was the most enjoyable evening he had spent in a long, long time.

Over coffee and dessert, he decided he had to come clean about the secret he was holding. "Bailey…"

She smiled at him. "Yes?"

"I have a confession to make."

Some of the sparkle left her expression. "Oh?"

"I heard what you said to Cade. About your father."

Color flushed her cheeks and then faded away, leaving her pale. "I see."

"I'm sorry. I didn't want to embarrass you yesterday."

"But it's okay tonight?" The words had a bite to them.

He shrugged. "I need to have honesty between us. It's important to me. You don't have to explain, but I *am* sorry that your childhood was so difficult. I really appreciate what you said to Cade. It was very generous of you."

She crossed her arms, the posture unconsciously defensive. "I had food and shelter growing up. Lots of kids don't have that much."

"True. But love is important. Perhaps your father didn't know how to show you what was in his heart."

"I told myself that when I was a teenager. I took a psychology class in high school. Learned a little bit about how pain can make people turn inward. But it didn't really help to know the reason why. My father and I barely speak. A couple of awkward meals at the holidays. The obligatory birthday gifts. I tried for years to get him to open up to me, but he's a stone wall with no apparent desire to change."

"He's missing out," Gil said soberly.

Bailey exhaled and took a drink of water, her hand trembling visibly. "Thank you."

After a moment's awkward silence, she leaned forward and clasped her hands on the table. Her beautiful brown eyes were earnest. "If there's a possibility that you and I are going to become…*intimate*…I wonder if I may ask you a personal question."

"Of course."

"Does Cade remember his mother at all?"

He hesitated. This wasn't a road he had expected to go down. But since he had inadvertently overheard Bailey's extremely personal confession to Cade, it seemed only fair that Gil should reciprocate. "No," he said slowly. "She died before his first birthday. Took her own life." Even now, it hurt to say the words. And since Bailey had dossiers on half the people in town, she probably already knew that.

"Oh, Gil. I am so sorry." Bailey took one of his hands in her two smaller ones and held it tightly.

He squeezed her fingers, warmed by her genuine sympathy. "It was a long time ago. And to be honest, our marriage was doomed from the beginning, though I didn't realize it for a long time. My wife had severe emotional problems that she hid well."

"You don't have to explain," Bailey said, still holding his hand.

"It's okay. I want to tell you. It might help you understand why I'm so protective of Cade. When things started to go wrong in my marriage, I urged Sherrie to go with me to counseling. In the safety of that situation she was able to reveal that she had been abused as a young teenager. I found it almost impossible to believe at first, but her parents were part of a religious cult that 'married' young girls in the church to older men."

Bailey released him and sat back, her gaze stricken. "That's horrible."

"Yes. To her credit, Sherrie really did want a child, and she was so happy to be pregnant. But postpartum depression took a toll on her, and she was never able to recover."

"So you made Cade your priority."

"Don't paint me as noble," he said soberly. "There was more to it than that. My in-laws took me to court and tried to steal Cade away from me. Faced with the prospect of losing him, I realized how much I loved that little innocent baby."

"Thank God they didn't succeed."

"I went through a hellish eight months of court-ordered visits and psychological evaluations…"

She nibbled her lower lip, her eyes huge, her expression sober. "I'm beginning to see why you have a chip on your shoulder about government intervention."

"I suppose I do, but I came close to losing everything. My in-laws paid off a judge, and it nearly worked. Fortunately for me, I have a lot of friends in Royal and in the state at large. Powerful friends. In the end, justice prevailed, but it was a close call."

"I've admired you since I first came to Royal," Bailey said quietly. "Now, even more."

Six

Bailey was shaken by what she had heard. Imagining Gil without his son was a picture she didn't want to paint. The two of them were a tight family unit. Despite the absence of a female figure.

She had wondered from time to time if Gil were still in love with his dead wife…and if that was why he hadn't remarried. Apparently, the truth was more complex. He wanted to protect his son, and that included not letting Cade's little heart get broken time and again if his father indulged in short-lived relationships.

Bailey had to admire Gil's selflessness. But how long could a virile, healthy man suppress his sexual needs before he did something reckless? Like initiating an intimate relationship with a woman he barely knew…a woman just passing through.

Sitting across the table from him was like a romantic fantasy come to life. She seldom had opportunities for fine dining, and never with someone who looked like Gil. His expensive black suit showcased broad shoulders and a trim waist. A crisp white shirt and red tie completed the image of a successful businessman. Though he would have fit right in wearing tooled leather boots, he had chosen more traditional dress shoes for their date. She found that she missed his cowboy look, though this man was wildly appealing, as well.

But no matter how much she was drawn to him, the truth of their situation gave her pause. If she made unwise choices and things blew up in her face, she could face a formal reprimand from her boss, or even worse. She'd seen other colleagues terminated because they let their judgment be clouded by personal involvement on a case.

Beyond the professional implications, Bailey didn't want to be Gil's guilty pleasure. She didn't want to be filed under the category *secret dalliance* or *enjoyable mistake.* Not that he was hiding anything tonight. They were eating dinner in front of half the town, it seemed. But letting Cade know was another story.

Her suppositions were confirmed when Gil glanced at his watch and muttered in dismay. "It's almost time for me to pick up Cade," he said. "I didn't know it was so late. I'll run you home and come back to get him."

She and Gil had talked easily and at length, with a comfort that Bailey rarely found in relationships with the opposite sex. The time had flown by. Underlying all of the conversation was the unspoken subtext of what they both wanted.

"That's not necessary," she said. "Too much driving back and forth. Let me call Chance. I'm sure he won't mind sending one of the ranch hands into town to pick me up. Go get your son, Gil. Take him home to bed." The Straight Arrow and McDaniel's Acres, both south of town, were not that far apart. It made no sense for Gil to crisscross the county when the solution was simple.

Gil waved a hand for the checks and tucked both of their credit cards in the folio, frowning. "I invited you to dinner tonight. I'll take you home." He grimaced, clearly conflicted. "I suppose he's old enough to know that not every relationship ends in wedding bells. We might as well go get him together."

"I appreciate your chivalry," she said wryly. "But I don't need a grand gesture. I've already told you how I feel. You're a sexy, appealing man, and I find myself very attracted to you. That won't change simply because you have responsibilities."

The tightness in his jaw eased, and his expression lightened. "Thank you, Bailey." He stood and took her wrist to pull her to her feet. "But we'll go together."

Outside, the weather had taken a turn for the worse, or at least toward the more seasonable. Temperatures had dropped while they were eating, and now, wind-driven spritzes of raindrops dampened the air.

Bailey shivered, wishing she had remembered to bring a wrap. Gil shrugged out of his jacket and tucked it around her shoulders without asking. The fabric smelled like warm male. "Thank you," she said, drawing the lapels closer together.

The car was not far, so they made a run for it. Gil tucked her inside and ran around to the driver's seat. When they were both safely inside, they laughed, shaking water droplets from their hair. The windows fogged up almost immediately.

He didn't start the engine. Instead, he turned toward her and studied her intently. Her taut nipples pressed against the fabric of her dress, perhaps visible even through her thin bra. Not that Gil could see. But *she* knew.

"Do you need the heater?" he asked gruffly, his gaze dark and hungry.

She shook her head. "It's not that cold in the car."

Their stilted, prosaic conversation might have been funny if she hadn't been wound so tightly. Her skin hummed with the need to feel his touch. Fortunately for her, Gil must have been on the same page.

"Come here, Bailey." They were sitting in the front of his fancy, enormous truck. The wide bench seat presented all sorts of intriguing possibilities.

She scooted closer, barely noticing when his jacket slipped away. "Why?" she asked. "Do I need to warm you up?"

His lips quirked in what might have been a grin had he not been so focused on finding her mouth with his. "Any warmer," he groaned, "and I'll be in danger of getting arrested." He cupped the back of her neck in one big hand and used the other to anchor her chin. Lazily, with no apparent hurry, he kissed her. His lips were firm and warm and took without asking. He tasted faintly of coffee and whipped cream.

"Gil…" The word trailed off on a whimper when he released her chin and found her knee.

Slowly, he glided his palm up her thigh. His whole body jerked when he discovered the edge of her stocking and the tiny satin rosette that was her garter. "Sweet heaven," he groaned. "You little tease."

She nipped his chin with sharp teeth. "I spend a lot of time on the job," she murmured, loosening his tie and unbuttoning two buttons at his throat. "When I dress up, I like feminine lingerie."

His fingers played with the edge of the stocking, his hand warm and hard. "Promise me something," he groaned, the words like ground glass.

She felt him trembling and understood the power she wielded. Both exultant and abashed, she struggled to find footing in the quicksand at her feet. Was this right for her? For Gil? What were they doing?

"Promise you what?" she asked. More than anything she wanted to take his hand and push it higher. But they were in a public parking lot, and it was time to pick up Cade.

"Promise me you'll wear this the first time we're together." He caressed the bare skin around her garter with his fingertip. Everything inside her went hot and shaky. She felt reckless, and that was enough to slow her down. Bailey Collins was never reckless. Not in her job and not in her personal life.

Someone had to be strong in the midst of insanity. This time it had to be her. With great regret, she removed his hand and slid to her side of the vehicle as far as she could go. "Will there be a time like that?" she asked.

"God, I hope so," he said, banging his fist on the steering wheel. "Because if I don't have you soon, I can't be held responsible for what happens."

He was exaggerating. She knew that. But the desperation in his voice was real and unmistakable "Look at your watch," she pleaded. "We have to go."

That he obeyed her was no victory. She wanted to stay with him in the intimate confines of the truck cab. In fact, she would have stayed there all night if he had asked. Though she hadn't fooled around like that as a high school kid, the idea held a certain appeal to a woman whose love life had been barren of late.

On the brief drive to Gil's cousin's house, silence reigned. The swish of the windshield wipers was the only sound. At their destination, Gil parked by the curb and hopped out. Minutes later, he returned, carrying a sleeping Cade. At Gil's motion, she leaned across the seat and opened his door.

Gently, his face unreadable, he scooted Cade to the middle and belted him into his booster seat. The boy's body was limp. When he slumped in Bailey's direction, she put her left arm around him and held him close. He smelled like peanut butter and little-boy sweat.

Gil climbed in and stared at his son. "He's dead to the world."

"Just as well," Bailey said. "Maybe this will all seem like a dream to him."

"Thank you for understanding. Most women would be offended."

"Not me. You're a father first and foremost. I respect that. Cade is a very lucky boy." She kissed the top of the child's head. "Take me home, Gil."

Gil drove more slowly than usual, fully aware that he was distracted. Bailey's care and consideration for his son impacted Gil in ways he couldn't explain. His brain ran in circles, torn between imagining intimacy with Bailey one second and wondering how he could ever test a relationship with a woman without dragging his son into it.

At McDaniel's Acres he pulled to a stop in front of the ranch house and put the truck in Park. Bailey put a hand on his arm. "Don't get out. You can't leave him here alone."

Gil shook his head. "He's fine." He went around the truck and opened Bailey's door, holding her hand to help her out. Remembering what she was wearing beneath that demure black dress made him hard all over again. "Good night, Bailey." He slid his hands beneath her thick, silky hair and anchored her head for his kiss.

She leaned into him, her lips eager and soft, her breasts crushed against his chest. Though he knew her to be tough and capable, when he held her like this, he wanted to protect her at all costs. The danger inherent in her job was never far from his mind.

He wedged a thigh between her legs, pulling her hips against his, letting her feel the extent of his need. "I'm working on an idea," he said. "Will you trust me?"

She toyed with his belt buckle. "Of course." The breathless note in her voice told him all he needed to know. He wasn't in this alone.

"Tomorrow. At the club. I'll explain."

"Yes." She ran her hand over the late-day stubble on his chin. He opened his mouth and bit gently on one of her fingertips.

The erotic action was a big mistake. The rush of lust almost crippled him. Backing away from her the way he would an angry rattler, he put the body of the truck between them. It was good that his son was asleep in the cab of the truck. Otherwise, Gil just might have taken Bailey standing up.

His forehead broke out in a cold sweat thinking about it. "Sleep well," he said, knowing that he wouldn't.

Bailey walked halfway up the steps, then turned to look at him. "I had fun tonight." Her voice carried on the night breeze. "Good night, Gil."

He got into the truck and leaned his forehead against the steering wheel, his heart slugging in his chest as if he'd run a marathon. Something was going to have to change. And soon....

Bailey entered the house quietly, though since it was not yet ten, likely no one was asleep. Chance McDaniel stood in the lobby chatting with a couple of gray-headed ladies from Ohio. Bailey had met them when she first arrived. Learning to ride a horse was a big item on their bucket list, and Chance's patient staff was helping that dream come true.

The owner of the dude ranch excused himself when he saw her enter and crossed the floor. "Everything okay?"

Her face must have reflected some of her turmoil. She flushed. "Fine. No problem."

He lifted an eyebrow. "Was that Gil Addison's truck I saw out front?"

Her flush deepened. "It was. We had dinner together."

Chance's smile was more of a grimace. "I suppose that means at least one of us is no longer on your suspect list."

"A man is innocent until proven guilty," she said.

Chance shook his head, his gaze hooded. "Doesn't feel that way from where I'm standing."

Bailey headed for the stairs, wishing she had the luxury of becoming friends with Chance. Already, in the short time she had been around, she felt like he was a man who could be trusted. But hard evidence was composed of facts and not feelings. Until she could completely clear his name from the suspect list, she couldn't get too friendly. It was impossible to imagine Chance committing a kidnapping. But she knew better than most that some people hid unimaginable secrets. Chance didn't. She was almost positive. Hopefully, soon she could prove it.

Upstairs, she stripped out of the one nice dress she had brought with her to Royal and stared at her reflection in the mirror. The tiny undies and demibra that matched the garter belt were intensely feminine. Closing her eyes, she tried to imagine the look on Gil's face if he saw her like this. His raw passion elated her, made her feel special and wanted.

In the shower, she imagined Gil at her side, his face all planes and angles as he stared at her with male determination. His body was intensely masculine, strong and rugged. The juxtaposition of his tenderness with Cade and his ruthless pursuit of Bailey should have confused her, but in a way, it made perfect sense. He was a man of deep emotions, whether it be love for his son or hunger for the woman in his arms.

She wouldn't be the woman in his *life*, not long-term. But if the fates were kind, she would certainly enjoy exploring her sensual side with him until it was time for her to leave.

Sliding her soapy fingers over her slick breasts, she inhaled sharply as arousal pumped through her veins like thick honey. Her nipples were taut nubs, their ache an ever-present reminder that she was young and in need of a man's touch.

Dragging the washcloth between her legs, she winced as her body demanded attention. It didn't take more than a few languid strokes before she came with a low moan and rested her forehead against the tile as her heartbeat slowly returned to normal.

On shaky legs, she got out and dried off, already anticipating the following day. What did Gil have in mind? And how long would they have to wait?

She was almost asleep when the cell phone on the bedside table vibrated suddenly. Snatching it up, she glanced at the screen. Though she had only dialed it once before, she recognized Gil's number. "Hello."

"Bailey. I just looked at the clock. I'm sorry. Were you asleep?"

"Not quite." She shifted, sitting up against the headboard. "Is something wrong?"

The silence on the other end of the phone lengthened. "Define wrong."

"Is Cade okay?"

Gil's voice was hoarse. "He's fine. Never even woke up when I carried him to his bed."

"That's good."

"Yeah." The awkward conversation was going nowhere. "I wish our evening could have lasted longer," he said.

She knew exactly what he meant. "Me, too." Suddenly, something struck her. "Are *you* in bed?" she asked, not sure if she wanted to know or not.

"Yes. And wishing you were here beside me."

She swallowed hard. The man was nothing if not honest. "I need you to be sure, Gil. Things will be complicated, and I don't want you to resent me when this is all over."

"I wasn't very nice to you at first, was I? And you're not sure if I fully trust you."

She heard the regret in his voice. "You were entitled to your opinion. In your place, I might have been just as aggravated. It's never easy to be questioned about a crime. It makes innocent people jittery. I understand."

"I don't want you to think I'm taking advantage of you. I really like you, Bailey. In spite of your job."

She smiled, smoothing her free hand over the soft, faded pattern of the double wedding ring quilt on her bed. "I like you, too, Gil. In spite of your bullheadedness."

"Touché."

His chuckle warmed her. "I'm not having phone sex with you," she said firmly, yet willing to be persuaded.

"Trust me, Bailey, when we finally have sex, it's going to be a helluva lot more exciting than mere words. I'm going to let you turn my world upside down and then return the favor."

Her breath caught as her legs moved restlessly against the sheets. "You're awfully confident."

"It has nothing to do with confidence. You and I are two of a kind. We're loners. Who feel things deeply and have a strong sense of responsibility toward those who depend on us. I think that's why I felt something for you the first day we met. You're not only beautiful and sexy, but you care about things. About people. About a little boy who wants a mother...."

"You know I'm not applying for that job, right?"

"I know. But how do you feel about the boy's father?"

Bailey sucked in a breath. Perhaps it was easier to be honest when he wasn't staring at her face to face. "I want to spend time with you, Gil...in all sorts of ways...."

He said something short and sharp that she couldn't quite hear. And then his voice echoed over the connection more strongly. "Not all women are as honest as you," he said.

She smiled, knowing he couldn't see. "Have I shocked you?"

"Only in the best possible way." He paused. "Go to sleep, Bailey. I'll see you tomorrow."

"Tomorrow..."

She fell asleep thinking about all the possibilities tied up in that one wonderful word.

Seven

Bailey worked her way through one drawer after another, her pile of file folders growing along with her list of questions. She'd been at the club all day, and Gil had never once shown his face. When she had arrived at ten as usual that morning, the club receptionist met her and handed over a key, saying that Mr. Addison had been detained.

Bailey tried not to brood over hurt feelings, but her reaction to Gil's absence was beginning to make her question whether it was wise to get involved with him at all. She didn't want to analyze his every move for evidence of whether or not he really cared. Fear of making an embarrassing misstep in their relationship kept her on edge.

At a quarter to five she began packing up her things, prepared to go home and pore over the new information she had gleaned. Still, nothing and no one jumped out at her as a likely suspect. But there were a lot of club members who had connections to Alex, and Bailey was pretty sure that given the chance to talk to them she might be able to make progress with her case.

When Gil walked into the small office, again without announcing his presence beforehand, she sucked in a sharp breath, but otherwise managed to face him with a neutral expression. Her hands continued to move, tidying up the work space, but her body was rigid.

Gil didn't look any happier than she felt. "I had five phone calls today," he said abruptly. "All of them wondering why I've allowed a woman I'm dating to spend time at the club without me present."

She winced. "So they know what I'm doing?"

"Not specifically. It's my fault for giving the receptionist my key. She's a nice woman, but she can't keep her mouth shut."

"What did you tell them?"

"I thought about making up a story, but frankly, you're a state investigator. Everyone in town knows it. Sooner or later, people were going to put two and two together. It was one thing for you to be seen eating lunch with Cade and me at the club. But I should have thought through the implications of you being here on your own today."

"So you told them the truth."

He nodded his head. "I did. And I can't repeat most of what was said in return. People don't like knowing that their personal business is being opened up to an outsider, especially one with government connections."

"I'm sorry, Gil."

"It's not your fault." He shrugged, his expression rueful. "You're merely doing your job. I can handle a little heat, Bailey. It's you I'm worried about."

"I told you...I can take care of myself."

"Alex Santiago would have told me the same thing,

and look what happened to him. Some nutcase decided to kidnap him."

"There had to be a reason. Some connection we're not seeing."

"Yes. And because we can't point to the perpetrator yet, the danger is still very real. What if someone tries to dissuade you from probing any further?"

"I take precautions. That's one reason I'm not staying in town. Chance's place is as safe as anywhere I can think of. Too many people around for anyone to get to me unnoticed. Not to mention the fact that I can keep an eye on Chance."

Gil ran a hand across the back of his neck, his face a thundercloud. "He has nothing to hide, Bailey. I'll be damn glad when this is all over."

"Not me," she said quietly. "At least not entirely. Because that means I'll have to head home."

His jaw tightened as the truth of her words sank in. Whatever time the two of them shared was likely to be very brief. Her heart shied away from that knowledge. Leaving Royal was a reality she didn't want to contemplate. Especially not now that Gil had admitted he wanted her.

He frowned as he took her shoulders in his hands and squeezed gently. "*Please* be careful, Bailey."

She moved closer into his embrace, kissed his cheek, and sighed. "I'm always careful." For long seconds, they stood there quietly as something fragile and precious bloomed. To have the right to lean on him, even symbolically, was very sweet. His hard frame seemed to shelter hers, even though she was quite capable of caring for herself.

The pull of his masculinity called to a part of her she often kept out of sight. Being "girlie" was the last thing she needed in her line of work. But with Gil, she felt herself letting down barriers. Softening. Needing.

"Tell me," she said, idly running her fingers over his collarbone. "What is this idea you were working on?"

He set her at arm's length, his expression unreadable. "You want to interview club members—right?"

"Yes. Maybe half a dozen or more."

"The thing is, Bailey, I can't stop you from doing what you were sent here to do, but I also can't condone using the club for those interviews. The TCC is where guys come to get away from life. To chill out and kick back. They have a right to their privacy. But…"

"But what?"

"But I think it might go down better if we do it at my place. I'll contact whomever you tell me and invite them out to the Straight Arrow tomorrow night. I won't lie. I'll tell them flat out why they're coming. But I'll throw some steaks on the grill and open a case of beer, and hopefully, we can mitigate any negative backlash."

"You'd do that for me?" What he was suggesting made perfect sense. Neutral territory.

He kissed her nose. "It's not that big a deal. But, yes."

"What about Cade? Will he be there?"

"Actually…"

For the first time since she had known him, Gil looked uncomfortable.

"What? What are you not telling me?"

"I have friends in Midland with a little boy exactly Cade's age. They're planning a sleepover birthday for their son and they want Cade to come. I'm driving him up there in the morning."

She fidgeted, not sure if she was reading him correctly.

Gil's smile was crooked. "I hope you'll pack a bag and stay at the Straight Arrow with me once our guests are gone."

* * *

Twenty-four hours later, Bailey drove out the familiar road to Gil's sprawling ranch, wondering how she had gone from being a hardworking investigator to a woman contemplating a night with her lover in one dizzying swoop.

The juxtaposition of professional and personal in the upcoming evening made her skittish. It was important that she come across as businesslike and competent when she interviewed Gil's friends and acquaintances. If any of them got wind of what Gil had planned for later, her credibility would be shot.

But there was no real cause for alarm. Gil didn't want gossip any more than Bailey did. For his son's sake, if nothing else.

When she arrived, Gil greeted her at the door. Two high-end pickup trucks were already parked out front. "Come on in," he said. "I thought you could go ahead and get started before dinner. We'll set you up in the front parlor. It was always my mom's holy of holies, but I think it will give you the privacy you need."

As they traversed the narrow hallway to the back of the house, Gil suddenly dragged her to a halt and pushed her against the antique wallpaper for a hard, hungry kiss. "I missed you today," he muttered, his hips anchoring her to the unyielding surface.

She returned the kiss eagerly, inhaling the scent of starched cotton and well-oiled leather. Gil was dressed casually in jeans, cowboy boots and a white shirt with the sleeves rolled up. He radiated tough masculinity, and despite her advanced degrees and the level to which she had risen in her career, it was humbling and embarrassing to admit that she was definitely turned on by his macho swagger.

"I missed you, too," she said primly. "And I want you

to know how much I appreciate all you've done to set this up tonight."

He nibbled the side of her neck. "You can thank me later. There's a full moon tonight. The view from my bedroom window is spectacular."

The breath caught in her throat as he hit a particularly sensitive spot. "Promises, promises…" She swallowed back an embarrassing moan. "There are vehicles out front. I assume we're not alone?"

As a protest, it was weak.

Gil rested his forehead against hers, his thumbs brushing the thin cotton of her blouse where it glided over her breasts. "You make me want to forget everything. That's dangerous."

"Should I apologize?" Her arms linked around his neck, feeling his warmth, his solidness.

"Come on," he said gruffly. "Let's get this over with."

Gil had to hand it to Bailey. She knew how to be charming. Her manner with the men he had invited hit just the right note. Neither authoritative nor tentative, she invited the guests to speak with her in private one by one. And as each man returned from the parlor, no one seemed particularly bent out of shape by Bailey's informal interrogation.

Over dinner, Gil surveyed the assorted group of men. Only two on his list had begged off. Sheriff Nathan Battle, who was on duty, and Paul Windsor, who was out of town on a business trip.

The rest had varying degrees of history with Alex Santiago. Douglas Firestone, Ryan Grant, the twins—Josh and Sam Gordon, Zach Lassiter, and Beau Hacket. With the possible exception of Hacket, Gil liked and respected every man present. And even Hacket, despite his son's recent vandalism of the child care center at the club, hardly seemed the type to kidnap anybody.

Fortunately, the medium-rare steaks were a big hit, the beer held out, and Bailey had the good sense to excuse herself from the table before the party became rowdy. By the time the evening wound down around ten, Gil was fairly certain that none of his guests really remembered why they had come. Each one went home with his belly full and perhaps a forbidden cigar or two smoked on the way out.

Gil closed and locked the front door, leaning against it with a sigh. As male bonding went, the evening was a home run.

But all he could think about was getting Bailey naked.

He found her in the parlor, her laptop open, her head bent studiously over a legal pad of notes. "Did you get anything good?" he asked, sprawling in a chair that was more comfortable than it looked.

She glanced up at him, her teeth worrying her bottom lip. "I have no idea. They all claim to like Alex. Firestone does admit to arguing with him, but insists it was nothing significant. Hacket tried to schmooze me and pretend that he's a saint. But overall, I came up with nothing that I didn't already know or suspect."

He saw the frustration on her face. "I invited Chance, but he was reluctant to come."

"I know. He glares at me when he thinks I'm not looking." She rubbed her temples with her index fingers. "I've had plenty of opportunity to talk to him, and if he's the kind of man to commit a felony, I'll be very surprised."

"Men in love do strange things."

"Is he? In love, I mean? You know him better than I do."

"I don't know. He and Cara were very close. But once Alex came on the scene, she had eyes for nobody else."

"So with Alex gone, Chance might try to make his move?"

"Even if he does, it still doesn't mean he had anything to do with Alex's disappearance."

"True…"

She stood up and stretched her arms toward the ceiling. "Enough of this. I'm officially off the clock until tomorrow."

Gil linked his hands behind his head. "I like the sound of that."

Hands on hips, she stared at him.

"What?" he asked, raising an eyebrow.

"Will I seem hopelessly inexperienced if I tell you I'm nervous?"

He rolled to his feet and walked toward her, grinning when she backed up and nearly toppled an antique glass pitcher. "There's nothing to be nervous about."

"That's what you think. I'm having trouble with the shift from work to play."

He tucked her hair behind her ears, glad that she had left it loose tonight. "I can help with that." Scooping her into his arms, he ignored her squeak of protest. "We're alone at last. I thought they would never leave." Striding out of the room and up the stairs, he felt his heart beating faster and faster, though carrying his burden was no strain. "In case it matters," he said, nuzzling her ear, "you're the first woman I've ever invited for a sleepover."

Bailey clung to Gil's neck, mortified that he had picked her up. She was not a petite woman, yet he seemed completely at ease. In the midst of being flustered by his romantic gesture, she was also taken aback by the casual way he told her this night was special.

In the doorway to his bedroom, he paused. "Last chance to say no." His dark eyes held not a flicker of humor.

She ran her thumb along his chiseled jawline. "I don't want to say no. I need you, Gil. I want you. Even if this night is all we have."

His slight frown told her he didn't like that last bit, but she was trying to be practical. Cade couldn't be shuttled off to friends and neighbors all the time, and Gil didn't want to parade his love life in front of his son. Any way you looked at it, tonight's encounter was not likely to be repeated.

Gil strode toward the bed and set her on her feet. He held her hands, his expression unreadable. "I've watched you for weeks," he murmured. "And even when I told myself you were an officious pain in the ass, I knew in my heart that I wanted you."

"All I saw was the disapproval," she confessed. "It hurt that you thought so little of me. And you seemed angry all the time."

"A defense," he said simply. "I hoped you would leave and I could forget the way your hair shines with fire in the sunlight or the way your long legs carry you across a crowded street."

Bailey's heart fluttered. Poetry from the man who was pragmatic and straightforward. He didn't dress it up or spout it effusively, thus making the quiet, sincere words all the more powerful.

She swallowed. "I had no idea."

"You weren't supposed to. I've done my damnedest to stay away from you. But when you called me about access to the club, I knew I was a goner." His smile was lopsided. "A man can only have so much self-control, and you tested mine to the limit. Turns out, I'm not as strong as I thought."

"I wish I could tell you I'm sorry about that, but I'm not. I've had an embarrassing crush on you since we first met."

"Nice to know." He grinned, the flash of white teeth literally taking her breath away. Gil bore great responsibilities and had a serious streak a mile wide. But this man, this lighthearted, teasing man, looked younger and happier than she had ever seen him.

She tugged her hands free and punched him in the arm. "You have to know that every woman in town thinks you're a hottie."

His smile faded, replaced by a searing look in his deep brown eyes that made her toes curl. "The only woman whose opinion interests me is you, Bailey." He curled an arm around her waist and dragged her closer. "But I think I'm done talking."

Wild elation streaked through her veins. His arms were hard and strong, binding her without mercy. She kissed him recklessly, clumsily, as if somewhere a clock counted down the seconds they could be together. The air in the room was charged.

"Take off your boots," she demanded. Her fuddled brain knew the priceless antique quilt on Gil's bed shouldn't be damaged. He released her only long enough to obey, toeing off each one and facing her in his sock feet.

He should have looked more vulnerable, less of a threat. But somehow that wasn't the case. "Any other orders?" he asked, the words mild despite his hot, determined expression.

She nodded slowly. "Now the belt."

Like the boots, the belt was constructed of expensive hand-tooled leather. Gil unfastened the buckle and made a production of sliding the length of cowhide through each loop. When it was free, he coiled it and tossed it on a chair.

His jaw flexed. His chest rose and fell rapidly with each labored breath. "Whatever you want, Bailey."

The way he looked at her made her body go lax with arousal, even as her hands fisted helplessly at her sides. Her thighs pressed together. Where her body prepared for his, she was damp and ready. She had known sexual desire in the past, but never this writhing hunger that turned her insides into an ache that consumed her.

Paralyzed suddenly by the knowledge that she wasn't really a femme fatale, she fell silent.

Gil seemed to read her hesitation. "You were on a roll," he muttered. "Don't stop now."

Apparently her bent for bossiness entertained him. She shifted from one foot to the other, realizing suddenly that her clothes were far too tight, much too hot. "The shirt," she said. "Unbutton it slowly."

Eight

She had created a monster. Straitlaced Gil Addison showed a definite talent for stripping. If he had loosened his shirt buttons any more slowly, Bailey might have lost it and ripped the fabric apart with her two hands. But she had asked and he had answered, so all she could do was watch as he tormented her.

When the shirt hung open, he stopped. She hadn't requested that he take it off, and he was obeying the letter of the law. His silence rattled her. What was he thinking? The uncertainty dried up any further desire to script this encounter. Her momentary lead in the dance no longer appealed.

They were separated by a distance of only three or four feet. Close enough for her to see the shadow of late-day stubble on his chin. The evidence of his masculinity underlined the differences between them. Bailey knew how to use a weapon and could even bring most men down using her training in martial arts.

Many people would describe her as tough.

But Gil…Gil was the real deal. His sleek, long-limbed body rippled with muscle. His olive skin gleamed with health and vigor. He was a man capable of defending those he loved. At the peak of his physical strength and power.

Bailey's heart twisted. Hard. What would it be like to be loved by Gil Addison? Clearly, he had loved his dead wife once upon a time. And of course he loved his parents and his son. But to be a woman loved by a man like Gil… that would be an incredible thing. In the present context, though, that thought was a fantasy, one she might as well put out of her mind.

Tonight was about human need. Sex. That was all. She and Gil were drawn to each other, because they both spent too many nights alone. So during this brief moment in time, they were going to cling to each other and enjoy the pleasures of carnal excess.

Perhaps Gil was more intuitive than she realized, for he abandoned his sexy pose and stalked her, backing her up until her hips hit the bed. "You aren't saying much," he taunted. "Cat got your tongue?"

She curled an arm around the bedpost, clinging in hopes that her shaky legs wouldn't give out. "Just admiring the view." It wouldn't do to let him know how much seeing his beautiful body in the privacy of his bedroom rattled her.

He shrugged out of the shirt and let it fall. Taking her free hand, he placed it flat over his heart. "Feel what you do to me."

The rapid thud of his heartbeat was unmistakable. Without thinking, she rubbed gently, as though she could absorb his life force through her fingertips. Touching him was both intimate and arousing.

Gil groaned and closed his eyes. Was it possible that he was as turned on as she was? Experimentally, she scraped her thumbnail across one flat, brown nipple. Gil put his hand over hers, trapping it against his hot skin. "Don't poke the tiger, Bailey. I have plans for tonight, and they don't involve coming too soon like a callow teenager."

His blunt speaking made her cheeks flame. "I want to please you. I need to know what you like."

"You *do* please me, in every way. I love your strength and your integrity. And I love the way you treat my son."

"He's lucky to have a dad like you."

Gil caressed her cheek, his gaze hooded. "I spend much of my time being Cade's father. I know that role inside and out. Tonight…" He paused and she saw the muscles in his throat contract. "Tonight I'm just a man. A man who wants *you*."

She slipped her arms around his neck, appreciating the distinction, even if it wasn't wholly true. Gil could have any woman he wanted, but in a town like Royal, such a relationship would be tricky. Sleeping with Bailey was less complicated. She understood that.

Resting her head on his shoulder, she whispered the bare, honest truth. "I want you to make love to me Gil. More than I've ever wanted another man. Don't make us wait any longer."

Gil felt the sting of strong emotion in his throat and his eyes. Bailey Collins was the most fascinating, unconsciously sensual woman he had ever met. Now that she was here—in his bedroom, about to make a number of his more torrid fantasies come to life—all he could think about was how soon he was going to lose her.

He slammed the door on those images. Who and what he needed was right in front of him…literally. Bailey was warm and real and so very, very beautiful. Running his hands though her hair, he imagined what it was going to look like spread across his pillow. "In other circumstances, I might insist that anticipation is half of the pleasure. But tonight, I'm in no mood to delay anything at all." He unfolded her arms from around his neck. "My turn, lovely Bailey."

As her cheeks turned the color of a ripe tomato, he undressed her bit by bit, supporting her arm as she stepped out of her clothes. His surmise had been right on target. She wore naughty undies beneath, this time pale pink trimmed in mocha lace. The tiny bikini panties and matching bra were ultrafeminine, reminding him that despite the toughness she exhibited in her job, Bailey was all woman.

She seemed reluctant to dispense with the final layer that shielded her full nudity. So he matter-of-factly shucked his jeans and boxers and socks in a couple of quick moves. Bailey's eyes widened. The expression on her face was gratifying.

He was fully erect, and aching to possess her. But first he was going to have to coax her into relaxing. "I don't know what you're thinking," he complained. "Is that deer-in-the-headlights look you're giving me because you've changed your mind or because I'm going too fast?"

She licked her lips, arms crossed beneath her breasts. "Neither," she said quietly. "I'm enjoying the moment."

"Could you possibly enjoy the moment under the covers? I'm getting cold feet."

That made her giggle, and some of the rigidity left her posture. "I'm on board with that."

He tugged her close for a quick kiss and then turned back the covers on the large, wide bed. His sheets were soft white cotton, scented with sunshine. The housekeeper was a big fan of using a clothesline, and truth be told, Gil liked it. The smell made him think of being a kid.

When he helped Bailey crawl beneath the sheet and the quilt, however, childhood was the last thing on his mind.

His brain blanked for a moment, all his senses absorbing the novel and gratifying sensation of feeling Bailey's arms and legs tangle with his. She was soft, so soft. He held her tightly, burying his face in her hair.

"I've imagined this moment for weeks," he admitted, flattening his palm on her belly and teasing her navel with his pinkie. It would almost have been enough just to hold her. To revel in the knowledge that she had come to him of her own free will and *wanted* to share his bed.

Bailey kissed his chin, her hands roving across his pecs and his shoulders. "Does it measure up?"

He wedged a thigh between hers and groaned as his thick, almost painful shaft rubbed against her leg. "I'm not sure. I'm having trouble believing this is real. I don't want to wake up in a minute and find out I was dreaming."

Without warning, her hand closed around his erection. "I'm real," she said. "We're real. Here. Together."

When she began stroking him, his eyes closed involuntarily. He had been leaning over her on one elbow, but now he fell back on the bed, his hands fisting in the sheet. *Holy hell.* It wasn't the effects of extended abstinence making him insane. It was the way she touched him. Her gentle movements were exactly right.

The first sexual encounter between a man and a woman was supposed to be fraught with pitfalls, neither partner knowing the other's preferences. Bailey was putting paid to that idea. Everything she did was gut-level perfect. Now she was the one leaning over *him*, her silky hair falling around them as she kissed him softly. Kiss/stroke. Kiss/stroke. The sequence made him dizzy with lust.

His sex quivered every time her lips found his. He held the back of her neck to deepen the kiss and to make sure she didn't stop what she was doing. But soon, far too soon, he had to call a halt. Sucking in raw lungfuls of air, he shook his head, half-crazed with hunger. "Enough," he croaked. He hovered on a knife-edge of arousal.

As he predicted, the moon had found its way into his bedroom, the silver orb framed by his window. The drapes were open. Shafts of white light spilled over Bailey's face, giving her the look of an ice queen. But no ice queen ever emanated the kind of warmth that could save a man's life. Gil hadn't fully understood the depths of his loneliness until he brought Bailey to his home and to his bed.

He had told himself repeatedly over the past few years that being Cade's father was more important than anything. And it was. A sacred obligation. But Gil was neither a monk nor a saint, and in this instant he realized how sterile he had allowed his life to become.

Every cell in his body cried out at the indulgence of touching Bailey, of kissing her. Like flowers blooming wildly in the once-barren desert after a storm, he found himself drunk with pleasure. She rolled with him in the bed, laughing softly as they bumped noses.

"This is nice," she said, the voice more prim than her actions. "I never knew Gil-the-sex-maniac existed."

"You're not naked," he complained.

Sitting up, she reached behind her back and unfastened her bra, dropping it at the foot of the bed. Now, the moon painted two perfect breasts with a magical palette of light and shadow. Bailey dragged her hair over one shoulder, her head cocked as she tried to read his expression. He, unlike his partner, was cast in semi-gloom.

"Is this what you had in mind?"

"Getting there," he muttered. He slid his hand between her smooth thighs and stroked the center of her panties. The scent of her came to him, warm and heady. "These, too." Rising to his knees, he shoved the offending scrap of nylon down her hips.

Bailey lay back, arms above her head, and let him finish the job. The moon took her natural beauty and made it supernatural, as though a fairy or a sprite had come to him in a mirage. Touching her was the only way to prove she wouldn't fade away.

Kneeling between her legs, he leaned forward and mapped her body like a blind man, his caresses making her whimper and stir restlessly. Her face, her throat. Each lovely breast. The narrow span of her waist. The flare of her hips.

He stopped there, breathing hard. Running through the back of his mind was the knowledge that he was missing something very important, something key to this moment.

Bailey put a hand on his thigh. "Do you have condoms?" she asked softly.

He sensed that the question embarrassed her. "Yes." Leaving her momentarily was unthinkable, but he would never do something she would regret. After sheathing himself in latex, he went back to her, his hands shaking as he sprawled on his side.

She turned her head to look at him, her lips curved in a smile that made him want to drag her beneath him like a caveman. But his evolved side held sway...barely. Tonight was about more than his sexual starvation. It was about pleasing Bailey.

He parted her sex with gentle fingers and tested her readiness. Warmth and wetness met his touch. Inserting two fingers into her tight passage, he played with her until she began to beg.

"Now, Gil. Please. Now."

Surprisingly, her urgency enabled him to chain his own impatience. Though his arousal pulsed and throbbed like a raw, aching nerve, he found himself entranced with tormenting Bailey. Locating the tiny nub that was her nerve center, he rubbed softly, exulting when she cried out and arched her back as the climax rolled over her.

When she was limp and still, he began all over again.

Bailey didn't know what she had done in a previous life to deserve such a night of enchantment, but she wasn't about to complain. Her world had narrowed to the confines of Gil Addison's bed. Nothing beyond that perimeter mattered for the next few hours.

Her body sated with pleasure, she struggled to focus her fuzzy thought processes. She was aware that Gil watched her, hawk-like, his features masked in the semidarkness. His back was to the window, so while *he* could look his fill of her nakedness painted in lunar glow, she was less able to gauge his mood.

She lifted a hand and let it fall. "You've destroyed me," she said, the words slurred. Her orgasm had been intense, unprecedented. To realize that he could draw such a response from her was daunting. What if tonight's affair ruined her for other men?

When he touched her again, she flinched.

Laughing softly, he spread her legs and positioned the head of his sex at her core. "I want you to remember every second of this night," he said hoarsely. "Because I'm going to make love to you until neither of us can remember our names."

Bailey believed him implicitly. Heat radiated from his big body, warming her chilled skin. Now that her pulse had settled back to normal, the room was cool.

Gently he stroked her swollen folds with his shaft. She was so sensitized that the caress was almost too much. Incredibly, as he brushed her intimately, her body began to thrum again with the need for him, the urgency to have him inside her.

Suddenly, desperately, she wanted to turn on a light.
She wanted to catch every moment of the insanity, to revel
in every nuance of expression that crossed his face as he
pleasured both of them.

Her breath caught when he cupped her bottom and
canted her hips. "Now," he promised, the single syllable
guttural. "Now, Bailey."

He was thick and hard. Her flesh yielded to his penetra-
tion slowly. On the heels of her earlier climax, this claiming was overwhelming. She shook her head from side to
side, incredulous that such feelings were real. Nothing in
her past had prepared her for Gil.

He held her tenderly as he took her with the confidence
of a man who knew what he wanted. What she wanted.
Kisses interspersed with raw lunges that took him all the
way to the mouth of her womb. His arms quivered as he
kept his weight from crushing her into the bed.

She wrapped her legs around his waist, feeling the
power, the potency. Her fingernails dug into his shoulders, marking him as hers. She could fall in love with him
so easily... For many weeks she had watched him from afar,
seeing the respect people afforded him, witnessing the joy
in his son's face, understanding the position and influence
Gil wielded in the community.

Tonight, though, her feelings went far beyond admiration. Gil had taken her heart. Perhaps he didn't even know
it. Perhaps it didn't even matter. For a stolen moment in
time the only real measure was how they each gave and
received pleasure.

She clung to him as he thrust wildly, his force shaking
the bed. A tendril of heat curled in her lower abdomen,
spread throughout her pelvis and burst into full flame as
she pitched over a sharp edge in the midst of Gil's hoarse
shout of completion.

* * *

They must have dozed in the aftermath. When she opened her eyes, the moon had shifted and was barely visible in the corner of the window. The room was quiet. Gil lay half on top of her, his face buried in the sheet. Despite the chill in the air, they were both sticky with sweat.

She eased to one side, wincing when he muttered in his sleep. Stealthily, she moved an inch at a time until she could free herself and slide from the bed. After using the bathroom and freshening up, she pondered the possibility of a hot shower. The lure was impossible to resist. A thick terrycloth robe hung on the back of the door, so she dropped it on the floor in arms' reach and turned on the water.

Soon, steam filled the roomy enclosure. Clearly, Gil had spent money on modernization at some point. Bailey applauded his choice. The bold turquoise and amber tiles reminded her of Spain's artistic influence in Texas architecture.

The water was hot and reviving, chasing the chill from her bones. She didn't bother with her hair, keeping it mostly dry. Though Gil had invited her to spend the night, she was already feeling anxious about "the morning after." Perhaps it would be better to say farewell and head on home very soon. Things that seemed perfectly natural and normal under the hypnotic effects of moonlight could develop into awkward realities in the cold light of day. She didn't want to spoil a perfect memory with an uncomfortable goodbye that left her feeling empty and lonelier than when she started.

Suddenly, the frosted-glass shower door opened and Gil's big body appeared in the opening. "Room for one more?"

Nine

Gil caught the play of emotions that skittered across his lover's face. Surprised pleasure. Shy embarrassment. Wary uncertainty.

She nodded. "Of course."

There was no *of course* about any of this. He and Bailey were breaking new ground, and he sensed that she had gotten cold feet in more ways than one. Giving her a moment to adjust to his presence, he took the soap and turned his back as he washed himself. His sex was hard and ready, but he wouldn't rush her. This was too important.

When he felt two hands on his back, rubbing his soap-slicked skin, he closed his eyes and smiled. "That feels good," he groaned, resting his head against the wall, feeling the hot, stinging spray pound his skin.

Bailey's arms encircled his waist from behind. He sucked in a sharp breath when he felt the press of her soft breasts on his back. "I was thinking about going home now," she said.

Gil jerked in shock and spun to face her, nearly depositing both of them on the slippery floor. He grabbed her upper arms to steady her. "What the hell are you talking about?"

Her eyes were huge. She shrugged helplessly. "You have employees and obligations. Tomorrow morning things will be different."

"Different, how?" His temper simmered.

"You know…weird."

He ran a finger down her nose and shook his head with a sigh. "Why do women have to be so complicated?" He turned off the water and pulled her into his arms, deliberately pressing his erection against the notch where her legs met.

"Life is complicated. *I'm* pretty simple."

He felt her shiver. "As much as I'd like to debate that last point, I think I need to warm you up. Put on my robe and I'll build a fire."

As they both dried off, he tried not to look at her, but it was like telling sailors not to gaze at sirens on the rocks. His gaze tracked her every graceful movement. The moment when she shrouded her nude form in his enveloping robe was a major disappointment.

The fireplace in his bedroom was original to the house and, like the other three scattered throughout his home, cost a fortune to insure. He rarely took the time to use this one, because many nights he was late coming to bed.

Now, though, he was glad of the ambience.

In his peripheral vision he was aware of Bailey climbing back into bed and huddling under the covers. In addition to growing up on a ranch, Gil had been a Boy Scout, so he soon had a roaring blaze that popped and crackled and began to fill the room with cozy warmth.

He rose from a squatting position and found her watching him, unmistakable arousal in her eyes. Her lips parted. Her breath came quickly. Men were rarely as modest as women, so it gave him not a second's pause to stride toward the bed, naked and determined. She couldn't hide what she was feeling. Not now.

When he scooted in beside her, she squawked as his cold feet made contact with her legs. He dragged her close, spooning her and kissing the nape of her neck. "I'm not letting you leave, Bailey. So get that out of your head. If you're worried about waking up tomorrow morning, perhaps I'll keep you up all night so it won't be an issue." He shuddered as he thought of the possibilities. "I don't have a problem with that."

She laughed softly, wriggling onto her side so she could face him. "You don't lack confidence, do you?" Reaching out, she ran her thumb over his bottom lip. Which seemed to Gil like an open invitation to nibble the tip of her finger. He sucked it into his mouth and felt the pull in his groin.

Breathing hard as he pulled back, he brushed aside the lapel of the robe she wore, baring her breasts. "It's not confidence if it's a fact. Every time I get near you, I get hard."

"Gil!"

He nuzzled her nose. "What, Bailey?"

She shook her head, surveying him with a slight smile. "I never knew you could be this way."

"I'm guessing you saw me as an uptight, judgmental, obstructive pain in the ass."

The smile broadened. "You said it, not me. But that's not all. I knew you were a gorgeous man and a loving father, so that balanced out your less stellar qualities."

"I'm sorry I made your job difficult."

"You're hardly the first. I'm rarely a popular person."

"I can't believe that. Criminals probably line up for the opportunity to be alone with you in a tiny interrogation room."

"You've been watching too many cop shows on television. I do a lot behind the scenes, but it's rarely glamorous."

He stroked her hair from her forehead, tucking it behind her ear. "I'm glad you're here tonight," he said, deadly serious.

Her gaze searched his. "Me, too."

This time, he was clearheaded, but no less hungry. He retrieved protection, rolled it on, and returned to her side. Slowly, wanting to draw out the moment, he moved over her and into her. Bailey lifted her hips and took him deep, her wide-eyed gaze holding mysteries he was unable to fathom. Did she feel the earth move? Was she already thinking about leaving him tomorrow?

The warm, tight clasp of her flesh on his made him woozy. He closed his eyes, concentrating on the lazy slide in and out. Bailey tried to urge him on with incoherent pleas. But he was set on a course that was as immovable and inexorable as the tides. What had started out as something of a one-night stand was shifting and changing. His brain shied away from the implications, even as he grappled with his need for her.

He had a son to consider. And a home in Royal. But the woman beneath him, her body soft and yet strong, had bewitched him. How could he go on with life as usual, knowing what he was giving up?

She was no happy homemaker in apron and pearls. Bailey was a competent career woman. Based in Dallas. Where she would have ample opportunities for advancement.

His body said with finality that the time for analysis

was over. His jaw tightened and his legs quivered as the urge to come struck furiously and without quarter. Dimly, he heard Bailey cry out as she found completion. His own climax was more of a tornado, snatching him up, ass over heels, and dropping him into a void of sated bliss so dark and deep he wanted to revel in it forever.

They stayed in bed this time, too exhausted to move. Bailey's head lay on his chest. One of her arms curled across his waist. He floated on a sea of contentment that was unprecedented. In that moment, he believed anything was possible.

Bailey stroked his chest idly, her fingers tracing the line of hair that ran from his collarbone to his groin. So mellow was he that her first quiet question didn't even cause him heartburn.

She sighed softly, her eyes shielded by long lashes. "Will you tell me more about your wife?"

He kissed her forehead. "Not much left to tell. We married young. She had serious emotional problems. Her parents were wackos who subjected her to an unimaginable adolescence."

"Does Cade ask about her?"

"He used to, from time to time. Now he's more interested in finding Mrs. Addison Number Two."

"Has he ever visited his maternal grandparents?"

Gil stiffened. "Not a chance in hell. My wife took an overdose of pills but lingered long enough to beg me not to ever let our son near her parents or their way of life. The custody case drew statewide attention. I think the cult—for lack of a better word—that my in-laws embraced began to worry that the government might take a closer look at them, so they moved the entire group over the border into Mexico."

"I'm so sorry, Gil. It must have been a nightmare for you."

"It was a long time ago."

She was quiet for a few minutes, and then she sat up in the bed. "If you have one more of those little packets, I think I'm in the mood to see the view from the top."

When Bailey awoke the next morning, the spot beside her was empty. In an instant, full recollection of what she had done rolled over her in a mix of exhilaration and panic. Raising up on her elbows, she saw a note on Gil's pillow written in dark scrawl on a scrap of paper:

Didn't want things to be "weird," so I'm giving you your space.

He had signed his name and added a crooked smiley face. She smiled, half-sorry he wasn't with her, but more than a little relieved to have a moment to compose herself. Lying in Gil's bed felt deliciously decadent. She was usually an early riser, eager to start the day. But for once, she allowed herself a few minutes to revel in the memories of last night.

Becoming Gil's lover had been eye-opening. Never had she dreamed that inside his no-nonsense exterior was a tiger ready to pounce. He had wooed her, coaxed her, seduced her. And she had been a willing participant every step of the way.

The scent of his skin still clung to her pillowcase. When her body reacted to the images that masculine fragrance evoked, she knew it was time to get up.

After a quick shower, she dried her hair and dressed in the clean clothes she had packed in her overnight case. She made the bed, repacked her things, and carried the bag with her downstairs to set it by the front door. Coming face-to-face with the housekeeper was a bit of a shock, but the older woman never batted an eyelash. She smiled kindly and offered to scramble some eggs or make whatever Bailey wanted for breakfast.

Settling for black coffee seemed the safest choice. Bailey's stomach fluttered with nerves. Even now, dressed and in control somewhat, the prospect of seeing Gil was nerve-racking. He was a contained man, a private man, and though he had opened up to her last night in a very intimate way, she did not delude herself into thinking that she knew him well. They hadn't been together long enough for that.

The housekeeper seemed flustered that Gil's guest wasn't interested in eating, so to keep the peace, Bailey accepted a plate of toast and carried it and her coffee out onto the back porch. The morning was chilly, but her blazer, the one at which Gil turned up his nose, was warm enough to warrant an alfresco meal.

It was a shock to find that her host had entertained the same idea. He sat on a cushioned wicker love seat, his phone and iPad on the glass-topped table beside him. When Bailey stepped out on the porch, he jumped to his feet. "Join me," he said, his smile warm.

She would rather have chosen the chair across from him, but that didn't seem to be an option. Her stomach tightened as she sat down at Gil's urging, hip to hip with the man who had wakened her twice during the night for lovemaking. Despite her best efforts, her cheeks reddened.

He rested an arm across the back of the seat, his fingers stroking her shoulder lightly. "Did you sleep well?" His voice was a low rumble, the words husky and intimate.

She set the plate of toast, uneaten, on the table, and gulped her coffee, not caring that it scalded her tongue. "Yes." Staring out across Gil's beautiful ranch, she pretended an intense interest in the view.

His fingers moved to her neck, just below her ear. "You're shy," he accused, humor in his tone.

The innocent caress turned her insides into a soft, yearning puddle of need, reminding her of the danger she faced. She was no more willing than any other woman to have her heart broken. "I'm thirty-three years old. I'm not shy."

"Then what is it? Look at me, Bailey."

She half turned, studying the face that had become dear to her. His chiseled good looks added up to so much more than a handsome man. His integrity, his decency, his willingness to do the right thing by his son...all those things touched her heart and made her love him.

Staring into his eyes, she tried not to let him see the revelation that had knocked her sideways. When had she first known the truth about her feelings? Only last night? Or had her regard for him grown almost imperceptibly in the weeks she had studied him in his element? Even during that first interview when he had been angry and borderline obstructive, she had been drawn to his masculinity, to his aura of command, and even to his arrogance.

Some men used their power and influence to ride roughshod over women and anyone they perceived as weak or inferior in any way. But Gil was different. He used his strength and capabilities to protect and support both his son and his wide circle of friends.

It hadn't escaped her notice that Gil was extremely popular in Royal. He was admired by women and respected by men. The truth was, in all her interviews, no one had ever spoken harshly or critically of Gil. He must have a few enemies or naysayers...most men in his position would. But if he did, she hadn't come across them yet.

Perhaps her mental "checkout" hadn't been as long as it seemed. Because Gil waited patiently, his dark-eyed gaze a little too perceptive for her comfort. She didn't want him to know the truth. She didn't want him to think she was angling for something permanent. She didn't want him to think she would be kind to his son to win points.

"I enjoyed last night," she said quietly, her mouth dry and her throat constricted. "But I do have a job I need to attend to. It's late. I have to get back to town."

He frowned. "That's it?"

"What do you mean?"

"You can just walk away after last night?"

Her fists clenched. "What do you want me to say, Gil? It was wonderful. But we both have responsibilities."

"I'm tired of being responsible," he said, the words flat. "What I want is to go back upstairs with you and close the door."

Her heart raced. The image he conjured was unbearably tempting. "So would I," she said. "But that's not really an option, and you know it. Please let me go, Gil."

Something vibrated in his big frame and flashed in his eyes. Anger. Desire. He jumped to his feet and paced. "I'd rather you stay away from the club for a few days. Until some of the gossip and complaints die down."

She nodded. "I was almost done, anyway."

He folded his arms across his chest, looking more combative than amorous. "So why do you need to work today?"

"You are a stubborn man."

He shrugged. "I know what I want."

"If you must know, I had planned to speak with Alex again. The doctors only allowed me a brief moment with him when he was found, and of course, he remembered nothing."

"You think that has changed?"

"No. But perhaps on his home turf I can pick up some small clue…anything we might have missed earlier."

The ring of a cell phone interrupted them. Bailey glanced at Gil's phone where it lay on the table. "It's the sheriff."

"I'd better take this. Nate doesn't call to chitchat."

Bailey listened unashamedly during the extremely brief conversation. When Gil hung up, she quizzed him. "Anything wrong?"

He nodded, sober-faced. "Alex was rushed to emergency during the middle of the night with an excruciating headache. And now there's some kind of uproar at the hospital. Nate asked me to get in touch with you and let you know."

Her mind raced. "Is Alex critical?"

"I'm not sure. Nate was in a rush and didn't take the time to explain. Do you think we should head over there?"

She nodded. "I certainly want to. Especially since Sheriff Battle was being mysterious. When do you have to pick up Cade?"

"Not until mid-afternoon. I'll drive you to the hospital."

"Thank you. But I'll take my own car. I don't know how long I'll be there. I don't want to be stranded when you leave."

He didn't like her choice. She could tell. But he didn't argue further. Instead, he pulled her to her feet, wrapped his arms around her and kissed her. Her arms circled his waist, feeling the heat of his body, the power, the ripple of muscle in his lower back.

His mouth was hungry, but gentle. They were essentially on display, though no one appeared to be close by at the moment. The broad light of day was far less protective of secrets, however, and far less private than a shadowy bedroom and a moonlit mattress.

She kissed him back, unable to resist. The way he held her conveyed so many things that hadn't been put into words. In his embrace, she felt not only desire, but also a tenderness that disarmed her.

His tongue teased the recesses of her mouth, making her knees wobble and her stomach tighten with pleasure. When she tasted him in return, he cursed quietly and set her away from him. The lines of his face were carved in frustration and thwarted need. "We're not done with this. Make no mistake."

Ten

Gil brooded on the way to the hospital, his hands wrapped around the steering wheel in a death grip. Only a short time ago he had awakened feeling jubilant and sexually sated and better than he had in a long, long time. A sleeping Bailey lay nude in his arms, her leg angled across his thighs, her hair a dark cinnamon cloud around her face.

He had held her close in the predawn darkness, deeply grateful for whatever path led her to him. She walked alone in life, it seemed. Halfway estranged from her father. No other close family. Though Gil admired her self-sufficiency, he wished she would not discount the possibility that her current assignment put her in danger.

The urge and desire to protect her was strong. As was the need to stake a claim somehow. That last bit didn't make sense. Bailey was not involved with anyone else sexually or otherwise. She might be staying at Chance's dude ranch, but Gil had no real worries on that score.

Even if Chance made a move on her, Bailey would never get involved with someone who might be key in her investigation.

But still the urge remained.

Gil knew that some bridge had been crossed last night. Over the years, particularly when Cade was too small to realize that his dad was gone overnight, Gil had spent an evening with an amenable woman and had his sexual needs fulfilled. It hadn't taken very long for him to realize that such encounters left a sour taste in his mouth.

Apparently, he wasn't cut out for casual sex.

As a young man, before he had fully understood the extent of his wife's emotional trauma, he'd had every reason to believe that he and Sherrie would spend a life together at the Straight Arrow, potentially filling the house with a number of children.

Once the truth came out, Sherrie withdrew, both physically and emotionally. Despite Gil's every effort, he had been unable to reach her. The loneliness of living in such a marriage hit hard, and had only increased tenfold after Sherrie's death.

Not even to himself had Gil admitted the great void in his life. It seemed ungrateful and almost wicked to complain when he had so many blessings. A happy, healthy son. A family property that generated a very comfortable lifestyle. A wide circle of friends.

But a man needed a woman in his bed at night. A woman by his side. A partner who would share dreams and sorrows and joy and troubles. Bailey seemed convinced that she was only passing through. And in truth, Gil had believed they had little basis for a long-term relationship. Their lives were so different.

But after last night…well…after last night, Gil was prepared to move heaven and earth to prove to her that she was wrong. He had no clear plan, no road map for avoiding the obstacles in their way. Nevertheless, he wasn't prepared to walk away from an experience and a woman who had made him rethink his monastic lifestyle.

A cynical person might point out that sexual euphoria was no basis for making serious life decisions. That simply because Gil had made love to Bailey Collins five times in one night didn't mean they were soul mates. That he was thinking with his male anatomy and not his brain.

Throughout history, sexual mistakes had brought down men with as much or more to lose than Gil. Sex often made fools of those who had the hubris to think they were invincible. Gil got it. He really did. But stubbornly, he believed his situation was different. That he and Bailey were different. They had connected last night with a fire and an intimacy that was as rare as it was stingingly real.

His thinking was muddled. There were things to be sorted out. And he felt as if he had a hangover, though he was stone-cold sober. But the future seemed brighter this morning. And for now, that was enough.

At the hospital, he parked and went to find Bailey. Royal Memorial was a modern, well-equipped facility outfitted with the latest in technology. Though Royal might not have the population of bigger towns and cities in Texas, there was plenty of money to go around, and the citizens had chipped in to endow various wings and such with generous gifts.

Bailey was waiting for him in the lobby. She had already checked with the information desk for the room number, so when Gil joined her, they headed for the bank of elevators.

"He's in a regular room," she said. "That's a good sign."

Gil kissed her cheek, hugging her briefly with one arm. They were alone in the elevator as they rode up. "I'm very proud of you, Bailey. Alex is a lucky man to have you on his side."

Her small smile was gratified. "Thank you. But until we bring this to a close, I won't be able to relax."

They got off on the third floor. A doctor was just coming out of Alex's room. Bailey flashed her badge and asked for an update.

The physician shook his head. "Not much to tell. We're running some tests, but the headache is most likely tied to the concussion. Not to mention the fact that Santiago is trying so hard to force himself to remember. I've cautioned him to back off. To rest. To give his brain time to heal. But patience isn't his strong suit."

Gil had known the doctor for many years. The man was, in fact, a longtime friend of Gil's parents. "Nate said there's some kind of commotion going on."

The doctor raised a bushy eyebrow, his expression slightly harried. "That's why we wanted to alert Ms. Collins. You might say there are some new developments in the case. And unfortunately, the sheriff was summoned away on an emergency."

Gil saw Bailey tense. "What kind of developments?" she asked.

"Mr. Santiago's father and sister have arrived from Mexico. The sheriff examined their credentials thoroughly before we allowed them to have access, though he has posted security guards, as you can see. Alex is awake and resting comfortably at the moment. We did give him something for pain, so he's a little groggy."

Gil put a hand at Bailey's back, following her into the room. By the window stood an imposing man with short, jet-black hair who bore a striking resemblance to the patient in the bed. The older man, probably in his mid-fifties, wore an expensive gold wristwatch and the kind of clothes that were made by a personal tailor. His brown eyes were not warm. Instead they had the flat, mud-like appearance of stagnant water.

Sitting in a chair by the bed was a striking young woman with long black hair. Her figure was curvaceous to say the least. A large, intricate necklace of thin gold filigree inset with deep burgundy rubies accentuated modestly revealed cleavage. The color of the stones was passionate. But their fire was not reflected in her face. She seemed exhausted.

"Who are you?" she asked, her voice deeply accented. "And why are you in my brother's room?"

Bailey stepped forward, hand extended. "I'm Bailey Collins, state investigator. I've been assigned to work the case involving Mr. Santiago's disappearance. And this is Gil Addison, president of the Texas Cattleman's Club."

The Latin beauty shook Bailey's hand briefly, her ample bosom confined in a jade silk dress. "Pardon my frankness, Ms. Collins, but from what Alex tells us about his ordeal, your progress in the case is, how do you say it… zippo. Nada."

Gil had to admire Bailey's self-control. She took the criticism without flinching. "I understand your frustration. But I can assure you that we are narrowing the field of suspects day by day. We *will* find out who did this." She paused. "I know the sheriff took a look at your identification, but I must ask to see it, as well. I'll need to scan it into our database as a precaution. I hope you understand that I can't merely take your word as to your connection with Alex."

The beautiful woman shot a look at the stranger by the window. "This is all his fault. Ask *him* about our IDs."

The older man ignored her.

Alex interrupted, his face etched in discomfort, his voice subdued. "Why would they lie?"

Gil watched in silence as Bailey eyed the visitors. After a brief hesitation, when Gil had the impression she was weighing her options, she offered her hand to the man, as well. "I'm pleased to meet you, Mr. Santiago."

The man's eyes flashed and he ignored her overture, forcing her to drop her arm. "Enough pretense," he hissed. "The IDs I showed the sheriff are fakes. My name is not Santiago. I am Rodrigo del Toro." His voice resonated with arrogance and pride and a thick Spanish accent. "This is my daughter, Gabriella, and the man in the bed is my son, Alejandro."

Gil tensed. "Alex lied to us?" Alex had never talked about his background, particularly not the fact that he had family in Mexico.

Alex, looking almost frail despite his fierce masculinity, winced. "It's damned hard to answer that since I can't remember a damn thing."

Gabriella slapped his hand despite the fact that it was attached to an IV. "Language, *mi hermano.*"

"Sorry." Alex grimaced. "I don't know who you people are, and I don't know why everyone thinks I'm Alex Santiago." His face reddened. "I'm trying. Hell, I'm trying!" The monitor beeped as Alex's blood pressure spiked.

A nurse came running, her brows drawn together in a frown. "I must ask all of you to leave the room. Mr. Santiago needs to rest. There is a small conference room at the end of the corridor. Feel free to continue your conversation there."

Alex's father and sister each kissed him on the cheek with muttered apologies, and walked out. As Gil watched, Bailey approached the bed and laid a hand on Alex's shoulder. "It's not your job to figure this out," she said softly. "There are a host of people looking out for you, and many professionals working on your case. I need you to quit worrying about things and concentrate on getting well."

Alex's jaw tightened, his hands gripping the sheet at his hips. "I have no clue if that man and woman are related to me or not. I remember you asking me questions when I was found. Do you really not know who did this to me?"

"I don't. But I will. Let me do my job. And in the meantime, try not to push yourself to remember. Everything will sort itself out in the end."

Bailey approached the conference room with a sense of exhilaration. This new information had the potential to break her case wide open. Gil walked at her side, his quiet presence comforting.

Once seated at the small table, Bailey and Gil faced the del Toros. Neither of Alex's family members looked encouraging, though they did hand over their real driver's licenses and passports, albeit grudgingly. But Bailey had been stonewalled by the best, and she wasn't afraid of a little conflict. She pulled a small notebook and pen from her purse. Ordinarily, she would do an audio recording of an interview in addition to entering notes straight into her laptop. But she hadn't come prepared for that scenario, and even if she had, she doubted if the two people eyeing her with varying degrees of hostility would agree to going on the record at this point.

Before Bailey could pose a question, Gabriella leaned forward, her anger clear, though it was not perhaps directed at Bailey. "My father is to blame for this *horrible* situation. He sent Alex here as a spy. No wonder my brother was kidnapped."

Bailey turned to Rodrigo. "Is this true?"

The intimidating del Toro had ice in his gaze. She imagined that a man like him resented being cross-examined by a woman.

He leaned back in his chair, simulating calm, though his posture was rigid. "I assume that what I tell you is in confidence?"

She shook her head. "Not at all. If what you divulge to me is relevant to my investigation, I have to share salient points with other members of law enforcement. But you should realize…the more I know of the truth, the more quickly we can solve this case."

The scowl on his cold but handsome face darkened. "I sent my son to Royal to gather information about Windsor Energy. My company, Del Toro Oil, is interested in a corporate takeover."

For several long beats, silence reigned in the room. A quick glance at Gil told Bailey that he was as shocked as she was.

Gabriella's dark eyes shone with tears. Her voice quivered. "It was the most wicked idea. *Madre de Dios*, Father. Alex could have been killed."

Bailey fixed her attention on Gabriella's father, speaking sternly. She felt sympathy for the sobbing woman, but she also knew this was a chance she couldn't afford to miss. "Start from the beginning, Mr. del Toro. When was the last time you talked to your son?"

"From the accounts I have read in your newspapers, a couple of days before he disappeared. At the time, I did not know anything was wrong. We had agreed to be in contact only infrequently, because I wanted to keep a low profile."

"What did you talk about that day? Was it privileged information?"

His jaw tightened. "No. We argued. He told me that he had *una novia*, that he had proposed marriage to her."

"And you didn't approve?"

Del Toro pounded a fist on the metal table, once. But with enough force to make his daughter jump. "I am one of the richest men in Mexico, Ms. Collins. Alejandro is my only son. He is destined to marry someone of his class and background. Not the daughter of a man whose business I plan to grind into the dust."

"Charming," Bailey muttered. "So the woman of whom you speak is Cara Windsor?"

"Yes. She bewitched my son somehow. Alejandro has always honored and obeyed his father. Suddenly, he was shouting at me. Insisting that he could no longer carry out my plan, because he had to prove to this Cara person that his love for her was real. We have telenovelas in my country, Ms. Collins, somewhat akin to your soap operas. I have seen the overly romantic drivel that passes for true love. But the real world is not so easily manipulated. I expect loyalty and obedience from my son."

"How did your conversation end?" Bailey was chilled by the man's hauteur.

"He hung up on me. I did not know until almost a week later that he had disappeared."

"Why didn't you come forward immediately?"

"My son is resourceful. And I did not want to tip my hand. I assumed that he would show up eventually."

"And when he didn't?"

"I was packed and ready to hop on a plane when the news service indicated that Alex had been found."

"But without his memory."

"True. These things, however, are usually temporary. I had great hope that he would recall his purpose in coming to Texas and would carry on with the job at hand."

"And when it became clear that his amnesia was not going to clear up overnight?"

His jaw tightened. "I realized I had no choice but to come here and identify my son."

"When you walked into the room, did he show any signs of recognizing either one of you?"

Gabriella spoke up. She had been standing with her back to them, gazing out the window. She turned now, her cheeks streaked with moisture. "Alex knows nothing." Her voice was thick. "My beloved brother knows nothing."

The tears started again. Bailey's heart went out to the young woman. Though Bailey had no siblings of her own, she could only imagine what it must be like to have a loved one regard you as a stranger.

She tapped her pen on the pad, her brain whirling with questions. "Do you plan to stay here in Royal for any length of time?"

"I will not leave until my Alex is fully recovered." Gabriella's words were adamant. Her father appeared less sure.

"We will see what happens," he said.

"You may be very unpopular," Bailey pointed out. "Alex made many friends in his time here, but no one likes a mole."

"A mole?" he asked.

Though both del Toros spoke immaculate English, perhaps the slang did not translate. "An informant. A corporate spy."

Gabriella wrapped her arms around her waist, her lashes spiky. "We need additional security for my brother, Ms. Collins. Now that the truth has come out, he will have more enemies. And whoever kidnapped him will no doubt realize that he is an extremely valuable asset, a bargaining chip if you will. They may try again."

"That will be a problem," Bailey said. "My employers are chronically understaffed."

Del Toro glared at his daughter. "Money is no object. I will hire bodyguards for Alejandro. And perhaps investigators of my own."

Bailey was startled to see Gil stand up, his face a thundercloud. "Watch your step, del Toro," he said, the words low and vibrating with anger. "This woman has spent more hours than you can imagine trying to find out why your son was kidnapped and by whom. You *will* give her the respect she is due."

The older man bristled, but he looked at Bailey and waved a hand. "I meant no insult. I am sorry if I gave offense."

As apologies went, it was weak, but Bailey accepted it at face value. She was stunned by Gil's impassioned defense of her work. Stunned and deeply touched. But she didn't need Gil fighting her battles. To allow him to do so would make her look weak.

She stood, gathering her things. "My job and my reputation are very important to me. And I have given my all to this case, though it isn't necessary for Mr. Addison to point that out." She scowled at Gil before continuing to address Alex's presumed family. "I appreciate your cooperation, Mr. del Toro. Ms. del Toro. I will have someone return your identification papers in the next hour or two. I assume you both will be staying with Alex?"

"If he will have us." Gabriella managed a weak smile.

Her father rose to his feet, as well. "My family will be together. And all of my resources are at your disposal, Ms. Collins. The sooner my son's attackers are behind bars, the sooner we can return home."

Eleven

Gil took Bailey's elbow as they walked across the parking lot. "Well, that was a surprise."

She nodded, her face troubled. "I felt like I was making definite progress with the investigation up until today, but del Toro's revelations put things in a whole new light."

"Does this mean Chance is off the hook?"

"I know you don't want to think he had anything to do with Alex's kidnapping. But I learned a long time ago that a surprising number of seemingly nice, normal people are capable of committing terrible sins in the heat of the moment. Chance certainly had motive."

"Because Cara broke his heart? You don't know that."

"True. And he doesn't act like he has a broken heart. But he could be hiding both his feelings and his guilt."

"We'll have to agree to disagree on the subject of Chance McDaniel," Gil said as he backed her up against the truck, his hips pinning hers to the door. No one was anywhere around. He bent his head and kissed her, sliding a hand around the back of her neck. "I wanted to stay in bed with you this morning," he confessed, his heart pumping as arousal brought his erection to full throttle.

Bailey's brown-eyed gaze clung to his. "I appreciated the privacy *and* your note. It was awkward enough as it was running into your housekeeper. I felt like I had a scarlet *A* on my chest."

He frowned. "Surely she didn't say anything to embarrass you." The woman had worked for him almost a decade, but he'd fire her on the spot if she had been rude to Bailey.

"Oh, no. She was lovely. But since you told me you'd never had a woman stay over, I felt extremely conspicuous."

"My housekeeper is not paid to speculate about my private life."

"People are human, Gil. She's probably discreet, because you're a good employer, but I *know* she was curious. Anyone would be."

"Change of subject," he insisted, kissing the side of her neck. "Tell me how soon we can be alone again."

Her wince gave him warning of what was to come. "With this new evidence," she said, "I have to buckle down on the case. I'll be spending time interviewing Alex's father and sister, assuming their story pans out. And I have to take a look at all my old notes in light of this new evidence. I can't have any distractions. You understand, don't you?"

She looked up at him so beseechingly, he had no choice but to swallow his disappointment and give her the support she deserved.

"I understand," he said, kissing the top of her head. "But I don't have to like it."

Bailey stroked her thumb across his bottom lip, her

fingertips cool against his skin. "I'll make it up to you. I promise."

He backed away from her, reminding himself that he was a grown man capable of delayed gratification. "I'll hold you to that," he said gruffly.

Fortunately for Gil, he was a busy man with many responsibilities. Even so, the subsequent week and a half dragged by with agonizing slowness. He and Bailey talked on the phone every day. Often more than once. But it was a poor substitute for having her in his bed…for feeling her naked body pressed against his. Somehow, without him even noticing, Bailey had become indispensable to his happiness. Without her, the days seemed dull, even with the presence of his precious son.

It didn't help that Cade asked about her constantly. The boy was single-minded in his determination to see her again. Gil made vague promises, but in truth, he had no idea when Bailey would be back under his roof.

On day eleven, he took matters into his own hands. Tracking her down took most of the morning. He finally found her vehicle parked at the courthouse…and waited with admirable patience for her to exit the building. When she saw him, her expression changed, but he couldn't pinpoint the mix of emotions that danced across her face.

Walking to meet her when she descended the steps, he slung an arm around her shoulders and steered her in the direction of his truck. He had parked in an adjacent alley, taking advantage of the shade from a large building, a spot that had the added benefit of giving them a modicum of privacy. "When was the last time you had a day off?"

"That's your best pickup line?" she quipped, smiling at him with joy in her eyes.

"Answer the question." He hadn't known for sure that

she would be glad to see him. Witnessing her pleasure erased some of the misery of the past ten days.

Bailey toyed with the buttons on his shirt, her fingers warming his skin through the fabric. "I don't remember."

"That's what I thought. You need a break. I know for a fact that you've been working dawn to dusk."

"And what would I do with this free day?" She glanced at her watch. "Now that it's almost lunchtime?"

Gil was getting desperate. Making love to Bailey... repeatedly...had not slaked his hunger for her at all. If anything, he wanted her more, because now he knew what it was like to have her in his bed. The memories made him sweat. Not to mention the fact that he was, at the moment, hard and hurting.

Bailey made no effort to move. Obviously she was aware that his erection nudged eagerly at her lower abdomen. He shuddered, dangerously close to ripping open the door of the truck and shoving her on the front seat.

He cleared his throat. "Cade spent the night with my friends again. I have to pick him up. In Midland. At four." He was barely able to string words together. "Come with me."

Her head shake was instantaneous. "Your parental instincts were good...thinking you needed to protect your son. I don't want to do anything to hurt him."

"I was wrong. I'll be honest with him."

"And say what?"

"That I like you. A lot. And I like spending time with you. But that your job and your home are in Dallas."

"What are we doing here, Gil?"

In her eyes he saw a mixture of resignation and sadness. Both emotions hit him hard, because he was responsible for putting them there. He stroked her hair from her face, cupping her cheek in his right hand. "Let's not analyze it, Bailey. I'm a man. You're a woman. Let's take a drive on a beautiful sunny afternoon and worry about tomorrow later."

"That's a dangerously open-ended philosophy for a man like you. Or a woman like me, for that matter."

He made himself step backward. "I won't coerce you. But I hope you'll say yes."

She waited long enough for his gut to tighten. Finally, she nodded. "I suppose it couldn't hurt. But again, we both have a vehicle."

He groaned. "I'll pick you up at Chance's place in forty-five minutes. Change into something that will be comfortable for a picnic." The day was not as hot as it had been earlier in the week, but still wonderfully pleasant for January.

"Who supplies the food?"

"My invitation, my responsibility."

She went up on tiptoes and kissed him square on the mouth, ducking away before he could grab her. "There's that nasty word again...*responsibility*."

Gil swiped the back of his hand across his forehead. Bailey's kisses, even quick ones, were lethal. "Believe me, Bailey. Taking care of you and your needs is pure pleasure."

Bailey didn't have much time to dither over her wardrobe. But she did intend to prove to Gil that she wasn't all business all the time. He had used the word *comfortable*. Men, however, were clueless at times about what was appropriate. If Bailey and Gil were picking up Cade at the home of a family friend, there was a good chance Bailey would be meeting someone. And she didn't plan to do so in old jeans and a T-shirt.

The outfit she picked out was one that packed easily, but

was comfy and fashionable at the same time. The short-sleeved, burgundy knit shirtdress was striped with navy and ended several inches above her knees. She paired it with navy leggings trimmed at the ankle with lace. Black espadrilles matched the black headband she used to push back her unruly hair. When she looked in the mirror after changing clothes hastily, the woman staring back at her definitely looked in the mood to play hooky.

Throwing a few things into a black tote, she gave her hair one last brushing and a warning to behave. Gil had seen her plenty of times with her hair confined for work. But because today he wanted her to let down her hair and goof off, she decided to indulge him both literally and metaphorically. The only thing left was to grab up a black cashmere cardigan in case the weather turned colder later.

Gil was right on time. No surprise there. She walked down the wide front steps of the ranch house and tried not to bounce like a giddy teenage girl. The prospect of a few hours away from work—in the company of the man with whom she had shared such dizzying intimacy—made her happy. A profound emotion, but one that was at its core plain and simple.

He helped her into the front seat of the truck and went around to the driver's side. "There's a belt in the center," he said, his lips quirking in a mocking smile.

Bailey smoothed her skirt over her thighs and put her tote at her feet. "I'm fine right here," she said, staying well toward the passenger door. Midland was fifty miles away. Boundaries had to be observed if they planned to make it on time.

As they pulled out onto the highway, Gil shot her a look, his expression amused. "You look cute today, Collins. I like it."

She rummaged in her tote for a water bottle and took a

long drink. "As much as I appreciate the compliment, I do want to point out that you promised to feed me."

"Patience, woman. The hamper's behind us, filled with all sorts of goodies."

She peered over her shoulder at the small space behind. Cade's little booster seat occupied one corner…a large rattan picnic basket, the other. "And how long do I have to wait?"

"There's a spot about twenty miles down the road where Cade and I like to stop. The property actually belongs to me, but I've never done anything with it. A tiny wet-weather stream cuts in in half. I thought you might like to have lunch beneath a little copse of cottonwood trees."

"You do know it's January. And all the leaves are gone."

"Use your imagination. I have a quilt."

"And sunscreen?"

"I'll cover you with my body."

Her jaw dropped and her face flamed. She'd been holding her own until that last comment. Now she lapsed into silence, her blood pumping with excitement. Surely Gil was joking.

Without asking, she reached forward and turned on his satellite radio. Picking an upbeat contemporary channel, she hummed along, relieved to have something to fill the silence. At times like this she realized that Gil was a man with one thing on his mind.

The turnoff to Gil's property was unmarked, nothing more than a narrow, rutted side road. The big truck handled the terrain comfortably, though Bailey was jostled rather more than she expected. If not for the seat belt, she would have ended up in Gil's lap.

When he finally stopped, at least four or five miles down the road, he rolled down the windows and cut the engine. "This is it."

The scene was peaceful, though remote. No one would disturb them. If another vehicle did approach, they would hear it coming long before it arrived. Above, puffy white clouds scudded across a sky the color of a robin's egg. A light breeze stirred the occasional flurry of dried leaves. With no power lines to mark the landscape, it almost seemed as if they had been transported back in time.

Bailey pressed her knees together, her hands clasped in her lap. "Very pretty."

Gil slung an arm across the steering wheel and turned to face her. "You look like a scared rabbit."

Bailey lifted her chin. "You flatter yourself."

His lopsided smile reached inside her chest and squeezed her heart. "I won't apologize for wanting you, Bailey. You're a very desirable woman."

Her cheeks were hot enough to fry an egg. She wasn't accustomed to talking about sex so matter-of-factly. She had been raised by a father who never did a thing to acknowledge that his daughter might need some education about her body and other personal matters. Nor did he offer her books or anything else to guide her in the murky waters of boy-girl relationships.

She'd been forced to stumble along on her own.

But she had managed. Refusing to let Gil know she was feeling off-balance, she managed a genuine smile. "You promised me a picnic. Food first. Flirting later."

"You've got your priorities muddled," he grumbled. But he grinned as he unloaded their supplies.

Bailey hopped down from the truck and helped spread the quilt. Gil's housekeeper had managed to put together a mouthwatering array of food, especially given the short notice. Chicken salad, fruit salad, homemade bread and oatmeal raisin cookies made Bailey's mouth water.

She was astonished to see Gil unpack a padded container that held china plates, crystal flutes and real silver-ware. "Wow. I was expecting paper and plastic."

He poured her a glass of champagne. "I may be a little rusty when it comes to dating, but I think I remember a few of the finer points when trying to impress a woman."

She sipped the champagne, recognizing that the taste alone declared it to be ridiculously expensive. "We're not dating, Gil." She had information he wasn't going to like to hear. So there was no reason to play games. "But I appreciate the effort."

He ignored her insistence on clinging to reality, choosing instead to serve a plate and hand it to her. "Dig in. I don't want you passing out from hunger on my watch."

They ate in silence for several minutes. A comfortable silence that acknowledged the beauty of the day and their unspoken contentment in sharing a stolen moment in time. Bailey sat cross-legged, her plate in her lap, while Gil sprawled on his side, his big body ranged comfortably as he propped himself on an elbow and ate one-handed.

The food was good. But after a while, it sat like a stone in her stomach. She believed in the concept of carpe diem, she really did. But she was also a realist. For every wonderful minute she spent with Gil, there would be a corresponding experience of pain when this whatever-it-was came to an abrupt end.

It was foolish and self-destructive to ruin a lovely interlude with such maudlin thoughts. Life didn't have to be perfect to be enjoyable. Happiness came in snatches, sometimes almost unnoticed. She wouldn't ask of Gil more than he was able to give.

When they were done eating, she helped him pack everything back in its spot. They had barely spoken a dozen words during the meal. Gil stood and carried the hamper and the dish tote back to the truck. Bailey pulled her knees to her chest and encircled them with her arms. For one brief moment, she allowed herself to wonder what it would be like if Gil were hers. Permanently.

She already knew he was an incredible father and an intuitive lover. It wasn't a stretch to imagine him as a loving husband, as well. He had softened toward her, given more of himself than she had expected. Closing her eyes, she entertained the fantasy of a rosy future.

Gil sat down beside her, his hip inches from hers. "Whatever you're thinking about must not be too pleasant. You have a tiny frown between your eyebrows." He rubbed the spot with a fingertip. "This picnic was supposed to be fun."

Shaking off her weird mood, she laid her head on his shoulder. "It *is* fun," she said honestly. "I get so wrapped up in my work, I sometimes forget how nice it is to do nothing at all."

"You've given a lot of yourself to your career."

Was there a veiled criticism in those words, or was she being overly sensitive? "I suppose I've let my job act as a substitute for family. I do have many good friends, but we all work together, so that has a downside. I'm rarely able to leave my cases when I go home at the end of the day. Not like someone who works in a factory or a department store. I'm always thinking about the next step."

"You care deeply about things, Bailey. I like that about you."

She linked her fingers with his, resting their hands on his thigh. Today he wore dark dress pants with a lightweight cotton pullover sweater in a shade of blue that echoed the hue of the sky.

His words of praise made her uncomfortable. Perhaps because she had grown up without that kind of verbal support. But also because she was hiding something from Gil. News she had received only today.

"Did you bring me out here so we could have sex?" she asked, the words far more calm that the riotous emotions pinballing inside her.

He squeezed her hand, his thumb massaging her palm. "It might have crossed my mind."

This would be their last chance. She knew it, and she was pretty sure Gil knew it, too. Their lives were too complicated to carry on an affair, clandestine or otherwise. Especially in a place like Royal where even the walls had ears. Turning to face him, she cupped his neck in her hands and pulled him closer for a kiss. "I was hoping you would say that."

Her blunt statement sent shock skittering across his face before it was replaced by hunger and determination. He reached into his pocket and extracted a series of condom packets hooked together. "I wasn't making any assumptions, but it never hurts to be prepared."

"Don't tell me. You were an Eagle Scout."

"Guilty as charged." He unbuttoned the top two buttons of her dress. "I also learned how to unhook a girl's bra with one hand, but that wasn't a Scout badge. More of an extracurricular activity."

"You're not such a straight arrow after all, are you Mr. Addison? I'm seeing you in a whole new light."

He eased her down onto her back with her cooperation. The sun blinded her, so she was forced to close her eyes.

His lips caressed her ear as he whispered. "You have no idea."

Twelve

Gil studied Bailey's face…the creamy skin, feminine nose, stubborn chin. In the broad light of day, her hair caught every ray of sun and glowed red with fire. Her slightly parted lips were the color of pale pink roses. Beneath her soft dress, her chest rose and fell rapidly.

In his head, the clock was ticking. He'd called his friends and asked for an hour of grace. Cade was having a blast and wouldn't begrudge the later arrival time.

Selfishness. All selfishness. Because Gil couldn't bear to let her go. Not without one last chance to bury himself in the tight, hot clasp of her body. To hear her cry out when he sent her flying. To lie with her in the aftermath and count the beats of his heart.

She had kicked off her shoes when she sat pretzel-fashion to eat her lunch. Now he studied her narrow, highly arched feet, bemused that the sight of them made him wonder for the first time if he had such a fetish. Her small toenails were painted the same color as her lips.

A tiny smile curved her lips. "I have my eyes closed, so I can't be sure. But it seems as if you've lost your way."

He stood and pulled her to her feet. "Your skin is turning pink. Let me move the quilt." With trembling hands, he dragged it into the patch of shade cast by the truck. "That's better."

When he turned back around, Bailey had pulled her dress over her head and stood facing him clad only in a lacy black bra and the leggings that clung to her shapely limbs.

He put a fist to his chest. "Be still my heart."

"Not that I'm criticizing, but it seems like one of us needs to remember the clock."

"I don't have to be there 'til five. I called them."

Her eyebrows went up, her expression scandalized. "You asked your friends if you could be late so that you and I could fool around in the middle of nowhere?"

He shrugged, not the least bit repentant. "That's about it."

She threw herself across the small space separating them, forcing him to catch her by the waist and lift her against his chest. He staggered backward, but caught himself.

Laughing down at him, her eyes sparkling with an innocent joy he'd rarely seen compared to her serious side, she rested her hands on his shoulders. "I do like this naughty version of Gil Addison. Very much."

For that, she deserved a kiss. Slowly, he let her slide down his body…like the hero's maneuver in a romantic chick flick. Her breasts nestled against his chest, giving him a mouthwatering view that was more provocative than total nudity. When her feet touched the quilt, they were both breathless. He tunneled the fingers of one hand in her hair, grabbing a handful and pulling her close. "And I do like this bra."

She rested her cheek on his shoulder. "I'm waiting to see your fancy maneuver." Grabbing his left hand, she brought it to her lips. "Show me what you've got."

To his eternal embarrassment, it took him three tries to unfasten the bra clasp one-handed.

Bailey just laughed. "I think I'm glad you aren't any better than that. No woman likes to be part of a crowd."

He pulled her down to the quilt again, this time knowing that nothing was going to stand in his way. "You'll never be one of a crowd, honey." She didn't know how true that was, but now was not the time to convince her with words.

He knelt over her, dragging the belt from around his waist and tossing it aside. Thankful that he hadn't worn his boots today, he kicked off his shoes and socks and unfastened his trousers. His erection bobbed thick and ready, tenting the thin fabric of his boxers.

Bailey licked her lips. "This feels wicked," she murmured.

"What does?"

She waved a hand. "Doing it outside in broad daylight."

"All the better to see you with, my dear."

"So that makes you the Big Bad Wolf?"

He grinned, shucking the pants but leaving the boxers for now. His sweater was far too warm, so he dispensed with it, as well. Bailey's interested gaze studied him from head to toe and all points in between. Her unconcealed perusal aroused him even more, if that were possible.

"You could say that," he said calmly. "I do have an inclination to gobble you up. Lift your fanny, woman." He peeled her leggings down and off, exposing thighs and calves that were long and shapely. The black lace panties he revealed matched the bra that now lay nearby.

He shook his head, trying to dispel a rush of dizziness, possibly caused by all the blood that had traveled south.

Bailey bent one knee, placing her foot flat on the quilt. The new position was provocative to say the least. "You okay?"

He nodded, hands on his thighs. "I need a minute. Looking at you may give me a heart attack."

"Very funny."

"I'm not kidding," he insisted. "Have you seen yourself in a mirror? You're a knockout, Bailey."

"It's the champagne talking. I may have to drive to Midland. I think you're delusional."

Trapping her thighs between his, he straddled her waist. The rocky ground beneath the quilt was hell on his knees, but the pain was a good thing if it kept him from rushing the moment. "Don't argue with me. I'm always right."

"You like to think so."

"If I kiss you, will it shut you up?"

"Why don't you try it and see?"

He crouched over her, stroking her curves with hands that trembled. Though the afternoon was plenty warm, small nipples pebbled at his touch. Despite her saucy bravado, he detected a hint of shyness even now. Her eyelids fluttered shut as he played with her breasts.

Her hips moved restlessly. He recognized the signs and felt the same urgency. "I want to make love to you," he said, the words ragged and hoarse. He felt as if he could barely draw a breath.

As she lifted up on her elbows without warning, she brushed the underside of his erection. "Then we're both going to get what we want." Her smile was pure female mischief.

Wiggling her hips, she used one hand to remove her last tiny scrap of underwear. He stood and followed suit. Donning a condom, he dropped down beside her and splayed a hand on her belly. "You dazzle me," he said roughly, with perfect truth. When he had fallen in love with his wife-to-be, he had been no more than a callow young man, hardly aware of the pitfalls that could loom in a relationship.

His marriage, or rather its failure, had almost broken him. When Sherrie ended her life, Gil had drowned in pain and guilt. During Cade's brief lifetime, things had gradually improved, because Gil had willed it to be so. But he had been convinced deep down inside that he would never have another chance at love.

Yet without warning, Bailey Collins had burst into his life. First he had resented her. Then he had wanted her. And now...he could barely even describe to himself what it was that he was feeling.

Bailey smiled at him wistfully, her eyes dark, mysterious. Was she even a fraction as hungry as he was?

Her hand wrapped around his erection, moving gently up and down, her fingers circling the head of his shaft. "I will always be glad I came to Royal," she whispered. Her voice broke on the last word.

"Don't say that. Don't write an epitaph before we're done."

Her eyes glittered with moisture. "Time's running out, Gil. Come here and give us both what we need."

He obeyed blindly, because joining his body with hers was what he wanted more than his next breath. Touching her gently, he felt the slick heat that signaled her readiness. He thrust slowly, closing his eyes at the sensation of rightness. Somehow he had to make this new turn in his life work. Somehow...

The sun moved inexorably in the sky. Already the rays

burned his back, the patch of shade shrinking. Each of his senses was painfully heightened. Bailey's skin was soft and warm everywhere he touched. The sound of their breathing mingled and floated away on the breeze. He smelled the fragrance of her perfume and the scent of his own sweat.

He withdrew briefly, though it cost him. Lightly, he teased the tiny spot that gave her the most pleasure. Her back arched off the quilt and she cried out as she climaxed, her body beautiful in its sensual abandon.

Before the last ripple of her orgasm faded, he entered her again, this time with far less finesse. Wildly he took her, over and over, until he felt a scalding rush of heat that ripped through his gut and drew a harsh shout from his parched throat at the end as he came endlessly, his head buried in the curve of her neck.

Bailey peeked through half-closed lashes, eyeing the buzzard that circled far overhead. Had she and Gil been comatose that long? She lifted her hand and squinted at her watch. Almost four o'clock. By the time they put themselves to rights and finished the drive to Midland, Cade would be waiting on them.

She nudged her lover's shoulder. "Gil."

"Hmm?" He didn't stir.

"We have to go."

"I bought us an extra hour," he mumbled.

"We've used that and more. I'm serious. Move, Addison."

He levered himself up on one elbow and blinked. "Crankiness is not a nice trait in a woman," he said. "Maybe you could work on that."

His droll humor made her smile. "Duly noted."

He helped her to her feet and she leaned into him, relishing the intimate feel of skin-to-skin contact.

Gil pinched her bottom. "I'd kill for a shower."

"Yes, well…you're the one who opted for alfresco she-nanigans."

"You're the only person I know who could use that word with a straight face." He kissed her nose.

"It's a perfectly good word."

"Do they teach you that in law enforcement training?" He lowered his voice. *"I've got a sixty-two fifty-one down at the Motel Six. Shenanigans without a license."*

She burst out laughing. "You are so full of it. Get dressed before someone comes to arrest us."

They were woefully unprepared for the aftermath of their romp. Fortunately, Gil remembered a container of wet wipes in the glove box. With the aid of those and the items in her purse, Bailey was able to restore her appearance to some semblance of dignity and decorum. Though she had left home looking perky and fresh, she was now definitely disheveled.

It didn't help that Gil kept trying to snitch her bra or tweak unprotected body parts. And that was not the only distraction standing in her way. Who could help noticing the breadth of his muscled shoulders or the fact that even now, he was semierect. As if his hunger had been only partially sated by their coupling.

But at last, they finally climbed back into the truck and headed out to the highway. When they made it onto even pavement, Gil shot her a look. "I have a favor to ask."

She pulled down the visor mirror and checked her reflection, wetting her finger to remove a tiny bit of something stuck to her eyebrow. "I'm pretty sure you used up all your markers back in Dry Gulch."

"I'm serious."

"Okay." She closed the mirror. "Tell me."

"I'm meeting up with a friend tomorrow morning and

helicoptering three counties over to check on some stud bulls we hope to buy. I use a high school girl in town to babysit Cade in the evenings whenever I need her. But it occurred to me that he would really enjoy spending part of the day with you. Chance has activities for children out at the ranch, doesn't he?"

"Yes. But you don't have to do this. I don't need a grand gesture to prove that you trust me with your son. It isn't necessary."

"So you don't want to hang out with him?"

She sighed. "Of course I do."

"Then what's the problem?"

Now seemed as good a time as any to share the news she had been sitting on since midday. "I talked to my boss when I went home to change clothes."

"You called him?" Gil's jaw was tight.

"No. He called me. Apparently as soon as we left the hospital, Rodrigo del Toro did some digging and went up the chain of command. He informed my boss that he would assume responsibility for the investigation since he had unlimited funds and Alex was safely back at home."

The word Gil said under his breath was harsh. "So that's it? The state drops the case without a resolution?"

"No, of course not. But del Toro doesn't like working with a woman, and he holds the purse strings right now, unfortunately. They'll send someone else to step in for me here in Royal. And besides, I'm needed back in Dallas to take over a new case."

"When?" It wasn't her imagination. He was pale beneath his tan.

She swallowed, feeling on the defensive and not sure why. "This coming Thursday. I have to wrap up all my notes and file a final report."

"I see."

The next few miles passed in uneasy silence. She didn't understand Gil's reaction. It was no secret that her assignment in Royal was temporary. Perhaps Gil was angry because Alex's kidnapper hadn't been apprehended.

"I don't think you have to worry about public safety," she said, after at least fifteen minutes had elapsed on the dashboard clock. "We're almost ninety percent sure that Alex was targeted specifically. This isn't some rogue criminal who poses a threat to the general population. And now that Mr. del Toro is here—with money to spare for security details—I think any real danger is minimal."

"For Alex's sake, I hope you're right." Even after her earnest reassurances, his shoulders were still rigid, his hands white-knuckled on the steering wheel.

She bit her lip. Confrontation had never been her strong suit. But in ten minutes or so, the talkative Cade would be joining them. Before that happened, Bailey wanted to clear the air.

"You seem upset," she said.

Gil's scowl was dark. When he took his eyes off the road for a brief moment to look at her directly, the turbulence in his gaze shocked her. "And you're not?"

"I don't understand."

With a jerk of the steering wheel and a flurry of gravel, he pulled off onto the side of the road and shoved the gearshift into Park. Turning to face her, he shocked her with the vehemence of his icy tone. "Maybe I can explain it in words that make sense to a by-the-book government type."

"That's not fair," she said, tears stinging her eyes.

"Too bad, because that's how I see it." He was furious, that much was clear. "Your boss summons you, and it doesn't bother you at all that you and I are in the middle of a—"

She punched him in the chest, halting the flow of heated

sarcasm. "I *know* what we're in the middle of," she cried. "But we both know the statistics on long-distance relationships."

His lips twisted, his expression bleak. "So we were merely scratching an itch?"

"Don't be crude." She was shaking. Wrapping her arms around her waist, she held on to a thread of composure. "When we were together before…and again today. It was wonderful."

"The sex, you mean." His eyes were flat, accusing.

"What do you want from me, Gil?"

The silence lengthened. "Nothing, Bailey. Nothing at all."

Thirteen

She didn't know what to do. Never in a million years had she expected this reaction to her announcement. Inside, she grieved for the moment she would have to say goodbye. Of *course* she was sad. The thought of leaving Gil was tearing her apart. But moaning about it wouldn't help.

He moved back out onto the highway, merging with the traffic and eating up the miles to Midland.

The hostile silence shredded her nerves. "Tell me about your friends," she said. Anything to pass the time until Cade would join them. With the little boy in the truck as a buffer, the trip home wouldn't be so bad. At the moment, however, her head was throbbing, and she needed a distraction sooner rather than later.

For several long seconds she thought Gil was going to ignore her request. But finally, he inhaled and exhaled, and some of the tension left him. "We all went to college together," he said. "Got married about the same time. Had a son about the same time. They were an incredible support to me after Sherrie was gone. Food. Companionship. Advice when I asked. A shoulder to cry on."

"I can't imagine you letting down your guard enough to admit you needed help." It was a true statement, but as soon as the words left her mouth she realized they came out sounding sarcastic. Fortunately, Gil didn't take offense.

"I was a mess," he said with raw honesty. "I was still adjusting to being a parent, and I was terrified I would do something wrong. Plus, the guilt about Sherrie was overwhelming."

"It wasn't your fault."

"Doesn't matter how true that is or how many times you tell yourself so, the burden is crushing when someone you love commits suicide. I felt like a complete failure."

Only hours ago she would have slid across the seat and put her arm around him. Now, she didn't feel as if she had the right. "I'm glad they were there for you."

"My parents were, too. They still lived in Royal back then."

Bailey stared out the window. She was under no illusions that her father would ever rush to her aid in a similar situation. The divide between them was much too large to cross.

Perhaps that was why she hadn't let Gil see the depth of her despair about leaving Royal…about leaving him. She had learned early on in life to pull herself up by her bootstraps and deal with hardships on her own. Self-sufficiency had been one of the few things of value her father gave her. That and the certainty that if she ever had a child of her own, she would wrap him or her in love that would never be doubted.

In the midst of her soul-searching, the truck rolled to a stop in front of an attractive two-story home in an upper-middle-class neighborhood. Bailey touched Gil's arm. "I'm going to stay here." He had already told her he didn't plan to linger.

Gil frowned. "Don't be ridiculous. Come meet my friends."

She shook her head. "They're an important part of your life. If I go in with you, they'll make assumptions. Let's not complicate things."

"Lord, you're stubborn."

"Go get Cade. I'll be fine."

He stalked away, clearly displeased. Her decision was the right one, though. If Gil showed up with a woman in tow, his friends would think something was going on. And it wasn't. She and Gil were having recreational sex. To fill a void in their lives.

Wanting more didn't make it so.

As Gil walked back to the truck with Cade, he ruffled his son's hair. "I have a surprise for you."

"What is it?" Cade looked tired and not quite as bouncy as usual. No doubt the boys had stayed up far too late.

"I brought a friend with me."

Gil opened the truck door and helped Cade climb into the back. The boy grinned hugely when he saw who sat in the passenger seat. "Hi, Miss Bailey. Wish I could sit up front with you."

She leaned over the seat and patted his knee. "We have to obey the law. Wouldn't want Sheriff Battle to arrest us."

Gil climbed in behind the wheel. "What is this obsession you have with being arrested?" he asked, the words barely audible.

Wincing, she remembered using the very same words only an hour before…when she and Gil had stood stark naked beneath the afternoon sun. She closed her eyes, still able to see in her mind's eye the two of them tangled together on an old, dusty quilt.

Ignoring Gil's provocative mutter was her only option. "I have an idea," she said. "Why don't I ride in the back with Cade? That way he won't be all alone."

Cade squealed with delight even as his father's face darkened with frustration. "If that's what you want."

Cade chattered nonstop three-fourths of the way back to Royal, and then without warning fell sound asleep, his little body slumping against Bailey's shoulder trustingly.

Her eyes met Gil's in the rearview mirror. "Poor thing is exhausted."

"Well, I haven't slept much for the past ten days. And you don't seem to be worried about me."

"Gil!"

"I'm not going to let you pretend nothing happened, Bailey. Things are different now."

"How?"

Fortunately for her, the question stumped him. Either that or he wasn't willing to talk about it in front of his son. Her blunt question put an end to any conversation at all. She leaned her head against the window and dozed, enjoying the feel of Gil's son pressed up against her side.

It was getting dark when they made it out to McDaniel's Acres. Lights in the farmhouse created a welcoming glow. Cade never stirred when Gil opened the passenger door and helped Bailey climb out of the backseat.

When her feet hit the ground, he continued to hold her. "We have to talk about this. But now is not the time."

Her heart swelled with hope and longing. Was he going to tell her something important? Something that could change her life forever? For the better?

She knew he was right about timing. Serious conversation required privacy. But when he bent his head and kissed her so very gently, she wanted to blurt out the truth. *I love you, Gil.*

Any anger and frustration he felt had melted away or had been stuffed into a box marked Don't Spoil the Moment.

She strained against him, feeling the urgent hunger that was never far from the surface. He didn't try to hide his arousal. Knowing he needed and wanted her was almost enough. But not entirely.

Wrapping her arms around his neck, she tried to read a deeper meaning into his tenderness. Did he feel anything for her beyond simple lust?

At last he released her. Breathing harshly, he rubbed a thumb over her cheekbone. "Don't fret, sweetheart. Everything is going to be okay. I promise."

What did that mean? What was he planning?

Before she could press for answers, he was gone...the taillights of his truck shining red in the gathering darkness as he headed home with his young son.

She walked up the steps slowly. Would it matter if she asked her boss for one more week? Or would that simply prolong the pain of walking away from Gil?

It startled her to realize that Chance was sitting on the front porch swing. And he was not alone. Cara Windsor stood abruptly. To Bailey's trained eye and with the illumination from the porch light, it was easy to see that the beautiful blonde had been crying.

Before Bailey could do more than say a quick hello, the other woman dashed down the steps, got into her car and drove away.

Chance spread his arms across the back of the swing, his long legs outstretched. "Was that Gil I saw bringing you home?"

Her cheeks flamed. She and Gil had kissed on the far

side of the truck. Chance couldn't have seen much. But it was still embarrassing. "Yes. I rode with him to Midland to pick up Cade."

"Cute kid."

"Yes."

"I hope you haven't planted doubts in Gil's head about me."

What could she say to that? "Gil makes his own decisions. And he's very loyal to his friends."

"Yes, he is. But men can do irrational things when a woman is involved."

Here was her opportunity. She dropped her tote on the floor and leaned against a post. "Is that what you did, Chance? To be with Cara?"

The smile faded from his face. "Things aren't always what they seem, Bailey. To be honest, I had no idea I was still on your list."

"She's not wearing her engagement ring anymore, is she? I like you, Chance. But it's hard to overlook the fact that she's been hanging around here instead of helping her fiancé regain his memory. Is there anything you want to tell me?"

He stood in one fluid motion and faced her, topping her by several inches. His move could have been threatening. But in her gut she knew it wasn't. "You've already questioned me, Bailey. Twice, if I remember correctly. And I told you everything I know about Alex's disappearance. Which is pretty much zero."

"And was everything you told me about Cara the truth? Did you perhaps leave out some pertinent details?"

"I did not. There's nothing more to tell."

"That tête-à-tête I interrupted a few minutes ago didn't look like nothing. Why don't you tell me what you were talking about? Why was she crying? Was it because the man she thought she loved doesn't even know who she is? Is that it?"

He folded his arms across his chest, his expression grim. "Cara's business is her own. If you want answers, you'll have to ask her."

"She didn't look like she wanted to talk to me."

"Perhaps not."

"I'm not the bad guy in this equation. Unless of course you really are guilty. In which case, you're out of luck. Because I never give up until I solve a case." She winced inwardly, because technically, that wasn't true. Not this time. Thanks to her boss, she was not going to have the satisfaction of finishing *this* investigation.

"At the risk of looking guilty when I change the subject, I'd like to give you some advice."

"Okay. I'll bite. What is it?"

"Gil Addison is a hell of a nice guy. And he's had some rough knocks. He deserves to be happy more than most anyone I know."

"And this concerns me how?"

"Don't let your passion for the truth hurt him. If you're not serious about a relationship, then walk away."

She pondered Chance's pointed remarks as she climbed the staircase to the second floor where her room was located. Was she giving up too easily? Did Gil believe he and Bailey had a deeper connection than she was giving them credit for?

Tossing her tote and sweater on the bed, she pulled her phone from her pocket and saw that she had a text from the man who filled her thoughts so completely.

Is it possible for u to meet me at the club in the morning...11:00 a.m....so I can hand over my rambunctious son??

She frowned as she curled up on the window seat. Under the circumstances, she would rather not see Gil again until she'd had time to process her emotions. But she had made a promise, and she couldn't disappoint the child caught in the middle of an adult conflict.

No problem. 11 it is. What will he want for lunch?

Gil's reply was swift.

Anything that ends with ice cream.

She tapped the keys.

So the diner would be good?

Definitely.

Resisting the urge to ask him what he meant earlier when he said everything would be okay, she added one last note.

See you then…

She set the cell phone on the bedside table and began changing out of her dress and leggings. Moments later, the text alert dinged again. Curious, she glanced at the screen.

My bed looks empty without you…

Torn between caution and excitement, she debated answering. Perhaps he would think she was in the shower if she didn't respond.

A second *ding* heralded another message.

I know you're reading this. I can feel your anxiety all the way over here. Quit worrying.

Easy for him to say. Since she couldn't think of an appropriate answer, she stood there staring at the prompt...

What we have is more than good sex, and you know it.

Her lips curled in a reluctant smile. How long would he carry on a one-sided conversation?

It's going to be a long, uncomfortable night. Every time I close my eyes and think of you, sleep is the last thing on my mind...

Finally, bravely, she replied with what was in her heart.

I miss you, Gil...

This time the long silence was on his end.
After two full minutes, his answer came.

I miss you, too, sweetheart. Sleep well...

Gil plugged his phone into the charger and prowled his bedroom, pacing from one side to the other. He'd told Bailey the truth. Everywhere he looked he saw her. Naked, sprawled across his mattress. Laughing. Panting. Crying out when he made her come.

How could two incredible sexual encounters turn his entire world upside down? Before he had gotten to know this woman, he had learned to live with loneliness, with sexual deprivation. Hard work and dedication to his son's welfare had enabled him to forget—most of the time—

that he was a man in his prime, a man who had the same needs as any other man.

Now that the genie was out of the bottle, though, there was no way he could go back to the way things were. He stopped dead in the middle of the room, struck with the knowledge that he was falling in love with Bailey Collins already. His subconscious must have known long before now, because the intensity of what he was feeling didn't happen overnight.

He'd been so busy stonewalling her and arguing with her that it had taken him all this time to admit she was exactly the woman he wanted. She was tough and strong and not afraid to do what was right. She was gentle with his son and passionate in Gil's arms.

The fact that she wore boring suits with naughty undies enchanted him. Knowing that she was a positive, upbeat person in spite of her sterile upbringing only added to his admiration of her character.

He couldn't wait to see her again. Was the emotion he had seen in her eyes this afternoon more than simple hunger?

Was it possible that Bailey cared about him in return?

He considered himself a fairly intuitive person, though he'd be the first to admit that women were complex creatures. Was Bailey leaving because Gil had given her no reason to stay?

From her perspective, he'd done nothing concrete to say that he wanted her in his life permanently. It shamed him that she could believe he saw her as no more than a good time.

The fact that she had a job and a life in another city complicated things. Was there any point in trying the long-distance thing for a while? Gil couldn't walk away from the ranch that was his son's heritage and his family's roots.

Not to mention the fact that the Straight Arrow provided a considerable number of jobs.

But was it fair to ask Bailey to give up everything and Gil nothing? He had a lot of thinking to do and not much time to do it. With Bailey being summoned home on Thursday, he had less than a week to analyze his gut feelings and make a plan. And then there was Cade. Gil was pretty sure what Cade's reaction would be, but he needed to sit down with his son and tell him what was going on. That his father wanted to include Bailey in their family.

Imagining the three of them as a unit healed a lingering hurt in Gil's soul. A dream had been stolen from him tragically long ago. Now he had a chance to start over, to have the traditional family he had always envisioned.

As he showered and climbed into bed, he realized that he was far too wired to sleep. By this time tomorrow night, God willing, he and Bailey would have an understanding. Perhaps he could fly to Dallas with her when she went back and they could shop for a ring.

He would use any means in his power to make her happy. Everything was going to be perfect.

Fourteen

Bailey arrived in town fifteen minutes early. She was genuinely looking forward to spending the day with Cade, but even more than that, she wanted to see Gil. His mysterious promises had lit a tiny flame of hope deep inside her, hope that he felt the same connection, the same craving to make their relationship more than a passing fancy.

When Gil's familiar big truck pulled up at the club, he and Cade hopped out. The two males were dressed similarly, both wearing jeans and cowboy boots with light rain jackets. The skies were dull, and the forecast called for showers.

Gil's coat was black to match his hair. Cade's was bright blue and reflected his eyes.

The boy ran across the pavement. "Hi, Miss Bailey! I get to stay with you today."

She grinned, kneeling to hug him. "Yes, you do. And

I'm excited about that. I thought we'd start with lunch if that's okay with you."

"Yes, ma'am." Cade beamed.

Gil touched the child's shoulder. "Take my phone and sit on the bench over there for a minute, please. You can play that new game we bought. I need to talk to Bailey."

Cade did as he was told, leaving Bailey and Gil to face each other. She felt self-conscious about being seen by club members, given their location. When Gil smiled at her, though, all that faded away.

He reached out to touch her, but apparently thought better of it at the last minute, because he retracted his hand. "I want to kiss you, but I don't want to embarrass you," he said.

"It *is* a fairly public spot. Maybe later?"

"No maybe about it." His gaze roved her face, his eyes burning with hunger. "I didn't sleep worth a damn."

"Me either."

They stared at each other.

He raked a hand through his hair. "I want us to talk. Tonight. Serious stuff."

"Sounds scary, but okay."

"When you bring Cade home this afternoon, stay for dinner." He paused, a spark of devilment in his brown eyes. "And breakfast. You can stay in the guest room if it will make you feel better. But you should know that Cade sleeps like the dead."

"Won't it look odd if I bring a suitcase with me?"

"Throw a few things in a shopping bag. He won't pay any attention, I promise."

Joy bubbled in her chest. There was no mistaking his meaning. This was as good as a declaration. "In that case, I'd love to come."

He glanced at his watch. "I've got to get going. You'll

be okay with him? If he gets too rowdy, time-out usually works."

"Don't worry. We'll be fine."

Bailey held Cade's hand as his father backed out of a parking space and drove away with a wave. She glanced down at her charge. "You ready to eat?"

Cade nodded enthusiastically. "I'm starving."

The kid could put away a lot of food. After consuming a full-size hamburger and a mountain of ketchup-laden fries, he declared himself ready for dessert.

"What does your father allow you to have?"

"Two scoops of ice cream with chocolate sauce and one cherry."

"A man who knows his own mind."

Cade cocked his head. "What does that mean?"

She grinned. "It means you are definitely your father's son."

After a brief rain shower that left the air sticky and the ground damp, the skies began to clear. Out at McDaniel's Acres, Cade was in his element. He had grown up on a ranch, so much of the activity was familiar to him. But because Chance's place was geared toward tourists, there were extras to entertain a young boy. Pony rides, a miniature rodeo-themed playground, and best of all, a new litter of puppies out in the barn, just begging for someone to play with them.

Fortunately the little canines were old enough to be away from their mother some of the time. Cade sat entranced, holding two of the six in his lap. They were mixed breed, part hound and part terrier.

For a young child, Cade was remarkably patient. He stroked their ears and talked to them with such sweetness that Bailey was hard-pressed not to get teary-eyed. She'd never been allowed to have pets as a child. A moment like this was one she would have treasured.

Cade looked up at her. "Which one is your favorite?" he asked, very serious.

Bailey studied the pups carefully. "That one," she said. "The smallest one with the black patch on his ear."

"He looks like a pirate."

"I agree. If he belonged to me, I think I'd call him Captain Jack."

"Do you have any pets, Miss Bailey?"

She shook her head. "I have to travel a lot for my job, and it wouldn't be fair to leave an animal at home alone."

Cade looked up at her with his trademark grin. "Whenever you're at my house, I'll share my pets with you. I have two dogs and a hamster."

"That's a very nice offer."

"Dad told me before he left today that he asked you to come to dinner at our house tonight."

She gnawed her lip. "Yes." She wasn't sure she was ready for this conversation.

"Do you like him?"

It was ridiculous that she felt her cheeks warm. "Of course I do. Lots of people like your dad. He's a nice man."

Cade rolled his eyes, looking like one of the precocious kids from the Disney Channel. "Miss Bailey, you know what I mean. Do you want him to be your boyfriend?"

She squatted beside him, hands on her knees. "I thought we talked about this."

"I'm not asking for a new mom. I just want to know if you like him."

The kid should be a lawyer when he grew up. She studied his innocent face, his features so like his father's. "Some subjects are for grown-ups, Cade. It's not that I don't want to answer your question. But what you're asking me is a private thing. Between your dad and me. Do you understand?"

His sigh was theatrical. "I guess so." He rubbed the puppy's head, his eyes downcast. "He likes you."

Oh, crap. How dignified was it to pump a kid for information? But the temptation was too much. "How do you know?"

Cade's expression was earnest when he looked up at her. "I heard him singing in the shower this morning."

Bailey frowned. "So?"

"So my dad never sings in the shower."

"Maybe he was in a good mood."

"I told you. He doesn't sing in the shower."

Clearly, Cade's logic made perfect sense to him. But Bailey was befuddled. "I'll take your word for it," she said. Reminding herself that she was a mature adult, she derailed the provocative conversation. "Let's go back to the house. Chance's cook promised to fix a snack for you."

Cade stood up, a piece of hay stuck to his pink, round cheek. He tucked his small hand in hers as they walked back to the main house. "I like you, too, Miss Bailey. Thanks for babysitting me today."

An hour later, Bailey took Cade up to her room and washed his face and hands and removed the worst of the mud from his shoes. She couldn't return him to his father looking like a ragamuffin. "We'd better head out," she said. "If I'm late getting you home, I'll be on your dad's bad list."

Cade giggled. "Dad says people aren't bad. But sometimes they do bad things. Is that how you get on the list?"

She picked up his jacket and the small cowboy hat Chance had given him. "I suppose so. Your dad is a very wise man." And a darned good father. Cade's maturity and grounded personality didn't happen by accident. It was the result of unwavering love and the confidence he possessed that his father would always protect him.

Her car was warm from sitting in the sun. She cranked up the air and then made sure Cade was properly strapped into his booster seat in the back. His eyelids were drooping. He considered himself too old for a nap, but he had played hard today.

As the crow flew, the trip from Chance's ranch to Gil's wasn't all that far. But the only way to get from one to the other was to drive the several miles out to the highway, hang a right for another six or seven miles, and finally, traverse the long road out to Gil's house.

The whole trip took thirty minutes or so. Cade, bless his heart, was conked out before she even got to the main highway. Keeping the radio turned low, she hummed along to a favorite song, feeling her pulse race at the thought of being with Gil again.

Imagining what he wanted to talk about was tantalizing. But she kept her anticipation in check. It was a long time until Cade would be tucked in tonight. By the time she and Gil talked, it would be late. After that, would he expect intimacy? With his son asleep down the hall? Or would they go their separate ways?

She couldn't imagine that. Not after yesterday. Gil looked at her with such intensity in his gaze that she was under no illusions about what he was thinking. He was a virile man. A sexy, masculine alpha male. And he wanted *her*.

The knowledge was exciting. But she felt restless and nervous. The sting of continuous desire was a unique experience. She didn't know it was possible to feel such gut-level need and still be so uncertain about the future. Would tonight be a watershed moment? Or was she making too many assumptions?

Suddenly, seemingly out of nowhere, a car pulled out to pass her. She grimaced. Impatient drivers were the worst. In slow motion it seemed, she glanced in the rearview mirror to look at Cade and almost simultaneously realized that the vehicle beside her was not merely crowding her accidentally. The driver jerked his wheel sharply and sideswiped her, pushing her toward the side of the road.

Her training clicked into gear. She had to outrun them. But even as she stepped on the gas, she despaired. The car responded sluggishly, the front right tire hung up in the ditch. With shaking hands she grabbed her cell phone and texted 9-1-1 to Gil…and seconds later to Nate. Then, *dialing* 9-1-1, she dropped the phone on the front seat and left the call open.

Her heart in her stomach, she prayed that Cade would stay asleep. The thought of him being scared made her angry. When she determined that her car would go no farther, she put it in Park. Bitterly regretting that she had not brought her service weapon, she debated her options. If at all possible, she would not let whoever had disabled the vehicle get near Cade.

At the moment, there was no movement from the other car. It had stopped, as well.

She glanced at Cade. His thumb was in his mouth and he clutched the small plastic pony that was his favorite. But still he slept.

Adrenaline flooded her stomach with sickening force as the door of the other car swung open and a man exited the vehicle. He wore a ski mask. Walking rapidly, he closed the distance between them. Though his arm was not outstretched, he had a gun in his hand pointed at the ground.

"Get out of the car," he said loudly, standing several feet away, nothing but glass between them.

"What do you want? I have money." She reached for her purse. "Credit cards. Cash. Take it and leave me alone."

"Let me see both of your hands."

Her brain raced. Did he know she was trained law enforcement? Was this Alex's kidnapper? Slowly, wanting to draw his attention away from Cade, she held up her arms.

The man's posture was rigid. "Get out."

If she did as he asked, Cade would be completely helpless.

The man took two steps closer. "Now," he shouted. "Or I shoot the kid." He placed the muzzle of the weapon against the glass of the back window.

Bailey glanced desperately at the boy in her charge. "Cade," she whispered. Knowing she couldn't take a chance that the man was bluffing, she unlocked the door and stood up. The assailant charged her and struck the side of her head, and her world went black.

Gil flew down the street toward the sheriff's office. He'd been in the chopper, still a long way out from the airport when Bailey's text came through. His return call to her went straight to voice mail.

Parking his truck haphazardly, half on, half off the sidewalk, he jumped out and ran toward the building just as Nate pulled up in a squad car, sirens blazing. Gil stared at his friend, his heart pumping like a madman's. Before Nate could speak, Gil grabbed his arm. "What in the hell is going on? I got a 9-1-1 text from Bailey."

"Me, too."

"Damn." Fear like he had never known swept over Gil. It was a hell of a time to figure out that his love for Bailey was neither halfhearted nor theoretical.

The door to the building burst open and Nate's second in command ran to meet them. "A 9-1-1 call came in about forty-five minutes ago. From Ms. Collins. She left the connection engaged so we could listen in. As crazy as it sounds, it appears that someone tried to carjack her. We sent personnel out immediately."

Nate frowned. "Where?"

"We located her cell phone signal. She was about halfway between McDaniel's Acres and Mr. Addison's place."

Fury choked Gil. "Where in the hell were you, Nate?"

"On a domestic disturbance call north of town. Woman took a butcher knife to her husband. I got back as soon as I could."

The cell phone at the young man's hip crackled. He answered it, and the blood drained from his face. "I understand. Thank you."

Gil felt a great yawning void in his chest. "Tell me," he said hoarsely. "Tell me."

The twenty-something kid swallowed visibly. "They found the car. Ms. Collins was lying in the road…unconscious. Nasty blow to the head."

"And my son?"

The younger man was pale as milk. "He's gone, Mr. Addison. No sign of him."

Gil reeled mentally, though he kept himself upright by sheer strength of will. Everything seemed very far away, the street sounds muffled.

Nate took his shoulders and got in his face. "Steady, man. We're going to find him."

"He's only a baby." Gil had spent the past five years making sure his son was happy and healthy. "How could this happen?"

The deputy spoke up, his voice shaky. "We have a team going over the crime scene. They're very good."

Nate still held Gil's shoulders. "Why don't you go to the hospital and check on Bailey? I'll text or call you every half hour. We have a protocol, and we're going to be all over this. Trust me, Gil. I'll search for that boy as if he were my own son."

Gil wanted to argue. He wanted to get in his car and comb the county. But without a lead, he was stonewalled. "You have to find him. I can't lose my son. I can't lose my son."

Nate released him, but still frowned. "I'm not sure you should be driving."

Gil glanced at his car. "I'm fine," he said dully. "I'm fine. I want to go with you." Everything inside him screamed in agony. The woman he loved was hurt...badly. But Cade needed him. The cruel impossibility of helping them both sliced him to shreds.

Nate hesitated, obviously weighing the pros and cons of letting Gil ride shotgun. "It's boring work," he said. "We'll be there for a while."

"Doesn't matter. I might be able to help."

"Fine. Let's go."

Gil saw nothing of the familiar scenery as it flashed by his window. When Nate screeched to a halt in front of three other squad cars and a van, Gil saw Bailey's car. Bile rose in his throat, but he choked it back.

They got out, and he strode beside his friend, stopping only when he saw the unmistakable stain of blood on the ground. *God in heaven*.

Nate quizzed the detective in charge. "Tell me what you know."

A female officer, her eyes shadowed as she glanced at Gil, spoke calmly and concisely.

"The damage to the victim's car indicates that some-one sideswiped her, forcing her off the road. We have decent tire tracks, as well as several shoeprints. Assailant was likely male.

"Any blood *inside* her car?"

"No."

Gil walked on shaky legs toward the vehicle and peered inside. "His booster seat is gone."

Nate followed him. "That's a good sign. Whoever took the boy means no harm."

Just then another officer climbed out of the mobile lab in the van and jogged up to them, his face red from exertion. "We found this, sir." He handed it to Nate. "It's a tracking device. No telling how long it's been on her car. We're trying to find the manufacturer."

Fifteen

Nate cursed as Gil's blood congealed. Gil squeezed the bridge of his nose, his fear mounting. "I told her that what she was doing put her in danger. She wouldn't listen."

Nate shook his head. "This may have nothing to do with Alex's disappearance."

But Gil could hear the uncertainty in the sheriff's voice. The timing was too much of a coincidence. Someone could have kidnapped Cade, knowing that the wealthy Alex Santiago would pay to ransom a child's life. And now that Gil knew the truth about Alex… Good Lord. If the attacker knew the truth, also, then he or she was aware that del Toro was one of the richest men in Mexico.

Gil cleared his throat. "A kidnapping for ransom would be a best-case scenario. If that's what happened, they won't hurt him." But Gil's innocent son would still be scared and alone. *Goddamn it.*

Nate pulled out his phone and dialed. "I'm calling the

hospital. If Bailey wakes up...*when* Bailey wakes up," he said more forcefully, "she may be able to give us a description of the car and the attacker. In the meantime, we'll put out an Amber Alert."

"But with no vehicle description and no way to tell who Cade is with, that will be pretty useless." Gil's fury was misplaced. Nate was trying to help. They all were.

Gil spun on his heel and strode down the road, away from the vehicles, away from the image of his son being dragged from the car, away from the sickening vision of Bailey lying in the dusty road.

When he had put several hundred yards between himself and the uniforms, he stopped, eyes scrunched closed against the piercing pain that threatened to explode his skull. *Dear God,* he prayed. *Protect them...please...* His brain was in such turmoil, those were the only words he could articulate. Over and over. *Protect them. Protect them.*

Nate followed him moments later. "I need to know what he was wearing."

Gil rattled off the requested information, trying not to think about how he had helped Cade get dressed only that morning, the little boy chattering excitedly about his day with Bailey.

Nate answered a call and listened intently. When he hung up, he touched Gil's arm in a brief gesture of reassurance. "Bailey's going to be okay. She has a severe concussion and required several stitches. It was a bad wound, but she's stable. The head nurse will call me when they have further news."

"I don't know what to do." The six words ripped his throat like sharp glass. His whole adult life he had been a man in control, the one to whom everyone else turned in a crisis. What kind of father stood by helplessly while his child faced God knew what evil?

"I think you should go to the hospital now. Call me with updates about Bailey, and I'll keep you apprised of our progress here. It's going to be critical that we find out what she knows."

Gil understood the sense of what Nate was saying. But he had the odd and terrible notion that he needed to stay right here. At the spot where his son was last alive and well. As if by some miracle, Cade might teleport back to Bailey's car and this whole thing would be a dream.

He nodded slowly, his hands fisted at his sides. The sense of helplessness was suffocating. But if he could not help his son in the short term, his only other option was to be with Bailey.

He had closed his mind to the possibility that she could have been killed. He couldn't process that thought in the midst of his son's disappearance. The brain could only handle so much trauma before it shut down. Bailey was fine. And she would understand his delay.

Leaving the crew on the scene to search for any last clues, Gil and Nate headed back into town. Gil got out of the squad car and stood on the sidewalk. It was a beautiful evening. All around them traffic bustled. People smiled and waved. The world went on.

But for Gil, time had stopped.

Nate hugged him. An unusual enough occurrence that Gil was both shocked and taken off guard by the other man's compassion.

Nate stepped back, preparing to go inside. "I'll keep you posted, and you do the same."

Gil nodded.

"Talk to someone at the hospital. You may be in shock. You won't do anyone any good if you collapse."

"I'm fine. Really." It was true. He was encased in ice now. Nothing could touch him. He had a plan and a mission. Watch over Bailey. Find out what she knew.

Leaving a concerned Nate staring after him, Gil strode to his truck, climbed in and started the ignition. For a moment, he couldn't remember which way he needed to go to find the hospital. Realizing that Nate still watched him, Gil took a deep breath and shifted into drive. He backed up, pulled into traffic, and rounded the corner.

Five minutes later, he pulled off into a narrow alley, put his head on the steering wheel and sobbed.

Had it been only a couple of weeks since Gil and Bailey had visited Alex? Kissing her in the parking lot seemed like a dream now...a bittersweet dream. Tonight was supposed to have been a threshold for them, a day of reckoning. Instead, anticipation had crumbled into sickening fear for his son.

Gil walked into the hospital, sparing only a fleeting thought to wonder if Alex had been discharged. Thinking about Santiago...or del Toro...or whatever his name was made Gil's anger rise again. It wasn't Alex's fault that Cade was gone. Gil knew that intellectually. But it was easier to shift his fury onto Alex than to admit that he had failed his son.

The waiting room was empty. Gil approached the pleasant-faced older woman volunteering at the information desk. "Bailey Collins. Can you tell me her room number?"

"Are you family?"

He ground his teeth. "She has no family in the area. I'm her friend."

"I'll need to check with the nurse..."

He gripped the edge of the desk, closing his eyes briefly and reaching for patience. "Ms. Collins and I are in a relationship. Do you understand what I mean? I have to know what's going on."

The lady in the pink smock flushed, her eyes wide. "I'm just following rules, sir. But I will take you at your word."

While Gil waited, the woman made a brief phone call, then hung up. She smiled hesitantly. "Ms. Collins is not in the room. She's having a CT scan and a couple of other tests as a precaution. As soon as she's back, they'll let me know."

Gil swallowed, feeling light-headed. "Thank you." Numb and filled with a black void of despair, he dropped into an uncomfortable chair on the far side of the room. A TV on the opposite wall, thankfully muted but with closed captioning on, played old reruns of *The Andy Griffith Show*. Opie was small in this episode, maybe Cade's age. He had broken his arm falling out of a tree, and Sheriff Andy was carrying him into the hospital.

Seeing the tears on Opie's face broke through Gil's calm, letting in a torrent of rage and terror. He dropped forward, head in his hands, elbows on his knees, and prayed.

An hour later, a doctor approached him. Gil leaped to his feet, swaying when spots danced in front of his eyes. He had skipped lunch knowing that the housekeeper was preparing a big spread for tonight's dinner with Bailey, hosted by Cade and himself.

It was after eight now.

The man stared at him with the same compassion Gil had seen in Nate's eyes. "Mr. Addison?"

"Yes."

"Your friend is back in the room resting."

"May I see her?"

"Only for a moment. She's had something to help her relax and sleep. We're monitoring the concussion."

"Are you aware of the situation?" Gil asked, his throat tight with a combination of frustration and dread.

The doctor nodded. "You need her to wake up. I get it. But you have to understand that her body needs rest and peace to heal. If she regains consciousness right now, she'll have to relive everything that happened, and she'll become agitated. At this critical juncture, I can't allow that. I'm sorry, Mr. Addison. Hopefully if her vital signs are good tomorrow, I can reconsider."

When the man departed, Gil pulled himself together and followed the directions back to the Bailey's room. Standing in the doorway, he felt his vision blur. Struggling to stand up straight, he moved toward the bed.

She lay still as death, her skin unnaturally pale. A large bandage covered an area that included her temple. An IV was secured in the hand that rested atop the sheet. Gil stared at that hand, remembering how it had caressed him.

Knowing Bailey, she would have done everything to save Cade. But it hadn't been enough. Bailey hadn't saved him, and neither had his father.

Emotion roiled in him, hot and deep. This was the woman to whom he wanted to propose marriage. By all rights he should be sitting at her elbow, promising to remain by her side.

But though every cell in his body wanted to hold her and comfort her, a sick guilt held him back. How could he think about loving Bailey when the only other person he loved with equal intensity was out there somewhere? Alone. Terrified.

A male nurse stepped in to check BP and temp and adjust the flow of medication. "She's doing as well as can be expected, sir. It was a nasty wound."

Gil leaned against the wall. No one told him she had cut her face. A neat line of stitches closed a gash on her forehead. She must have hit a rock or some other sharp object when she fell.

"Should I leave my number?" he asked, his lips numb as he formed the words. He felt as if he were outside his body observing.

The man nodded, moving about the bed with efficient, gentle motions. "Write it on the board, if you will. Someone will get in contact with you if there is any change. If you'll permit me to give you some advice, sir, I'd suggest you go home and get some rest. You look pretty bad. Visiting hours start at ten in the morning. There's nothing you can do for her now."

Gil didn't remember walking back to his truck, but he found himself behind the wheel. In some dim corner of his brain, he realized that he was impaired. Driving as slowly as a geriatric en route to Sunday church, he made his way home, determined not to hurt anyone else.

Though it was cold, he sat on the back porch to call Nate. But there was no news. The investigation was ongoing. They were doing everything they could to find Cade.

The housekeeper had gone home. She left instructions for heating dinner. Gil fixed a plate of chicken casserole and ate five or six bites. Moments later he was in the bathroom throwing up.

He couldn't walk upstairs. He couldn't look into his son's bedroom. He couldn't look at the bed where he and Bailey had made love with such happy abandon.

His soul in ashes, he stretched out on the sofa in the living room and slung an arm over his eyes.

Bailey didn't want to wake up. Somewhere just off-stage, pain waited, deep and vicious. She clung to the drug-induced fog, well aware that the alternative was not something she wished to face.

Hours passed. Maybe weeks. She didn't know. She didn't care. Nothing could hurt her in this wonderful co-coon.

But eventually, her cowardice was challenged. Professional voices, sympathetic but demanding, insisted she accept reality. Swimming toward the surface, she noted the various aches and pains that held her down. The crushing throb in her skull was the worst.

She opened her eyes cautiously. The light was bright. Too bright. Turning her head slowly, she focused her eyes on the man sitting by her bed. Frowning, she tried to decipher what was wrong with the picture. "Nate?" she croaked.

The sheriff jumped to his feet, looking down at her with an indecipherable expression. "Let me get the nurse," he said.

"No, wait." She frowned. "Why are you here?"

He rubbed a hand over his chin. "I wanted to see how you're doing."

"Gil?" The omission of his name seemed ominous.

"He's on his way." The answer was too quick, too hearty.

She closed her eyes, sifting through the layers of memory. A hospital. Something had happened. Suddenly, the truth crashed down on her. A wail ripped from her throat. "Cade," she cried, her head pounding. "What happened to Cade?"

Nate went white, and suddenly the room was filled with medical personnel. Seconds later, the fog returned…

Gil and Nate stood at the foot of the bed. Bailey's doctor was there, as well. The older man's expression was grim. "We've backed off the sedative. You'll have to be quick.

This morning her BP skyrocketed when she realized what had happened."

"What if she can't help us?" It was Gil's worst fear. He had hung all his hopes on the fact that Bailey would be able to explain things when she woke up.

Nate shifted from foot to foot, his gaze watchful. "We'll work with what we have."

Slowly, almost imperceptibly, Bailey returned to consciousness. The first sign that she was at all aware of her surroundings was the frown that creased the space between her eyebrows.

The doctor looked at the monitor. "She's in pain. As soon as you have what you need, I'll give her more meds."

Gil shuddered. What they were about to do seemed little shy of torture. "You have to do it," he muttered to Nate. "I can't. I'll step over here where she won't see me."

Nate stared at him. "I understand."

As Gil watched, Bailey opened her eyes. Only for a few seconds. But in a moment, she tried again, this time focusing on Nate.

He spoke softly, reassuringly. "Hey, there, Bailey. Glad to see you're back with us."

Her lips trembled. "I'm so sorry."

Nate touched her hand. "Steady. I need to know if you can help me. Do you remember?"

Her expression destroyed Gil. He had never seen such agony on a woman's face.

"Yes," she whispered.

Nate nodded, his face calm, his eyes kind. "Someone ran you off the road and hit you on the head."

"Yes."

"Who was it?"

"I don't know. He wore a ski mask."

"Anyone else in the car?"

"I think so, but I'm not sure."

"And the vehicle?"

"A beige sedan…newer model. Maybe a Honda. The plate was dirty, but it was Mexican, I think. Had a 367 at the beginning."

"Anything else, honey?"

"It all happened so fast. They didn't want money. Cade was in the car asleep. I had to do something…" Tears welled in her eyes and spilled down her cheeks. "Oh, God." She sobbed aloud, groaning as her involuntary movements caused her discomfort.

Nate squeezed her hand. "Relax, Bailey. It's okay. You may remember something else later. Everything's going to be okay. I promise."

The doctor pushed something in the IV and Bailey's body visibly relaxed.

Nate exhaled. "Well, at least we have something. It's a start."

Gil shook his head, his heart sick. "It's damn little."

"Faith, Gil. Keep the faith."

Sixteen

The next time Bailey awoke, she knew exactly where she was and why. Gil sat beside her bed, his eyes closed, his face gray with exhaustion. She wet her dry, chapped lips. "May I have a drink, please?"

He roused instantly, poured water from an insulated pitcher, and stuck a straw in it. Holding it for her, he helped her take several sips. "You look a little better," he said.

"You don't have to stay with me. I know you have responsibilities at the ranch. And you need to help Nate look for…" Her throat hurt. She couldn't say the last word.

He shrugged. "They tell me civilians only get in the way."

She closed her eyes, processing what he wasn't saying. "You're angry with me."

"No." The answer was quick. "But I warned you that the investigation was dangerous."

His calm stoicism made her feel worse. Inside, he had

to be a mess. And all because he had entrusted Bailey with his son's care, and she had allowed him to be kidnapped.

"Is there any word about Cade?" She could barely voice the question. Because she knew the answer in her heart. Gil wouldn't be here if Cade had been found. He would be with his son.

Gil's expression was grim. "Not yet. Nate has brought in off-duty officers from other counties. I'm footing the bill for the extra help. They will find Cade."

"You sound so sure."

His gaze met hers square on, and for the first time, she saw the extent of his torment. "I can't allow room for doubt. I won't." His voice was raw.

Tears burned her eyes, but she blinked them away. "I never should have let myself get close to you or to Cade. We're all paying for my selfishness."

His scowl deepened. "We both made mistakes. Both lost sight of our primary goals. You had a job to do, and I had a son to protect. Have a son," he corrected swiftly, the words cracking.

A masculine voice in the hall caught her attention. It sounded like the sheriff. Gil stood up. "I'm going to grab a cup of coffee. I'll be right back." He pulled the door partway closed as he walked out.

The men conversed in low voices, obviously thinking Bailey could not hear them. But she was able to catch words here and there, enough to piece together what was being said.

They were arguing about possible theories. Judging from Nate's line of thought, he was still expecting a ransom note. She strained to listen. Gil was audibly upset, his voice growing louder.

Suddenly, the voices moved away and the hall was silent. Bailey shrank back in the bed, tears filling her eyes and spilling across her cheeks. Gil would never forgive her, even if and when Cade was found. Her actions had brought harm to Gil's family. One moment she'd been standing on the cusp of something wonderful, and now it was all gone.

The pain made it hard to breathe. She loved Gil Addison and his son. But she had lost them both. Shaking and cold, she punched the button to summon the nurse.

Moments later, the woman entered the room, her expression concerned. "Are you hurting? It's not time for medicine yet."

Bailey *was* hurting. Her dreams had shattered into a million pieces. Now was a heck of a time to learn that a heart truly could break.

She gripped a handful of the sheet, her breathing choppy. "Is it okay if I limit my visitors?"

The woman frowned. "Of course. Is there a problem?"

"I'm willing to see the sheriff. But no one else. Please."

The woman's eyes were kind. "Would you like me to ask the chaplain to come by?"

"No." Bailey's throat was so tight she could barely speak. "Thank you." She couldn't bear to look into Gil's eyes and see his anger and disappointment and fear. It was better to make a clean break.

"I'll make sure your wishes are noted at the nurse's station and on your door."

"Thank you."

The woman left. Bailey turned her head to stare out the window. The sun was shining brightly, in direct opposition to her bleak mood. How soon would she be able to travel? Her boss needed her back in Dallas, and Bailey wanted to go home. If there was more work to be done in Royal, she would ask to be reassigned. She couldn't come back here.

In her heart, though, she knew she would not be able to leave until she had the assurance that Cade was back in his father's arms…safe and happy. Thinking about the alternative was unbearable. Surely a ransom note would arrive soon. One victim with no memory, one child too young to plan an escape, and Bailey—who had been unconscious when the child was taken. It was an impossible situation.

Her brief burst of energy faded, leaving her drowsy and deeply sad. Cade had trusted her. Gil had trusted her. And she had failed them both. The knowledge haunted her.

She drifted into sleep, her dreams dark and threatening. Suddenly, she was back on the road between Chance's place and Gil's ranch…

She felt the cold slither of fear. The rapid beat of her heart. She stared at the man. He was tall. Maybe older. But the ski cap obscured everything important. Think, Bailey. Think. She focused on the car. It was ordinary. A figure sat in the passenger seat. Again, she saw Cade, sweet innocent Cade in the backseat. Then, something brutally hard hit her head. She crumpled, the ground coming up to meet her.

Bailey woke with a start even as the recollection of panic pushed adrenaline through her veins. The bland sterility of the hospital room was recognizable and reassuring. With shaking hands, she pushed the button to call the nurse.

Gil sat beside Nate in the squad car as they sped through town. "I don't understand. Why didn't she call *me?*" he asked

"Don't know." Nate slowed down for a stop sign, noted the empty side streets, and kept going. He had his lights flashing, but the sirens were off. At the hospital, they parked in a restricted zone. Both of them jogged toward the front of the hospital.

On Bailey's floor, a nurse with salt-and-pepper hair stopped them. "Hello, Sheriff. Mr. Addison."

Gil shifted from one foot to the other, impatient to hear what Bailey had to say. And to see for himself if she was improving. "We're here to see Bailey," he said, wanting to add, *Get out of my way, woman.*

"I'm sorry, sir. Ms. Collins has restricted her visitors."

Gil looked at her blankly. "What the hell does that mean?"

The nurse frowned at his language.

Nate touched his arm. "Take it easy." He addressed the woman calmly. "I had a message that Ms. Collins wanted to see me."

"She does. But Mr. Addison, I'm sorry. You can sit in the waiting room down the hall."

Gil felt his temper rise. He was on a short fuse from worry and lack of sleep. "I think there's been some kind of mistake," he said, injecting ice into his voice.

The woman didn't budge. "She was very clear. Only the sheriff."

Gil's eyebrows shot upward, incredulity in his exclamation. "I was here a few hours ago. What's this about?"

Nate gave him a glance. "Keep your mind on the goal, buddy. Let me go in and see what she has to say."

Relief washed over Bailey when she saw Nate's head poke around her door.

"You ready to see me?" he asked.

She nodded. "Pull up a chair."

When Nate made himself comfortable, Bailey managed a smile, though she hoped it didn't look as false at it felt to her. "I think I remembered something. It may amount to nothing. So don't get your hopes up. But then again, it might be a lead."

He leaned forward, elbows on his knees. "Tell me."

"I'm almost positive there *was* another person in the car that ran me off the road...a woman in the passenger seat. I remember seeing long hair. And today, something clicked. What if this has nothing to do with Alex? What if Gil's in-laws took the boy?"

Nate's gaze sharpened. "That's an angle we haven't considered."

"Were you in Royal when Gil's wife died?"

"Yes."

"So you remember that his wife's parents tried to get custody of Cade? And nearly succeeded?"

"True. But Gil hasn't heard from them in almost five years. I still think someone might have been sending you a signal to get out of Royal."

"You're probably right. But it won't hurt to check this out, will it?"

"I won't waste any time." He got to his feet, leaned down, and kissed her gently on the forehead. "Thank you. Now concentrate on getting better. That's an order."

"Yes, sir."

He stopped at the door and turned, his expression no longer as excited. "Why won't you see Gil?

"My reasons are private."

"You might want to cut him some slack. He's been through hell. Worried about you. Sick about Cade."

"I understand what's at stake here. But I'm not Gil's responsibility. He needs to focus on his son." She was proud of the even tenor of her voice and the calm expression on her face.

Nate shrugged. "I've seen the way he looks at you, Bailey. What's a man to do when the two people he cares most about are in harm's way at the same time?"

"I'm not upset with him, Nate, truly. Cade needs to come first. That's as it should be."

The sheriff looked as if he wanted to argue with her, but the clock was on her side. "You have a new lead to follow," she said. "Quit wasting time here."

"Can I let Gil come in to see you?"

She shook her head, her chest tight. "No, thank you. I'm going to take a nap. Please let me know when you have any news."

The door shut behind him, and finally she could release the tears that had been building.

If Gil had learned nothing else in this crisis, it was that he didn't like twiddling his thumbs. A man needed action to feel that he was making progress. *Hurry up and wait* was a special kind of torture.

One of the deputies brought him a cup of coffee. "There's a cot in the back room, Mr. Addison. It may be a while before we hear anything. Maybe you could sleep for an hour or so."

Gil managed a smile. "Thank you. I'm fine." He'd lost track of the number of hours he had been awake. Sleep had been nothing more than moments of lost consciousness every now and then. His eyes were gritty. His body ached. And a great yawning emptiness filled the space where his heart had been.

He had truly thought Bailey would be part of his life. But now he wasn't sure. Had she picked up on his ambivalence? His guilt over wanting her when Cade was missing? God, he felt as if he were being stretched on a rack. In dark moments when the fear for his son threatened to make him go mad, he escaped into his memories, seeing pictures of Bailey in his bed.

The images sustained him and gave him hope. But now

he had lost Bailey, too. If he had to, he would give his life for either one of them, his son or his lover. But what if he didn't get that chance? What if his life was reduced to nothing but emptiness? Would he ever recover?

Nate answered a phone call, his demeanor intense. He looked almost as tired as Gil. But a weary smile lit his face when he hung up. "They have the full license number. And the vehicle it's associated with belongs to your wife's parents. We've sent the information out statewide, and across the border, as well. It shouldn't be long now."

"Unless they've ditched the car and are hiding out."

"They must have been keeping tabs on you for a long time. When they realized you were getting close to Bailey, they started tracking her, as well. I'm betting they planned every possible scenario. A deserted road would have seemed like their golden opportunity."

Gil leaned against the wall, his body suddenly limp with fatigue. "Tell me we'll find him, Nate."

"We will," the other man replied, the two words allowing no room for doubt. "We will."

The next time Bailey awoke, the sky outside her window was dark, and Nate had returned.

She scanned his face. "Any news?"

He shook his head. "No. But we're cautiously optimistic. Your theory about the grandparents was right on target. What we *don't* know is whether they took Cade immediately across the border or if they've hidden out somewhere here in the states to avoid detection. The Mexican authorities are assisting every way they can."

"I see." It was a tiny comfort to know that she had been able to provide some help, after all. But it wasn't enough. The larger question loomed. Was Cade safe? Dear God, let it be so.

Nate yawned, and she glanced at the clock on the wall. "Please go home if you can," she said. "I'm feeling much better, and the night staff nurses are wonderful. I'd appreciate it if you would keep me updated."

He stood and stretched. "Of course."

"Thank you for all you've done."

He gave her a lopsided smile. "Gil is my friend. And you're a very nice woman. It's what we do here in Royal."

After he left, she pondered his words. It was true. She had seen it time and again since she had been assigned here. The community was tight-knit. And they would go out of their way for one of their own. What must it be like to have that kind of security? That depth of loyalty?

Her friends back in Dallas were all great people. But they were spread out across the city. Bailey didn't live with the kind of neighborly closeness that thrived here in Royal.

She was lucky that for the moment they were including her in the circle. It was a warm feeling. And one she wouldn't mind replicating.

The nurse came in to check her vital signs and also to give her a pain pill. Bailey had insisted on reducing the dosage. She didn't like being so drugged, and the throbbing in her head had subsided somewhat, at least enough that she could sleep. She punched her pillow into a more comfortable shape and tucked her hand under her cheek. When she turned out the light, she felt entirely alone.

Seventeen

Gil loitered at the end of the hallway until he was sure his presence would go unnoticed. Bailey's room was dark. He slipped inside and quietly pulled a chair close to the bed. Gently, he touched her head.

Stroking her hair lightly so as not to wake her, he whispered the words he had wanted to say long before now. "I love you, Bailey."

Though he had barely made a sound, she moved restlessly in the bed and opened her eyes. "Gil? How did you get in here?"

A tiny light on the panel above the bed was the only illumination in the room, but it was enough for him to see the wariness in her expression.

He shrugged, unrepentant. "I sneaked in when no one was looking." He took her hand. "How are you feeling?"

"Much better. I think they're going to release me in the morning."

"Why did you shut me out, sweetheart?

She withdrew visibly. "I want you to go." Her voice quivered.

"Please, honey. Tell me the truth."

Her big eyes were tragic. "I can't bear to see the look on your face. I know you blame me. And you have every right."

If he had ever felt more like scum in his life, he couldn't remember it. Shame made him drop his head, his forehead resting on her arm. She was so brave and so strong, and he had hurt her by not reassuring her from the outset that he didn't hold her responsible.

"Oh, Bailey. I don't deserve you. What a jackass I am, my love. I've been angry at the world and scared out of my mind and weaving on my feet with fatigue. But I should have realized you would feel this way. You're so very conscientious. I don't blame you. I would *never* blame you. I know you would protect Cade with your life."

She stroked his hair, a tentative, tender caress that was evidence of her generous spirit. "You're not just saying that to make me feel better?"

He sat up and stared at her sternly. "The kidnapping could have happened if he had been with me. Now stop worrying."

"I won't stop worrying until we have some good news."

"Is it good news to hear that I love you?"

She paled. "You're delirious."

"Not in the slightest. Tired, yes. And frightened for you and my son, yes. But completely in my right mind. I was all set to propose when things went south."

She stared at him, mute.

"I didn't think it would be such a shock," he said. "Surely you knew we were headed in this direction."

She shook her head. "No. I thought we were break-ing up."

He grinned despite his exhaustion. "Well, think again. I want you in my life. I need you and Cade needs you."

"I don't think I can talk about this yet. It feels wrong."

He sobered. "I understand. But don't make me stay away from you. I can't bear that on top of everything else."

Her bottom lip quivered as she reached out to grip his hand with hers. "He's coming back to us. We have to be-lieve that."

Gil's cell phone vibrated in his pocket, startling him. He answered it, his heart in his throat. Two minutes later, he hung up, his eyes damp. Inhaling a harsh breath, he leaned over and kissed Bailey...hard. "Nate's team has found Cade," he said, his voice gruff.

Her lips opened and closed. Tears trickled from her beautiful eyes. "He's okay?"

"Completely." He shuddered, swamped by a wave of re-lief so strong it made him dizzy. "My in-laws were hiding out with him in Del Rio, hoping to slip across the border into Mexico when the furor died down."

"Poor little man. He must be so confused."

"We'll make sure he sees a counselor. And we'll smother him with love." He nudged her hip. "Move over, gorgeous." He raised the head of the bed and leaned back against the pillows, gathering her in his right arm, tucking her against his chest. "Nate is driving him back to Royal early in the morning. I want you to be there with me at the Straight Arrow, Bailey, to welcome him home. If the doc-tor thinks you're well enough to be released."

She nestled into his embrace. "Oh, yes," she said. "I wouldn't miss it for the world."

Eight hours later, Bailey sat on Gil's front porch wrapped in a quilt, waiting for Nate's squad car to come into sight. When it did, she stood up, the tears flowing again. She hated feeling so weak and emotional, but her relief and joy were profound.

Gil put a hand on her shoulder. "Save your strength, honey. I'll bring him to you."

The car pulled to a stop at the foot of the steps, and a door flew open. "Daddy!" Cade ran toward his father, the two males meeting halfway in a boisterous hug that was beautiful to watch. Seeing Gil reunited with his son healed a deep crack in Bailey's heart. She may not have solved the case of Alex's kidnapping, but that failure paled in comparison to this victory.

Moments later she saw Gil whisper something in Cade's ear. The child looked up and saw Bailey. His mouth rounded in an *O* of surprise and his little face crumpled. "Miss Bailey," he wailed, running up the remainder of the steps. "You're okay." He threw himself at her, and Bailey winced as she tried to catch him without jarring her injury.

Hugging Cade tightly, she rested her cheek against his dark hair. "I'm pretty tough," she said. "And you were awfully brave."

Gil eased his son away. "We have to be careful with Miss Bailey, Cade. Her head is still getting well."

After that, Cade insisted on seeing her bandages, and of course, they all had to thank Nate profusely. It was almost an hour later before she was finally alone with Gil. Cade had run to his room to play with his toys. His father scooped Bailey into his arms and carried her up the stairs to his bedroom. She could hear the steady beat of his heart beneath her cheek.

"You smell good," she said, burrowing her nose in the crisply starched fabric of his white cotton shirt. In honor of Cade's homecoming, he had worn his best Stetson and his fanciest pair of cowboy boots.

Gil flipped back the quilt and the top sheet and laid her gently on the soft mattress. "Don't flirt with me," he begged. "I'm trying to remind myself that your recovery has a long way to go."

"I want to sleep with you tonight," she whispered.

A dark flush tinged his cheekbones. "Sleep only. I won't be responsible for putting you back in the hospital."

She tugged his hand. "Lie down beside me."

He kicked off his boots, removed his belt, and stretched out on his back, careful not to jostle her head. He closed his eyes and breathed deeply. "I feel so damn good, I may just float up to the ceiling."

Linking her fingers with his, she smiled up at the surface in question. "I'd miss you," she said.

After a long silence, he spoke again, this time with no humor at all in his voice. "I've been waiting to hear you say something very important, Bailey."

She froze, the words stuck in her throat. It was a huge commitment. Turning her life upside down. Giving up everything she knew. "You're asking if I love you?"

"Yes."

Why was it that she could face down an armed assailant without flinching, but taking this leap petrified her? She'd been on her own for a long time. Self-reliant. Depending on no one. Her emotionally unavailable father had taught her that.

But Gil Addison was an entirely different kind of parent. And an entirely different kind of man. He cared. And he wasn't afraid to show it.

The question was, could she be as brave? She turned on her side and put a hand on his chest, covering his heart. "I do care about you, Gil. How could I not?"

Her wording was not lost on him, because he grimaced.

"Thank God. For a while there, I thought you only wanted me for sex."

She laughed softly. "Well, that *is* a definite plus."

He lifted up on his elbow, head propped on his hand. His crooked smile was the kind of thing that made good girls get in trouble. "As flattering as that is to hear, I want more than your luscious body. I know we have problems to sort out, but we'll manage it. I love you, sweetheart, heart and soul and everything in between. I want to make a family with you and Cade. I realize you probably didn't bargain for getting hitched to a guy with a kid. But he's a pretty great kid, and he adores you."

"I adore *him,* but are you absolutely sure about this marriage idea?"

"One hundred percent. I know you're very good at your job, but maybe Nate could use you here in Royal. Alex still doesn't remember anything, and del Toro is throwing his weight around with no real success. Even in an unofficial capacity, your skills would be important. You'd be the one doing the sacrificing. I get that. And I know it's not fair. But the Straight Arrow is Cade's birthright."

Even though her head throbbed and she felt weak, her heart soared. "I wouldn't mind learning how to be Cade's mom. That would keep me plenty busy for a while."

"Is that a yes?" His hand toyed with the buttons on her blouse, his thumb brushing her nipple through the fabric.

A sweet trickle of arousal swam in her veins, making her light-headed and giddy. "All the single women in town will be gunning for me if I lasso Royal's most eligible bachelor," she teased.

"You can take them," he said. "I have faith in you."

She searched his face, wanting desperately to believe she had found her happy ending. "You won't change your mind? It might be the endorphins talking."

He nudged her to her back again and laid his head on her flat belly, his fingers stroking the center seam of her soft khaki pants. "I've never been more sure of anything in my life. Would you mind terribly if we made a few babies together?"

She smiled, though he couldn't see. "It might take a lot of effort on your part." His intimate touch made her shiver.

"I think I can handle it. But we have one more hurdle, Bailey. One glaring omission. When a man lays his heart on the line, it seems like he's entitled to a little sweet talk in return."

"I see."

"But only if you mean it." He sat up, one knee raised, and stared at her with some anxiety. "I know I'm pushing you…taking advantage of you in a vulnerable condition. But I…"

She put a hand over his mouth, her gaze intent. "I do love you, Gil Addison. For now and forever. Come here and kiss me."

As kisses went, it was a doozy. Deep and wet and hungry. They were both breathless when it ended, and a certain part of Gil's anatomy was hard as stone.

He stared down at her, dark eyes flashing. "How long until those stitches come out?"

"Seven more days, give or take."

"Can you plan a wedding in seven days?"

"People will think we *have* to get married," she said, daring to tease him when he was primed for action.

He lifted her hand to his lips, his handsome face solemn. "We *do* have to get married," he said softly. "Because I'm not willing to live another minute without you in my life and in my bed."

Bailey blinked, totally undone by the sight of this rough and tough cowboy baring his soul to her. "Then I believe my answer is yes, dear Gil. Because I feel the same way. There's just one more thing…"

One wicked eyebrow lifted. "Yes, my love?"

"On our wedding night, I want you to wear the Stetson to bed…"

And as it happens…he did.

* * * * *

"You can't be serious."

"I'm completely serious." Elliot's fingers twisted in Lucy Ann's ponytail.

"Let. Go. Now," she said, barely able to keep herself from hauling him in for a kiss. "Sex will only complicate matters."

"Or it could simplify things." He released her hair slowly, his stroke tantalizing all the way down her arm.

"Lucy Ann?" His bourbon-smooth tones intoxicated her parched senses. "What are you thinking?"

"My aunt said the same thing about the bonus of friends becoming…more."

He laughed softly, the heat of his breath broadcasting how close he'd moved to her. "Your aunt has always been a smart woman. Although, I sure as hell didn't talk to her about you and I becoming lovers."

"You need to quit saying things like that. You and I need boundaries for this to work."

His gaze fell to her mouth for an instant that stretched to eternity. "We'll have to agree to disagree."

* * *

For the Sake of Their Son
is part of The Alpha Brotherhood series: Bound by an oath to make amends, these billionaires can conquer anything…but love.

FOR THE SAKE
OF THEIR SON

BY
CATHERINE MANN

MILLS & BOON

Published in Great Britain 2014
by Mills & Boon, an imprint of Harlequin (UK) Limited,
Eton House, 18-24 Paradise Road, Richmond, Surrey, TW9 1SR

© 2014 Catherine Mann

ISBN: 978 0 263 91453 5

51-0114

Harlequin (UK) Limited's policy is to use papers that are natural, renewable and recyclable products and made from wood grown in sustainable forests. The logging and manufacturing processes conform to the legal environmental regulations of the country of origin.

Printed and bound in Spain
by Blackprint CPI, Barcelona

USA TODAY bestselling author **Catherine Mann** lives on a sunny Florida beach with her flyboy husband and their four children. With more than forty books in print in over twenty countries, she has also celebrated wins for both a RITA® Award and a Booksellers' Best Award. Catherine enjoys chatting with readers online—thanks to the wonders of the internet, which allows her to network with her laptop by the water! Contact Catherine through her website, www.catherinemann.com, find her on Facebook and Twitter (@CatherineMann1) or reach her by snail mail at PO Box 6065, Navarre, FL 32566, USA.

For my children.

One

Elliot Starc had faced danger his whole life. First at the hands of his heavy-fisted father. Later as a Formula One race car driver who used his world travels to feed information to Interpol.

But he'd never expected to be kidnapped. Especially not in the middle of his best friend's bachelor party.

Mad as hell, Elliot struggled back to consciousness, only to realize his wrists were cuffed. Numb. He struggled against the restraints while trying to get his bearings, but his brain was still disoriented. Last he remembered, he'd been in Atlanta, Georgia, at a bachelor party and now he was cuffed and blindfolded, for God's sake. What the hell? He only knew that he was in the back of a vehicle that smelled of leather and luxury. Noise offered him little to go on. Just the purr of a finely tuned engine. The pop of an opening soda can. A low hum of music so faint it must be on a headset.

"He's awake," a deep voice whispered softly, too softly to be identified.

"Damn it," another voice hissed.

"Hey," Elliot shouted, except it wasn't a shout. More of a hoarse croak. He cleared his throat and tried again. "Whatever the hell is going on here, we can talk ransom—"

A long buzz sounded. Unmistakable. The closing of a privacy window. Then silence. Solitude, no chance of shouting jack to anyone in this…

A limo, perhaps? Who kidnapped someone using a limousine?

Once they stopped, he would be ready, though. The second he could see, he wouldn't even need his hands. He was trained in seven different forms of self-defense. He could use his feet, his shoulders and his body weight.

He would be damned before he let himself ever be helpless in a fight.

They'd pulled off an interstate at least twenty minutes ago, driving into the country as best he could tell. He had no way of judging north, south or west. He could be anywhere from Florida to Mississippi to South Carolina, and God knows he had enemies in every part of the world from his work with Interpol and his triumphs over competitors in the racing world.

And he had plenty of pissed-off ex-girlfriends…. He winced at the thought of females and Carolina so close together. Home. Too many memories. Bad ones—with just a single bright spot in the form of Lucy Ann Joyner, but he'd wrecked even that.

Crap.

Back to the present. Sunlight was just beginning to filter through the blindfold, sparking behind his eyes like shards of glinting glass.

One thing was certain. This car had good shock absorbers. Otherwise the rutted road they were traveling would have rattled his teeth.

Although his teeth were clenched mighty damn tight right now.

Even now, he still couldn't figure out how he'd been blindsided near the end of Rowan Boothe's bachelor party in an Atlanta casino. Elliot had ducked into the back to find a vintage Scotch. Before he could wrap his hand around the neck of the bottle, someone had knocked him out.

If only he knew the motive for his kidnapping. Was someone after his money? Or had someone uncovered his secret dealings with Interpol? If so, did they plan to exploit that connection?

He'd lived his life to the fullest, determined to do better than his wrong-side-of-the-tracks upbringing. He only had one regret: how his lifelong friendship with Lucy Ann had crashed and burned more fiercely than when he'd been sideswiped at the Australian Grand Prix last year—

The car jerked to a halt. He braced his feet to keep from rolling off onto the floor. He forced himself to stay relaxed so his abductors would think he was still asleep.

His muscles tensed for action, eager for the opportunity to confront his adversaries. Ready to pay back. He was trained from his work with Interpol, with lightning-fast instincts honed in his racing career. He wouldn't go down without a fight.

Since he'd left his dirt-poor roots behind, he'd been beating the odds. He'd dodged juvie by landing in a military reform school where he'd connected with a lifelong group of friends. Misfits like himself who disdained rules while living by a strict code of justice. They'd grown up to take different life paths, but stayed connected through their friendship and freelance work for Interpol. Not that they'd been much help to him while someone was nabbing him a few feet away from the bachelor party they were all attending.

The car door opened and someone leaned over him. Something tugged at the back of his brain, a sense that he should know this person. He scrambled to untangle the mystery before it was too late.

His blindfold was tugged up and off, and he took in the inside of a black limo, just as he'd suspected. His abductors, however, were a total surprise.

"Hello, Elliot, my man," said his old high school pal Malcolm Douglas, who'd asked him to fetch that bottle of Scotch back at the bachelor party. "Waking up okay?"

Conrad Hughes—another traitorous bastard friend—patted his face. "You look plenty awake to me."

Elliot bit back a curse. He'd been kidnapped by his own comrades from the bachelor party. "Somebody want to tell me what's going on here?"

He eyed Conrad and Malcolm, both of whom had been living it up with him at the casino well past midnight. Morning sunshine streamed over them, oak trees sprawling behind them. The scent of Carolina jasmine carried on the breeze. Why were they taking him on this strange road trip?

"Well?" he pressed again when neither of them answered. "What the hell are you two up to?" he asked, his anger barely contained. He wanted to kick their asses. "I hope you have a good reason for taking me out to the middle of nowhere."

Conrad clapped him on the back. "You'll see soon enough."

Elliot angled out of the car, hard as hell with his hands

cuffed in front of him. His loafers hit the dirt road, rocks and dust shifting under his feet as he stood in the middle of nowhere in a dense forest of pines and oaks. "You'll tell me now or I'll beat the crap out of both of you."

Malcolm lounged against the side of the black stretch limo. "Good luck trying with your hands cuffed. Keep talking like that and we'll hang on to the key for a good long while."

"Ha—funny—not." Elliot ground his teeth in frustration. "Isn't it supposed to be the groom who gets pranked?"

Conrad grinned. "Oh, don't worry. Rowan should be waking up and finding his new tattoo right about now."

Extending his cuffed wrists, Elliot asked, "And the reason for this? I'm not the one getting married."

Ever.

Malcolm pushed away, jerking his head to the side, gesturing toward the path leading into the dense cluster of more pine trees with an occasional magnolia reaching for the sun. "Instead of telling you why, we'll just let you look. Walk with us."

As if he had any choice. His friends clearly had some kind of game planned and they intended to see it through regardless. Sure, he'd been in a bear of a mood since his breakup with Gianna. Hell, even before that. Since Lucy Ann had quit her job as his assistant and walked out of his life for good.

God, he really needed to pour out some frustration behind the wheel, full out, racing to…anywhere.

A few steps deeper into the woods, his blood hummed with recognition. The land was more mature than the last time he'd been here, but he knew the area well enough. Home. Or rather it used to be home, back when he was a poor kid with a drunken father. This small South Carolina farm town outside of Columbia had been called God's land.

Elliot considered it a corner of hell.

Although hell was brimming with sunshine today.

He stepped toward a clearing and onto a familiar dirt driveway, with a ranch-style cabin and a fat oak at least a hundred years old in the middle. A tree he'd played under as a kid, wishing he could stay here forever because this little haven in hell was a lot safer than his home.

He'd hidden with Lucy Ann Joyner here at her aunt's farmhouse. Both of them enjoying the sanctuary of this place, even if only for a few hours. Why were his buds taking him down this memory lane detour?

Branches rustled, a creaking sound carrying on the breeze, drawing his gaze. A swing dangled from a thick branch, moving back and forth as a woman swayed, her back to them. He stopped cold. Suddenly the meaning of this journey was crystal clear. His friends were forcing a confrontation eleven months in the making since he and Lucy Ann were both too stubborn to take the first step.

Did she know he was coming? He swallowed hard at the notion that maybe she wanted him here after all. That her decision to slice him out of her life had changed. But if she had, then why not just drive up to the house?

He wasn't sure the past year could be that easily forgotten, but his gut twisted tight over just the thought of talking to her again.

His eyes soaked in the sight of her, taking her in like parched earth with water. He stared at the slim feminine back, the light brown hair swishing just past her shoulders. Damn, but it had been a long eleven months without her. His lifelong pal had bolted after one reckless— incredible—night that had ruined their friendship forever.

He'd given her space and still hadn't heard from her.

In the span of a day, the one person he'd trusted above everyone else had cut him off. He'd never let anyone get that close to him—not even his friends from the military reform school. He and Lucy Ann had a history, a shared link that went beyond a regular friendship.

Or so he'd thought.

As if drawn by a magnet, he walked closer to the swing, to the woman. His hands still linked in front of him, he moved silently, watching her. The bared lines of her throat evoked memories of her jasmine scent. The way her dress slipped ever so slightly off one shoulder reminded him of years past when she'd worn hand-me-downs from neighbors.

The rope tugged at the branch as she toe-tapped, back and forth. A gust of wind turned the swing spinning to face him.

His feet stumbled to a halt.

Yes, it was Lucy Ann, but not just her. Lucy Ann stared back at him with wide eyes, shocked eyes. She'd clearly been kept every bit as much in the dark as he had. Before he could finish processing his disappointment that she hadn't helped arrange this, his eyes took in the biggest shocker of all.

Lucy Ann's arms were curved around an infant swaddled in a blue plaid blanket as she breast-fed him.

Lucy Ann clutched her baby boy to her chest and stared in shock at Elliot Starc, her childhood friend, her former boss. Her onetime lover.

The father of her child.

She'd scripted the moment she would tell him about their son a million times in her mind, but never had it played out like this, with him showing up out of the blue. Handcuffed? Clearly, he hadn't planned on coming to see her. She'd tempted fate in waiting so long to tell him, then he'd pulled one of his disappearing acts and she couldn't find him.

Now there was no avoiding him.

Part of her ached to run to Elliot and trust in the friendship they'd once shared, a friendship built here, in the wooded farmland outside Columbia, South Carolina. But another part of her—the part that saw his two friends lurking and the handcuffs on her old pal—told her all she needed to know. Elliot hadn't suddenly seen the light and come running to apologize for being a first-class jerk. He'd been dragged kicking and screaming.

Well, screw him. She had her pride, too.

Only the baby in her arms kept her from bolting altogether into her aunt's cabin up the hill. Lucy Ann eased Eli from her breast and adjusted her clothes in place. Shifting her son to her shoulder, she patted his back, her eyes staying locked on Elliot, trying to gauge his mood.

The way his eyes narrowed told her loud and clear that she couldn't delay her explanation any longer. She should have told him about Eli sooner. In the early days of her pregnancy, she'd tried and chickened out. Then she'd gotten angry over his speedy rebound engagement to the goddess Gianna, and that made it easier to keep her distance a while longer. She wouldn't be the cause of breaking up his engagement—rat bastard. She would tell him once he was married and wouldn't feel obligated to offer her anything. Even though the thought of him marrying that too-perfect bombshell heiress made her vaguely nauseous.

Now, Elliot was here, so damn tall and muscular, his sandy brown hair closely shorn. His shoulders filled out the black button-down shirt, his jeans slung low on his hips. His five o'clock shadow and narrowed green eyes gave him a bad-boy air he'd worked his whole life to live up to.

She knew every inch of him, down to a scar on his elbow he'd told everyone he got from falling off his bike but he'd really gotten from the buckle on his father's belt during a beating. They shared so much history, and now they shared a child.

Standing, she pulled her gaze from him and focused on his old boarding school friends behind him, brooding Conrad Hughes and charmer Malcolm Douglas. Of course they'd dragged him here. These days both of them had sunk so deep into a pool of marital bliss, they seemed to think everyone else wanted to plunge in headfirst. No doubt they'd brought Elliot here with just that in mind.

Not a freakin' chance.

She wasn't even interested in dipping her toes into those waters and certainly not with Elliot, the biggest playboy in the free world.

"Gentlemen, do you think you could uncuff him, then leave so he and I can talk civilly?"

Conrad—a casino owner—fished out a key from his pocket and held it up. "Can do." He looked at Elliot. "I trust you're not going to do anything stupid like try to start a fight over our little prank here."

Prank? This was her life and they were playing with it. Anger sparked in her veins.

Elliot pulled a tight smile. "Of course not. I'm outnumbered. Now just undo the handcuffs. My arms are too numb to hit either of you anyway."

Malcolm plucked the keys from Conrad and opened the cuffs. Elliot massaged his wrists for a moment, still silent, then stretched his arms over his head.

Did he have to keep getting hotter every year? Especially not fair when she hadn't even had time to shower since yesterday thanks to her son's erratic sleeping schedule.

Moistening her dry mouth, Lucy Ann searched for a way to dispel the awkward air. "Malcolm, Conrad, I realize you meant well with this, but perhaps it's time for you both to leave. Elliot and I clearly have some things to discuss."

Eli burped. Lucy Ann rolled her eyes and cradled her son in the crook of her arm, too aware of the weight of Elliot's stare.

Malcolm thumped Elliot on the back. "You can thank us later."

Conrad leveled a somber steady look her way. "Call if you need anything. I mean that."

Without another word, both men disappeared back into the wooded perimeter as quickly as they'd arrived. For the first time in eleven months, she was alone with Elliot.

Well, not totally alone. She clutched Eli closer until he squirmed.

Elliot stuffed his hands in his pockets, still keeping his distance. "How long have you been staying with your aunt?"

"Since I left Monte Carlo." She'd been here the whole time, if he'd only bothered to look. Where else would she go? She had money saved up, but staying here made the most sense economically.

"How are you supporting yourself?"

"That's not your business." She lifted her chin. He had the ability to find out anything he wanted to know about her if he'd just looked, thanks to his Interpol connections.

Apparently, he hadn't even bothered to try. And that's what hurt the most. All these months, she'd thought he would check up on her. He would have seen she was pregnant. He would have wondered.

He would have come.

"Not my business?" He stalked a step closer, only a hint of anger showing in his carefully guarded eyes. "Really? I think we both know why it is so very much my business."

"I have plenty saved up from my years working for you." He'd insisted on paying her an outlandish salary to be his personal assistant. "And I'm doing virtual work to subsidize my income. I build and maintain websites. I make enough to get by." Her patience ran out with this small talk, the avoidance of discussing the baby sleeping in her arms. "You've had months to ask these questions and chose to remain silent. If anyone has a right to be angry, it's me."

"You didn't call either, and you have a much more compelling reason to communicate." He nodded toward Eli. "He is mine."

"You sound sure."

"I know you. I see the truth in your eyes," he said simply.

She couldn't argue with that. She swallowed once, twice, to clear her throat and gather her nerve. "His name is Eli. And yes, he's your son, two months old."

Elliot pulled his hands from his pockets. "I want to hold him."

Her stomach leaped into her throat. She'd envisioned this moment so many times, but living in it? She never could have imagined how deeply the emotions would rattle her. She passed over Eli to his father, watching Elliot's face. For once, she couldn't read him at all. So strange, considering how they'd once been so in sync they could finish each other's sentences, read a thought from a glance across a room.

Now, he was like a stranger.

Face a blank slate, Elliot held their son in broad, capable hands, palmed the baby's bottom and head as he studied the tiny cherub features. Eli still wore his blue footed sleeper from bedtime, his blond hair glistening as the sun sent dappled rays through the branches. The moment looked like a fairy tale, but felt so far from that her heart broke over how this should have, could have been.

Finally, Elliot looked up at her, his blasé mask sliding away to reveal eyes filled with ragged pain. His throat moved in a slow gulp of emotion. "Why did you keep this—Eli—from me?"

Guilt and frustration gnawed at her. She'd tried to contact him but knew she hadn't tried hard enough. Her pride… Damn it all. Her excuses all sounded weak now, even to her own ears.

"You were engaged to someone else. I didn't want to interfere in that."

"You never intended to tell me at all?" His voice went hoarse with disbelief, his eyes shooting back down to his son sleeping against his chest so contentedly as if he'd been there all along.

"Of course I planned to explain—after you were married." She dried her damp palms on her sundress. "I refused to be responsible for breaking up your great love match."

Okay, she couldn't keep the cynicism out of that last part, but he deserved it for his rebound relationship.

"My engagement to Gianna ended months ago. Why didn't you contact me?"

He had a point there. She ached to run, but he had her son. And as much as she hated to admit it to herself, she'd missed Elliot. They'd been so much a part of each other's lives for so long. The past months apart had been like a kind of withdrawal.

"Half the time I couldn't find you and the other half, your new personal secretary couldn't figure out where you were." And hadn't that pissed her off something fierce? Then worried her, because she knew about his sporadic missions for Interpol, and she also knew his reckless spirit.

"You can't have tried very hard, Lucy Ann. All you had to do was speak with any of my friends." His eyes narrowed. "Or did you? Is that why they brought me here today, because you reached out to them?"

She'd considered doing just that many times, only to balk at the last second. She wouldn't be manipulative. She'd planned to tell him face-to-face. And soon.

"I wish I could say yes, but I'm afraid not. One of them must have been checking up on me even if you never saw the need."

Oops. Where had that bitter jab come from?

He cocked an eyebrow. "This is about Eli. Not about the two of us."

"There is no 'two of us' anymore." She touched her son's head lightly, aching to take him back in her arms. "You ended that when you ran away scared after we had a reckless night of sex."

"I do *not* run away."

"Excuse me if your almighty ego is bruised." She crossed her arms over her chest, feeling as though they were in fifth grade again, arguing over whether the basketball was in or out of bounds.

Elliot sighed, looking around at the empty clearing. The limo's engine roared to life, then faded as it drove away without him. He turned back to Lucy Ann. "This isn't accomplishing anything. We need to talk reasonably about our child's future."

"I agree." Of course they had to talk, but right now her

heart was in her throat. She could barely think straight. She scooped her baby from his arms. "We'll talk tomorrow when we're both less rattled."

"How do I know you won't just disappear with my son?" He let go of Eli with obvious reluctance.

His son.

Already his voice echoed with possessiveness.

She clasped her son closer, breathing in the powder-fresh familiarity of him, the soft skin of his cheek pressed against her neck reassuringly. She could and she would manage her feelings for Elliot. Nothing and no one could be allowed to interfere with her child's future.

"I've been here all this time, Elliot. You just never chose to look." A bitter pill to swallow. She gestured up the empty dirt road. "Even now, you didn't choose. Your friends dumped you here on my doorstep."

Elliot walked a slow circle around her, his hand snagging the rope holding the swing until he stopped beside her. He had a way of moving with such fluidity, every step controlled, a strange contradiction in a man who always lived on the edge. Always flirting with chaos.

Her skin tingled to life with the memory of his touch, the wind teasing her with a hint of aftershave and musk.

She cleared her throat. "Elliot, I really think you should—"

"Lucy Ann," he interrupted, "in case it's escaped your notice, my friends left me here. Alone. No car." He leaned in closer, his hand still holding the rope for balance, so close she could almost feel the rasp of his five o'clock shadow. "So regardless of whether or not we talk, for now, you're stuck with me."

Two

Elliot held himself completely still, a feat of supreme control given the frustration racing through his veins. That Lucy Ann had hidden her pregnancy—his son—from him all this time threatened to send him to his knees. Somehow during this past year he'd never let go of the notion that everything would simply return to the way things had been before with them. Their friendship had carried him through the worst times of his life.

Now he knew there was no going back. Things between them had changed irrevocably.

They had a child together, a boy just inches away. Elliot clenched his hand around the rope. He needed to bide his time and proceed with caution. His lifelong friend had a million great qualities—but she was also stubborn as hell. A wrong step during this surprise meeting could have her digging in her heels.

He had to control his frustration, tamp down the anger

over all that she'd hidden from him. Staying levelheaded saved his life on more than one occasion on the racetrack. But never had the stakes been more important than now. No matter how robbed he felt, he couldn't let that show.

Life had taught him well how to hide his darker emotions.

So he waited, watching her face for some sign. The breeze lifted a strand of her hair, whipping it over his cheek. His pulse thumped harder.

"Well, Lucy Ann? What now?"

Her pupils widened in her golden-brown eyes, betraying her answering awareness a second before she bolted up from the swing. Elliot lurched forward as the swing freed. He released the rope and found his footing.

Lucy Ann glanced over her shoulder as she made her way to the graveled path. "Let's go inside."

"Where's your aunt?" He followed her, rocks crunching under his feet.

"At work." Lucy Ann walked up the steps leading to the prefab log cabin's long front porch. Time had worn the redwood look down to a rusty hue. "She still waits tables at the Pizza Shack."

"You used to send her money." He'd stumbled across the bank transaction by accident. Or maybe his accountant had made a point of letting him discover the transfers since Lucy Ann left so little for herself.

"Well, come to find out, Aunt Carla never used it," Lucy Ann said wryly, pushing the door open into the living room. The decor hadn't changed, the same brown plaid sofa with the same saggy middle, the same dusty Hummel figurines packed in a corner cabinet. He'd forgotten how Carla scoured yard sales religiously for the things, unable to afford them new.

They'd hidden here more than once as kids, then as

teenagers, plotting a way to escape their home lives. He eyed the son he'd barely met but who already filled his every plan going forward. "Your aunt's prideful, just like you."

"I accepted a job from you." She settled Eli into a portable crib by the couch.

"You worked your butt off and got your degree in computer technology." He admired the way she never took the easy way out. How she'd found a career for herself.

So why had she avoided talking to him? Surely not from any fear of confrontation. Her hair swung forward as she leaned into the baby crib, her dress clinging to her hips. His gaze hitched on the new curves.

Lucy Ann spun away from the crib and faced him again. "Are we going to keep making small talk or are you going to call a cab? I could drive you back into town."

"I'm not going anywhere."

Her eyebrows pinched together. "I thought we agreed to talk tomorrow."

"You decided. I never agreed." He dropped to sit on the sofa arm. If he sat in the middle, no telling how deep that sag would sink.

"You led me to believe…" She looked around as if searching for answers, but the Hummels stayed silent. "Damn it. You just wanted to get in the house."

Guilty as charged. "This really is the best place to discuss the future. Anywhere else and I'll have to be on the lookout for fans. We're in NASCAR country, you know. Not Formula One, but kissing cousins." He held up his hands. "Besides, my jackass buddies stranded me without my wallet."

She gasped. "You're joking."

"I wish." They must have taken it from his pocket while he was knocked out. He tamped down another surge of anger over being manipulated. If he'd just had some warning...

"Why did they do this to you—to both of us?" She sat on the other arm of the sofa, the worn width between them.

"Probably because they know how stubborn we are." He watched her face, trying to read the truth in the delicate lines, but he saw only exhaustion and dark circles. "Would you have ever told me about the baby?"

"You've asked me that already and I've answered. Of course I would have told you—" she shrugged "—eventually."

Finally he asked the question that had been plaguing him most. "How can I be sure?"

Shaking her head, she shrugged again. "You can't. You'll just have to trust me."

A wry smile tugged the corner of his mouth. "Trust has never been easy for either of us." But now that he was here and saw the truth, his decision was simple. "I want you and Eli to come with me, just for a few weeks while we make plans for the future."

"No." She crossed her arms over her chest.

"Ah, come on, Lucy Ann. Think about my request before you react."

"Okay. Thinking..." She tapped her temple, tapping, tapping. Her hand fell to her lap. "Still no."

God, her humor and spunk had lifted him out of hell so many times. He'd missed her since she'd stormed out of his life....

But he'd also missed out on a lot more in not knowing about his son.

"I can never regain those first two months of Eli's life." A bitter pill he wasn't sure how to swallow down. "I need a chance to make up for that."

She shook her head slowly. "You can't be serious about taking a baby on the road."

"I'm dead serious." He wasn't leaving here without them. He couldn't just toss money down and go.

"Let me spell it out for you then. Elliot, this is the middle of your racing season." She spoke slowly, as she'd done when they were kids and she'd tutored him in multiplication tables. "You'll be traveling, working, running with a party crowd. I've seen it year after year, enough to know that's no environment for a baby."

And damn it, she was every bit as astute now as she'd been then. He lined up an argument, a way to bypass her concerns. "You saw my life when there wasn't a baby around—no kids around, actually. It *can* be different. *I* can be different, like other guys who bring their families on the circuit with them." He shifted to sit beside her. "I have a damn compelling reason to make changes in my life. This is the chance to show you that."

Twisting the skirt of her dress in nervous fingers, she studied him with her golden-brown gaze for so long he thought he'd won.

Then resolve hardened her eyes again. "Expecting someone to change only sets us both up for disappointment."

"Then you'll get to say 'I told you so.' You told me often enough in the past." He rested a hand on top of hers to still the nervous fidgeting, squeezing lightly. "The best that happens is I'm right and this works. We find a plan to be good parents to Eli even when we're jet-setting around the world. Remember how much fun we used to have together? I miss you, Lucy Ann."

He thumbed the inside of her wrist, measuring the speed of her pulse, the softness of her skin. He'd done everything he could to put her out of his mind, but with no luck. He'd been unfair to Gianna, leading her to think he was free. So many regrets. He was tired of them. "Lucy Ann…"

She yanked her hand free. "Stop it, Elliot. I've watched you seduce a lot of women over the years. Your games don't work with me. So don't even try the slick moves."

"You wound me." He clamped a hand over his heart in an attempt at melodrama to cover his disappointment.

She snorted. "Hardly. You don't fool me with the pained look. It's eleven months too late to be genuine."

"You would be wrong about that."

"No games." She shot to her feet. "We both need time to regroup and think. We need to continue this conversation later."

"Fair enough then." He sat on the sofa, stretching both arms out along the back.

She stomped her foot. "What are you doing?"

He picked up the remote from the coffee table and leaned back again into the deepest, saggiest part. "Making myself comfortable."

"For what?"

He thumbed on the television. "If I'm going to stick around until you're ready to talk, I might as well scout the good stations. Any beer in the fridge? Although wait, it's too early for that. How about coffee?"

"No." She snatched the remote control from his hand. "And stop it. I don't know what game you're playing but you can quit and *go*. In case that wasn't clear enough, leave and come back later. You can take my car."

He took the remote right back and channel surfed without looking away from the flat screen. "Thanks for the generous offer of transportation, but you said we can't take Eli on the road and I only just met my son. I'm not leaving him now. How about the coffee?"

"Like hell."

"I don't need cream. Black will do just fine."

"Argh!" She slumped against the archway between the living room and kitchen. "Quit being ridiculous about the coffee. You know you're not staying here."

He set aside the remote, smiling as some morning talk show droned in the background. "So you'll come with me after all. Good."

"You're crazy. You know that, right?"

"No newsflash there, sweetheart. A few too many concussions." He stood. "Forget the suitcase."

"Run that by me again?"

"Don't bother with packing. I'll buy everything you need, everything new. Let's just grab a couple of diapers for the rug rat and go."

Her acceptance was becoming more and more important by the second. He needed her with him. He had to figure out a way to tie their lives together again so his son would know a father, a mother and a normal life.

"Stop! Stop trying to control my life." She stared at him sadly. "Elliot, I appreciate all you did for me in the past, but I don't need rescuing anymore."

"Last time I checked, I wasn't offering a rescue. Just a partnership."

If humor and pigheadedness didn't work, time to go back to other tactics. No great hardship really, since the attraction crackled between them every bit as tangibly now as it had the night they'd impulsively landed in bed together after a successful win. He sauntered closer. "As I recall, last time we were together, we shared control quite…nicely. And now that I think of it, we really don't need those clothes after all."

* * *

The rough upholstery of the sofa rasped against the backs of Lucy Ann's legs, her skin oversensitive, tingling to life after just a few words from Elliot. Damn it, she refused to be seduced by him again. The way her body betrayed her infuriated her down to her toes, which curled in her sandals.

Sure, he was beach-boy handsome, mesmerizingly sexy and blindingly charming. Women around the world could attest to his allure. However, in spite of her one unforgettable moment of weakness, she refused to be one of those fawning females throwing themselves at his feet.

No matter how deeply her body betrayed her every time he walked in the room.

She shot from the sofa, pacing restlessly since she couldn't bring herself to leave her son alone, even though he slept. Damn Elliot and the draw of attraction that had plagued her since the day they'd gone skinny-dipping at fourteen and she realized they weren't kids anymore.

Shutting off those thoughts, she pivoted on the coarse shag carpet to face him. "This is not the time or the place for sexual innuendo."

"Honey—" his arms stretched along the back of the sofa "—it's never a bad time for sensuality. For nuances. For seduction."

The humor in his eyes took the edge of arrogance off his words. "If you're aiming to persuade me to leave with you, you're going about it completely the wrong way."

"There's no denying we slept together."

"Clearly." She nodded toward the Pack 'n Play where their son slept contentedly, unaware that his little world had just been turned upside down.

"There's no denying that it was good between us. Very good."

Elliot's husky words snapped her attention back to his face. There wasn't a hint of humor in sight. Awareness tingled to the roots of her hair.

Swallowing hard, she sank into an old cane rocker. "It was impulsive. We were both tipsy and sentimental and reckless." The rush of that evening sang through her memory, the celebration of his win, reminiscing about his first dirt track race, a little wine, too much whimsy, then far too few clothes…. "I refuse to regret that night or call our…encounter…a mistake since I have Eli. But I do not intend to repeat the experience."

"Now that's just a damn shame. What a waste of good sexual chemistry."

"Will you please stop?" Her hands fisted on the arms of the wooden rocker. "We got along just fine as friends for thirty years."

"Are you saying we can be friends again?" He leaned forward, elbows on his knees. "No more hiding out and keeping big fat secrets from each other?"

His words carried too much truth for comfort. "You're twisting my words around."

"God's honest truth, Lucy Ann." He sighed. "I'm trying to call a truce so we can figure out how to plan our son's future."

"By telling me to ditch my clothes? You obviously missed class the day they taught the definition of truce."

"Okay, you're right. That wasn't fair of me." He thrust his hands through his hair. "I'm not thinking as clearly as I would like. Learning about Eli has been a shock to say the least."

"I can understand that." Her hands unfurled to grip the rocker. "And I am so very sorry for any pain this has caused you."

"Given that I've lost the first two months of my son's

life, the least you can do is give me four weeks together. Since you're working from home here, you'll be able to work on the road, as well. But if going on the race circuit is a deal breaker, I'll bow out this season."

She jolted in surprise that he would risk all he'd worked so hard to achieve, a career he so deeply loved. "What about your sponsors? Your reputation?"

"This is your call."

"That's not fair to make an ultimatum like that, to put it on me."

"I'm asking, and I'm offering you choices."

Choices? Hardly. She knew how important his racing career was to him. And she couldn't help but admit to feeling a bit of pride in having helped him along the way. There was no way she could let him back out now.

She tossed up her hands. "Fine. Eli and I will travel with you on the race circuit for the next four weeks so you can figure out whatever it is you want to know and make your plans. You win. You always do."

Winning didn't feel much like a victory tonight.

Elliot poured himself a drink from the wet bar at his hotel. He and Lucy Ann had struck a bargain that he would stay at a nearby historic home that had been converted into a hotel while she made arrangements to leave in the morning. He'd called for a car service to pick him up, making use of his credit card numbers, memorized, a fact he hadn't bothered mentioning to Lucy Ann earlier. Although she should have known. Had she selectively forgotten or had she been that rattled?

The half hour waiting for the car had been spent silently staring at his son while Eli slept and Lucy Ann hid in the other room under the guise of packing.

Elliot's head was still reeling. He had been knocked

unconscious and kidnapped, and found out he had an unknown son all in one day. He tipped back the glass of bourbon, emptying it and pouring another to savor, more slowly, while he sat out on the garden balcony where he would get better cell phone reception.

He dropped into a wrought-iron chair and let the Carolina moon pour over him. His home state brought such a mix of happy and sad memories. He was always better served just staying the hell away. He tugged his cell from his waistband, tucked his Bluetooth in his ear and thumbed autodial three for Malcolm Douglas.

The ringing stopped two buzzes in. "Brother, how's it going?"

"How do you think it's going, Douglas? My head hurts and I'm pissed off." Anger was stoked back to life just thinking about his friends' arrogant stunt, the way they'd played with his life. "You could have just told me about the baby."

Malcolm chuckled softly. "Wouldn't have been half as fun that way."

"Fun? You think this is some kind of game? You're a sick bastard." The thought of them plotting this out while he partied blissfully unaware had him working hard to keep his breath steady. He and his friends had played some harsh jokes on one another in the past, but nothing like this. "How long have you known?"

"For about a week," the chart-topping musician answered unrepentantly.

"A week." Seven days he could have had with his son. Seven days his best friends kept the largest of secrets from him. Anger flamed through him. Was there nobody left in this world he could trust? He clenched his hand around the glass tumbler until it threatened to shatter. "And you said nothing at all."

"I know it seems twisted, but we talked it through," he said, all humor gone, his smooth tones completely serious for once. "We thought this was the best way. You're too good at playing it cool with advance notice. You would have just made her mad."

"Like I didn't already do that?" He set aside the half-drunk glass of bourbon, the top-shelf brand wasted on him in his current mood.

"You confronted her with honesty," Malcolm answered reasonably. "If we'd given you time to think, you'd have gotten your pride up. You would have been angry and bullish. You can be rather pigheaded, you know."

"If I'm such a jackass, then why are we still friends?"

"Because I'm a jackass, too." Malcolm paused before continuing somberly. "You would have done the same for me. I know what it's like not to see your child, to have missed out on time you can never get back…"

Malcolm's voice choked off with emotion. He and his wife had been high school sweethearts who'd had to give up a baby girl for adoption since they were too young to provide a life for their daughter. Now they had twins—a boy and a girl—they loved dearly, but they still grieved for that first child, even knowing they'd made the right decision for her.

Although Malcolm and Celia had both known about *their* child from the start.

Elliot forked his hands through his buzzed hair, kept closely shorn since he'd let his thoughts of Lucy Ann distract him and he'd caught his car on fire just before Christmas—nearly caught himself on fire, as well.

He'd scorched his hair; the call had been that damn close.

"I just can't wrap my brain around the fact she's kept his existence from me for so long."

Malcolm snorted. "I can't believe the two of you slept together."

A growl rumbled low in his throat. "You're close to overstepping the bounds of our friendship with talk like that."

"Ahhh." He chuckled. "So you do care about her more than you've let on."

"We were…friends. Lifelong friends. That's no secret." He and Lucy Ann shared so much history it was impossible to unravel events from the past without thinking about each other. "The fact that there was briefly more…I can't deny that, either."

"You must not have been up to snuff for her to run so fast."

Anger hissed between Elliot's teeth, and he resisted the urge to pitch his Bluetooth over the balcony. "Now you have crossed the line. If we were sitting in the same place right now, my fist would be in your face."

"Fair enough." Douglas laughed softly again. "Like I said. You do care more than a little, more than any 'buddy.' And you can't refute it. Admit it, Elliot. I've just played you, my friend."

No use denying he'd been outmaneuvered by someone who knew him too well.

And as for what Malcolm had said? That he cared for Lucy Ann? Cared? Yes. He had. And like every other time in his life he'd cared, things had gone south.

If he wanted to sort through this mess and create any kind of future with Eli and Lucy Ann, he had to think more and care less.

Three

Lucy Ann shaded her eyes against the rising sun. For the third time in twenty-four hours a limousine pulled up her dusty road, oak trees creating a canopy for the long driveway. The first time had occurred yesterday when Elliot had arrived, then when he'd left, and now, he was returning.

Her simple semihermit life working from home with her son was drawing to a close in another few minutes.

Aunt Carla cradled Eli in her arms. Carla never seemed to age, her hair a perpetual shade halfway between gray and brown. She refused to waste money to have it colored. Her arms were ropy and strong from years of carting around trays of pizzas and sodas. Her skin was prematurely wrinkled from too much hard work, time in the Carolina sun—and a perpetual smile.

She was a tough, good woman who'd been there for Lucy Ann all her life. Too bad Carla couldn't have been her mother. Heaven knows she'd prayed for that often enough.

Carla smiled down at little Eli, his fist curled around her finger. "I'm sure I'm going to miss you both. It's been a treat having a baby around again."

She'd never had a child of her own, but was renowned for opening her home to family members in need. She wasn't a problem-solver so much as a temporary oasis. Very temporary, as the limo drew closer down the half-mile driveway.

"You're sweet to make it sound like we haven't taken over your house." Lucy Ann tugged her roller bag through the door, *kerthunking* it over a bump, casting one last glance back at the tiny haven of Hummels and the saggy sofa.

"Sugar, you know I only wish I could've done more for you this time and when you were young." Carla swayed from side to side, wearing her standard high-waisted jeans and a seasonal shirt—a pink Easter bunny on today's tee.

"You've always been there for me." Lucy Ann sat on top of her luggage, her eyes on the nearing limo. "I don't take that for granted."

"I haven't always been there for you and we both know it," Carla answered, her eyes shadowed with memories they both didn't like to revisit.

"You did the best you could. I know that." Since Lucy Ann's mother had legal guardianship and child services wouldn't believe any of the claims of neglect, much less allegations of abuse by stepfathers, there wasn't anything Lucy Ann could do other than escape to Carla— or to Elliot.

Her mother and her last stepfather had died in a boating accident, so there was nothing to be gained from dwelling on the past. Her mom had no more power over her than Lucy Ann allowed her. "Truly, Carla, the past is best left there."

"Glad to know you feel that way. I hope you learned that from me." Carla tugged on Lucy Ann's low ponytail. "If you can forgive me, why can't you forgive Elliot?"

Good question. She slouched back with a sigh. "If I could answer that, then I guess my heart wouldn't be breaking in two right now."

Her aunt hauled her in for a one-armed hug while she cradled the baby in the other. "I would fix this for you if I could."

"Come with us," Lucy Ann blurted. "I've asked you before and I know all your reasons for saying no. You love your home and your life and weekly bingo. But will you change your mind this time?" She angled back, hoping. "Will you come with us? We're family."

"Ah, sweet niece." Carla shook her head. "This is your life, your second chance, your adventure. Be careful. Be smart. And remember you're a damn amazing woman. He would be a lucky man to win you back."

Just the thought... No. "That's not why I'm going with him." She took Eli from her aunt. "My trip is only about planning a future for my son, for figuring out a way to blend Elliot's life with my new life."

"You used to be a major part of his world."

"I was his glorified secretary." A way for him to give her money while salving her conscience. At least she'd lived frugally and used the time to earn a degree so she could be self-sufficient. The stretch limo slowed along the last patch of gravel in front of the house.

"You were his best friend and confidant... And apparently something more at least once."

"I'm not sure what point you are trying to make, but

if you're going to make it, do so fast." She nodded to the opening limo door. "We're out of time."

"You two got along fabulously for decades and there's an obvious attraction. Why can't you have more?" Her aunt tipped her head, eyeing Elliot stepping from the vehicle. The car door slammed.

Sunshine sent dappled rays along his sandy-brown hair, over his honed body in casual jeans and a white polo that fit his muscled arms. She'd leaned on those broad shoulders for years without hesitation, but now all she could think about was the delicious feel of those arms around her. The flex of those muscles as he stretched over her.

Lucy Ann tore her eyes away and back to her aunt. "Have more?" That hadn't ended well for either of them. "Are you serious?"

"Why wouldn't I be?"

"He hasn't come looking for me for nearly a year. He let me go." Something that had hurt every day of the eleven months that passed. She waved toward him talking to his chauffeur. "He's only here now because his friends threw him on my doorstep."

"You're holding back because of your pride?" Her aunt tut-tutted. "You're throwing him and a possible future away because of pride?"

"Listen to me. *He* threw *me* away." She'd been an afterthought or nuisance to people her whole life. She wouldn't let her son live the same second-class existence. Panic began to set in. "Now that I think of it, I'm not sure why I even agreed to go with him—"

"Stop. Hold on." Carla grabbed her niece by the shoulders and steadied her. "Forget I said anything at all. Of course you have every reason to be upset. Go with him and figure out how to manage your son's future. And I'll always be here if you decide to return."

"If?" Lucy Ann rolled her eyes. "You mean when."

Carla pointed to the limo and the broad-shouldered man walking toward them. "Do you really think Elliot's going to want his son to grow up here?"

"Um, I mean, I hadn't thought…"

True panic set in as Lucy Ann realized she no longer had exclusive say over her baby's life. Of course Elliot would have different plans for his child. He'd spent his entire life planning how to get out of here, devising ways to build a fortune, and he'd succeeded.

Eli was a part of that now. And no matter how much she wanted to deny it, her life could never be simple again.

Elliot sprawled in the backseat of the limo while Lucy Ann adjusted the straps on Eli's infant seat, checking each buckle to ensure it fit with obvious seasoned practice. Her loose ponytail swung forward, the dome light bringing out the hints of honey in her light brown hair.

He dug his fingers into the butter-soft leather to keep from stroking the length of her hair, to see if it was as silky as he remembered. He needed to bide his time. He had her and the baby with him. That was a huge victory, especially after their stubborn year apart.

And now?

He had to figure out a way to make her stay. To go back to the way things were…except he knew things couldn't be exactly the same. Not after they'd slept together. Although he would have to tread warily there. He couldn't see her cheering over a "friends with benefits" arrangement. He'd have to take it a step at a time to gauge her mood. She needed to be reminded of all the history they shared, all the ways they got along so well.

She tucked a homemade quilt over Eli's tiny legs before shifting to sit beside him. Elliot knocked on the driver's window and the vehicle started forward on their journey to the airport.

"Lucy Ann, you didn't have to stay up late packing that suitcase." He looked at the discarded cashmere baby blanket she left folded to the side. "I told you I would take care of buying everything he needs."

His son would never ride a secondhand bike he'd unearthed at the junkyard. A sense of possessiveness stirred inside him. He'd ordered the best of the best for his child—from the car seat to a travel bed. Clothes. Toys. A stroller. He'd consulted his friends' wives for advice— easy enough since his buddies and their wives were all propagating like rabbits these days.

Apparently, so was he.

Lucy Ann rested a hand on the faded quilt with tiny blue sailboats. "Eli doesn't know if something is expensive or a bargain. He only knows if something feels or smells familiar. He's got enough change in his life right now."

"Is that a dig at me?" He studied her, trying to get a read on her mood. She seemed more reserved than yesterday, worried even.

"Not a dig at all. It's a fact." She eyed him with confusion.

"He has you as a constant."

"Damn straight he does," she said with a mama-bear ferocity that lit a fire inside him. Her strength, the light in her eyes, stirred him.

Then it hit him. She was in protective mode because she saw him as a threat. She actually thought he might try to take her child away from her. Nothing could be further from the truth. He wanted to parent the child *with* her.

He angled his head to capture her gaze fully. "I'm not trying to take him away from you. I just want to be a part of his life."

"Of course. That was always my intention," she said, her eyes still guarded, wary. "I know trust is difficult right now, but I hope you will believe me that I want you to have regular visitation."

Ah, already she was trying to set boundaries rather than thinking about possibilities. But he knew better than to fight with her. Finesse always worked better than head-on confrontation. He pointed to the elementary school they'd attended together, the same redbrick building but with a new playground. "We share a lot of history and now we share a son. Even a year apart isn't going to erase everything else."

"I understand that."

"Do you?" He moved closer to her.

Her body went rigid as she held herself still, keeping a couple of inches of space between them. "Remember when we were children, in kindergarten?"

Following her train of thought was tougher than maneuvering through race traffic, but at least she was talking to him. "Which particular day in kindergarten?"

She looked down at her hands twisted in her lap, her nails short and painted with a pretty orange. "You were lying belly flat on a skateboard racing down a hill."

That day eased to the front of his mind. "I fell off, flat on my ass." He winced. "Broke my arm."

"All the girls wanted to sign your cast." She looked sideways at him, smiling. "Even then you were a chick magnet."

"They just wanted to use their markers," he said dismissively.

She looked up to meet his eyes fully for the first time since they'd climbed into the limousine. "I knew that your arm was already broken."

"You never said a word to me." He rubbed his forearm absently.

"You would have been embarrassed if I confronted you, and you would have lied to me. We didn't talk as openly then about our home lives." She tucked the blanket more securely around the baby's feet as Eli sucked a pacifier in his sleep. "We were new friends who shared a jelly sandwich at lunch."

"We were new friends and yet you were right about the arm." He looked at his son's tiny hands and wondered how any father could ever strike out at such innocence. Sweat beaded his forehead at even the thought.

"I told my mom though, after school," Lucy Ann's eyes fell to his wrist. "She wasn't as...distant in those days."

The weight of her gaze was like a stroke along his skin, her words salve to a past wound. "I didn't know you said anything to anyone."

"Her word didn't carry much sway, or maybe she didn't fight that hard." She shrugged, the strap of her sundress sliding. "Either way, nothing happened. So I went to the principal."

"My spunky advocate." God, he'd missed her. And yet he'd always thought he knew everything about her and here she had something new to share. "Guess that explains why they pulled me out of class to interview me about my arm."

"You didn't tell the principal the truth though, did you?

I kept waiting for something big to happen. My five-year-old imagination was running wild."

For one instant in that meeting he had considered talking, but the thoughts of afterward had frozen any words in his throat like a lodged wad of that shared jelly sandwich. "I was still too scared of what would happen to my mother if I talked. Of what he would do to her."

Sympathy flickered in her brown eyes. "We discussed so many things as kids, always avoiding anything to do with our home lives. Our friendship was a haven for me then."

He'd felt the same. But that meeting with the principal had made him bolder later, except he'd chosen the wrong person to tell. Someone loyal to his father, which only brought on another beating.

"You had your secrets, too. I could always sense when you were holding back."

"Then apparently we didn't have any secrets from each other after all." She winced, her hand going to her son's car seat. "Not until this year."

The limo jostled along a pothole on the country road. Their legs brushed and his arm shot out to rest along the back of her seat. She jolted for an instant, her breath hitching. He stared back, keeping his arm in place until her shoulders relaxed.

"Oh, Elliot." She sagged back. "We're a mess, you and I, with screwed-up pasts and not much to go on as an example for building a future."

The worry coating her words stabbed at him. He cupped her arm lightly, the feel of her so damn right tucked to him. "We need to figure out how to straighten ourselves out to be good parents. For Eli."

"It won't be all that difficult to outdo our parents."

"Eli deserves a lot better than just a step above our

folks." The feel of her hair along his wrist soothed old wounds, the way she'd always done for him. But more than that, the feel of her now, with the new memories, with that night between them…

His pulse pounded in his ears, his body stirring…. He wanted her. And right now, he didn't see a reason why they couldn't have everything. They shared a similar past and they shared a child.

He just had to convince Lucy Ann. "I agree with you there. That's why it's important for us to use this time together wisely. Figure out how to be the parents he deserves. Figure out how to be a team, the partners he needs."

"I'm here, in the car with you, committed to spending the next four weeks with you." She tipped her face up to his, the jasmine scent of her swirling all around him. "What more do you want from me?"

"I want us to be friends again, Lucy Ann," he answered honestly, his voice raw. "Friends. Not just parents passing a kid back and forth to each other. I want things the way they were before between us."

Her pupils widened with emotion. "Exactly the way we were before? Is that even possible?"

"Not exactly as before," he conceded, easy enough to do when he knew his plans for something better between them.

He angled closer, stroking her ponytail over her shoulder in a sweep he wanted to take farther down her back to her waist. He burned all the way to his gut, needing to pull her closer.

"We'll be friends and more. We can go back to that night together, pick up from there. Because heaven help me, if we're being totally honest, then yes. I want you back in my bed again."

Four

The caress of Elliot's hand along her hair sent tingles all the way to her toes. She wanted to believe the deep desire was simply a result of nearly a year without sex, but she knew her body longed for this particular man. For the pleasure of his caress over her bare skin.

Except then she wouldn't be able to think straight. Now more than ever, she needed to keep a level head for her child. She loved her son more than life, and she had some serious fences to mend with Elliot to secure a peaceful future for Eli.

Lucy Ann clasped Elliot's wrist and moved it aside. "You can't be serious."

"I'm completely serious." His fingers twisted in her ponytail.

"Let. Go. Now," she said succinctly, barely able to keep herself from grabbing his shirt and hauling him in for a kiss. "Sex will only complicate matters."

"Or it could simplify things." He released her hair slowly, his stroke tantalizing all the way down her arm.

Biting her lip, she squeezed her eyes shut, too enticed by the green glow of desire in his eyes.

"Lucy Ann?" His bourbon-smooth tones intoxicated the parched senses that had missed him every day of the past eleven months. "What are you thinking?"

Her head angled ever so slightly toward his touch. "My aunt said the same thing about the bonus of friends becoming…more."

He laughed softly, the heat of his breath warming her throat and broadcasting just how close he'd moved to her, so close he could kiss the exposed flesh. "Your aunt has always been a smart woman. Although I sure as hell didn't talk to her about you and I becoming lovers."

She opened her eyes slowly, steeling herself. "You need to quit saying things like that or I'm going to have the car stopped right now. I will walk home with my baby if I have to. You and I need boundaries for this to work."

His gaze fell to her mouth for an instant that felt stretched to eternity before he angled back, leather seat creaking. "We'll have to agree to disagree."

Her exhale was shakier than she would have liked, betraying her. "You can cut the innocent act. I've seen your playboy moves over the years. Your practiced charm isn't going to work with me." Not again, anyway. "And it wouldn't have worked before if I hadn't been so taken away by sentimentality and a particularly strong vintage liqueur."

Furrows dug deep trenches in his forehead. "Lucy Ann, I am deeply sorry if I took advantage of our friendship—"

"I told you that night. No apologies." His apologies had been mortifying then, especially when she'd been hoping for a repeat only to learn he was full of regrets. He'd stung her pride and her heart. Not that she ever intended to let him know as much. "There were two of us in bed that night, and I refuse to call it a mistake. But it won't happen again, remember? We decided that then."

Or rather *he* had decided and *she* had pretended to go along to save face over her weakness when it came to this man.

His eyes went smoky. "I remember a lot of other things about that night."

Already she could feel herself weakening, wanting to read more into his every word and slightest action. She had to stop this intimacy, this romanticism, now.

"Enough talking about the past. This is about our future. Eli's future." She put on her best logical, personal-assistant voice she'd used a million times to place distance between them. "Where are we going first? I have to confess I haven't kept track of the race dates this year."

"Races later," he said simply as the car reached the airport. "First, we have a wedding to attend."

Her gut tightened at his surprise announcement. "A wedding?"

Lucy Ann hated weddings. Even when the wedding was for a longtime friend. Elliot's high school alumni pal—Dr. Rowan Boothe—was marrying none other than an African princess, who also happened to be a Ph.D. research scientist.

She hated to feel ungrateful, though, since this was the international event of the year, with a lavish ceremony in East Africa, steeped in colorful garb and local delicacies. Invitations were coveted, and media cameras hovered at a respectable distance, monitored by an elite security team that made the packed day run smoothly well into the evening. Tuxedos, formal gowns and traditional tribal wraps provided a magnificent blend of beauty that reflected the couple's modern tastes while acknowledging time-honored customs.

Sitting at the moonlit reception on the palace lawns by the beach, her baby asleep in a stroller, Lucy Ann sipped her glass of spiced fruit juice. She kept a smile plastered on her face as if her showing up here with Elliot and their son was nothing out of the ordinary. Regional music with drums and flutes carried on the air along with laughter and celebration. She refused to let her bad mood ruin the day for the happy bride and groom. Apparently, Elliot had been "kidnapped" from Rowan's bachelor party.

Now he'd returned for the wedding—with her and the baby. No one had asked, but their eyes all made it clear they knew. The fact that he'd thrust their messed-up relationship right into the spotlight frustrated her. But he'd insisted it was better to do it sooner rather than later. Why delay the inevitable?

He'd even arranged for formal dresses for her to pick from. She'd had no choice but to oblige him since her only formals were basic black, far too somber for a wedding. She'd gravitated toward simple wear in the past, never wanting to stand out. Although in this colorful event, her pale lavender gown wasn't too glaring. Still, she felt a little conspicuous because it was strapless and floor-length with a beaded bodice. Breast-feeding had given her new cleavage.

A fact that hadn't gone unnoticed, given the heated looks Elliot kept sliding her way.

But her mood was too sour to dwell on those steamy glances. Especially when he looked so mouth-wateringly handsome in a tuxedo, freshly shaven and smiling. It was as if the past eleven months apart didn't exist, as if they'd just shared the same bed, the same glass of wine. They'd been close friends for so long, peeling him from her thoughts was easier said than done.

She just wanted the marriage festivities to be over, then hopefully she would feel less vulnerable, more in control.

Weddings were happy occasions for some, evoking dreams or bringing back happy memories. Not for her. When she saw the white lace, flowers and a towering cake, she could only remember each time her mama said "I do." All four times. Each man was worse than the one before, until child services stepped in and said drug addict stepdaddy number four had to go if Lucy Ann's mother wanted to keep her child.

Mama chose hubby.

Lucy Ann finally went to live with her aunt for good— no more dodging groping hands or awkward requests to sit on "daddy's" lap. Her aunt loved her, cared for her, but Carla had others to care for, as well—Grandma and an older bachelor uncle.

No one put Lucy Ann first or loved her most. Not until this baby. She would do anything for Eli. Anything. Even swallow her pride and let Elliot back in her life.

Still, keeping on a happy face throughout the wedding was hard. All wedding phobia aside, she worked to appreciate the wedding as an event. She had to learn the art of detaching her emotions from her brain if she expected to make it through the next four weeks with her heart intact.

"Lucy Ann?" A familiar female voice startled her, and she set her juice aside to find Hillary Donavan standing beside her.

Hillary was married to another of Elliot's school friends, Troy Donavan, more commonly known as the

Robin Hood Hacker. As a computer-savvy teen he'd wreaked all sorts of havoc. Now he was a billionaire software developer. He'd recently married Hillary, an events planner, who looked as elegant as ever in a green Grecian-style silk dress.

The red-haired beauty dropped into a chair beside the stroller. "Do you mind if I hide out here with you and the baby for a while? My part in orchestrating this nationally televised wedding is done, thank heavens."

"You did a lovely job blending local traditions with a modern flair. No doubt magazine covers will be packed with photos."

"They didn't give me much time to plan since they made their engagement announcement just after Christmas, but I'm pleased with the results. I hope they are, too."

"I'm sure they are, although they can only see each other." Lucy Ann's stomach tightened, remembering her mother's adoring looks for each new man.

"To think they were professional adversaries for so long…now the sparks between them are so tangible I'm thinking I didn't need to order the firework display for a finale."

Lucy Ann pulled a tight smile, doing her best to be polite. "Romance is in the air."

"I hope this isn't going too late for you and the little guy." She flicked her red hair over her shoulder. "You must be exhausted from your flight."

"He's asleep. We'll be fine." If she left, Elliot would feel obligated to leave, as well. And right now she was too emotionally raw to be alone with him. Surely Hillary had to have some idea of how difficult this was for her, since the alum buddies had been party to the kidnapping.

Her eyes slid to the clutch of pals, the five men who'd been sent to a military reform school together.

Their bond was tight. Unbreakable.

They stood together at the beachside under a cabana wearing matching tuxedos, all five of them too damn rich and handsome for their own good. Luckily for the susceptible female population, the other four were now firmly taken, married and completely in love with their brides. The personification of bad boys redeemed, but still edgy.

Exciting.

The Alpha Brotherhood rarely gathered in one place, but when they did, they were a sight to behold. They'd all landed in trouble with the law as teens, but they'd been sent to a military reform school rather than juvie. Computer whiz Troy Donavan had broken into the Department of Defense's computer system to expose corruption. Casino magnate Conrad Hughes had used insider trading tips to manipulate the stock market. He'd only barely redeemed himself by tanking corporations that used child-labor sweatshops in other countries. World famous soft rock/jazz musician Malcolm Douglas had been sent away on drug charges as a teenager, although she'd learned later that he'd been playing the piano in a bar underage and got nabbed in the bust.

The groom—Dr. Rowan Boothe—had a history a bit more troubled. He'd been convicted of driving while drunk. He'd been part of an accident he'd taken the blame for so his overage brother wouldn't go to jail—then his brother had died a year later driving drunk into a tree. Now Rowan used all his money to start clinics in third-world countries.

They all had their burdens to bear, and that guilt motivated them to make amends now. Through their freelance work with Interpol. Through charitable donations beyond anything anyone would believe unless they saw the accounting books.

Now, they'd all settled down and gotten married, starting families of their own. Was that a part of what compelled Elliot to push for more with her? A need to fit in with his Alpha Brothers as they moved on to the next phase of their lives?

Lucy Ann looked back at Hillary. "Did you know what Malcolm and Conrad were up to yesterday?"

"I didn't know exactly, not until Troy told me, and they were already on their way. I can't say I approve of their tactics, but it was too late for me to do anything. You appear to be okay." Hillary leaned on her elbows, angling closer, her eyes concerned. "Is that an act?"

"What do you think?"

She clasped Lucy Ann's hand. "I'm sorry. I should have realized this calm of yours is just a cover. We're kindred spirits, you and I, ever organized, even in how we show ourselves to the world." She squeezed once before letting go. "Do you want to talk? Need a shoulder? I'm here."

"There's nothing anyone can do now. It's up to Elliot and me to figure out how to move forward. If I'd let him know earlier…"

"Friend, you and I both know how difficult it can be to contact them when the colonel calls for one of their missions. They disappear. They're unreachable." She smiled sadly. "It takes something as earth-shattering as, well, a surprise baby to get them to break the code of silence."

"How do you live with that, as a part of a committed relationship?"

She couldn't bring herself to ask what it felt like to be married to a man who kept such a chunk of his life separate. She'd known as a friend and as a personal assistant that Elliot's old headmaster later recruited previous students as freelancers for Interpol. She'd kept thoughts about that segmented away, since it did not pertain to her job or their life on the race circuit.

But now, there was no denying that her life was tied to Elliot's in a much deeper way.

"I love Troy, the man he is. The man he's always been," Hillary said. "We grow, we mature, but our basic natures stay the same. And I love who that man is."

Lucy Ann could almost—almost—grasp the promise in that, except she knew Hillary helped her husband on some of those missions, doing a bit of freelance work of her own.

Lucy Ann stared down into the amber swirl of her juice glass. "Is it so wrong to want an ordinary life? I don't mean to sound ungrateful, but *normal,* boring, well, I've never had that. I crave it for myself and my child, but it feels so unattainable."

"That's a tough one, isn't it? These men are many things, but normal—delightfully boring—doesn't show up anywhere on that list."

Where did that leave her? In search of what she couldn't have? Or a hypocrite for not accepting Elliot the way he had accepted her all her life? She ran from him. As much as she swore that he pushed her away, she knew. She'd run just as fast and hard as he'd pushed.

"Thank you for the advice, Hillary."

Her friend sighed. "I'm not sure how much help I've been. But if you need to talk more, I'm here for you. I won't betray your confidences."

"I appreciate that," Lucy Ann said, and meant it, only just realizing how few female friends she'd ever had. Elliot had been her best friend and she'd allowed that to close her off to other avenues of support.

"Good, very good. We women need to stick together, make a sisterhood pact of our own." She winked before ducking toward the stroller. "Little Eli is adorable, and I'm glad you're here."

Lucy Ann appreciated the gesture, and she wanted to trust. She wanted to believe there could be a sisterhood of support in dealing with these men—even though she wouldn't be married to Elliot. Still, their lives were entwined because of their child.

A part of her still wondered, doubted. The wives of Elliot's friends had reached out initially after she left, but eventually they'd stopped. Could she really be a part of their sisterhood?

"Thank you, Hillary," she said simply, her eyes sliding back to Elliot standing with his friends.

Her hand moved protectively over to the handle of her son's stroller, her throat constricting as she took in the gleaming good looks of her baby's father. Even his laugh seemed to make the stars shimmer brighter.

And how frivolous a thought was that?

She definitely needed to keep her head on straight and her heart locked away. She refused to be anyone's obligation or burden ever again.

Elliot hoped Rowan and Mariama's marriage ceremony would soften Lucy Ann's mood. After all, weren't weddings supposed to make women sentimental? He'd watched her chatting with his friends' wives and tried to gauge her reaction. She knew them all from her time working as his assistant, and seeing this big extended family connected by friendship rather than blood should appeal to her. They'd talked about leaving their pasts behind countless times as kids.

They could fit right in here with their son. A practical decision. A fun life.

So why wasn't she smiling as the bride and groom drove away in a BMW convertible, the bride's veil trailing in the wind?

Shouldering free of the crowd, Elliot made his way toward Lucy Ann, who stood on the periphery, their son in a stroller beside her. Even though he'd arranged for a nanny who'd once worked for a British duke, Lucy Ann said she couldn't let her son stay with a total stranger. She would need to conduct her own interview tomorrow. If the woman met her standards, she could help during Eli's naps so Lucy Ann could keep up with the work obligations she hadn't been able to put on hold. The encounter still made Elliot grin when he thought of her refusing to be intimidated by the very determined Mary Poppins.

He stopped beside Lucy Ann, enjoying the way the moonlight caressed her bare shoulders. Her hair was loose and lifting in the night wind. Every breath he took drew in hints of her, of Carolina jasmine. His body throbbed to life with a reminder of what they could have together, something so damn amazing he'd spent eleven months running from the power of it.

Now, fate had landed him here with her. Running wasn't an option, and he found that for once he didn't mind fate kicking him in the ass.

Elliot rested his hand on the stroller beside hers, watching every nuance of her reaction. "Are you ready to call it a day and return to our suite, or would you like to take a walk?"

She licked her lips nervously. "Um, I think a walk, perhaps."

So she wasn't ready to be alone with him just yet? A promising sign, actually; she wanted him still, even if she wasn't ready to act on that desire. Fine, then. He could use the moon and stars to romance her, the music from a steel drum band serenading them.

"A walk it is, then, Lucy dear," he asserted.

"Where can we go with a baby?"

He glanced around at the party with guests still dancing along the cabana-filled beach. Tables of food were still laden with half shares of delicacies, fruits and meats. A fountain spewing wine echoed the rush of waves along the shore. Mansions dotted the rocky seashore, with a planked path leading to docks.

"This way." He gestured toward the shoreline boardwalk, all but deserted this late at night. "I'll push the stroller."

He stepped behind the baby carriage. Lucy Ann had no choice but to step aside or they would be stuck hip to hip, step for step.

Five minutes later, they'd left the remnants of the reception behind, the stroller wheels rumbling softly along the wooden walkway. To anyone looking from the looming mansions above, lights shining from the windows like eyes, he and Lucy Ann would appear a happy family walking with their son.

Tonight more than ever he was aware of his single status. Yet again, he'd stood to the side as another friend got married. Leaving only him as a bachelor. But he was a father now. There was no more running from fears of becoming his father. He had to be a man worthy of this child. His child with Lucy Ann.

She walked beside him, the sea breeze brushing her gauzy dress along his leg in phantom caresses. "You're quite good at managing that stroller. I'm surprised. It took me longer than I expected to get the knack of not knocking over everything in my path."

He smiled at her, stuffing down a spark of anger along with the urge to remind her that he would have helped in those early days if she'd only let him know. "It's just like maneuvering a race car."

"Of course. That makes sense."

"More sense than me being at ease with a child? I'm determined to get this right, Lucy Ann, don't doubt that for a second." Steely determination fueled his words.

"You used to say you never wanted kids of your own."

Could those words have made her wary of telling him? There had been a time when they shared everything with each other.

He reminded her, "You always insisted that you didn't want children, either."

"I didn't want to risk putting any child in my mother's path." She rubbed her hand along her collarbone, the one she'd cracked as a child. "I'm an adult now and my mother's passed away. But we're talking about *you* and your insistence that you didn't want kids."

"I didn't. Then." If things hadn't changed, he still might have said the same, but one look in Eli's wide brown eyes and his world had altered in an instant. "I don't run away from responsibilities."

"You ran away before—" She stopped short, cursing softly. "Forget I said that."

Halting, he pulled his hands from the stroller, the baby sleeping and the carriage tucked protectively between them and the railing.

Elliot took her by the shoulders. Her soft bare shoulders. So vulnerable. So...*her*. "Say it outright, Lucy Ann. I left *you* behind when I left Columbia behind, when I let myself get sloppy and caught, when I risked jail because anything seemed better than staying with my father. For a selfish instant, I forgot about what that would mean for you. And I've regretted that every day of my life."

The admission was ripped from his throat; deeper still, torn all the way from his gut. Except there was no one but Lucy Ann to hear him on the deserted walkway. Stone houses dotted the bluff, quarters for guests and staff, all structures up on the bluff with a few lights winking in the night. Most people still partied on at the reception.

"I understand that you feel guilty. Like you have to make up for things. But you need to stop thinking that way. I'm responsible for my own life." She cupped his face, her eyes softening. "Besides, if you'd stayed, you wouldn't have this amazing career that also gave me a chance to break free. So I guess it all worked out in the end."

"Yet you ended up returning home when you left me." Hell, he should be honest now while he had the chance. He didn't want to waste an instant or risk the baby waking up and interrupting them. "When I stupidly pushed you away."

Her arm dropped away again. "I returned with a degree and the ability to support myself and my child. That's significant and I appreciate it." Her hands fisted at her sides. "I don't want to be your obligation."

"You want a life of your own, other than being my assistant. I understand that." He kept his voice low, which brought her closer to listen over the crash of waves below the boardwalk. He liked having her close again. "Let's talk it through, like we would have in the old days."

"You're being so—" she scowled "—so reasonable."

"You say that like it's a dirty word. Why is that a bad thing?" Because God help him, he was feeling anything but reasonable. If she wanted passion and emotion, he was more than willing to pour all of that into seducing her. He just had to be sure before he made a move.

A wrong step could set back his cause.

"Don't try to manipulate me with all the logical reasons why I should stay. I want you to be honest about what you're thinking. What you *want* for your future."

"When it comes to the future, I don't know what I want, Lucy Ann, beyond making sure you and Eli are safe, provided for, never afraid. I'm flying by the seat of my pants here, trying my best to figure out how to get through this being-a-father thing." Honesty was ripping a hole in him. He wanted to go back to logic.

Or passion.

Her chest rose and fell faster with emotion, a flush spreading across her skin in the moon's glow. "How would things have been different if I had come to you, back when I found out I was pregnant?"

"I would have proposed right away," he said without hesitation.

"I would have said no," she answered just as quickly.

He stepped closer. "I would have been persistent in trying to wear you down."

"How would you have managed that?"

The wind tore at her dress, whipping the skirt forward to tangle in his legs, all but binding them together with silken bands.

He angled his face closer to hers, his mouth so close he could claim her if he moved even a whisker closer. "I would have tried to romance you with flowers, candy and jewels." He watched the way her pupils widened with awareness as his words heated her cheek. "Then I would have realized you're unconventional and I would have changed tactics."

"Such as?" she whispered, the scent of fruit juice on her breath, dampening her lips. "Be honest."

"Hell, Lucy Ann, if you want honesty, here it is." His hand slid up her bare arm, along her shoulder, under her hair, to cup the back of her neck, and God, it felt good to touch her after so long apart. It felt right. "I just want to kiss you again."

Five

Lucy Ann gripped Elliot's shoulders, her fingers digging in deep by instinct even as her brain shouted "bad idea."

Her body melted into his, the hard planes of his muscular chest absorbing the curves of her, her breasts hypersensitive to the feel of him. And his hands… A sigh floated from her into him. His hands were gentle and warm and sure along her neck and into her hair, massaging her scalp. Her knees went weak, and he slid an arm down to band around her waist, securing her to him.

How could he crumble her defenses with just one touch of his mouth to hers? But she couldn't deny it. A moonlight stroll, a starlight kiss along the shore had her dreaming romantic notions. Made her want more.

Want him.

His tongue stroked along the seam of her mouth, and she opened without hesitation, taking him every bit as much as he took her. Stroking and tasting. There was a certain safety in the moment, out here in the open, since there was no way things could go further. Distant guest houses, the echoes of the reception carrying on the wind and of course the baby with them kept her from being totally swept away.

Her hands glided down his sides to tuck into his back pockets, to cup the taut muscles that she'd admired on more than one occasion. Hell, the whole female population had admired that butt thanks to a modeling gig he'd taken early in his career to help fund his racing. She'd ribbed him about those underwear ads, even knowing he was blindingly hot. She'd deluded herself into believing she was objective, immune to his sensuality, which went beyond mere good looks.

The man had a rugged charisma that oozed machismo.

Heaven help her, she wanted to dive right in and swim around, luxuriating in the sensations. The tingling in her breasts sparked through her, gathering lower with a familiar intensity she recognized too well after their night together.

This had to stop. Now. Because mistakes she'd made this time wouldn't just hurt her—or Elliot. They had a child to consider. A precious innocent life only a hand's reach away.

With more than a little regret, she ended the kiss, nipping his sensuous bottom lip one last time. His growl of frustration rumbled his chest against hers, but he didn't stop her. Her head fell to rest on his shoulder as she inhaled the scent of sea air tinged with the musk of his sweat. As Elliot cupped the back of her head in a broad palm, his ragged breaths reassured her he was every bit as affected by the kiss. An exciting and yet dangerous reality that confused her after the way they'd parted a year ago.

She needed space to think through this. Maybe watching the wedding and seeing all those happy couples had affected her more than she realized. Even just standing here in his arms with the feel of his arousal pressing against her stomach, she was in serious danger of making a bad choice if she stayed with him a moment longer.

Flattening her palms to his chest, Lucy Ann pushed, praying her legs would hold when he backed away.

She swayed for an instant before steeling her spine. "Elliot, this—" she gestured between them, then touched her kissed tender lips softly "—this wasn't part of our bargain when we left South Carolina. Or was it?"

The night breeze felt cooler now, the sea air chilly.

His eyes stayed inscrutable as he stuffed his hands in his tuxedo pockets, the harsh planes of his face shadowed by moonlight. "Are you accusing me of plotting a seduction?"

"*Plotting* is a harsh word," she conceded, her eyes flitting to the baby in his stroller as she scrambled to regain control of her thoughts, "but I think you're not above planning to do whatever it takes to get your way. That's who you are. Can you deny it?"

His eyes glinted with determination—and anger? "I won't deny wanting to sleep with you. The way you kissed me back gives me the impression you're on board with that notion."

Her heartbeat quickened with visions of how easy it would be to fall into bed with him. To pick up where they'd left off a year ago. If only she had any sense he wanted her for more than a connection to his son.

"That's the point, Elliot. It doesn't matter what *we* want. This month together is supposed to be about building a future for *Eli*. More of—" she gestured between them, her heart tripping over itself at just the mention of their kiss, their attraction "—playing with fire only risks an unstable future for our son. We need to recapture our friendship. Nothing more."

Her limbs felt weak at even the mention of *more*.

He arched an arrogant eyebrow. "I disagree that they're mutually exclusive."

"If you push me on this, I'll have to leave the tour and return to South Carolina." She'd seen too often how easily he seduced women. He was a charmer, without question, and she refused to be like her mother, swept away into reckless relationships again and again. She had a level head and she needed to keep it. "Elliot, do you hear me? I need to know we're on the same page about these next four weeks."

He studied her through narrowed eyes for the crash of four rolling waves before he shrugged. "I will respect your wishes, and I will keep my hands to myself." He smiled, pulling his hands from his pockets and holding them up. "Unless you change your mind, of course."

"I won't," she said quickly, almost too forcefully for her own peace of mind. That old Shakespeare quote came back to her, taunting her, *Methinks the lady doth protest too much.*

"Whoa, whoa, hold on now." Elliot patted the air. "I'm not trying to make you dig in your stubborn heels, so let's end this conversation and call it a day. We can talk more tomorrow, in the light of day."

"Less ambiance would be wise." Except she knew he looked hunky in any light, any situation.

Regardless of how much she wanted to go back, she realized that wasn't possible. They'd crossed a line the night they went too far celebrating his win and her completing her final exams.

It had never happened before she had a plan for her

own future. The catalyst had been completing her degree, feeling that for the first time since they were kids, she met him on an even footing. She'd allowed her walls to come down. She'd allowed herself to acknowledge what she'd been hiding all her adult life. She was every bit as attracted to Elliot Starc as his fawning groupies.

What if she was no different from her mother?

The thought alone had her staggering for steady ground. She grabbed the stroller just to be on the safe side. "I'm going back to the room now. It's time to settle Eli for the night. I need to catch up on some work before I go to sleep. And I do mean sleep."

"Understood," he said simply from beside her. "I'll walk back with you."

The heat of him reached her even though their bodies didn't touch. Just occupying the same space as him offered a hefty temptation right now.

She shook her head, the glide of her hair along her bared shoulders teasing her oversensitized skin. "I'd rather go alone. The palace is in sight and the area's safe."

"As you wish." He stepped back with a nod and a half bow. "We'll talk tomorrow on the way to Spain." He said it as a promise, not a request.

"Okay then," she conceded softly over her shoulder as she pushed the stroller, wheeling it toward the palace where they were staying in one of the many guest suites. Her body still hummed from the kiss, but her mind filled with questions and reservations.

She and Elliot had been platonic friends for years, comfortable with each other. As kids, they'd gone skinny-dipping, built forts in the woods, comforted each other during countless crises and disappointments. He'd been her best friend…right up to the moment he wasn't. Where had this crazy attraction between them come from?

The wheels of the stroller whirred along the walkway as fast as the memories spinning through her. That night eleven months ago when they'd been together had been spontaneous but amazing. She'd wondered if maybe there could be more between them. The whole friends-with-benefits had sounded appealing, taking it a day at a time until they sorted out the bombshell that had been dropped into their relationship: a sexual chemistry that still boggled her mind.

And yet Elliot's reaction the next day had made her realize there could be no future for them. Her euphoria had evaporated with the morning light.

She'd woken before him and gone to the kitchen to make coffee and pile some pastries on a plate. The front door to his suite had opened and she'd assumed it must be the maid. Anyone who entered the room had to have a key and a security code.

However, the woman who'd walked in hadn't been wearing a uniform. She—Gianna—had worn a trench coat and nothing else. If only it had been a crazed fan. But Lucy Ann had quickly deduced Gianna was the new female in Elliot's life. He hadn't even denied it. There was no misunderstanding.

God, it had been so damn cliché her stomach had roiled. Elliot came out of the bedroom and Gianna had turned paler than the towel around Elliot's waist.

He'd kept his calm. Apologized to Gianna for the awkward situation, but she'd burst into tears and run. He'd told Lucy Ann there was nothing between him and his girlfriend anymore, not after what happened the night before with Lucy Ann.

But she'd told him he should have let Gianna know that first, and she was a hundred percent right. He'd agreed and apologized.

That hadn't been enough for her. The fact that he could be seeing one woman, even superficially, and go to bed with another? No, no and hell, no. That was something she couldn't forgive. Not after how all those men had cheated on her mom with little regard for vows or promises. And her mother kept forgiving the first unfaithful jerk, and then the next.

If Elliot could behave this way now, how could she trust him later? What if he got "swept away" by someone else and figured he would clue her in later? She'd called him dishonorable.

And in an instant, with that one word, a lifetime friendship crumbled.

She'd thrown on her clothes and left. Elliot's engagement to Gianna a month later had only sealed Lucy Ann's resolve to stay away. They hadn't spoken again until the day he'd shown up in Carla's yard.

Now, after more impulsive kisses, she found herself wanting to crawl right back into bed with him. Lucy Ann powered the stroller closer to the party and their quarters, drawing in one deep breath of salty air after another, willing her pulse to steady. Wishing the urge to be with Elliot was as easily controlled.

With each step, she continued the chant in her brain, the vow not to repeat her mother's mistakes.

Wind tearing at his tuxedo jacket, Elliot watched Lucy Ann push the stroller down the planked walkway, then past the party. He didn't take his eyes off her or his son until he saw they'd safely reached the palace, even though he now had bodyguards watching his family 24/7. His family?

Hell, yes, his family.

Eli was his son. And Lucy Ann had been his only real

family for most of his life. No matter how angry he got at her for holding back on telling him about Eli, Elliot also couldn't forgive himself for staying away from her. He'd let her down in a major way more than once, from his teenage years up to now. She had reason not to trust him.

He needed to earn back her trust. He owed her that and so much more.

His shoulders heaving with a sigh, he started toward the wedding reception. The bride and groom had left, but the partying would go long into the night. It wasn't every day a princess got married. People would expect a celebration to end all celebrations.

A sole person peeled away from the festivities and ambled toward him. From the signature streamlined fedora, he recognized his old school pal Troy Donavan. Troy was one of the originals from their high school band, the Alpha Brotherhood, a group of misfits who found kindred spirits in one another and their need to push boundaries, to expose hypocrisy—the greatest of crimes in their eyes.

Troy pulled up alongside him, passing him a drink. "Reconciliation not going too well?"

"What makes you say that?" He took the thick cut glass filled with a locally brewed beer.

"She's returning to her room alone after a wedding." Troy tipped his glass as if in a toast toward the guests. "More people get lucky after weddings than any other event known to mankind. That's why you brought Lucy Ann here, isn't it? To get her in the romantic mood."

Had he? He'd told himself he wanted her to see his friends settling down. For her to understand he could do the same. But he wasn't sure how much he felt like sharing, especially when his thoughts were still jumbled.

"I brought Lucy Ann to the wedding because I couldn't

miss the event. The timing has more to do with how you all colluded to pull off that kidnapping stunt."

"You're still pissed off? Sorry, dude, truly," he said, wincing. "I thought you and Malcolm talked that all out."

"Blah, blah, blah, my good pals wanted to get an unguarded reaction. I heard." And it still didn't sit well. He'd trusted these guys since high school, over fifteen years, and hell, yeah, he felt like they'd let him down. "But I also heard that Lucy Ann contacted the Brotherhood over a week ago. That's a week I lost with my son. A week she was alone caring for him. Would you be okay with that?"

"Fair enough. You have reason to be angry with us." Troy nudged his fedora back on his head. "But don't forget to take some of the blame yourself. She was your friend all your life, and you just let her go. You're going to have a tough as hell time convincing her you've magically changed your mind now and you would have wanted her back even without the kid."

The truth pinched. "Tell me something I don't know."

"Okay then. Here's a bit of advice."

"Everyone seems full of it," Elliot responded, tongue in cheek.

Troy laughed softly, leaning back against a wrought-iron railing. "Fine. I'm full of it. Always have been. Now, on to my two cents."

"By all means." Elliot knocked back another swallow of the local beer.

"You're a father now." Troy rolled his glass between his palms. "Be that boy's father and let everything else fall into place."

A sigh rattled through Elliot. "You make it sound so simple."

Troy's smile faded, no joking in sight. "Think how different our lives would have been with different parents.

Things came together when Salvatore gave us direction. Be there for your son."

"Relationships aren't saved by having a child together." His parents had gotten married because he was on the way. His mother had eventually walked out and left him behind.

"True enough. But they sure as hell are broken up by fighting over the child. Be smart in how you work together when it comes to Eli and it might go a long way toward smoothing things out with Lucy Ann." Troy ran a finger along the collar of his tuxedo shirt, edging a little more air for himself around his tie. "If not, you've got a solid relationship with your kid, and that's the most important thing."

Was his focus all wrong by trying to make things right with Lucy Ann? Elliot had to admit Troy's plan made some sense. The stakes were too important to risk screwing up with his son. "When did you get to be such a relationship sage?"

"Hillary's a smart woman, and I'm smart enough to listen to her." His sober expression held only for a second longer before he returned to the more lighthearted Troy they were all accustomed to. "Now more than ever I need to listen to Hillary's needs since she's pregnant."

"Congratulations to you both." Elliot clapped Troy on the back, glad for his friend even as he wondered what it might have been like to be by Lucy Ann's side while she was expecting Eli. "Who'd have predicted all this home and hearth for us a few years ago?"

"Colonel Salvatore's going to have to find some new recruits."

"You're not pulling Interpol missions?" That surprised him. Elliot understood Hillary's stepping out of fieldwork while pregnant. But he wouldn't have thought Troy would ever back off the edge.

"There are other ways I can help with my tech work. Who knows, maybe I'll even take on the mentorship role like Salvatore someday. But I'm off the clock now and missing my wife." Troy walked backward, waving once before he sprinted toward the party.

Elliot knew his friend was right. The advice made sense. Focus on the baby. But that didn't stop him from wanting Lucy Ann in his bed again. The notion of just letting everything fall into place was completely alien to his nature. He'd never been the laid-back sort like Troy. Elliot needed to move, act, win.

He needed Lucy Ann back in his life.

For months he'd told himself the power of Lucy Ann's kiss, of the sex they'd shared nearly a year ago, had been a hazy memory distorted by alcohol. But now, with his body still throbbing from the kiss they'd just shared, his hair still mussed, the memory of their hands running frenetically—hungrily—over each other, he knew. Booze had nothing to do with the explosive chemistry between them. Although Gianna's arrival had sure as hell provided a splash of ice water on the morning-after moment.

He'd screwed up by not breaking things off with Gianna before he let anything happen between him and Lucy Ann. He still wasn't sure why he and Gianna had reconciled afterward. He hadn't been fair to either woman. The dishonor in that weighed on him every damn day.

At least he'd finally done right by Gianna when they'd broken up. Now, he had to make things right with Lucy Ann.

Their kiss ten minutes ago couldn't lead to anything more, not tonight. He accepted that. It was still too early in his campaign to win her over. But a kiss? He could have that much for now at least. A taste of her, a hint of what more they could have together.

A hint of Lucy Ann was so much more than everything with any other woman.

She was so much a part of his life. Why the hell had he let her go?

This didn't have to be complicated. Friendship. Sex. Travel the world and live an exciting life together. He had a fortune at his disposal. They could stay anywhere, hire teachers to travel with them. Eli would have the best of everything and an education gleaned from seeing the world rather than just reading about it. Surely Lucy Ann would see that positively.

How could she say no to a future so much more secure than what they'd grown up with? He'd been an idiot not to press his case with her last time. But when she'd left before, he'd thought to give her space. This time, he would be more persistent.

Besides, last time he'd been a jerk and tried to goad her into returning by making the news with moving on—a total jackass decision he never would have made if he'd thought for a second that Lucy Ann might be pregnant.

Now, he would be wiser. Smoother.

He would win her over. They'd been partners before. They could be partners again.

Lucy Ann peered out the window of the private jet as they left Africa behind.

Time for their real journey to begin. It had been challenging enough being together with his friends, celebrating the kind of happily ever after that wasn't in the cards for her. But now came the bigger challenge—finding a way to parent while Elliot competed in the Formula One circuit. A different country every week—Spain, Monaco, Canada, England. Parties and revelry and yes, decadence, too. She felt guilty for enjoying it all, but she couldn't deny that she'd missed the travel, experiencing different cultures without a concern for cost. Plus, his close-knit group of friends gave them a band of companionship no matter what corner of the earth he traveled to during racing season.

She sank deeper into the luxury of the leather sofa, the sleek chrome-and-white interior familiar from their countless trips in the past, with one tremendous exception. Their son was secured into his car seat beside her, sleeping in his new race car pj's with a lamb's wool blanket draped over his legs. She touched his impossibly soft cheek, stroking his chubby features with a soothing hand, cupping his head, the dusting of blond hair so like his father's.

Her eyes skated to Elliot standing in the open bulkhead, talking to the pilot. Her former best friend and boss grew hotter with each year that passed—not fair. That didn't stop her from taking in the sight of him in low-slung jeans and a black button-down shirt with the sleeves rolled up. Italian leather loafers. He looked every bit the world-famous race car driver and heartthrob.

How long would Elliot's resolution to build a family life for Eli last? Maybe that's what this trip was about. Proving to *him* it couldn't be done. She wouldn't keep his son from him, but she refused to expose her child to a chaotic life. Eli needed and deserved stability.

And what did she want?

She pressed a hand to her stomach, her belly full of butterflies that had nothing to do with a jolt of turbulence. Just the thought of kissing Elliot last night… She dug her fingers into the supple leather sofa to keep from reaching for him as he walked toward her.

"Would you like something to eat or drink?" he asked, pausing by the kitchenette. "Or something to read?"

She knew from prior trips that he kept a well-stocked library of the classics as well as the latest bestsellers loaded on ereaders for himself and fellow travelers. In school, he'd always won the class contest for most books read in a year. He told her once those stories offered him an escape from his day-to-day life.

"No, thank you. The brunch before we left was amazing."

True enough, although she hadn't actually eaten much. She'd been so caught up in replaying the night before. In watching his friends' happy marriages with their children and babies on the way until her heart ached from all she wanted for her son.

For herself, as well.

Elliot slid onto the sofa beside her, leaning over her to adjust the blanket covering Eli's legs. "Tell me about his routine."

She sat upright, not expecting that question at all. "You want to know about Eli's schedule? Why?"

"He's my son." His throat moved with a long swallow of emotion at the simple sentence. "I should know what he needs."

"He has a mom, and he even has a nanny now." The British nanny was currently in the sleeping quarters reading or napping or whatever nannies did when they realized mothers needed a breather from having them around all the time.

Elliot tapped Lucy Ann's chin until she looked at him again. "And he has a dad."

"Of course," she agreed, knowing it was best for Eli,

but unused to sharing him. "If you're asking for diaper duty, you're more than welcome to it."

Would he realize her halfhearted attempt at a joke was meant to ease this tenacious tension between them? They used to be so in tune with each other.

"Diaper duty? Um, I was thinking about feeding and naps, that kind of thing."

"He breastfeeds," she said bluntly.

His eyes fell to her chest. The stroke of his gaze made her body hum as tangibly as the airplane engines.

Elliot finally cleared his throat and said, "Well, that could be problematic for me. But I can bring him to you. I can burp him afterward. He still needs to be burped, right?"

"Unless you want to be covered in baby spit-up." She crossed her arms over her chest.

He pulled his eyes up to her face. "Does he bottle-feed, too? If so, I can help out that way."

Fine, he wanted to play this game, then she would meet him point for point. "You genuinely think you can wake up during the night and then race the next day?"

"If you can function on minimal sleep, then so can I. You need to accept that we're in this together now."

He sounded serious. But then other than his playboy ways, he was a good man. A good friend. A philanthropist who chose to stay anonymous with his donations. She knew about them only through her work as his assistant.

"That's why I agreed to come with you, for Eli and in honor of our friendship in the past."

"Good, good. I'm glad you haven't forgotten those years. That friendship is something we can build on. But I'm not going to deny the attraction, Lucy Ann." He slid his arm along the back of the sofa seat, stretching his legs out in front of him. "I can't. You've always been pretty, but you looked incredible last night. Motherhood suits you."

"Flattery?" She picked up his arm and moved it to his lap. "Like flowers and candy? An obvious arm along the back? Surely you've got better moves than that."

"Are you saying compliments are wasted on you?" He picked up a lock of her hair, teasing it between two fingers. "What if I'm telling the truth about how beautiful you are and how much I want to touch you?"

She rolled her eyes, even though she could swear electricity crackled up the strand of hair he held. "I've watched your moves on women for years, remember?"

"It's not a move." He released the lock and smoothed it into the rest before crossing his arms. "If I were planning a calculated seduction for you, I would have catered a dinner, with a violin."

She crinkled her nose. "A violin? Really?"

"No privacy. Right." His emerald eyes studied her, the wheels in his brain clearly churning. "Maybe I would kiss you on the cheek, distract you by nuzzling your ear while tucking concert tickets into your pocket."

"Concert tickets?" She lifted an eyebrow with interest. They'd gone to free concerts in the park when they were teenagers.

"We would fly out to a show in another country, France or Japan perhaps."

She shook her head. "You're going way overboard. Too obvious. Rein it in, be personal."

"Flowers…" He snapped his fingers. "No wait. A single flower, something different, like a sprig of jasmine because the scent reminds me of you."

That silenced her for a moment. "You know my perfume?"

He dipped his head toward her ever so slightly as if

catching a whiff of her fragrance even now. "I know you smell like home in all the good ways. And I have some very good memories of home. They all include you."

Damn him, he was getting to her. His words affected her but she refused to let him see that. She schooled her features, smiling slightly. "Your moves have improved."

"I'm only speaking the truth." His words rang with honesty, his eyes heated with attraction.

"I do appreciate that about you, how we used to be able to tell each other anything." Their friendship had given her more than support. He'd given her hope that they could leave their pasts behind in a cloud of dust. "If we can agree to be honest now, that will work best."

"And no more secrets."

She could swear a whisper of hurt smoked through his eyes.

Guilt stabbed through her all over again. She owed him and there was no escaping that. "I truly am sorry I held back about Eli. That was wrong of me. Can you forgive me?"

"I have to, don't I?"

"No." She swallowed hard. "You don't."

"If I want us to be at peace—" he reached out and took her hand, the calluses on his fingertips a sweet abrasion along her skin "—then yes, I do."

She wasn't sure how that honest answer settled within her because it implied he wasn't really okay with what she'd done. He was only moving past it out of necessity. The way he'd shrugged off all the wrongs his father had done because he had no choice.

Guilt hammered her harder with every heartbeat, and she didn't have a clue how to make this right with him. She had as little practice with forgiveness and restitution as he did.

So she simply said, "Peace is a very good thing."

"Peace doesn't have to be bland." His thumb stroked the inside of her wrist.

Her pulse kicked up under his gentle stroking. "I didn't say that."

"Your tone totally implied it. You all but said 'boring.'" His shoulder brushed hers as he settled in closer, seducing her with his words, his husky tones every bit as much as his touch. "A truce can give freedom for all sorts of things we never considered before."

"News flash, Elliot. The kissing part. We've considered that before."

"Nice." He clasped her wrist. "You're injecting some of your spunky nature into the peace. That's good. Exciting. As brilliantly shiny as your hair with those new streaks of honey added by the Carolina sun."

Ah, now she knew why he'd been playing with her hair. "Added by my hairdresser."

"Liar."

"How do you know?"

"Because I'm willing to bet you've been squirrelling away every penny you make. I can read you—most of the time." He skimmed his hand up her arm to stroke her hair back over her shoulder. "While I know that you want me, I can't gauge what you intend to do about that, because make no mistake, I want us to pursue that. I said before that motherhood agrees with you and I meant it. You drove me crazy last night in that evening gown."

He continued to stroke her arm, but she couldn't help but think if she moved even a little, his hand would brush her breast. Even the phantom notion of that touch had her tingling with need.

She worked to keep her voice dry—and to keep from grabbing him by the shirtfront and hauling him toward her. "You're taking charming to a new level. I'm impressed."

"Good. But are you seduced?"

"You're good, and I'm enticed," she said, figuring she might as well be honest. No use denying the obvious. "But Elliot, this isn't a fairy tale. Our future is not going to be some fairy tale."

He smiled slowly, his green eyes lighting with a promise as his hand slid away. "It can be."

Without another word, he leaned back and closed his eyes. Going to sleep? Her whole body was on fire from his touch, his words—his seduction. And he'd simply gone to sleep. She wanted to shout in frustration.

Worse yet, she wanted him to recline her back on the sofa and make love to her as thoroughly as he'd done eleven months ago.

Six

By nightfall in Spain, Elliot wondered how Lucy Ann would react to their lodgings for the night. The limousine wound deeper into the historic district, farther from the racetrack than they normally stayed. But he had new ideas for these next few weeks, based on what Lucy Ann had said on the plane.

After the fairy-tale discussion, inspiration had struck. He'd forced himself to make a tactical retreat so he could regroup. Best not to risk pushing her further and having her shut him down altogether before he could put his plan into action to persuade her to stay longer than the month.

Once she was tucked into the back room on the airplane to nurse Eli, Elliot had made a few calls and set the wheels in motion to change their accommodations along the way. A large bank account and a hefty dose of fame worked wonders for making things happen fast. He just hoped his new agenda would impress Lucy Ann. Winning her over was becoming more pressing by the second. Not just for Eli but because Elliot's life had been damn empty without her. He hadn't realized just how much until he had her back. The way her presence made everything around him more vibrant. Hell, even her organized nature, which he used to tease her about. She brought a focus, a grounding and a beauty to his world that he didn't want to lose again.

Failure was not an option.

He'd made himself a checklist, just like he kept for his work. People thought he was impulsive, reckless even, but there was a science to his job. Mathematics. Calculations. He studied all the details and contingencies until they became so deeply ingrained they were instinct.

Still, he refused to become complacent. He reviewed that checklist before every race as if he were a rookie driver. Now he needed to apply the same principles to winning back Lucy Ann's friendship…and more.

Their new "hotel" took shape on the top of the hill, the Spanish sunset adding the perfect dusky aura to their new accommodations.

In the seat across from him, Lucy Ann sat up straighter, looking from the window to him with confusion stamped on her lovely face.

"This isn't where you usually stay. This is…a castle."

"Exactly."

The restored medieval castle provided safety and space, privacy and romance. He could give her the fairy tale while making sure Lucy Ann and their son were protected. He could—and would—provide all the things a real partner and father provided. He would be everything his father wasn't.

"Change of plans for our stay."

"Because…?"

"We need more space and less chance of interruptions." He couldn't wait to have her all to himself. Damn, he'd missed her.

"But pandering to the paparazzi plays an important role in your PR." She hugged the diaper bag closer to her chest; the baby's bag, her camera and her computer had been the only things she'd insisted on bringing with her from home.

"Pandering?" He forced himself to focus on her words rather than the sound of her voice. Her lyrical Southern drawl was like honey along his starved senses. "That's not a word I'm particularly comfortable with. Playing along with them, perhaps. Regardless, they don't own me, and I absolutely will not allow them to have access to you and our son on anything other than our own terms."

"Wow, okay." Her eyes went wide before she grinned wryly. "But did you have to rent a castle?"

He wondered if he'd screwed up by going overboard, but her smile reassured him he'd struck gold by surprising her.

"It's a castle converted to a hotel, although yes, it's more secure and roomier." Safer, but also with romantic overtones he hoped would score points. "I thought in each place we stay, we could explore a different option for traveling with a child."

"This is…an interesting option," she conceded as the limousine cruised along the sweeping driveway leading up to the towering stone castle. Ivy scrolled up toward the turrets, the walls beneath baked brown with time. Only a few more minutes and the chauffeur would open the door.

Elliot chose his words wisely to set the stage before they went inside. "Remember how when we were kids, we hid in the woods and tossed blankets over branches? I called them forts, but you called them castles. I was cool with that as long as I got to be a knight rather than some pansy prince."

They'd climbed into those castle forts where he'd read for hours while she colored or drew pictures.

"Pansy prince?" She chuckled, tapping his chest. "You *are* anti-fairy-tale. What happened to the kid who used to lose himself in storybooks?"

He captured her finger and held on for a second before linking hands. "There are knights in fairy tales. And there are definitely castles."

"Is that what this is about?" She left her hand in his. "Showing me a fairy tale?"

"Think about coming here in the future with Eli." He stared at his son's sleeping face and images filled his head of their child walking, playing, a toddler with his hair and Lucy Ann's freckles. "Our son can pretend to be a knight or a prince, whatever he chooses, in a real castle. How freaking cool is that?"

"Very cool." A smile teased her kissable pink lips. "But this place is a long way from our tattered quilt forts in the woods."

His own smile faded. "Different from our childhood is a very good thing."

Her whole body swayed toward him, and she cupped his face. "Elliot, it's good that our child won't suffer the way we did, but what your father did to you…that had nothing to do with money."

Lucy Ann's sympathy, the pain for him that shone in her eyes, rocked the ground under him. He needed to regain control. He'd left that part of his life behind and he had no desire to revisit it even in his thoughts. So he deflected as he always did, keeping things light.

"I like it when you get prissy." He winked. "That's really sexy."

"Elliot, this isn't the time to joke around. We have some very serious decisions to make this month."

"I'm completely serious. Cross my heart." He pressed their clasped hands against his chest. "It makes me want to ruffle your feathers."

"Stop. It." She tugged free. "We're talking about Eli. Not us."

"That's why we're at a castle, for Eli," he insisted as the limousine stopped in front of the sprawling fortress. "Einstein said, 'The true sign of intelligence is not knowledge but imagination.' That's what we can offer our son with this unique lifestyle. The opportunity to explore his imagination around the world, to see those things that we only read about. You don't have to answer. Just think on it while we're here."

With the baby nursing, Lucy Ann curled up in her massive bed. She took comfort in the routine of feeding her child, the sweet softness of his precious cheek against her breast. With her life turning upside down so fast, she needed something familiar to hold on to.

The medieval decor wrapped her in a timeless fantasy she wasn't quite sure how to deal with. The castle had tapestries on the wall and sconces with bulbs that flickered like flames. Her four-poster bed had heavy drapes around it, the wooden pillars as thick as any warrior's chest. An arm's reach away waited a bassinet, a shiny reproduction of an antique wooden cradle for Eli.

Her eyes gravitated toward the tapestry across the room telling a love story about a knight romancing a maiden by a river. Elliot had chosen well. She couldn't help but be charmed by this place. Even her supper was served authentically in a trencher, with water in a goblet.

A plush, woven rug on the stone floor, along with

the low snap of the fire in the hearth, kept out the chilly spring night. The sound system piped madrigal music as if the group played in a courtyard below.

Through the slightly opened door, she saw the sitting room where Elliot was parked at a desk, his computer in front of him. Reviewing stats on his competitors? Or a million other details related to the racing season? She missed being a part of all that, but he had a new assistant, a guy who did his job so seamlessly he blended into the background.

And speaking of work, she had some of her own to complete. Once Eli finished nursing and went to bed there would be nothing for her to do but complete the two projects she hadn't been able to put on hold.

She'd expected Elliot to try to make a move on her once they got inside, but the suite had three bedrooms off the living area. One for her and one for him. The British nanny he'd hired had settled into the third, turning in after Lucy Ann made it clear Eli would stay with his mother tonight. While Mrs. Clayworth kept a professional face in place, the furrows along her forehead made it clear that she wondered at the lack of work on this job.

This whole setup delivered everything Elliot had promised, a unique luxury she could see her son enjoying someday. Any family would relish these fairy-tale accommodations. It was beyond tempting.

Elliot was beyond tempting.

Lucy Ann tore her eyes from her lifetime friend and onetime lover. This month was going to be a lot more difficult than she'd anticipated.

Desperate for some grounding in reality before she weakened, she reached for her phone, for the present, and called her aunt Carla.

* * *

She'd made it through the night, even if the covers on the bed behind her were a rumpled mess from her restless tossing and turning.

Lucy Ann sat at the desk at the tower window with her laptop, grateful to Carla for the bolstering. Too bad she couldn't come join them on this trip, but Carla was emphatic. She loved her home and her life. She was staying where she belonged.

Who could blame her? A sense of belonging was a rare gift Lucy Ann hadn't quite figured out how to capture yet. In South Carolina, she'd dreamed of getting out, and here she craved the familiarity of home.

Which made her feel like a total ingrate.

She was living the easy life, one any new mother would embrace. How ironic that at home she'd spent every day exhausted, feeling like Eli's naps were always a few minutes too short to accomplish what she needed to do. And now, she spent most of her time waiting for him to wake up.

She closed her laptop, caught up on work, dressed for the day, waiting to leave for Elliot's race. She still couldn't wrap her brain around how different this trip was from ones she'd shared with Elliot in the past. Staring out the window in their tower suite, she watched the sun cresting higher over the manicured grounds.

Last night, she'd actually slept in a castle. The restored structure was the epitome of luxury and history all rolled into one. She'd even pulled out her camera and snapped some photos to use for a client's web design. Her fingers already itched to get to the computer and play with the images, but Elliot was due back soon.

He'd gone to the track for prelim work, his race scheduled for tomorrow. Normally he arrived even earlier before an event, but the wedding had muddled his schedule. God, she hoped his concentration was rock solid. The thought of him in a wreck because she'd damaged his focus sent her stomach roiling. Why hadn't she considered this before? She should have told him about Eli earlier for so many reasons.

She was familiar with everything about his work world. She'd been his personal assistant for over a decade, in charge of every detail of his career, his life. And even in their time apart she'd kept up with him and the racing world online. Formula One racing in Spain alternated locations every year, Barcelona to Valencia and back again. She knew his preferences for routes like Valencia, with the street track bordering the harbor. She was used to being busy, in charge—not sitting around a castle twiddling her thumbs, eating fruit and cheese from medieval pottery.

Being waited on by staff, nannies and chauffeurs, being at loose ends, felt alien, to say the least. But she'd agreed to give him a chance this month. She would stick to her word.

As if conjured from her thoughts, Elliot appeared in the arched doorway between the living area and her bedroom. Jeans hugged his lean hips, his turtleneck shirt hugging a well-defined chest. Her mouth watered as she considered what he would do if she walked across the room, leaned against his chest to kiss him, tucked her hands in his back pockets and savored the chemistry simmering between them.

She swallowed hard. "Are you here for lunch?"

"I'm here for you and Eli." He held out a cashmere sweater of his. "In case you get chilly on our outing."

"Outing?" she asked to avoid taking the sweater until she could figure out what to do next.

She'd worn pieces of Elliot's clothes countless times over the years without a second thought, but the notion of wrapping his sweater around her now felt so intimate that desire pooled between her legs. However, to reject the sweater would make an issue of it, revealing feelings that made her too vulnerable, a passion she still didn't know how to control yet.

Gingerly, she took the sweater from him, the cashmere still warm from his touch. "Where are we going?"

He smiled mysteriously. "It's another surprise for you and Eli."

"Can't I even have a hint?" She hugged the sweater close, finding she was enjoying his game more than she should.

"We're going to play." He scooped his son up from the cradle in sure hands. "Right, Eli, buddy? We're going to take good care of your mama today. If she agrees to come with me, of course."

The sight of their son cradled in Elliot's broad hands brought her heart into her throat. She'd imagined moments like this, dreamed of how she would introduce him to their child. Day after day, her plan had altered as she delayed yet again.

And why? Truly, why? She still wasn't sure she understood why she'd made all the decisions she'd made these past months. She needed to use her time wisely to figure out the best way to navigate their future.

She tugged on the sweater. "Who am I to argue with such a tempting offer? Let's go play."

They left the suite and traveled down the sweeping stone stairway without a word, passing other guests as well as the staff dressed in period garb. The massive front doors even creaked as they swept open to reveal the waiting limousine.

Stepping out into the sunshine, she took in the incredible lawns. The modern-day buzz of cars and airplanes mixed with the historical landscaping that followed details down to the drawbridge over a moat.

The chauffeur opened the limo door for her. Lucy Ann slid inside, then extended her arms for her child. Elliot passed over Eli as easily as if they were a regular family.

Lucy Ann hugged her son close for a second, breathing in the baby-powder-fresh scent of him before securing Eli into his car seat. "Shouldn't you be preparing for race day?"

Getting his head together. Resting. Focusing.

"I know what I need to do," he answered as if reading her mind. He sat across from her, his long legs extended, his eyes holding hers. "That doesn't mean we can't have time together today."

"I don't want to be the cause of your exhaustion or lack of focus because you felt the need to entertain me." She'd been so hurt and angry for a year, she'd lost sight of other feelings. Race day was exciting and terrifying at the same time. "I've been a part of your world for too long to let you be reckless."

"Trust me. I have more reason than ever to be careful. You and Eli are my complete and total focus now."

There was no mistaking the certainty and resolve in his voice. Her fears eased somewhat, which made room for her questions about the day to come back to the fore. "At least tell me something about your plans for today. Starting with, where are we going?"

He leaned to open the minifridge and pulled out two water bottles. "Unless you object, we are going to the San Miguel de los Reyes Monastery."

She sat up straighter, surprised, intrigued. She took

the water bottle from him. "I'm not sure I understand your plan...."

"The monastery has been converted into a library. We've never had a chance to visit before on other trips." He twisted open his spring water. "In fact, as I look back, we both worked nonstop, all the time. As I reevaluate, I'm realizing now a little sightseeing won't set us behind."

"That's certainly a one-eighty from the past. You've always been a very driven man—no pun intended." She smiled at her halfhearted joke, feeling more than a little off balance by this change in Elliot. "I'll just say thank-you. This is a very thoughtful idea. Although I'm curious. What made you decide on this particular outing when there are so many more obvious tourist sites we haven't visited?"

"You sparked the idea when we were on the airplane, actually." He rolled the bottle between his palms. "You mentioned not believing in fairy tales anymore. That is why I chose the castle. Fairy tales are important for any kid...and I think we've both lost sight of that."

"We're adults." With adult wants and needs. Like the need to peel off his forest-green turtleneck and faded jeans.

"Even as kids, we were winging it with those fairy tales. Then we both grew jaded so young." He shrugged muscular shoulders. "So it's time for us to learn more about fairy tales so we can be good parents. Speaking of which, is Eli buckled in?"

"Of course."

"Good." He tapped on the window for the chauffeur to go. "Just in case you were wondering, I'm calling this the *Beauty and the Beast* plan."

They were honest-to-goodness going to a library. She sagged back, stunned and charmed all at once.

God, she thought she'd seen all his moves over the years—moves he'd used on other women. He'd always been more…boisterous. More obvious.

This was different. Subtle. Damn good.

"So I'm to be Belle to your beast."

"A Southern belle, yes, and you've called me a beast in the past. Besides, you know how much I enjoy books and history. I thought you might find some interesting photo opportunities along the way."

"You really are okay with a pedestrian stroll through a library." The Elliot she'd known all her life had always been on the go, scaling the tallest tree, racing down the steepest hill, looking for the edgiest challenge. But he did enjoy unwinding with a good book, too. She forgot about that side of him sometimes.

"I'm not a Cro-Magnon…even though I'm playing the beast. I do read. I even use a napkin at dinnertime." He waggled his eyebrows at her, his old playful nature more evident.

She wished she could have just slugged him on the shoulder as if they were thirteen again. Things had been simpler then on some levels—and yet not easy at all on others.

"You're right. I shouldn't have been surprised."

"Let's stop making assumptions about each other from now on about a lot of things. We've been friends for years, but even friends change, grow, even a man like me can mature when he's ready. Thanks to you and Eli, I'm ready now."

She wanted to believe him, to believe in him. She wanted to shake off a past where the people she cared about always let her down. Hundreds of times over the past eleven months she'd guessed at what his reaction would be if she told him about the baby.

She'd known he would come through for her. The part that kept haunting her, that kept her from trying… She could never figure out how she would know if he'd come through out of duty or something more.

The thought that she could yearn for more between the two of them scared her even now. She was much better off taking this one day at a time.

"Okay, Elliot—" she spread her arms wide "—I'm all-in…for our day at the monastery."

As she settled in for her date, she couldn't help wondering which was tougher: resisting the fairy-tale man who seemed content to ignore the past year or facing the reality of her lifelong friend who had every reason to be truly angry with her.

Regardless, at some point the past would catch up with both of them. They could only play games for so long before they had to deal with their shared parenthood.

Wearing a baseball cap with the brim tugged low, Elliot soaked in the sight of Lucy Ann's appreciation of the frescoes and ancient tomes as she filled a memory card with photos of the monastery turned library. He should have thought to do this for her sooner. The place was relatively deserted, a large facility with plenty of places for tourists to spread out. A school tour had passed earlier, but the echoes of giggles had faded thirty minutes ago. No one recognized him, and the bodyguards hung back unobtrusively. For all intents and purposes, he and Lucy Ann were just a regular family on vacation.

Why had he never thought to bring her to places like this before? He'd convinced himself he was taking care of her by offering her a job and a life following him around the world. But somehow he'd missed out on giving her so much more. He'd let her down when they were teenagers and he'd gotten arrested, leaving her alone to deal with her family. Now to find out he'd been selfish as an adult too. That didn't sit well with him.

So he had more to fix. He and Lucy Ann were bound by their child for life, but he didn't intend to take that part for granted. He would work his tail off to be more for her this time.

He set the brake on the stroller by a looming marble angel. "You're quiet. Anything I can get for you?"

She glanced away from her camera, looking back over her shoulder at him. "Everything's perfect. Thank you. I'm enjoying the peace. And the frescoes as well as the ornately bound books. This was a wonderful idea for how to spend the afternoon."

Yet all day long she'd kept that camera between them, snapping photos. For work? For pleasure?

Or to keep from looking at him?

Tired of the awkward silence, he pushed on, "If you're having fun, then why aren't you smiling?"

She lowered the camera slowly, pivoting to face him. Her eyes were wary. "I'm not sure what you mean."

"Lucy Ann, it's me here. Elliot. Can we pretend it's fifteen years ago and just be honest with each other?"

She nibbled her bottom lip for a moment before blurting out, "I appreciate what you're doing, that you're trying, but I keep waiting for the explosion."

He scratched over his closely shorn hair, which brought memories of sprinting away from a burning car. "I thought we cleared that up in the limo. I'm not going to wreck tomorrow."

"And I'm not talking about that now." She tucked the camera away slowly, pausing as an older couple meandered past looking at a brochure map of the museum. Once they cleared the small chapel area, she turned back to him and said softly, "I'm talking about an explosion of anger. You have to be mad at me for not telling you about Eli sooner. I accept that it was wrong of me not to try harder. I just keep wondering when the argument will happen."

God, was she really expecting him to go ballistic on her? He would never, never be like his father. He used his racing as an outlet for those aggressive feelings. He did what he needed to do to stay in control. Always.

Maybe he wasn't as focused as he claimed to be, because if he'd been thinking straight he would have realized that Lucy Ann would misunderstand. She'd spent her life on shaky ground growing up, her mother hooking up with a different boyfriend or husband every week. Beyond that, she'd always stepped in for others, a quiet warrior in her own right.

"You always did take the blame for things."

"What does that have to do with today?"

He gestured for her to sit on a pew, then joined her. "When we were kids, you took the blame for things I did—like breaking the aquarium and letting the snake loose in the school."

She smiled nostalgically. "And cutting off Sharilynn's braid. Not a nice thing to do at all, by the way."

"She was mean to you. She deserved it." He and Lucy Ann had been each other's champions in those days. "But you shouldn't have told the teacher you did it. You ended up cleaning the erasers for a week."

"I enjoyed staying after school. And my mom didn't do anything except laugh, then make me write an apology and do some extra chores." She looked down at her hands twisted in her lap. "Your father wouldn't have laughed if the school called him."

"You're right there." He scooped up her hand and held

on. It was getting easier and easier for them to be together again. As much as he hated revisiting the past, if it worked to bring her back into his life, he would walk over hot coals in hell for her. "You protected me every bit as much as I tried to protect you."

"But your risk was so much higher...with your dad." She squeezed his hand. "You did the knightly thing. That meant a lot to a scrawny girl no one noticed except to make fun of her clothes or her mom."

He looked up at Lucy Ann quickly. Somehow he'd forgotten that part of her past. He always saw her as quietly feisty. "What elementary school boy cares about someone's clothes?"

"True enough, I guess." She studied him through the sweep of long eyelashes. "I never quite understood why you decided we would be friends—before we started taking the blame for each other's transgressions."

Why? He thought back to that time, to the day he saw her sitting at the computer station, her legs swinging, too short to reach the ground. The rest of the class was running around their desks while the teacher stepped out to speak with a parent. "You were peaceful. I wasn't. We balanced each other out. We can have that again."

"You're pushing." She tugged her hand.

He held firm. "Less than a minute ago, you told me I have the right to be mad at you."

"And I have the right to apologize and walk away."

Her quick retort surprised him. The Lucy Ann of the past would have been passive rather than confrontational. Like leaving for a year and having his baby. "Yeah, you're good at that, avoiding."

"There." She looked up quickly. "Tell me off. Be angry. Do anything other than smile and pretend everything's okay between us while we tour around the world like some dream couple."

Her fire bemused him and mesmerized him. "You are the most confusing woman I have ever met."

"Good." She stood up quickly, tugging her camera bag back onto her shoulder. "Women have always fallen into your arms far too easily. Time to finish the tour."

Seven

Lucy Ann swaddled her son in a fluffy towel after his bath while the nanny, Mrs. Clayworth, placed a fresh diaper and sleeper on the changing table. After the full day touring, then dinner with the nanny so Lucy Ann could get to know her better, she felt more comfortable with the woman.

Elliot's thoughtfulness and care for their son's future touched her. He'd charmed Mrs. Clayworth, yet asked perceptive questions. The woman appeared soft and like someone out of a Disney movie, but over the hours it became clear she was more than a stereotype. More than a résumé as a pediatric nurse. She was an avid musician and a hiker who enjoyed the world travel that came with her job. She spent her days off trekking through different local sites or attending concerts.

Lucy Ann liked the woman more and more with every

minute that passed. "Mrs. Clayworth, so you really were a nanny for royalty? That had to have been exciting."

Her eyes twinkled as she held out her arms for Eli. "You have seen my list of references. But that's just about the parents." She tucked Eli against her shoulder with expert hands, patting his back. "A baby doesn't care anything about lineage or credentials. Only that he or she is dry, fed, cuddled and loved."

"I can see clearly enough that you have a gift with babies."

The nanny's patience had been admirable when, just after supper, Eli cried himself purple over a bout of gas.

"I had two of my own. The child care career started once they left for the university. I used to be a pediatric nurse and while the money was good, it wasn't enough. I had bills to pay because of my loser ex-husband, and thanks to my daughter's connections with a blue-blooded roommate, I lucked into a career I thoroughly enjoy."

Having lived the past months as a single mom, Lucy Ann sympathized. Except she had always had the safety net of calling Elliot. She'd had her aunt's help, as well. What if she'd had nowhere to go and no one's help? The thought made her stomach knot with apprehension. That didn't mean she would stay with Elliot just because of her bills—but she certainly needed to make more concrete plans.

"I want the best for my son, too."

"Well, as much as I like my job, you have to know the best can't always be bought with money."

So very true. Lucy Ann took Eli back to dress him in his teddy bear sleeper. "You remind me of my aunt."

"I hope that's a compliment." She tucked the towel into the laundry chute.

"It is. Aunt Carla is my favorite relative." Not that

there was a lot of stiff competition. She traced the appliquéd teddy bear on the pj's and thought of her aunt's closet full of themed clothes. "She always wears these chipper seasonal T-shirts and sweatshirts. She has a thick Southern accent and deep-fries everything, including pickles. I know on the outside it sounds like the two of you are nothing alike, but on the inside, there's a calming spirit about you both."

"Then I will most certainly take that as a compliment, love." She walked to the pitcher on the desk by the window and poured a glass of water. "I respect that you're taking your time to get to know me and to see how I handle your son. Not all parents are as careful with their wee ones."

Mrs. Clayworth placed the glass beside the ornately carved rocker thoughtfully, even though Lucy Ann hadn't mentioned how thirsty she got when she nursed Eli. Money couldn't buy happiness, but having extra hands sure made life easier. She snapped Eli's sleeper up to his neck.

"I do trust Elliot's judgment. I've known him all my life. We've relied on each other for so much." There had been a time when she thought there was nothing he could do that would drive a wedge between them. "Except now there's this new dynamic to adjust to with Eli. But then you probably see that all the time."

Lucy Ann scooped up her son and settled into the wooden rocker, hoping she wasn't the only new mother to have conflicted feelings about her role. As much as she loved nursing her baby, she couldn't deny the occasional twinge of sadness that the same body Elliot once touched with passion had been relegated to a far more utilitarian purpose.

"You're a new mum." Mrs. Clayworth passed a burp cloth. "That's a huge and blessed change."

"My own mother wasn't much of a role model." She adjusted her shirt, and Eli hungrily latched on.

"And this favorite aunt of yours?" The nanny adjusted the bedding in the cradle, draping a fresh blanket over the end, before taking on the many other countless details in wrapping up the day.

"She helped as much as she could, but my mother resented the connection sometimes." Especially when her mom was between boyfriends and lonely. Then suddenly it wasn't so convenient to have Lucy Ann hang out with Aunt Carla. "I've been reading everything I can find on parenting. I even took some classes at the hospital, but there are too many things to cover in books or courses."

"Amen, dear."

Having this woman to lean on was…incredible, to say the least. Elliot was clearly working the fairy tale–like life from all angles.

She would be pridefully foolish to ignore the resources this woman brought to the table. Isolating herself for the past eleven months had been a mistake. Lucy Ann needed to correct that tendency and find balance. She needed to learn to accept help and let others into her life. Starting now seemed like a good idea.

She couldn't deny that all this "playing house" with Elliot was beginning to chip away at her reservations and her resolve to keep her distance. Elliot had said they needed to use this time to figure out how to parent Eli. She knew now they also needed to use this time to learn how to be in the same room with each other without melting into a pool of hormones. Time to quit running from the attraction and face it. Deal with it.

"And that's where your experience comes in. I would

be foolish not to learn from you." Lucy Ann paused, patting Eli's pedaling feet. "Why do you look so surprised?"

"Mothers seek help from me, not advice. You are a unique one."

"Would you mind staying for a while so we can talk?"

"Of course. I don't mind at all."

Lucy Ann gestured to the wingback chair on the other side of the fireplace. "I'd like to ask you a few questions."

"About babies?" she asked, sitting.

"Nope, I'd like to ask your advice on men."

The winner's trophy always felt so good in his hands, but today…the victory felt hollow in comparison with what he really wanted. More time with Lucy Ann.

Elliot held the trophy high with one hand, his helmet tucked under his other arm.

His *Beauty and the Beast* plan had gone well. They'd spent a low-key day together. Her pensive expression gave him hope he was on the right path. If she was ready to check out and return to Columbia, there would have been decisiveness on her face. But he was making headway with her. He could see that. He just needed to keep pushing forward with his plans, steady on. And try like hell to ignore the urge to kiss her every second they were together.

A wiry reporter pushed a microphone forward through the throng of fans and press all shouting congratulations. "Mr. Starc, tell us about the new lady in your life."

"Is it true she was your former assistant?"

"Where has she been this year?"

"Did she quit or was she fired?"

"Lovers' spat?"

"Which designer deserves credit for her makeover?"

Makeover? What the hell were they talking about?

To him, she was Lucy Ann—always pretty and special. And even though she had come out of her shell some in the past year, that didn't change the core essence of her, the woman he'd always known and admired.

Sure, her new curves added a bombshell quality. And the clothes his new assistant had ordered were flashier. None of that mattered to him. He'd wanted her before. He wanted her still.

The wiry reporter shoved the mic closer. "Are you sure the baby is yours?"

That question pulled him up short in anger. "I understand that the press thinks the personal life of anyone with a little fame is fair game. But when it comes to my family, I will not tolerate slanderous statements. If you want access to me, you will respect my son and his mother. And now it's time for me to celebrate with my family. Interviews are over."

He heard his assistant hiss in protest over the way he'd handled the question. The paparazzi expected to be fed, not spanked.

Shouldering through the crowd, Elliot kept his eyes locked on Lucy Ann in his private box, watching. Had she heard the questions through the speaker box? He hoped not. He didn't want anything to mar the evening he had planned. She'd actually consented to let the nanny watch Eli. Elliot would have her all to himself.

He kept walking, pushing through the throng.

"Congratulations, Starc," another reporter persisted. "How are you planning to celebrate?"

"How long do you expect your winning streak to run?"

"Is the woman and your kid the reason your engagement broke off?"

He continued to "no comment" his way all the way up the steps, into a secure hallway and to the private viewing box in the grandstand where Lucy Ann waited with a couple of honored guests, local royalty and politicians he only just managed to acknowledge with a quick greeting and thanks for attending. His entire focus locked on Lucy Ann.

"You won," she squealed, her smile enveloping him every bit as much as if she'd hugged him. Her red wraparound dress clung to her body, outlining every curve.

He would give up his trophy in a heartbeat to tug that tie with his teeth until her dress fell open.

"I think we should go." Before he embarrassed them both in front of reporters and esteemed guests.

He couldn't wait to get her alone. All he'd been able to think about during the race was getting back to Lucy Ann so he could continue his campaign. Move things closer to the point where he could kiss her as he wanted.

"Right." She leaned to pluck her purse from her seat. "The after-parties."

"Not tonight," he said softly for her ears only. "I have other plans."

"You have responsibilities to your career. I understand that."

He pulled her closer, whispering, "The press is particularly ravenous today. We need to go through the private elevator."

Her eyebrows pinched together. "I'm not so sure that's the best idea."

Damn it, was she going to bail on him before he even had a chance to get started? He would just have to figure out a way around it. "What do you propose we do instead?"

She tugged his arm, the warmth of her touch reaching through his race jacket as she pulled him closer to the observation window. "You taught me long ago that the best way to get rid of the hungry press is to feed them tidbits."

The tip of her tongue touched her top lip briefly before she arched up on her toes to kiss him. He stood stock-still in shock for a second before—hell, yeah—he was all-in. His arms banded around her waist. She leaned into him, looping her arms his neck. He could almost imagine the cameras clicking as fast as his heartbeat, picking up speed with every moment he had Lucy Ann in his arms.

He didn't know what had changed her mind, but he was damn glad.

Her fingers played along his hair and he remembered the feel of her combing her hands through it the night they'd made love. He'd kept his hair longer then, before the accident.

Lucy Ann sighed into his mouth as she began to pull back with a smile. "That should keep the media vultures happy for a good long while." She nipped his bottom lip playfully before asking, "Are you ready to celebrate your win?"

Lucy Ann stepped out onto the castle balcony, the night air cool, the stone flooring under her feet even cooler but not cold enough to send her back inside. She walked to the half wall along the balcony and let the breeze lift her hair and ruffle through her dress before turning back to the table.

Elliot was showering off the scent of gasoline. He'd already ordered supper. The meal waited for them, savory Spanish spices drifting along the air.

There was no question that Elliot had ordered the dinner spread personally. The table was laden with her favorites, right down to a flan for dessert. Elliot remembered. She'd spent so much time as his assistant making sure to remember every detail of his life, she hadn't considered he'd been paying just as close attention to her.

She trailed her fingers along the edge of her water goblet. The sounds below—other guests coming and going, laughing and talking—mingled with the sound system wafting more madrigal tunes into the night. She didn't even have the nursery monitor with her for the first time since... She couldn't remember when. Mrs. Clayworth had already planned to watch Eli tonight since Lucy Ann had expected to go to an after-race party with Elliot.

Then she'd kissed him.

Halfway through that impulsive gesture, Lucy Ann realized that holding back was no longer an option. Sleeping with Elliot again was all but inevitable. The longer she waited, the more intense the fallout would be. They needed to figure out this crazy attraction now, while their son was still young enough not to know if things didn't work out.

Her stomach knotted with nerves. But the attraction was only getting stronger the longer she denied herself. It was only a matter of time—

As if conjured from that wish, Elliot stood in the balcony doorway, so fresh from the shower his short hair still held a hint of water. He'd changed into simple black pants and a white shirt with the sleeves rolled up. With the night shadows and flickering sconce lights he had a timeless air—the Elliot from the past mixing with the man he'd become.

She wanted them both.

Lucy Ann swallowed nervously and searched for something to say to break the crackling silence between them. "I can't believe the press actually left us alone after the race."

"We did slip away out a back entrance."

"That never stopped them before."

"I ordered extra security." He stalked toward her slowly. "I don't want anyone hassling you or Eli. Our lives are private now. I'm done playing the paparazzi game. At least we know this place is secure."

"As private as the woods we hid in as kids."

How many times had he made her feel safe? As if those quilted walls could hold out the world while they huddled inside reading books and coloring pictures like regular kids.

He stopped in front of her, his hand brushing back a stray lock of her hair. "Why did you kiss me after the race?"

"To keep the press content." To let other women know he was taken? "Because I wanted to."

He tugged the lock of hair lightly. "I meant why did you bite me?"

A laugh rolled free and rode the breeze. "Oh, that. Can't have everything going your way."

"You're more confident these days." His emerald eyes glinted with curiosity—and promise.

"Motherhood has given me purpose." Even now, the need to settle her life for her child pushed her to move faster with Elliot, to figure out one way or another.

To take what she could from this time together in case everything imploded later.

"I like seeing you more comfortable in your skin." He sat on the balcony half wall with unerring balance and confidence. "Letting the rest of the world see the woman you are."

As much as she feared trusting a man—trusting Elliot—she couldn't help but wonder if he would continue trying to spin a fairy-tale future for them long beyond tonight and ignore the fact that she had been the unnoticed Cinderella all her life. She wanted a man who noticed the real her—not the fairy tale. Not the fantasy. If she was honest, she was still afraid his sexual interest had come too late to feel authentic.

"You make me sound like I was a mouse before—someone in need of a makeover, like that reporter said."

He cursed softly. "You heard their questions?"

"The TV system in the private box was piping in feed from the winner's circle." She rolled her eyes. "It was a backhanded compliment of sorts."

"Don't ever forget I saw the glow long before."

She couldn't help but ask, "If you saw my glow, then why did it take you all those years to make a move on me?"

"If I remember correctly, you made the first move."

She winced, some of her confidence fading at the thought that they could have still been just friends if she hadn't impulsively kissed him that night they'd been drunk, celebrating and nostalgic. "Thanks for reminding me how I made a fool of myself."

"You're misunderstanding." He linked fingers with her, tugging her closer. "I've always found you attractive, but you were off-limits. Something much more valuable than a lover—those are a dime a dozen. You were, you are, my friend."

She wanted to believe him. "A dime a dozen. Nice."

"Lucy Ann, stop." He squeezed her hand. "I don't want to fight with you. It doesn't have to be that way for us this time. Trust me. I have a plan."

She'd planned to seduce him, keep things light, and he was going serious on her. She tried to lighten the mood again. "What fairy tale does this night come from?"

"It could be reality."

"You disappoint me." She leaned closer until their

chests just brushed. Her breasts beaded in response. "Tonight, I want the fairy tale."

He blinked in surprise. "Okay, fair enough." He stood, tugging her to the middle of the balcony. "We're in the middle of Cinderella's ball."

Appropriate, given her thoughts earlier. "Well, the clock is definitely ticking since Eli still wakes up in the middle of the night."

"Then we should make the most of this evening." The moonlight cast a glow around them, adding to the magical air of the night. "Are you ready for supper?"

"Honestly?" She swayed in time with the classical music.

"I wouldn't have asked if I hadn't wanted to know. I don't think you know how much I want to make you happy."

She stepped closer, lifting their hands. "Then let's dance."

"I can accommodate." He brought her hand to rest on his shoulder, his palm sliding warmly along her waist. "I owe you for homecoming our sophomore year in high school. You had that pretty dress your aunt made. She showed me so I could make sure the flowers on your wrist corsage matched just the right shade of blue."

"I can't believe you still remember about a high school dance." Or that he remembered the color of her dress.

"I got arrested for car theft and stood you up." He rested his chin on top of her head. "That tends to make a night particularly memorable."

"I knew it was really your friends that night, not you."

He angled back to look in her warm chocolate-brown eyes. "Why didn't you tell me you thought that?"

"You would have argued with me about some technical detail." She teased, all the while too aware of the freshly showered scent of him. "You were even more stubborn in those days."

"I *did* steal that car." He tugged her closer and stole her breath so she couldn't speak. "And it wasn't a technicality. I wanted to take you to the dance in decent wheels. I figured the used car dealership would never know as long as I returned it in the morning."

"I wouldn't have cared what kind of car we had that night."

"I know. But I cared. And ended up spending the night in jail before the car dealer dismissed the charges—God only knows why." He laughed darkly. "That night in jail was the best night's sleep I'd gotten in a long time, being out of my father's house."

God, he was breaking her heart. Their childhoods were so damaged, had they even stood a chance at a healthy adult relationship with each other? She rested her head on his shoulder and let him talk, taking in the steady beat of his pulse to help steady her own.

"I felt like such a bastard for sleeping, for being grateful for a night's break from my dad when I'd let you down."

Let her down? He'd been her port in the storm, her safe harbor. "Elliot," she said softly, "it was a silly dance. I was more worried about how your father would react to your arrest."

"I wanted to give you everything," he said, ignoring her comment about his dad. "But I let you down time after time."

This conversation was straying so far from her plans for seduction, her plans to work out the sensual ache inside her. "This isn't the sort of thing Prince Charming says to Cinderella at the ball."

"My point is that I'm trying to give you everything

now, if you'll just let me." He nuzzled her hair. "Just tell me what you want."

Every cell in her body shouted for her to say she wanted him to peel off her dress and make love to her against the castle wall. Instead, she found herself whispering, "All I want is for Eli to be happy and to lead a normal life."

"You think this isn't normal." His feet matched steps with hers as the music flowed into their every move.

A castle? A monastery library? "Well, this isn't your average trip to a bookstore or corner library, that's for sure."

"There are playgrounds here as well as libraries. We just have to find them for Eli."

Lucy Ann felt a stab of guilt. Elliot was thinking of their son and she'd been thinking about sex. "You make it sound so simple."

"It can be."

If only she could buy into his notion of keeping things simple long-term. "Except I never contacted you about being pregnant."

"And I didn't come after you like I should have. I let my pride get stung, and hurt another woman in the process."

She hadn't considered the fact that Gianna had been wronged in this situation. "What happens in the future if you find someone else…or if I do?"

"You want monogamy?" he asked. "I can do that."

"You say that so quickly, but you're also the one spinning fairy tales and games." She looked up at him. "I'm asking honest questions now."

She wondered why she was pushing so hard for answers to questions that could send him running. Was she on a self-destructive path in spite of her plans to be with him? Then again, this level of honesty between them had been a long time coming.

His feet stopped. He cupped her face until their eyes met. "Believe this. You're the only woman I want. You're sure as hell more woman than I can handle, so if you will stay with me, then monogamy is a piece of cake."

"Are you proposing?"

"I'm proposing we stay together, sleep together, be friends, lovers, parents."

He wasn't proposing. This wasn't Cinderella's ball after all. They were making an arrangement of convenience—to enjoy sex and friendship.

She didn't believe in fairy tales, damn it. So she should take exactly what he offered. But she intended to make sure he understood that convenience did not mean she would simply follow his lead.

Eight

Lucy Ann stepped out of his arms, and a protest roared inside Elliot. Damn it, was she leaving? Rejecting him in spite of everything they'd just said to each other? He set his jaw and stuffed his hands into his pockets to keep from turning into an idiot, a fool begging her to stay.

Except she didn't move any farther away. She locked eyes with him, her pupils wide—from the dark or from desire? He sure as hell hoped for the latter. Her hand went to the tie of her silky wraparound dress and she tugged.

His jaw dropped. "Um, Lucy Ann? Are you about to, uh—?"

"Yes, Elliot, I am." She pulled open the dress, revealing red satin underwear and an enticing expanse of creamy freckled skin.

His brain went on stun. All he could do was stare—and appreciate. Her bra cupped full breasts so perfectly his hands ached to hold and test their weight, to caress her until she sighed in arousal.

She shrugged and the dress started to slide down, down—

Out here.

In the open.

He bolted forward, a last scrap of sense telling him to shield her gorgeous body. He clasped her shoulders and pulled her to him, stopping the dress from falling away. "Lucy Ann, we're on a balcony. Outside."

A purr rippled up her throat as she wriggled against his throbbing erection. "I know."

Her fragrance beckoned, along with access to silky skin. His mouth watered. That last bit of his sense was going to give up the fight any second.

"We need to go back into our suite."

"I know that, too. So take me inside. Your room or mine. You choose as long as we're together and naked very soon." She leaned into him, her breasts pressing against his chest. "Unless you've changed your mind."

The need to possess tensed all his muscles, the adrenaline rush stronger than coming into a final turn neck and neck.

"Hell, no, I haven't changed my mind. We'll go to my room because there are condoms in my nightstand. And before you ask, yes, I've been wanting and planning to take you to bed again every minute of our journey." He scooped her up into his arms and shouldered the doors open into their suite. The sitting area loomed quiet and empty. "Thank God Mrs. Claymore isn't up looking for a midnight snack."

Her hair trailing loose over his shoulder, Lucy Ann kissed his neck in a series of nibbles up to his ear. "You're supposed to be the race car driver who lives on the edge, and yet you're the one being careful. That's actually quite romantic."

"For you. Always careful for you." Except he hadn't been. He'd left her alone as a teen, gotten her pregnant and stayed away for nearly a year. He refused to let her down again in any way. She deserved better from him.

Lucy Ann deserved the best. Period.

She slid her hand behind his head and brought him closer for a kiss. He took her mouth as fully as he ached to take her body. With every step closer to his bedroom, his body throbbed harder and faster for her. The last few steps to the king-size bed felt like a mile. The massive headboard took up nearly the whole wall, the four posters carved like trees reaching up to the canopy. He was glad now he'd brought her here, a place they'd never been, a fantasy locale for a woman who deserved to be pampered, adored.

Treasured.

He set her on her feet carefully, handling her like spun glass. She tossed the dress aside in a silky flutter of red.

Nibbling her bottom lip and releasing it slowly, seductively, Lucy Ann kicked her high heels off with a flick of each foot. "One of us is *very* overdressed."

"You don't say."

"I do." She hooked her finger in the collar of his shirt and tugged down. Hard. Popping the buttons free in a burst that scattered them along the floor.

Ooooo-kay. So much for spun glass. His libido ramped into high gear. "You seem to be taking charge so nicely I thought you might help me take care of that."

He looked forward to losing more buttons in her deft hands.

"Hmm," she hummed, backing toward the bed until her knees bumped the wooden steps. "If I'm taking charge, then I want you to take off the rest of your clothes while I watch."

"I believe I can comply with that request." Shrugging off his destroyed shirt, he couldn't take his eyes from her as she settled onto the middle of the gold comforter, surrounded by tapestry pillows and a faux-fur throw. He toed off his loafers, his bare feet sinking into the thick Persian rug.

She reclined on the bed, pushing her heels into the mattress to scoot farther up until she could lean against the headboard. "You could have continued your underwear model days and made a mint, you know."

His hands stopped on his belt buckle. "You're killing the mood for me, Lucy Ann. I prefer to forget that brief chapter of my life."

"Briefs?" She giggled at her own pun. "You're right. You're definitely more of a boxers kind of guy now."

Fine, then. She seemed to want to keep this lighthearted, avoiding the heavier subjects they'd touched on while dancing. Now that he thought of it, they'd never gotten around to dinner, either. Which gave him an idea, one he'd be better off starting while he still had his clothes on.

"Stay there, just like that," he said. "I'll be right back."

Belt buckle clanking and loose, he sprinted out to the balcony. He picked up the platter of fruit and cheese and tucked the two plates of flan on top. Balancing the makeshift feast, he padded toward their room, careful not to wake the nanny or Eli.

Backing inside, he elbowed the door closed carefully. Turning, he breathed a sigh of relief to find Lucy Ann waiting. He hadn't really expected her to leave…except for a hint of an instant he'd thought about how quickly she'd run from what they shared last time.

She tipped her head to the side, her honey-streaked brown hair gliding along her shoulder like melted caramel. "You want to eat dinner now?"

He gave her his best bad boy grin. "If you're my plate, then yes, ma'am, I think this is a fine time for us to have supper."

"Okay then. Wouldn't want to mess up our clothes." She tugged off her bra and shimmied out of her panties, her lush curves bared and... Wow.

He almost dropped the damn tray.

Regaining his footing, he set the food on the edge of the bed without once taking his eyes off the long lines of her legs leading up to her caramel curls. He was definitely overdressed for what he had in mind.

He tugged off his slacks along with his boxers. His erection sprang free.

She smiled, her eyes roving over him in an appreciative sweep that made him throb harder. "Elliot?"

"Yes?" He clasped her foot in his hand, lifting it and kissing the inside of her ankle where a delicate chain with a fairy charm surprised him on such a practical woman. What else had he missed about Lucy Ann in the year they'd been apart?

"Do you know what would make this perfect?"

He kissed the inside of her calf. "Name it. I'll make it happen."

"More lights."

He looked up from her leg to her confident eyes reflecting the bedside lamp. "Lights?"

"It's been quite a while since I saw you naked, and last time was rather hurried and with bad lighting."

She was a total and complete turn-on. Everything about her.

"Can do," he said.

He placed her leg back on the bed and turned on the massive cast-iron chandelier full of replica candles that supplemented the glow of the bedside lamp. The rich colors of the bed and the heavy curtains swept back on either side somehow made Lucy Ann seem all the more pale and naked, her creamy flesh as tempting as anything he'd ever seen. The feel of her gaze on him heated his blood to molten lava, his whole body on fire for her.

But no way in hell would he let himself lose control. He took the time to reach for the bedside table, past his vintage copy of *Don Quixote*. Dipping into the drawer, he pulled out a condom. He dropped it on the bed before hitching a knee on the edge and joining her on the mattress. Taking his time, even as urgency thrummed through him, he explored every curve, enjoying the way goose bumps rose along her bared flesh.

She met him stroke for stroke, caress for caress, until he couldn't tell for certain who was mirroring whom. Their hands moved in tandem, their sighs syncing up, until they both breathed faster. He lost track of how long they just enjoyed each other, touching and seeking their fill. At some point, she rolled the condom over him, but he only half registered it since pleasure pulsed through him at her touch—and at the feel of her slick desire on his fingertips as he traced and teased between her legs.

Holding himself in check grew tougher by the second so he angled away, reaching for the platter of food on the corner of the bed.

He pushed the tray along the bed to put it in better reach. Then he plucked a strawberry and placed the plump fruit between his teeth. He slid over her, blanketing her. He throbbed between her legs, nudging, wanting. He leaned closer and pressed the strawberry to her mouth. Her lips parted to close over the plump fruit until they met in a kiss.

She bit into the strawberry and he thrust inside her. The fruity flavor burst over his taste buds at the same time sensation sparked through him. Pleasure. The feel of her clamping around him, holding him deep inside her as a "yes" hissed between her teeth. Her head pressed back into the bolster, her eyes sliding closed.

He moved as her jaw worked, chewing the strawberry. Her head arched back, her throat gliding with a slow swallow. Her breasts pushed upward, beading tight and hard.

Inviting.

Leaning on one elbow, he reached for another berry. He squeezed the fruit in his fist, dribbling the juice over her nipple. She gasped in response. He flicked his tongue over her, tasting her, rolling the beaded tip in his mouth until she moaned for more. The taste of ripe fruit and a hint of something more had him ready to come apart inside her already.

Thrusting over and over, he pushed aside the need to finish, hard and fast. Aching to make this last, for her and for him.

How could he possibly have stayed away from her for so long? For any time at all? How could he have thought for even a second he could be with anyone other than her? They were linked together. They always had been, for as far back as he could remember.

She was his, damn it.

The thought rocketed through him, followed closely by her sighs and moans of completion. Her hands flung out, twisting in the comforter, her teeth sinking deep into her bottom lip as she bit back the cry that might wake others.

Seeing the flush of pleasure wash over her skin

snapped the reins on his restraint and he came, the hot pulse jetting from him into her. Deeper, and yet somehow not deep enough as he already wanted her again.

As his arms gave way and he sank to rest fully on top of her, he could only think, damn straight, she was his.

But he hadn't been able to keep Lucy Ann before. How in the hell was he going to manage to keep the new, more confident woman in his arms?

A woman who didn't need anything from him.

Tingling with anticipation, Lucy Ann angled toward Elliot. "I need another bite now or I am absolutely going to pass out."

She gripped his wrist and guided his spoonful of flan toward her mouth as he chuckled softly. She closed her lips over it and savored the creamy caramel pudding. All of her senses were on hyperalert since she and Elliot had made love—twice. The scent of strawberries still clung to the sheets even though they'd showered together, making love in the large stone spa before coming back to bed.

Eventually, she would have to sleep or she would be a completely ineffective mother. But for now, she wasn't ready to let go of this fantasy night, making love with Elliot in a castle.

The luxurious sheets teased her already-sensitive skin, and she gave herself a moment to soak in the gorgeous surroundings. Beyond Elliot. The man was temptation enough, but he'd brought her to this decadent haven where she could stare up at carvings of a Dionysian revel on the bedposts or lose herself in the images of a colorful, wall-sized tapestry depicting a medieval feast. The figures were almost life-size, gathered around a table, an elegant lord and lady in the middle and an array of characters all around from lecherous knight to teasing serving maid. Even the scent of dried herbs and flowers that emanated from the linens immersed her in a fantasy world.

One she never wanted to end.

She scooped her spoon through the flan and offered a bite to her own sexy knight. "I have to say our dance tonight ended much better than our sophomore homecoming ever could have."

"You're right about that." He dipped his spoon into the dessert for her, picking up the rhythm of feeding each other. "Lady, you are rocking the hell out of that sheet."

He filled her whole fairy-tale fantasy well with his broad shoulders and muscular chest, the sheet wrapped around his waist. There was a timeless quality about this place that she embraced. It kept her from looking into the future. She intended to make the absolute most of this chance to be together.

They'd had sex before. They knew each other's bodies intimately. Yet there was a newness about this moment. She looked different now that she'd had a baby. Her body had changed. *She* had changed in other ways, as well. She had a growing confidence now, personally and professionally.

Lucy Ann searched Elliot's eyes…and found nothing but desire. His gaze stroked over her with appreciation and yes, even possession—stoking the heat still simmering inside her.

"I have to confess something." She angled forward to accept the next bite he fed her.

His face went somber in a flash even as he took the spoonful of flan she brought to his mouth. He swallowed, then said, "Tell me whatever you need to. I'm not going anywhere."

She carefully set her utensil onto the platter by the last strawberry, her body humming with the memory of the moment they'd shared the fruit, the moment he'd thrust inside her. The intensity of it all threatened to overwhelm her. She desperately needed to lighten the moment before they waded into deeper waters.

"I may like simplicity in many parts of my life—" she paused for effect, then stretched out like a lazy cat until the sheet slithered away from her breasts "—but I am totally addicted to expensive linens."

"God, Lucy Ann." He hauled her against his side, her nipples beading tighter at the feel of his bare skin. "You scared the hell out of me with talk of confessions."

"I'm serious as a heart attack here." She rested her cheek on his chest, the warmth of him seeping into her. "Every night when I crawled into bed—and trust me, cheap mattresses also suck a lot more than I remembered—those itchy sheets made me long for Egyptian cotton."

"Ahhh, now I understand." He tugged the comforter over them. "The fairy tale here is *The Princess and the Pea*. I will be very sure you always have the best mattresses and sheets that money can buy." He patted her butt.

"My prince," she said, joking to keep talk of the future light for now, all the while knowing that inevitably they would have to steer the conversation in another direction. "I don't think I ever said congratulations on your win today. I'm sorry you missed out on the parties tonight."

"I'm not sorry at all." He stroked back her hair, extending the length with his fingers and letting damp strands glide free. "This is exactly where I wanted to be. Celebrating with you, without clothes—best party ever."

"You do deserve to celebrate your success though. You've come a long way through sheer determination." She hooked a leg over his, enjoying the way they fit.

"Although I have to say, I've always been surprised you chose Formula One over the NASCAR route, given your early days racing the dirt-track circuit."

Why had she never thought to question him about this before? She'd simply followed, accepting. He'd always taken the lead in life and on the track.

He'd begun racing with adults at fourteen years old, then picked it up again when he graduated from the military high school in North Carolina. He was a poster boy for the reformative success of the school even without people knowing he periodically helped out Interpol.

Elliot rested his chin on her head, his breath warm on her scalp. "I guess I have a confession of my own to make. I wanted to go to college and major in English. But I had to make a living. I went back to racing after school because my credit was shot."

English? It made sense given the way he'd always kept a book close at hand, and yet she couldn't believe he'd never mentioned that dream. A whole new side of Elliot emerged, making her wonder what else he'd kept secret.

"Because of your arrest history?"

His chest rose and fell with a heavy sigh. "Because my father took out credit cards in my name."

Her eyes closing, she hugged an arm tighter around him. "I'm so sorry. Nothing should surprise me when it comes to that man, but it still sucks to hear. I'm just so glad you got away from him."

"You should be mad at me for leaving you," he repeated, his voice hoarse. "I let you down."

"I don't agree." She kissed his chest before continuing. "You did what you needed to. I missed you when they sent you to North Carolina, but I understood."

"All the same, you were still hurt by what I did. I could see that then. I can even feel it now. Tell me the truth."

So much for keeping things light. They would always have to cycle around to the weightier stuff eventually. "I understand why you needed a way out, believe me, I do. I just wish you'd spoken to me, given me an opportunity to weigh in and figure out how we could both leave. That place was bearable with you around. Without you…"

She squeezed her eyes closed, burying her face in his chest, absorbing the vibrant strength of him to ward off the chill seeping into her bones.

"I like to think if I could go back and change the past that I would. Except I did the same thing all over again. I let you go. You deserve to be put first in someone's life, someone who won't let you down."

Where was he going with this? Where did she *want* him to go?

After that, he stayed silent so long she thought for a moment he had drifted off midthought, then his hand started to rove along her spine slowly. Not in a seductive way; more of a touch of connection.

He kissed the top of her head, whispering into her hair still damp from their shared shower, "I didn't want to leave you back in high school. You have to know that." His voice went ragged with emotion. "But I didn't have anything to offer you if we left together. And I couldn't stay any longer. I just couldn't see another way out except to get arrested."

She struggled to sift through his words, to understand what he was trying to tell her. "You stole cars on purpose, hoping the cops would catch you?"

"That pretty much sums it up." His hand slid to rest on her hip, his voice strangely calm in contrast to his racing heart. "After that first night in jail, I started stealing cars on a regular basis. I didn't expect to be so good at it. I thought I would get caught much earlier."

"Why did you want to get caught?" she repeated, needing to understand, wondering how she didn't know this about him. She'd thought they told each other everything.

"I figured jail was safer than home," he said simply. "I didn't worry so much about myself with my dad, but I worried what he would do to the people around me."

"You mean me and your mother?"

He nodded against her head. "Remember when we went on that trip to the beach and my old rebuilt truck broke down?"

"You mean when the tires fell off." Only his incredible reflexes had kept them from crashing into a ditch. It had been a near miss.

"Right. When the first one fell off, I thought what crappy luck. Then the second one came off, too...."

Her stomach lurched at the memory. "We were lucky we didn't get T-boned in traffic. You had fast instincts, even then."

His arms twitched around her, holding her too tightly. "I found out that my father had taken out a life insurance policy on me."

She gasped, rising up on her elbows to look him in the eyes. His expression was completely devoid of emotion, but she could see the horror that must be on her face reflected in his eyes.

"Elliot, do you really believe your father tried to kill you?"

"I'm sure of it," he said with certainty, pushing up to sit, the covers rustling and twisting around their legs.

"You had to have been so scared."

Why hadn't he told her? Although the second she finished that thought, she already knew the answer. He didn't want to put her at risk. Debating the fact now, insisting he should have told the police, seemed moot after so long. Better to just listen and figure out why he was telling her this now.

"I didn't have the money to strike out on my own. I knew the odds of teens on the street." His head fell back against the carved headboard. "I figured the kids in juvie couldn't be as bad as my old man."

"Except you were sent to military reform school instead."

Thank heavens, too, since his life had been turned around because of his time in that school, thanks to his friends and the headmaster. The system did work for the best sometimes. Someone somewhere had seen the good deep inside of Elliot.

"I finally caught a lucky break." He cupped the back of her head, his fingers massaging her scalp. "I'm just so damn sorry I had to leave you behind. I see now I should have figured out another way."

"It all worked out—"

"Did it?" he asked, his eyes haunted. "Your mom's boyfriends… We've talked about so much over the years but we've never discussed that time when I was away."

Slowly, she realized what he was asking, and the thought that he'd worried about her, about that, for all these years… Her heart broke for him and the worries he'd had. She wondered if that's why he'd been so protective, giving her a job, keeping her with him—out of guilt?

"Elliot, the guys my mom saw were jerks, yes, and a few of them even tried to cop a feel, but none of them were violent. Some may have been perverts but they weren't rapists. So I was able to take care of myself by avoiding them. I escaped to Aunt Carla's until things settled down or until Mom and her latest guy broke up."

"You shouldn't have had to handle it yourself, to hide from your own home." Anger and guilt weighted his words and tightened his jaw until the tendons flexed along his neck. "Your mother should have been there for you. *I* should have been there."

She didn't want him to feel guilty or to feel sorry for her. Angling up, she cupped his face in her hands. "I don't want you to feel obligated to be my protector."

"I don't know what else I can be for you." His voice was ragged with emotion, his eyes haunted.

They could have been teenagers again, the two of them clinging to each other because there was so little else for them. So much pain. So much betrayal by parents who should have valued them and kept them safe. Her shared past with Elliot wrapped around her so tightly she felt bound to him in a way she couldn't find words to explain but felt compelled to express, even if only physically.

Soaking in the feel of bare flesh meeting flesh, Lucy Ann kissed Elliot, fully, deeply. She savored the taste of flan and strawberries and *him*. A far more intoxicating combination than any alcohol.

And he was all hers, for tonight.

Nine

Their tongues met and tangled as Lucy Ann angled her mouth over Elliot's. They fit so seamlessly together as she tried to give him some sort of comfort, even if only in the form of distraction. Sex didn't solve problems, but it sure made the delaying a hell of a lot more pleasurable. Her mind filled with the sensation of him, the scents of them together.

His hands banded around her waist, and he urged her over him. She swung her leg over his lap, straddling him. His arousal pressed between her legs, nudging against the tight bundle of nerves at her core.

She writhed against him, her body on fire for him. "I need… I want…"

"Tell me, Lucy Ann," he said between kisses and nips, tasting along her neck, "tell me what you want."

She didn't even know what would settle out their lives or how to untangle the mess they'd made of their world.

Not to mention their emotions. "Right now, I just need you inside me."

"That's not what I meant." He held her with those mesmerizing green eyes, familiar eyes that had been a part of her life for as long as she could remember.

"Shh, don't ruin this." She pressed two fingers to his lips. She didn't want to risk their conversation leading down a dangerous path as it had eleven months ago.

Even thinking about their fight chilled her. That argument had led to the most painful time in her life, the time without the best friend she'd ever had. They couldn't go that route again. They had Eli to consider.

And as for their own feelings?

She shied away from those thoughts, determined to live in the moment. She shifted to reach in the bedside table drawer for another condom. He plucked it from between her fingers and sheathed himself quickly, efficiently, before positioning her over him again. Slowly, carefully—blissfully—she lowered herself onto him, taking the length of him inside her until he touched just... the right...spot.

Yessss.

Her eyelids grew heavy but the way he searched her face compelled her to keep her eyes open, to stare back at him as she rolled her hips to meet his thrusts. Every stroke sent ripples of pleasure tingling through her as they synced up into a perfect rhythm. Her palms flattened against his chest, her fingers digging into the bunched muscles twitching under her touch. A purr of feminine satisfaction whispered free as she reveled in the fact that she made him feel every bit as out of control as he made her feel.

His hands dug into her hips then eased, caressing up her sides then forward to cup her breasts. She sighed at the gentle rasp of his callused fingers touching her so instinctively, his thumbs gliding over nipples until she feared she would come apart now. Too soon. She ached for this to last, to hang on to the blissful forgetfulness they could find in each other's arms. She flowed forward to cover him, moving slower, holding back.

Elliot's arms slid around her, and he drew her earlobe between his teeth. Just an earlobe. Yet her whole body tensed up with that final bit of sensation that sent her hurtling into fulfillment. Her nails dug into his shoulders, and she cried out as her release crested.

He rolled her over, and she pushed back, tumbling them again until the silver tray went crashing to the floor, the twang of pewter plates clanking. He kissed her hard, taking her cries of completion into his mouth. As orgasm gripped her again and again, his arms twitched around her, his body pulsing, his groans mingling with hers until she melted in the aftermath.

Panting, she lay beside him, her leg hitched over his hip, an arm draped over him. Her whole body was limp from exhaustion. She barely registered him pulling the comforter over her again.

Maybe they could make this friendship work, friendship combined with amazing sex. Being apart hadn't made either of them happy.

Could this be enough? Friendship and sex? Could they learn to trust each other again as they once had?

They had the rest of the month together to figure out the details. If only they could have sex until they couldn't think about the future.

His breath settled into an even pattern with a soft snore. What a time to realize she'd never slept with him before. She'd seen him nap plenty of times, falling asleep with a book on his chest, but never once had she stayed through the night with him.

For now, it was best she keep it that way. No matter how tempted she was to indulge herself, she wouldn't make the mistakes of her past again. Not with Eli to think about.

Careful not to wake her generous, sexy lover, she eased from the bed, tiptoeing around the scattered cutlery and dishes that looked a lot like the disjointed parts of her life. Beautiful pieces, but such a jumbled mess there was no way to put everything back together.

"Lucy Ann?" Elliot called in a groggy voice. He reached out for her. "Come back to bed."

She pulled on her red wraparound dress and tied it quickly before gathering her underwear. "I need to go to Eli. I'll see you in the morning."

Her bra and panties in her hand, she raced from his room and tried to convince herself she wasn't making an even bigger mess of her life by running like a coward.

"Welcome to Monte Carlo, Eli," Elliot said to his son, carrying the baby in the crook of his arm, walking the floor with his cranky child while everyone else slept. He'd heard Eli squawk and managed to scoop him up before Lucy Ann woke.

But then she was sprawled out on her bed, looking dead to the world after their trip to Monte Carlo—with a colicky kid.

The day had been so busy with travel, he hadn't had a chance to speak to Lucy Ann alone. But then she hadn't gone out of her way to make that possible, either. If he hadn't known better, he would have thought she was hiding from him.

Only there was no reason for her to do so. The sex

last night had been awesome. They hadn't argued. Hell, he didn't know what was wrong, but her silence today couldn't be missed.

Compounding matters, Eli had become progressively irritable as the day passed. By the time his private plane had landed in Monte Carlo, Elliot was ready to call a doctor. Lucy Ann and the nanny had both reassured him that Eli was simply suffering from gas and exhaustion over having his routine disrupted.

Of course that only proved Lucy Ann's point that a child shouldn't be living on the road, but damn it all, Elliot wasn't ready to admit defeat. Especially not after last night. He and Lucy Ann were so close to connecting again.

He'd hoped Monte Carlo would go a long way toward scoring points in his campaign. He owned a place here. A home with friends who lived in the area. Sure it was a condominium and his friend owned a casino. But his friend was a dad already. And the flat was spacious, with a large garden terrace. He would have to add some kind of safety feature to the railing before Eli became mobile. He scanned the bachelor pad with new eyes and he saw a million details in a different light. Rather than fat leather sofas and heavy wooden antiques, he saw sharp edges and climbing hazards.

"What do you think, Eli?" he asked his son, staring down into the tiny features all scrunched up and angry. "Are you feeling any better? I'm thinking it may be time for you to eat, but I hate to wake your mama. What do you say I get you one of those bottles with expressed milk?"

Eli blinked back up at him with wide eyes, his fists and feet pumping.

He'd always thought babies all looked the same, like

tiny old men. Except now he knew he could pick out Eli from dozens of other babies in a heartbeat.

How strange to see parts of himself and Lucy Ann mixed together in that tiny face. Yet the longer he looked, the more that mixture became just Eli. The kid had only been in his life for a week. Yet now there didn't seem to be a pre-Eli time. Any thoughts prior to seeing him were now colored by the presence of him. As if he had somehow already existed on some plane just waiting to make an appearance.

Eli's face scrunched up tighter in that sign he was about to scream bloody murder. Elliot tucked his son against his shoulder and patted his back while walking to the fridge to get one of the bottles he'd seen Lucy Ann store there.

He pulled it out, started to give it to his son...then remembered something about cold bottles not being good. He hadn't paid a lot of attention when his friends took care of baby stuff, but something must have permeated his brain. Enough so that he tugged his cell phone from his pocket and thumbed speed dial for his buddy Conrad Hughes. He always stayed up late. Conrad had said once that life as a casino magnate had permanently adjusted his internal clock.

The phone rang only once. "This is Hughes. Speak to me, Elliot."

"I need advice."

"Sure, financial? Work? Name it."

"Um, babies." He stared at the baby and the bottle on the marble slab counter. Life had definitely changed. "Maybe you should put Jayne on the line."

"I'm insulted," Conrad joked, casino bells and music drifting over the airwaves. "Ask your question. Besides, Jayne's asleep. Worn out from the kiddo."

"The nanny's sick and Lucy Ann really needs to sleep in." He swayed from side to side. "She's been trying to keep up with her work, the baby, the traveling."

"And your question?"

"Oh, right. I forgot. Sleep deprivation's kicking in, I think," he admitted, not that he would say a word to Lucy Ann after the way she was freaking out over him having a wreck.

"Happens to the best of us, brother. You were just the last man to fall."

"Back to my question. When I give the baby a bottle of this breast milk from the refrigerator, do I heat it in the microwave? And I swear if you laugh, I'm going to kick your ass later."

"I'm only laughing on the inside. Never out loud." Conrad didn't have to laugh. Amusement drenched his words.

"I can live with that." As long as he got the advice.

"Run warm water over the bottle. No microwave. Do not heat it in water on the stove," Conrad rattled off like a pro. "If he doesn't eat it all, pour it out. You can't save and reuse it. Oh, and shake it up."

"You're too good at this," Elliot couldn't resist saying as he turned on the faucet.

"Practice."

"This has to be the strangest conversation of my life." He played his fingers through the water to test the temperature and found it was warming quickly. He tucked the bottled milk underneath the spewing faucet with one hand, still holding his son to his shoulder with the other.

"It'll be commonplace before you know it."

Would it? "I hope so."

The sound of casino bells softened, as if Conrad had

gone into another room. "What about you and Lucy Ann?"

Elliot weighed his answer carefully before saying simply, "We're together."

"Together-together?" Conrad asked.

Elliot glanced through the living area at the closed bedroom door and the baby in his arms. "I'm working on it."

"You've fallen for her." His friend made it more of a statement than a question.

So why couldn't he bring himself to simply agree? "Lucy Ann and I have been best friends all our lives. We have chemistry."

Best friends. His brothers all called themselves best friends, but now he realized he'd never quite paired up with a best bud the way they all had. He was a part of the group. But Lucy Ann was his best friend, always had been.

"You'd better come up with a smoother answer than that if you ever get around to proposing to her. Women expect more than 'you're a great friend and we're super together in the sack.'"

Proposing? The word *marriage* hadn't crossed his mind, and he realized now that it should have. He should have led with that from the start. He should have been an honorable, stand-up kind of guy and offered her a ring rather than a month-long sex fest.

"I'm not that much of an idiot."

He hoped.

"So you are thinking about proposing."

He was now. The notion fit neatly in his brain, like the missing piece to a puzzle he'd been trying to complete since Lucy Ann left a year ago.

"I want my son to have a family, and I want Lucy Ann to be happy." He turned off the water and felt the bottle. Seemed warm. He shook it as instructed. "I'm just not sure I know how to make that happen. Not many long-term role models for happily ever after on my family tree."

"Marriage is work, no question." Conrad whistled softly on a long exhale. "I screwed up my own pretty bad once, so maybe I'm not the right guy to ask for advice."

Conrad and Jayne had been separated for three years before reuniting.

"But you fixed your marriage. So you're probably the best person to ask." Elliot was getting into this whole mentor notion. Why hadn't he thought to seek out some help before? He took his son and the bottle back into the living room of his bachelor pad, now strewn with baby gear. "How do you make it right when you've messed up this bad? When you've let so much time pass?"

"Grovel," Conrad said simply.

"That's it?" Elliot asked incredulously, dropping into his favorite recliner. He settled his son in the crook of his arm and tucked the bottle in his mouth. "That's your advice? Grovel?"

"It's not just a word. You owe her for being a jackass this past year. Like I said before. Relationships are work, man. Hard work. Tougher than any Interpol assignment old headmaster Colonel Salvatore could ever give us. But the payoff is huge if you can get it right."

"I hope so."

"Hey, I gotta go. Text just came in. Kid's awake and Jayne doesn't believe in nighttime nannies. So we're in the walking dead stage of parenthood right now." He didn't sound at all unhappy about it. "Don't forget. Shake the milk and burp the kid if you want to keep your suit clean."

Shake. Burp. Grovel. "I won't forget."

Lucy Ann blinked at the morning sun piercing the slight part in her curtains. She'd slept in this room in Elliot's posh Monte Carlo digs more times than she could remember. He'd even had her choose her own decor since they spent a lot of off-season time here, too.

She'd chosen an über-feminine French toile in pinks and raspberries, complete with an ornate white bed—Renaissance antiques. And the best of the best mattresses. She stretched, luxuriating in the well-rested feeling, undoubtedly a by-product of the awesome bed and even more incredible sex. She couldn't remember how long it had been since she'd woken up refreshed rather than dragging, exhausted. Certainly not since Eli had been born—

Blinking, she took in the morning sun, then gasped. "Eli!"

She jumped from the bed and raced over to the portable crib Elliot had ordered set up in advance. Had her baby slept through the night? She looked in the crib and found it empty. Her heart lurched up to her throat.

Her bare feet slipping on the hardwood floor, she raced out to the living room and stopped short. Elliot sat in his favorite recliner, holding their son. He looked so at ease with the baby cradled in the crook of his arm. An empty bottle sat on the table beside them.

Elliot toyed with his son's foot. "I have plans for you, little man. There are so many books to read. *Gulliver's Travels* and *Lord of the Rings* were favorites of mine as a kid. And we'll play with Matchbox cars when you're older. Or maybe you'll like trains or airplanes? Your choice."

Relaxing, Lucy Ann sagged against the door frame in relief. "You're gender stereotyping our child."

Glancing up, Elliot smiled at her, so handsome with a five o'clock shadow peppering his jaw and baby spit-up dotting his shoulder it was all she could do not to kiss him.

"Good morning, beautiful," he said, his eyes sliding over her silky nightshirt with an appreciation that all but mentally pulled the gown right off her. "Eli can be a chef or whatever he wants, as long as he's happy."

"Glad to hear you say that." She padded barefoot across the room and sat on the massive tapestry otto-man between the sofa and chairs. "I can't believe I slept in so late this morning."

"Eli and I managed just fine. And if I ran into prob-lems, I had plenty of backup."

"I concede you chose well with the nanny." She wasn't used to taking help with Eli, but she could get addicted to this kind of assistance quickly. "Mrs. Clayworth's amaz-ing and a great help without being intrusive."

"You're not upset that I didn't wake you?"

She swept her tangled hair back over her shoulders. "I can't think any mother of an infant would be upset over an extra two hours of sleep."

"Glad you're happy, Sleeping Beauty." His heated gaze slid over the satin clinging to her breasts.

"Ah, your fairy-tale romancing theme."

He arched an eyebrow. "You catch on fast. If you were to stay with me for the whole racing season, we could play Aladdin and his lamp."

His talk of the future made her…uncomfortable. She was just getting used to the shift in their relationship, adding a sexual level on a day-to-day basis. So she ig-nored the part about staying longer and focused on the fairy tale. "You've been fantasizing about me as a belly dancer?"

"Now that you mention it…"

"Lucky for us both, I'm rested and ready." She curled her toes into the hand-knotted silk Persian rug that would one day be littered with toys. "You're going to be a wonderful father."

As the words fell from her mouth she knew them to be true, not a doubt in her mind. And somehow she'd slid into talking about the future anyway.

"Well, I sure as hell learned a lot from my father about how not to be a dad." His gaze fell away from her and back to their child. "And the things I didn't learn, I intend to find out, even if that means taking a class or reading every parenting book on the shelves since I never had much of a role model."

Clearly, he was worried about this. She leaned forward to touch his knee. "Does that mean I'm doomed to be a crummy mother?"

"Of course not." He covered her hand with his. "Okay, I see your point. And thanks for the vote of confidence."

"For what it's worth, I do think you've had a very good role model." She linked fingers with him. "The colonel. Your old headmaster has been there for you, the way my aunt has for me. Doing the best they could within a flawed system that sent them broken children to fix."

"I don't like to think of myself as broken." His jaw clenched.

"It's okay, you know—" she rubbed his knee "—to be sad or angry about the past."

"It's a lot easier to just speed around the track, even smash into walls, rather than rage at the world." His throat moved with a long swallow.

"I'm not so sure I like that coping mechanism. I would

be so sad if anything happened to you." And wasn't that the understatement of the year? She had to admit, though, she'd been worrying more about him lately, fearing the distractions she brought to his life, also fearing he might have beat the odds one time too many.

He squeezed her hand, his eyes as serious as she'd ever seen them. "I would quit racing. For you."

"And I would never ask you to do that. Not for me."

"So you would ask for Eli?"

She churned his question around in her mind, unable to come up with an answer that didn't involve a lengthy discussion of the future.

"I think this is entirely too serious a conversation before I've had breakfast."

Scooping up her son from Elliot's arms, she made tracks for the kitchen, unable to deny the truth. Even though she stayed in the condo, she was running from him now every bit as much as she'd run eleven months ago.

Ten

Steering through the narrow streets of Monte Carlo, Elliot drove his new Mercedes S65 AMG along the cliff road leading to the Hughes mansion. His Maserati wouldn't hold a baby seat, so he'd needed a sedan that combined space and safety with his love of finely tuned automobiles. He felt downright domesticated driving Lucy Ann and their son to a lunch with friends. She was meeting with Jayne Hughes and Jayne's baby girl while he went over to the track.

Last time he'd traveled this winding road, he'd been driving Jayne and Conrad to the hospital—Conrad had been too much of a mess to climb behind the wheel of his SUV. Jayne had been in labor. She'd delivered their baby girl seventeen minutes after they'd arrived at the hospital.

How strange to think he knew more about his friend's first kid coming into the world than he knew about the birth of his own son.

His fingers clenched around the steering wheel as they wound up a cliff-side road overlooking the sea. "Tell me about the day Eli was born."

"Are you asking me because you're angry or because you want to know?"

A good question. It wouldn't help to say both probably came into play, so he opted for, "I will always regret that I wasn't there when he came into this world, that I missed out on those first days of his life. But I understand that if we're going to move forward here, I can't let that eat at me. We both are going to have to give a little here. So the answer to your question is, I want to know because I'm curious about all things relating to Eli."

She touched his knee lightly. "Thank you for being honest."

"That's the only way we're going to get through this, don't you think?"

He glanced over at her quickly, taking in the beautiful lines of her face with the sunlight streaming through the window.

Why had it taken him so long to notice?

"Okay…" She inhaled a shaky breath. "I had an appointment the week of my due date. I really expected to go longer since so many first-time moms go overdue. But the doctor was concerned about Eli's heart rate. He did an ultrasound and saw the placenta was separating from the uterine wall— Am I getting too gross for you here?"

"Keep talking," he commanded, hating that he hadn't been there to make things easier, less frightening for her. If he hadn't been so pigheaded, he would have been there to protect her. Assure her.

"The doctor scheduled me for an immediate cesarean section. I didn't even get to go home for my toothbrush," she joked in an attempt to lighten the mood.

He wasn't laughing. "That had to be scary for you. I wish I could have been with you. We helped each other through a lot of tough times over the years."

"I did try to call you," she confessed softly, "right before I went in. But your phone went straight to voice mail. I tried after, too...I assumed you were off on an Interpol secret 'walkabout' for Colonel Salvatore."

"I was." He'd done the math in his head. Knew the case he'd been working at the time.

"I know I could have pushed harder and found you." She shook her head regretfully. "I didn't even leave a message. I'm so sorry for that. You may be able to move past it, but I'm not sure I'll ever forgive myself."

He stayed silent, not sure what to say to make this right for both of them.

"What would we have done if Malcolm and Conrad hadn't kidnapped you from the bachelor party?"

Damn good question. "I like to think I would have come to my senses and checked on you. I don't know how the hell I let eleven months pass."

"Or how you found a fiancée so fast," she blurted out. "You proposed to another woman barely three months after we slept together. Yes, that's a problem for me."

He weighed his words carefully. "This may sound strange, but Gianna was the one who got shortchanged. I obviously didn't care about her the way I should have. I wasn't fair to her."

Her smile was tight. "Excuse me if I'm not overly concerned about being fair to Gianna. And from what I read in the news, she broke things off with you. Not the other way around. If she hadn't left, would you have married her?"

Stunned, he downshifted around a corner. She'd read about his breakup? She'd left, but kept tabs on him. If only he'd done the same with her, he would have known about Eli. As much as Elliot wanted to blame a remote Interpol stint for keeping him out of touch, he knew he should have followed up with Lucy Ann.

Then why hadn't he? She'd been so good to him, always there for him, always forgiving him. Damn it, he didn't deserve her— Could that have been part of why he'd stayed away? Out of guilt for taking so much from her all their lives?

That she could think he still wanted Gianna, especially after what he and Lucy Ann had just shared... Incomprehensible.

"No. I didn't want to marry her. We broke off the engagement. I knew it was inevitable. She just spoke first."

She nodded tightly. "Fine, I appreciate your honesty. I'm still not totally okay with the fact that you raced right back to her after we... Well, I'm just not okay with it. But I'm working on it."

Conrad had told him to grovel. Elliot scrounged inside himself for a way to give her what she needed.

"Fair enough. At least I know where I stand with you." He stared at the road ahead, struggling. Groveling was tougher than he'd expected after the way his father had beaten him to his knees so many times. "That was the hardest part about growing up with my old man. The uncertainty. I'm not saying it would have been okay if he'd punched me on a regular basis. But the sick feeling in my gut as I tried to gauge his moods? That was a crappy way to live."

"I'm so sorry." Her hand fell to rest on his knee again. This time she didn't pull away.

"I know. You saved my sanity back then." He placed his hand over hers. "I always knew it was you who let the air out of my dad's tires that time in sixth grade."

She sat upright. "How did you know?"

"Because you did it while I was away on that science fair trip. So I couldn't be blamed or catch the brunt of his anger." He rubbed her hand along the spot on her finger where he should have put a ring already. "Do I have the details correct?"

"That was the idea. Couldn't have your father get away with everything."

"He didn't. Not in the end." There'd never been a chance to make peace with his bastard of an old man—never a chance to confront him, either.

"I guess there's a sad sort of poetic justice that he died in a bar fight while you were off at reform school."

Her words surprised him. "You're a bloodthirsty one."

"When it comes to protecting the people in my life? Absolutely."

She was freaking amazing. He couldn't deny the rush of admiration for the woman she'd become—that she'd always been, just hidden under the weight of her own problems.

And on the heels of that thought, more guilt piled on top of him for all the ways he'd let her down. Damn it all, he had to figure out how to make this right with her. He had to pull out all the stops as Conrad advised.

Full throttle.

He had to win her over to be his wife.

Lucy Ann sat on the terrace with Jayne Hughes, wondering how a woman who'd been separated for three years could now be such a happily contented wife and new mother. What was her secret? How had they overcome the odds?

There was no denying the peaceful air that radiated off the bombshell blonde with her baby girl cradled in a sling. The Hughes family split their time between their home in Monte Carlo and a home in Africa, where Jayne worked as a nurse at a free clinic her husband funded along with another Alpha Brother. She made it all look effortless whether she was serving up luncheon on fine china or cracking open a boxed lunch under a sprawling shea butter tree.

Lucy Ann patted her colicky son on his precious little back. He seemed to have settled to sleep draped over her knees, which wasn't particularly comfortable, but she wasn't budging an inch as long as he was happy.

Jayne paused in her lengthy ramble about the latest addition to the pediatrics wing at the clinic to tug something from under the plate of petits fours. "Oh, I almost forgot to give you this pamphlet for Elliot."

"For Elliot?" She took it from Jayne, the woman's short nails hinting at her more practical side. "On breast-feeding?"

"He called Conrad with questions the other night." She adjusted her daughter to the other breast in such a smooth transition the cloth baby sling covered all. "I don't know why he didn't just look it up on Google. Anyhow, this should tell him everything he needs to know."

"Thank you." She tucked the pamphlet in her purse, careful not to disturb her son. "He didn't tell me he called your husband for help."

"He was probably too embarrassed. Men can be proud that way." She sipped her ice water, sun glinting off the Waterford crystal that Lucy Ann recalled choosing for a wedding gift to the couple.

There'd been a time when tasks like that—picking out expensive trinkets for Elliot's wealthy friends—had made her nervous. As if the wrong crystal pattern could call her out as an interloper in Elliot Starc's elegant world.

But it had taken walking away from the glitz and glamour to help her see it for what it really was…superficial trappings that didn't mean a lot in the long run. Lucy Ann was far more impressed with Jayne's nursing capabilities and her motherhood savvy than with what kind of place setting graced her table.

"There's a lot to learn about parenting," Lucy Ann acknowledged. "Especially for someone who didn't grow up around other kids." She would have been overwhelmed without Aunt Carla's help.

And wasn't it funny to think that, even though she'd traveled the globe with Elliot for a decade, she'd still learned the most important things back home in South Carolina?

"I think it's wonderful that he's trying. A lot of men would just dump all the tough stuff onto a nanny." Jayne shot a glance over her shoulder through the open balcony doors, somehow knowing Conrad had arrived without even looking.

"I just suggested that it wouldn't hurt to let someone else change the diapers," said Mr. Tall, Dark and Brooding. "Who the hell wants to change a diaper? That doesn't make me a bad human being."

Lucy Ann had to admit, "He has a point."

Jayne set her glass down. "Don't encourage him."

Conrad chuckled as he reached for his daughter. "Lucy Ann, let me know when you're done. I promised Elliot I would drive you and the kidlet back to the condo. He said he's running late at the track. Have fun, ladies. The princess and I are going to read the *Wall Street Journal*."

Conrad disappeared back into the house with his daughter, words about stocks and short sales carrying on the wind spoken in a singsong tone as if telling her a nursery rhyme.

Lucy Ann leaned back in the chair and turned her water glass on the table, watching the sunlight refracting prisms off the cut crystal. "I envy your tight-knit support group. Elliot and I didn't have a lot of friends when we were growing up. He was the kid always in trouble so parents didn't invite him over. And I was too shy to make friends."

"You're not shy anymore," Jayne pointed out.

"Not that I let people see."

"We've known you for years. I would hope you could consider us your friends, too."

They'd known each other, but she'd been Elliot's employee. It wasn't that his friends had deliberately excluded her, but Conrad had been separated for years, and only recently had the rest of them started marrying. She knew it would be easier for all of them if she made the effort here.

"We'll certainly cross paths because of Eli," Lucy Ann said simply.

"And Elliot?"

The conversation was starting to get too personal for her comfort. "We're still working on that."

"But you're making progress."

"Have you been reading the tabloids?"

"I don't bother with those." Jayne waved dismissively. "I saw the way you two looked at each other when Elliot dropped you off."

In spite of herself, Lucy Ann found herself aching to talk to someone after all, and Jayne seemed the best candidate. "He's into the thrill of the chase right now. Things will go back to normal eventually."

"I'm not so sure I agree. He seems different to me." Jayne's pensive look faded into a grin. "They all have to grow up and settle down sometime."

"What about—" She didn't feel comfortable discussing the guys' Interpol work out in the open, so she simply said, "Working with the colonel after graduation and following a call to right bigger wrongs? How do they give that up to be regular family guys?"

"Good question." Jayne pinched the silver tongs to shuffle a petit four and fruit onto a dessert plate. "Some still take an active part once they're married, but once the children start coming, things do change. They shift to pulling the strings. They become more like Salvatore."

"Mine is a bit wilder than yours." When had she started thinking of Elliot as *hers*? Although on some level he'd been hers since they were children. "I mean, seriously, he crashes cars into walls for a living."

"You've known that about him from the start. So why are things different now?"

"I don't know how to reconcile our friendship with everything else that's happened." The whole "friends with benefits" thing was easier said than done.

"By 'everything else' you mean the smoking hot sex, of course." Jayne grinned impishly before popping a grape in her mouth.

"I had forgotten how outspoken you can be."

"Comes with the territory of loving men like these. They don't always perceive subtleties."

True enough. Lucy Ann speared a chocolate strawberry and willed herself not to blush at the heated memories the fruit evoked. "Outspoken or not, I'm still no closer to an answer."

Jayne nudged the gold-rimmed china plate aside and leaned her arms on the table. "You don't have to reconcile the two ways of being. It's already done—or it will be once you stop fighting."

Could Jayne be right? Maybe the time had come to

truly give him a chance. To see if he was right. To see if they could really have a fairy-tale life together.

Fear knotted her gut, but Lucy Ann wasn't the shy little girl anymore. She was a confident woman and she was all-in.

Elliot shrugged out of his black leather jacket with a wince as he stepped into the dark apartment. He'd done his prelim runs as always, checklists complete, car scrutinized to the last detail, and yet somehow he'd damn near wiped out on a practice run.

Every muscle in his body ached from reactionary tensing. Thank goodness Lucy Ann hadn't been there as she would have been in the past as his assistant. He didn't want her worrying. He didn't want to risk a confrontation.

He tossed the jacket over his arm, walking carefully so he wouldn't wake anyone up. His foot hooked on something in the dark. He bit back a curse and looked down to find…a book? He reached to pick up an ornately bound copy of *Hansel and Gretel*. He started to stand up again and looked ahead to find a trail of books, all leading toward his bedroom. He picked up one book after the other, each a different fairy tale, until he pushed open his door.

His room was empty.

Frowning, he scanned the space and… "Aha…"

More books led to the bathroom, and now that he listened, he could hear the shower running. He set the stack on the chest of drawers and gathered up the last few "crumbs" on his trail, a copy of *Rapunzel* and a Victorian version of *Rumpelstiltskin*. Pushing his way slowly into the bathroom, he smiled at the shadowy outline behind the foggy glass wall. The multiple showerheads shot spray over Lucy Ann as she hummed. She didn't seem to notice he'd arrived.

He peeled off his clothes without making a sound and padded barefoot into the slate-tiled space. He opened the door and stepped into the steam. Lucy Ann stopped singing, but she didn't turn around. The only acknowledgment she gave to his arrival was a hand reaching for him. He linked fingers with her and stepped under the warm jets. The heat melted away the stress from his muscles, allowing a new tension to take hold. He saw the condom packet in the soap dish and realized just how thoroughly she'd thought this through.

He pressed against her back, wrapping his arms around her. Already, his erection throbbed hard and ready, pressed between them.

He sipped water from just behind her ear. "I'm trying to think of what fairy tale you're fantasizing about, and for water, I can only come up with the *Frog Prince*."

Angling her head to give him better access to her neck, she combed her fingers over his damp hair. "We're writing our own fantasy tonight."

Growling his approval, he slicked his hands over her, taking in the feel of her breasts peaking against his palms. His blood fired hotter through his veins than the water sluicing over them. He slipped a hand between her thighs, stroking satin, finding that sweet bundle of nerves. Banding his arm tighter around her waist, he continued to circle and tease, feeling her arousal lubricate his touch. She sagged back against him, her legs parting to give him easier access.

With her bottom nestled against him, he held on to control by a thread. Each roll of her hips as she milked the most from her pleasure threatened to send him over the edge. But he held back his own release, giving her hers. He tucked two fingers inside her, his thumb still working along that pebbled tightness.

Her sighs and purrs filled the cubicle, the jasmine scent of her riding the steam. Every sound of her impending arousal shot a bolt of pleasure through him, his blood pounding thicker through his veins. Until, yes, she cried out, coming apart in his arms. Her fingernails dug deep into his thighs, cutting half-moons into his flesh as she arched into her orgasm.

He savored every shiver of bliss rippling her body until he couldn't wait any longer. He took the condom from the soap tray and sheathed himself. He pressed her against the shower stall wall, her palms flattened to the stone. Standing behind her, he nudged her legs apart and angled until… He slid home, deep inside her, clamped by damp silken walls as hot and moist as the shower.

Sensation engulfed him, threatened to shake the ground under him as he pushed inside her again and again. Things moved so damn fast… He was so close… Then he heard the sound of her unraveling in his arms. The echoes of her release sent him over the edge. Ecstasy rocked his balance. He flattened a hand against the warm wall to keep from falling over as his completion pulsed until his heartbeat pounded in his ears. Shifting, he pulled out of her, keeping one arm around her.

Slowly, his world expanded beyond just the two of them, and he became aware of the water sheeting over them. The patter of droplets hitting the door and floor.

Tucking her close again, he thought about his near miss at the track today and all the relationship advice from his friends. He'd waited too long these past eleven months to make sure she stayed with him. Permanently. He wouldn't let another minute pass without moving forward with their lives.

He nuzzled her ear. "What kind of house do you want?"

"House?" she asked, her knees buckling.

He steadied her. "I want to build a real house for us, Lucy Ann. Not just condos or rented places here and there."

"Umm…" She licked her lips. The beads on her temple mingled perspiration with water. "What city would you choose?"

He had penthouse suites around the world, but nowhere he stayed long enough to call home. And none of them had the room for a boy to run and play.

"I need a home. We need a home for our son."

"You keep assuming we'll stay together."

Already his proposal was going astray. Could be because most of the blood in his brain was surging south. "Where do you want to live? I'll build two houses next door if that's the way you want it." Living near each other would give him more time to win her over, because he was fast realizing he couldn't give her up. "I have connections with a friend who restores historic homes."

She turned in his arms, pressing her fingers to his lips. "Can we just keep making love instead?"

Banding her wrist in his hand, he kissed it, determined not to let this chance slip away, not to let *her* slip away again. "Let's get married."

She leaned into him, whispering against his mouth as she stroked down between them, molding her palm to the shape of him. "You may have missed the memo…" She caressed up and down, again and again. "But you don't have to propose to get me to sleep with you."

He angled away, staring straight in her eyes, her eyelashes spiky wet. "I'm not joking, so I would appreciate it if you took my proposal seriously."

"Really? Now?" She stepped back, the water showering between them. "You mean this. For Eli, of course."

"Of course Eli factors into the equation." He studied her carefully blank expression. "But it's also because you and I fit as a couple on so many levels. We've been friends forever, and our chemistry... Well, that speaks for itself. We just have to figure out how not to fight afterward and we'll have forever locked and loaded."

The more he talked, the more it felt right.

"Forever?" Her knees folded, and she sat on the stone seat in the corner, her hair dripping water. "Do you think that's even possible for people like you and me?"

"Why shouldn't it be?" He knelt in front of her.

"Because of our pasts." She stroked over his wet hair, cupping his neck, her eyes so bittersweet they tore him to bits. "Our parents. Our own histories. I refuse to spend the rest of my life wondering when the next Gianna is going to walk through the door."

Gianna? He hadn't even thought of her other than when Lucy Ann mentioned her. But looking back, he realized how bad his engagement would have looked to her, how that must have played a role in her keeping quiet about the pregnancy.

This was likely where the groveling came in. "I'm sorry."

"For which part? The engagement? Or the fact you didn't contact me— Hell, forget I said that." She leaned forward to kiss him.

If they kissed, the discussion would be over, opportunity missed. He scooped her up in his arms and pivoted, settling her into his lap as he sat on the stone seat in the corner.

She squawked in protest but he pressed on. "You expected me to follow you? Even after you said—and I quote—'I don't ever want to lay eyes on your irresponsible ass ever again'?"

"And you've never said anything in the heat of the moment that you regretted later?"

Groveling was all well and good, but he wasn't taking the full blame for what shook down these past months. "If you regretted those words, it sure would have been helpful if you'd let me know."

"This is my whole point. We're both so proud, neither one of us could take the steps needed to repair the damage we did. Yes, I am admitting that we both were hurt. Even though you seemed to recover fast with Gianna—" she gave him that tight smile again "—I acknowledge that losing our friendship hurt you, as well. But friendship isn't enough to build a marriage on. So can we please go back to the friends-with-benefits arrangement?"

"Damn it, Lucy Ann—"

She traced his face with her fingers. "Do you know what I think?" She didn't wait for him to answer. "I think you don't believe in fairy tales after all. The dates, the romance… It has actually been a game for you after all. A challenge, a competition. Something to win. Not Cinderella or Sleeping Beauty."

"I suspect I've been led into a trap." He'd thought he'd been following all the right signs and taking the steps to fix this, but he'd only seemed to dig a bigger hole for himself.

"Well, you followed my bread crumbs." Her joke fell flat between them, her eyes so much sadder than he'd ever dreamed he could make them.

"So you're sure you don't want to marry me?"

She hesitated, her pulse leaping in her neck. "I'm sure I don't want you to propose to me."

Her rejection stunned him. Somehow he'd expected her to say yes. He'd thought… Hell, he'd taken her for granted all over again and he didn't know how to fix this. Not now. He needed time to regroup. "If I agree to stop pressing for marriage, can we keep having incredible sex with each other?"

"'Til the end of the month."

"Sex for a few weeks? You're okay with sleeping together with an exit strategy already in place?"

"That's my offer." She slid from his lap, stepping back. Away. Putting distance between them on more than just one level. "Take it or leave it."

"Lucy Ann, I'm happy as hell to take you again and again until we're both too exhausted to argue." Although right now, he couldn't deny it. He wanted more from her. "But eventually we're going to have to talk."

Eleven

Lucy sprawled on top of Elliot in bed, satiated, groggy and almost dry from their shower, but not ready for their evening together to end. Elliot seemed content to let the proposal discussion go—for tonight. So this could well be the last uncomplicated chance she had to be with him.

The ceiling fan *click, click, clicked* away their precious remaining seconds together, the lights of Monaco glittering through the open French doors, the Cote d'Azur providing a breathtaking vista. Who wouldn't want to share this life with him? Why couldn't she just accept his proposal? She hated how his offer of marriage made her clench her gut in fear. She should be happy. Celebrating. This would be the easy answer to bringing up Eli together. They were best friends. Incredible lovers. Why not go with the flow? They could take a day to see Cannes with the baby, and she could snap pictures…savor the things she'd been too busy to notice in the early years of traveling with Elliot.

Yet something held her back. She couldn't push the word *yes* free. Every time she tried, her throat closed up. She trusted him…yet the thought of reliving the past eleven months again, of living without him…

Her fingers glided along his closely shorn hair. "You could have been killed that day your hair got singed."

"You're not going to get rid of me that easily," he said with a low chuckle and a stroke down her spine.

Ice chilled the blood in her veins at his words. "That wasn't funny."

"I'm just trying to lighten the mood." He angled back to kiss the tip of her nose, then look into her eyes. "I'm okay, Lucy Ann. Not a scratch on me that day."

She'd been in South Carolina when it had happened, her belly swelling with his child and her heart heavy with the decision of when to tell him about the baby. "That doesn't make it any less terrifying."

He grinned smugly. "You do care."

"Of course I care what happens to you. I always have. There's no denying our history, our friendship, how well we know each other." How could he doubt that, no matter what else they'd been through? "But I know something else. You're only interested in me now because I'm telling you no. You don't like being the one left behind."

Breathlessly, she finished her rant, stunned at herself. Her mouth had been ahead of her brain. She hadn't even realized she felt that way until the words came rolling out.

"That's not a very nice thing to say," he said tightly.

"But is it true?" She cupped his face.

He pulled her hands down gently and kissed both palms. "I already offered to stop racing. I meant it. I'm a father now and I understand that comes with responsibilities."

Responsibilities? Is that what they were to him? But then, in a way, that's what she'd always been since he got out of reform school, since he'd offered her a job as his assistant even though at the time she hadn't been qualified for the job. He'd given it to her out of friendship—and, yes, the sense of obligation they felt to look out for each other.

That had been enough for a long time, more than either of them had gotten from anyone else in their lives. But right now with her heart in her throat, obligation didn't feel like nearly enough to build a life on.

She slid off him, the cooling breeze from the fan chilling her bared flesh. "Do whatever you want."

"What did I say wrong? You want me to quit and I offer and now you're angry?"

"I didn't say I want you to quit." She opted for the simpler answer. "I understand how important your career is to you. You have a competitive nature and that's not a bad thing. It's made you an incredibly successful man."

"You mentioned my competitiveness earlier. Lucy Ann, that's not why I—"

She rolled to her side and pressed her fingers to his mouth before he could get back to the proposal subject again. "You've channeled your edginess and your drive to win. That's not a bad thing." She tapped his bottom lip. "Enough talk. You should rest up now so you're focused for the race."

And so she could escape to her room, away from the building temptation to take what he offered and worry about the consequences later. Except with Elliot's muscled arm draped over her waist, she couldn't quite bring herself to move out of his embrace. His hand moved along her back soothingly. Slowly, her body began to relax, melting into the fantastic mattress.

"Lucy Ann? You're right, you know." Elliot's words were so low she almost didn't hear him.

"Right about what?" she asked, groggy, almost asleep.

"I like to win— Wait. Scratch that. I *need* to win."

Opening her eyes, she didn't move, just stared at his chest and listened. There was no escaping this conversation. Wherever it led them.

"There are two kinds of people in the world. Ones who have known physical pain and those who never will. Being beaten…" He swallowed hard, his heart hammering so loudly she could feel her pulse sync up with his, racing, knowing just what that word *beating* meant to him growing up. "That does something to your soul. Changes you. You can heal. You can move on. But you're forever changed by that moment you finally break, crying for it to stop."

His voice stayed emotionless, but what he said sliced through her all the more because of the steely control he forced on himself.

Her hand fluttered to rest on his heart as she pressed a kiss to his shoulder. "Oh, God, Elliot—"

"Don't speak. Not yet." He linked his fingers with hers. "The thing is, we all like to think we're strong enough to hold out when that person brings on the belt, the shoe, the branch, or hell, even a hand used as a weapon. And there's a rush in holding out at first, deluding yourself into believing you can actually win."

She willed herself to stay completely still, barely breathing, while he poured out the truth she'd always known. She'd even seen the marks he'd refused to acknowledge. Hearing him talk about it, though, shredded her heart, every revelation making her ache for what he'd suffered growing up. She also knew he wouldn't accept her sympathy now any more than he had then. So she gave him the only thing she could—total silence while he spoke.

"The person with the weapon is after one thing," he shared, referring to his father in such a vague sense as if that gave him distance, protection. "It isn't actually about the pain. It's about submission."

She couldn't hold back the flinch or a whimper of sympathy.

Elliot tipped her chin until she looked at him. "But you see, it's okay now. When I'm out there racing, it's my chance to win. No one, not one damn soul, will ever beat me again."

She held her breath, wrestling with what to do next, how they could go forward. This wasn't the time to pledge futures, but it also wasn't the time to walk away. Growing up, she'd always known how to be there for him. At this moment, she didn't have a clue.

The squawk of their son over the nursery monitor jolted them both. And she wasn't sure who was more relieved.

Her or Elliot.

Elliot barely tasted the gourmet brunch catered privately at a crowded café near the race day venue. With two hundred thousand people pouring into the small principality for the circuit's most famous event, there were fans and media everywhere. At least his friends and mentor seemed to be enjoying themselves. He wanted to chalk up his lack of enthusiasm to sleep deprivation.

Race day in Monaco had always been one of Elliot's favorites, from the way the sun glinted just right off the streets to the energy of the crowds. The circuit was considered one of the most challenging Formula One routes—narrow roads, tight turns and changing elevations made it all the more exciting, edgy, demanding.

And just that fast, Lucy Ann's words haunted him, how she'd accused him of searching out challenges. How she'd accused him of seeing her as a challenge. Damn it all, he just wanted them to build a future together.

What would she be thinking, sitting in the stands today with his school friends and their wives?

He glanced at her across the table, strain showing in the creases along her forehead and the dark smudges under her eyes. He wanted to take Eli from her arms so she could rest, but wasn't sure if she would object. He didn't want to cause a scene or upset her more.

With a mumbled excuse, he scraped back his chair and left the table. He needed air. Space.

He angled his way out of the room—damn, he had too many curious friends these days—and into the deserted patio garden in the back. All the patrons had flocked out front to the street side to watch the crowds already claiming their places to watch the race. But back here, olive trees and rosebushes packed the small space so densely he almost didn't see his old high school headmaster—now an Interpol handler—sitting on a bench sending text messages.

Colonel Salvatore sat beside his preteen son, who was every bit as fixated on his Game Boy as his father was on his phone. A couple of empty plates rested between them.

How had he missed them leaving the table? Damn, his mind wasn't where it was supposed to be.

Colonel Salvatore stood, mumbled something to his son, then walked toward Elliot without once looking up from his phone. The guy always had been the master of multitasking. Very little slipped by him. Ever.

The older man finally tucked away his cell phone and nodded. "We couldn't sit still," he said diplomatically, "so we're out here playing 'Angry Monkeys' or something like that."

"I'm sure you both enjoyed the food more here where it's quieter," he said diplomatically. "I could sure use parenting advice if you've got some to offer up."

Salvatore straightened his standard red tie. He wore the same color gray suit as always, like a retirement uniform. "Why don't you ask the guys inside?"

"They only have babies. They're new parents." Like him. Treading water as fast as he could and still choking. "You have an older boy."

"A son I rarely see due to my work schedule." He winced. "So again I say, I'm not the one to help."

"Then your first piece of advice would be for me to spend time with him."

"I guess it would." He glanced over at his son, whose thumbs were flying over the buttons. "Gifts don't make up for absence. Although don't underestimate the power of a well-chosen video game."

"Thank God we have the inside scoop with Troy's latest inventions." Maybe that's who he needed to be talking to. Maybe Troy could invent a baby app. Elliot shoved a hand over his hair, realizing how ridiculous the thought sounded. He must be sleep-deprived. "I'm a little short on role models in the father department—other than you."

Salvatore's eyebrows went up at the unexpected compliment. "Um, uh, thank you," he stuttered uncharacteristically.

"Advice then?"

"Don't screw up."

"That's it?" Elliot barked. "Don't screw up?"

"Fine, I'll spell it out for you." Salvatore smiled as if

he'd been toying with him all along. Then the grin faded. "You've had to steal everything you've ever wanted in life. From food to cars to friends—to your freedom."

"I'm past that."

"Are you?" The savvy Interpol handler leaned against the centuries-old brick wall, an ivy trellis beside him. "It's difficult for me to see beyond the boy you were when you arrived at my school as a teenager hell-bent on self-destructing."

"Self-destructing?" he said defensively. "I'm not sure I follow." He was all about winning.

"You stole that car on purpose to escape your father, and you feel guilty as hell for leaving Lucy Ann behind," Salvatore said so damn perceptively he might as well have been listening in on Elliot's recent conversations. "You expected to go to jail as punishment and since that didn't happen, you've been trying to prove to the world just how bad you are. You pushed Lucy Ann away by getting engaged to Gianna."

"When did you find time to get your psychology degree between being a headmaster and an Interpol handler?"

"There you go again, trying to prove what a smart-ass you are."

Damn it. Didn't it suck to realize how well he played to type? He took a steadying breath and focused.

"I'm trying to do the right thing by Lucy Ann now. I want to live up to my obligations."

"The right thing." The colonel scratched a hand over gray hair buzzed as short of Elliot's. "What is that?"

"Provide for our son… Marry her… Damn it, colonel, clearly you think I'm tanking here. Is it fun watching me flounder?"

"If I tell you what to do, you won't learn a thing. A

mentor guides, steers. Think of it as a race," he said with a nod—which Elliot knew from years in the man's office meant this conversation was over. Colonel Salvatore fished out his phone and headed back to sit silently beside his son.

Elliot pinched the bridge of his nose and pivoted toward the iron gate that led to the back street. He needed to get his head on straight before the race. Hell, he needed to get his head back on straight, period. Because right now, he could have sworn he must be hallucinating.

Beyond the iron gate, he saw a curly-haired brunette who looked startlingly like his former fiancée. He narrowed his eyes, looking closer, shock knocking him back a step as Gianna crossed the street on the arm of a Brazilian Formula One champion.

Lucy Ann usually found race day exciting, but she couldn't shake the feeling of impending doom. The sense that she and Elliot weren't going to figure out how to make things work between them before the end of their time together. Thank goodness Mrs. Clayworth had taken the baby back to the condo to nap, because Lucy Ann was beyond distracted.

Sitting in the private viewing box with Elliot's friends and the relatives of other drivers, she tried to stifle her fears, to reassure herself that she and Elliot could find a way to parent together—possibly even learn to form a relationship as a couple. That she could figure out how to heal the wounds from his past, which still haunted everything he did.

The buzz of conversation increased behind her, a frenzy of whispers and mumbles in multiple languages. She turned away from the viewing window and monitors broadcasting prerace hubbub, newscasters speaking in French, English, Spanish and a couple of languages she didn't recognize. She looked past the catering staff carrying glasses of champagne to the entrance. A gasp caught in her throat.

Gianna? Here?

The other woman worked her way down the steps, her dark curls bouncing. Shock, followed by a burst of anger, rippled through Lucy Ann as she watched Gianna stride confidently closer. Her white dress clung to her teeny-tiny body. Clearly those hips had never given birth. And Lucy Ann was long past her days of wearing anything white thanks to baby spit-up. Not that she would trade her son for a size-zero figure and a closet full of white clothes.

Above all, she did not want a scene in front of the media. Gianna's eyes were locked on her, her path determined. If the woman thought she could intimidate, she was sorely mistaken.

Lucy Ann shot to her feet and marched up the stairs, her low heels clicking. She threw her arms wide and said loud enough for all to hear, "Gianna, so glad you could make it."

Stunned, the woman almost tripped over her own stilettos. "Um, I—"

Lucy Ann hugged her hard and whispered in her ear, "We're going to have a quick little private chat and, above all, we will not cause a scene before the race."

She knew how fast gossip spread and she didn't intend to let any negative energy ripple through the crowd. And she definitely didn't intend for anyone to see her lose her calm. She hauled the other woman down the hall and into a ladies' room, locking the door behind them.

Once she was sure no one else was in the small sitting area or in the stalls, she confronted Elliot's former fiancée. "Why are you here?"

Gianna shook her curls. "I'm here with a retired Brazilian racer. I was simply coming by to say hello."

"I'm not buying that." Lucy Ann stared back at the other woman and found she wasn't jealous so much as angry that someone was trying mess with her happiness—hers, Elliot's and Eli's.

The fake smile finally faded from Gianna's face. "I came back because now it's a fair fight."

At least the woman wasn't denying it. "I'm not sure I follow your logic."

"Before, when I found out about you and the baby—"

Lucy gasped. "You knew?"

"I found out by accident. I got nosy about you, looked into your life…" She shrugged. "I was devastated, but I broke off the engagement."

"Whoa, hold on." Lucy Ann held up a hand. "I don't understand. Elliot said you broke up because of his Interpol work. That you couldn't handle the danger."

She rolled her dramatic Italian eyes. "Men are so very easy to deceive. I broke the engagement because I couldn't be the one to tell him about your pregnancy. I couldn't be 'that' woman. The one who broke up true love. The evil one in the triangle. But I also couldn't marry him knowing he might still want you or his child."

"So you left." Lucy Ann's legs gave way and she sagged back against the steel door.

"I loved him enough to leave and let him figure this out on his own."

If she'd really loved him, Gianna would have told him about his child, but then Lucy Ann figured who was she to throw stones on that issue? "Do you still love Elliot?"

"Yes, I do."

She searched the woman's eyes and saw…genuine heartache. "You're not at all what I expected."

Gianna's pouty smile faltered. "And you're everything I feared."

So where did they go from here? That question hammered through Lucy Ann's mind so loudly it took her a moment to realize the noise was real. Feet drummed overhead with the sound of people running. People screaming?

She looked quickly at Gianna, whose eyes were already widening in confusion, as well. Lucy Ann turned on her heels, unlocked the door and found mass confusion. Spectators and security running. Reporters rushing with their cameras at the ready, shouting questions and directions in different languages.

Lucy Ann grabbed the arm of a passing guard. "What's going on?"

"Ma'am, there's been an accident in the lineup. Please return to your seat and let us do our jobs," the guard said hurriedly and pulled away, melting into the crowd.

"An accident?" Her stomach lurched with fear.

There were other drivers. Many other drivers. And an accident while lining up would be slow? Right? Unless someone was doing a preliminary warm-up lap.... So many horrifying scenarios played through her mind, all of them involving Elliot. She shoved into the crush, searching for a path through to her viewing area or to the nearest telecast screen. Finally, she spotted a wide-screen TV mounted in a corner, broadcasting images of flames.

The words scrolling across the bottom blared what she already knew deep in her terrified heart.

Elliot had crashed.

Twelve

Her heart in her throat, Lucy Ann pushed past Gianna and shouldered through the bustling crush of panicked observers. She reached into her tailored jacket and pulled out her pass giving her unlimited access. She couldn't just sit in the private viewing area and wait for someone to call her. What if Elliot needed her? She refused to accept the possibility that he could be dead. Even the word made her throat close up tight.

Her low pumps clicked on the stairs as she raced through various checkpoints, flashing the access pass every step of the way.

Finally, thank God, finally, she ran out onto the street level where security guards created an impenetrable wall. The wind whipped her yellow sundress around her legs as she sprinted. Her pulse pounding in her ears, she searched the lanes of race cars, looking for flames. But she found no signs of a major explosion.

A siren's wail sliced through her. An ambulance navigated past a throng of race personnel spraying down the street with fire extinguishers. The vehicle moved toward two race cars, one on its side, the other sideways as if it had spun out into a skid. As much as she wanted to deny what her eyes saw, the car on its side belonged to Elliot.

Emergency workers crawled all over the vehicle, prying open the door. Blinking back burning tears, Lucy Ann strained against an arm holding her back, desperate to see. Her shouts were swallowed up in the roar of activity until she couldn't even hear her own incoherent pleas.

The door flew open, and her breath lodged somewhere in her throat. She couldn't breathe, gasp or shout. Just wait.

Rescue workers reached inside, then hauled Elliot out. Alive.

She sagged against the person behind her. She glanced back to find Elliot's Interpol handler, Colonel Salvatore, at her side. He braced her reassuringly, his eyes locked on the battered race car. Elliot was moving, slowly but steadily. The rescue workers tried to keep his arms over their shoulders so they could walk him to a waiting ambulance. But he shook his head, easing them aside and standing on his own two feet. He pulled off his helmet and waved to the crowd, signaling that all was okay.

The crowd roared, a round of applause thundering, the reverberations shuddering through her along with her relief. His gaze homed in on her. Lucy Ann felt the impact all the way to her toes. Elliot was alive. Again and again, the thought echoed through her mind in a continual loop of reassurance, because heaven help her, she loved him. Truly loved him. That knowledge rolled through her, settled into her, in a fit that told her what she'd known all along.

They'd always loved each other.

At this moment, she didn't doubt that he loved her back. No matter what problems, disagreements or betrayals they might have weathered, the bond was there. She wished she could rejoice in that, but the fear was still rooted deep inside her, the inescapable sense of foreboding.

Elliot pushed past the emergency personnel and… heaven only knew who else because she couldn't bring herself to look at anyone except Elliot walking toward her, the scent of smoke tingling in her nose as the sea breeze blew in. The sun shone down on the man she loved, bright Mediterranean rays glinting off the silver trim on his racing gear with each bold step closer.

She vaguely registered the colonel flashing some kind of badge that had the security cop stepping aside and letting her stumble past. She regained her footing and sprinted toward Elliot.

"Thank God you're okay." Slamming into his chest, she wrapped her arms around him.

He kissed her once, firmly, reassuringly, then walked her away from the sidelines, the crowd parting, or maybe someone made the path for them. She couldn't think of anything but the man beside her, the warmth of him, the sound of his heartbeat, the scent of his aftershave and perspiration.

Tears of relief streaming down her face, she didn't bother asking where they were going. She trusted him, the father of her child, and honestly didn't care where they went as long as she could keep her hands on him, her cheek pressed to his chest, the fire-retardant material of his uniform bristly against her skin. He pushed through a door into a private office. She didn't care whose or how he'd chosen the stark space filled with only a wooden desk, a black leather sofa and framed racing photos.

Briskly, he closed and locked the door. "Lucy Ann, deep breaths or you're going to pass out. I'm okay." His voice soothed over her in waves. "It was just a minor accident. The other guy's axle broke and he slammed into me. Everyone's fine."

She swiped her wrists over her damp eyes, undoubtedly smearing mascara all over her face. "When there's smoke—possibly fire—involved, I wouldn't call that minor."

Elliot cradled her face in his gloved hands. "My hair didn't even get singed."

"I'm not in a joking mood." She sketched jerky hands over him, needing to touch him.

"Then help me out." He stalled one of her hands and kissed her palm. "What can I say to reassure you?"

"Nothing," she decided. "There's nothing to say right now."

It was a time for action.

She tugged her hand free and looped her arms around his neck again and drew his face down to hers. She kissed him. More than a kiss. A declaration and affirmation that he was alive. She needed to connect with him, even if only on a physical level.

"Lucy Ann," he muttered against her mouth, "are you sure you know what you're doing?"

"Are you planning to go back to the race?" she asked, gripping his shoulders.

"My car's in no shape to race. You know that. But are you cert—"

She kissed him quiet. She was so tired of doubts and questions and reservations. Most of all, she couldn't bear for this to be about the past anymore. To feel more pain for him. For herself. For how damn awful their child-hoods had been—his even worse than hers.

Hell, she'd lived through those years with him, doing her best to protect him by taking the brunt of the blame when she could. But when the adults wouldn't step up and make things right, there was only so much a kid could do.

They were't children any longer, but she still couldn't stand to think of him getting hurt in any way. She would do anything to keep danger away, to make them both forget everything.

At this moment, that "anything" involved mind-blowing sex against the door. Fast and intense. No fun games or pretty fairy tales. This was reality.

She tugged at his zipper, and he didn't protest this time. He simply drew back long enough to tug his rac-ing gloves off with his teeth. With her spine pressed to the door, he bunched up her silky dress until a cool breeze blew across her legs. A second later, he twisted and snapped her panties free, the scrap of lace giving way to him as fully as she did.

But she took as much as she gave. She nudged the zipper wider, nudging his uniform aside until she re-leased his erection, steely and hot in her hand. Then, he was inside her.

Her head thunked against the metal panel, her eyes sliding closed as she lost herself in sensation. She glided a foot along his calf, up farther until her leg hitched around him, drawing him deeper, deeper in a frenzied meeting of their bodies.

All too soon, the pleasure built to a crescendo, a wave swelling on the tide of emotions, fear and adrenaline. And yes, love. She buried her face in his shoulder, trying to hold back the shout rolling up her throat. His hoarse encouragement in her ear sent pleasure crashing over her. Feeling him tense in her arms, shudder with his own completion, sent a fresh tingle of aftershocks through her. Her body clamped around him in an instinctive need to keep him with her.

With each panting breath, she drew in the scent of them. His forehead fell to rest against the door, her fingers playing with the close-shorn hair at the base of his neck. Slowly, her senses allowed in the rest of the world, the dim echo outside reminding her they couldn't hide in here forever.

They couldn't hide from the truth any longer.

Even as she took him now, felt the familiar draw of this man she'd known for as long as she could remember, she also realized she didn't belong here in this world now. She couldn't keep him because she couldn't stay.

No matter how intrinsic the connection and attraction between them, this wasn't the life she'd dreamed of when they'd built those fairy-tale forts and castles. In her fantasies, they'd all just looked like a real home. A safe haven.

She loved him. She always had. But she'd spent most of her adult life following him. It was time to take charge of her life, for herself and for her son.

It was time to go home.

As Elliot angled back and started to smile at her, she captured his face in her hands and shook her head.

"Elliot, I can't do this anymore, trying to build a life on fairy tales. I need something more, a real life, and maybe that sounds boring to you, but I know who I am now. I know the life I want to live and it isn't here."

His eyes searched hers, confused and a little angry. "Lucy Ann—"

She pressed her fingers to his mouth. "I don't want

to argue with you. Not like last time. We can't do that to each other again—or to Eli."

He clasped her hand, a pulse throbbing double time in his neck. "Are you sure there's nothing I can do to change your mind?"

God, she wanted to believe he could, but right now with the scent of smoke clinging to his clothes and the adrenaline still crackling in the air, she couldn't see any other way. "No, Elliot. I'm afraid not."

Slowly, he released her hand. His face went somber, resigned. He understood her in that same perfect and tragic way she understood him. He already knew.

They'd just said goodbye.

The next day, Elliot didn't know how he was going to say goodbye. But the time had come. He sat on Aunt Carla's front porch swing while Lucy Ann fed Eli and put him down for a nap.

God, why couldn't he and Lucy Ann have had some massive argument that made it easier to walk away, like before?

Instead, there had been this quiet, painful realization that she was leaving him. No matter how many fairy-tale endings he tried to create for her, she'd seen through them all. After their crazy, out-of-control encounter against the door, they'd returned to the hotel. She'd packed. He'd arranged for his private jet to fly them home to South Carolina.

Lucy Ann had made a token offer to travel on her own, not to disrupt his schedule—not to distract him. The implication had been there. The accident had happened because his life was fracturing. He couldn't deny it.

But he'd damn well insisted on bringing them back here himself.

The front door creaked open, and he looked up sharply. Lucy Ann's aunt walked through. He sagged back in his swing, relieved to have the inevitable farewell delayed for a few more minutes. He knew Lucy Ann would let him be a part of his son's world, but this was not how he wanted their lives to play out.

Carla settled next to him on the swing, her T-shirt appliquéd with little spring chickens. "Glad to know you survived in one piece."

"It was a minor accident," he insisted again, the wind rustling the oak trees in time with the groan of the chains holding the swing. The scent of Carolina jasmine reminded him of Lucy Ann.

"I meant that kidnapping stunt your friends staged. Turning your whole life upside down."

Right now, it didn't feel like he'd walked away unscathed. The weight on his chest pressed heavier with every second, hadn't let up since he'd been pulled from his damaged car. "I'll provide for Lucy Ann and Eli."

"That was never in question." She patted his knee. "I'm glad you got out of here all those years ago."

"I thought you wanted Lucy Ann to stay? That's always been my impression over the years."

"I do believe she belongs here. But we're not talking about her." She folded her arms over the row of cheerful chickens. "I'm talking about what you needed as a teenager. You had to leave first before you could find any peace here. Although, perhaps it was important for Lucy Ann to leave for a while, as well."

There was something in her voice—a kindred spirit? An understanding? Her life hadn't been easy either, and he found himself saying, "You didn't go."

"I couldn't. Not when Lucy Ann needed me. She was my one shot at motherhood since I couldn't have kids of my own." She shrugged. "Once she left with you, I'd already settled in. I'm on my own now."

"I just assumed you didn't want kids." He was realizing how little time he'd spent talking to this woman who'd given him safe harbor, the woman who'd been there for Lucy Ann and Eli. He didn't have much in the way of positive experience with blood relatives, but it was undoubtedly time to figure that out.

"I would have adopted," Carla confided, "but my husband had a record. Some youthful indiscretions with breaking and entering. Years later it didn't seem like it should have mattered to the adoption agencies that he'd broken into the country club to dump a bunch of Tootsie Rolls in the pool."

Elliot grinned nostalgically. "Sounds like he would have made a great addition to the Alpha Brotherhood."

And might Elliot have found a mentor with Lucy Ann's uncle as well if he'd taken the time to try?

"I wish Lucy Ann could have had those kinds of friendships for herself. She was lost after you left," Carla said pointedly. "She didn't find her confidence until later."

What was she talking about? "Lucy Ann is the strongest, most confident person I've ever met. I wouldn't have made it without her."

He looked into those woods and thought about the dream world she'd given him as a kid, more effective an escape than even his favorite book.

"You protected her, but always saw her strengths. That's a wonderful thing." Carla pinned him with unrelenting brown eyes much like her stubborn niece's. "But you also never saw her vulnerabilities or insecurities. She's not perfect, Elliot. You need to stop expecting her to be your fairy-tale princess and just let her be human."

What the hell was she talking about? He didn't have time to ask because she pushed up from the swing and left him sitting there, alone. Nothing but the creak of the swing and the rustle of branches overhead kept him company. There was so much noise in this ends-of-the-earth place.

Carla's words floated around in his brain like dust searching for a place to land. Damn it all, he knew Lucy Ann better than anyone. He saw her strengths and yes, her flaws, too. Everyone had flaws. He didn't expect her to be perfect. He loved her just the way she—

He loved her.

The dust in his brain settled. The world clarified, taking shape around those three words. He loved her. It felt so simple to acknowledge, he wondered why he hadn't put the form to their relationship before. Why hadn't he just told her?

The trees swayed harder in the wind that predicted a storm. He couldn't remember when he'd ever told anyone he loved them. But he must have, a long time ago. Kids told their parents they loved them. Although now that he thought about it, right there likely laid the answer for why the word *love* had dried up inside him.

He'd told himself he wanted to be a better parent than his father—a better man than his father. Now he realized being a better man didn't have a thing to do with leaving this porch or this town. Running away didn't change him. This place had never been the problem.

He had been the problem. And the time had come to make some real changes in himself, changes that would make him the father Eli deserved. Changes that would make him the man Lucy Ann deserved.

Finally, he understood how to build their life together.

* * *

The time was rapidly approaching to say goodbye to Elliot.

Her mind full of regrets and second thoughts, Lucy Ann rocked in the old bentwood antique in her room at Carla's, Eli on her shoulder. She held him to comfort herself since he'd long since settled into a deep sleep. She planned to find a place of her own within the next two weeks, no leaning on her aunt this time.

The past day since they'd left Monte Carlo after the horrifying accident had zipped by in such a haze of pain and worry. Her heart still hadn't completely settled into a steady beat after Elliot's accident. Right up to the last second, she'd hoped he would come up with a Hail Mary plan for them to build a real life together for Eli. She loved Elliot with all her heart, but she couldn't deny her responsibilities to her son. He needed a stable life.

To be honest, so did she.

There was a time she'd dreamed of escaping simple roots like the cabin in the woods, and now she saw the value of the old brass bed that had given her a safe place to slip away. The Dutch doll quilt draped over the footboard had been made for her by her aunt for her eighth birthday. She soaked in the good memories and the love in this place now, appreciating them with new eyes—but still that didn't ease the unbearable pain in her breaking heart as she hoped against all hope for a last-minute solution.

Footsteps sounded in the hall—even, manly and familiar. She would recognize the sound of Elliot anywhere. She had only a second to blink back the sting of tears before the door opened.

Elliot filled the frame, his broad-shouldered body that of a mature man, although in faded jeans and a simple gray T-shirt, he looked more like *her* Elliot. As if this weren't already difficult enough.

She smoothed a hand along Eli's back, soaking in more comfort from his baby-powder-fresh scent. "Did you want to hold him before you go?"

"Actually, I thought you and I could go for a walk first and talk about our future," he said, his handsome face inscrutable.

What else could there be left to say? She wasn't sure her heart could take any more, although another part of her urged her to continue even through the ache, just to be with him for a few minutes longer.

"Sure," she answered, deciding he must want to discuss visitation with Eli. She wouldn't keep him from his son. She'd made a horrible mistake in delaying telling Elliot for even a day. She owed him her cooperation now. "Yes, we should talk about the future, but before we do that, I need to know where you stand with Gianna. She approached me at the stadium just before your wreck." The next part was tougher to share but had to be addressed. "She said she's still in love with you."

His forehead furrowed. "I'm sorry you had to go through that, but let's be very clear. I do *not* love Gianna and I never did, not really. I did her a grave injustice by rebounding into a relationship with her because I was hurting over our breakup." The carefully controlled expression faded and honest emotion stamped itself clearly in his eyes. "That's a mistake I will not repeat. She is completely in the past. My future is with you and Eli. Which is what I want to speak with you about. Now, can we walk?"

"Of course," she said, relief that one hurdle was past and that she wouldn't have to worry about Gianna popping up in their lives again.

Standing, Lucy Ann placed her snoozing son in his portable crib set up beside her bed. She felt Elliot behind her a second before he smoothed a hand over their son's head affectionately, then turned to leave.

Wordlessly, she followed Elliot past the Hummel collection and outside, striding beside him down the porch steps, toward a path leading into the woods. Funny how she knew without hesitation this was where they would walk, their same footpath and forest hideout from their childhood years. Oak trees created a tunnel arch over the dappled trail, jasmine vines climbing and blooming. Gray and orange shadows played hide-and-seek as the sunset pushed through the branches. Pine trees reached for the sky. She'd forgotten how peaceful this place was.

Of course she also knew she'd walked the same course over the past year searching for this peace. Elliot's presence brought the moment to shimmering life as he walked beside her, his hands in his pockets. She assumed he had a destination in mind since they still weren't talking. A dozen steps later they came around a bend and—

Four of her aunt's quilts were draped over the branches, creating a fort just like the ones they'd built in the past. Another blanket covered the floor of their forest castle.

Lucy Ann gasped, surprised. Enchanted. And so moved that fresh tears stung her eyes.

Elliot held out a hand and she took it. The warmth and familiarity of his touch wrapped around her, seeping into her veins. She wasn't sure where he was going with this planned conversation, but she knew she couldn't turn back. She needed to see it through and prayed that somehow he'd found a way for them all to be together.

He guided her to their fort, and she sat cross-legged, her body moving on instinct from hundreds of similar hideaways here. He took his place beside her, no fancy trappings but no less beautiful than the places they'd traveled.

"Elliot, I hope you know that I am so very sorry for not telling you about Eli sooner," she said softly, earnestly. "If I had it to do over again, I swear to you I would handle things differently. I know I can't prove that, but I mean it—"

He covered her hand with his, their fingers linking. "I believe you."

The honesty in his voice as he spoke those three words healed something inside her she hadn't realized was hurting until now. "Thank you, Elliot. Your forgiveness means more to me than I can say."

His chest rose and fell with a deep sigh. "I'm done with racing. There's no reason to continue putting my life at risk in the car—or with Interpol, for that matter."

The declaration made her selfishly want to grasp at what he offered. But she knew forcing him into the decision would backfire for both of them. "Thank you for offering again, but as I said before, I don't want you to make that sacrifice for me. I don't want you to do something that's going to make you unhappy, because in the end that's not going to work for either of us—"

"This isn't about you. It isn't even about Eli, although I would do anything for either of you." He squeezed her fingers until she looked into his eyes. "This decision is about me. Interpol has other freelancers to call upon. I mean it when I say I'm through with the racing circuit. I don't need the money, the notoriety. The risk or the chaos. I have everything I want with you and Eli."

"But please know I'm not asking that sacrifice from you." Although, oh, God, it meant so much to her that he'd offered.

He lifted her hand and kissed the inside of her wrist.

"Being with you isn't a sacrifice. Having you, I gain everything."

Seeing the forgiveness that flooded his eyes, so quickly, without hesitation, she realized for the first time how much more difficult her deception must have been for him, given his past. All his life he'd been let down by people who were supposed to love him and protect him. His father had beaten him and for years he'd taken it to shield his mother. His mother hadn't protected him. Beyond that, his mother had walked out, leaving him behind. On the most fundamental levels, he'd been betrayed. He'd spent most of his adult years choosing relationships with women that were destined to fail.

And when their friendship moved to a deeper level, he'd self-destructed again by staying away. He'd been just as scared as she was about believing in the connection they'd shared the night they'd made love.

She knew him so well, yet she'd turned off all her intuition about him and run.

"Life doesn't have to be about absolutes. Your world or my world, a castle or a fort. There are ways to compromise."

Hope flared in his green eyes. "What are you suggesting?"

"You can have me." She slid her arms around his neck. "Even if we're apart for some of the year, we can make that work. We don't have to follow you every day, but Eli and I can still travel."

"I know you didn't ask me to give it up," he interrupted. "But it's what I want—a solid base for our son and any other children we have. I'm done running away. It's time for us to build a home. We've been dreaming of this since we tossed blankets over branches in the forest as kids. Lucy Ann," he repeated, "it's time for me to come home and make that dream come true. I love you, Lucy Ann, and I want you to be my wife."

How could she do anything but embrace this beautiful future he'd just offered them both? Her heart's desire had come true. And now, she was ready, she'd found her strength and footing, to be partners with this man for life.

"I've loved you all my life, Elliot Starc. There is no other answer than yes. Yes, let's build our life together, a fairy tale on our own terms."

The sigh of relief that racked his body made her realize he'd been every bit as afraid of losing this chance. She pressed her lips to his and sealed their future together as best friends, lovers, soul mates.

He swept back her hair and said against her mouth, "Right here, on this spot, let's build that house."

"Here?" She appreciated the sacrifice he was making, returning here to a town with so many ghosts and working to find peace. "What if we take our blankets and explore the South Carolina coast together until we find the perfect spot—a place with a little bit of home, but a place that's also new to us where we can start fresh."

"I like the way you dream, Lucy Ann. Sounds perfect." He smiled with happiness and a newfound peace. "We'll build that home, a place for our son to play, and if we have other children, where they can all grow secure." He looked back at her, love as tangible in his eyes as those dreams for their future. "What do you think?"

"I believe you write the most amazing happily ever after ever."

Epilogue

Elliot Starc had faced danger his whole life. First at the hands of his heavy-fisted father. Later as a Formula One race car driver who used his world travels to feed information to Interpol.

But he'd never expected to be kidnapped. Especially not in the middle of his son's second birthday party.

Apparently, about thirty seconds ago, one of his friends had snuck up behind him and tied a bandanna over his eyes. He wasn't sure who since he could only hear a bunch of toddlers giggling.

Elliot lost his bearings as two of his buddies turned him around, his deck shoes digging into the sand, waves rolling along the shore of his beach house. "Are we playing blind man's bluff or pin the tail on the donkey?"

"Neither." The breeze carried Lucy Ann's voice along with her jasmine scent. "We're playing guess this object."

Something fuzzy and stuffed landed in his hands.

Some kind of toy maybe? He frowned, no clue what he held, which brought more laughter from his Alpha Brotherhood buddies who'd all gathered here with their families. Thank goodness he and Lucy Ann had plenty of room in their home and the guest house.

He'd bought beach property on a Low Country Carolina island, private enough to attract other celebrities who wanted normalcy in their lives. He and Lucy had built a house. Not as grand as he'd wanted to offer her, but he understood the place was a reflection of how they lived now. She'd scaled him back each step of the way on upgrades, reminding him of their new priorities. Their marriage and family topped the list—which meant no scrimping on space, even if he'd had to forgo a few extravagant extras.

As for upgrades, that money could be spent on other things. They'd started a scholarship foundation. Lucy Ann's organizational and promotional skills had the foundation running like clockwork, doubling in size. They'd kept to their plans to travel, working their schedule around his life, which had taken a surprising turn. Since he didn't have to worry about money, thanks to his investments, he'd started college, working toward a degree in English. He was studying the classics along with creative writing, and enjoying every minute of it. Lucy Ann had predicted he would one day be a college professor and novelist.

His wonderful wife was a smart woman and a big dreamer.

There was a lot to be said for focus. Although with each of the brothers focused on a different part of the world, they had a lot of ground covered. Colonel Salvatore had taught them well, giving them a firm foundation to build happy, productive lives even after their Interpol days were past.

Famous musician Malcolm Douglas and his wife were

currently sponsoring a charity tour with their children in tow, and if it went as well as they expected, it would be an annual affair. The Doctors Boothe had opened another clinic in Africa last month along with the Monte Carlo mega-rich Hughes family—their daughters along for the ribbon-cutting. Computer whiz Troy Donavan and his wife, Hillary, had a genius son who kept them both on their toes.

"Elliot." Lucy Ann's whisper caressed his ear. "You're not playing the game."

He peeled off his blindfold to find his beautiful wife standing in front of him. His eyes took in the sight of her in a yellow bikini with a crocheted cover-up. "I surrender."

She tucked her hand in his pocket and stole the toy from his hand, tucking it behind her back. "You're not getting off that easily."

Colonel Salvatore chuckled from a beach chair where he wore something other than his gray suit for once—gray swim trunks and T-shirt, but still. Not a suit. But they were all taking things easier these days. "You never did like to play by the rules."

Aunt Carla lifted a soda in toast from her towel under a beach umbrella. "I can attest to that."

Elliot reached toward Lucy Ann for the mysterious fuzzy toy. "Come on. Game over."

She backed up, laughing. "Catch me if you want it now."

She was light on her feet, and he still enjoyed the thrill of the chase when it came to his wife. Jogging a few yards before he caught her, Elliot swept her up into his arms and carried her behind a sand dune where he could kiss her properly as he'd been aching to do all day. Except his house was so full of friends and family.

With the waves crashing and sea grass rustling, Elliot kissed her as he'd done thousands of times and looked forward to doing thousands more until they drew their last breath. God, he loved this woman.

Slowly, he lowered her feet to the ground, and she molded her body to his. If there wasn't a party going on a few yards away, he would have taken this a lot further. Later, he promised himself, later he would bring her out to a cabana and make love to her with the sound of the ocean to serenade them—his studies in English and creative writing were making him downright poetic these days.

For now though, he had a mission. He caressed up her arm until he found her hand. With quick reflexes honed on the racetrack, he filched the mystery toy from her fingers. Although he had to admit, she didn't put up much of a fight.

He slid his hand back around, opened his fist and found…a baby toy. Specifically, a fuzzy yellow rabbit. "You're—"

"Pregnant," she finished the sentence with a shining smile. "Four weeks. I only just found out for sure."

They'd been trying for six months, and now their dream to give Eli a brother or a sister was coming true. He hugged her, lifting her feet off the ground and spinning her around.

Once her feet settled on the sand again, she said, "When we were kids, we dreamed of fairy tales. How funny that we didn't start believing them until we became adults."

His palm slid over her stomach. "Real life with you and our family beats any fairy tale, hands down."

* * * * *

A sneaky peek at next month…

PASSIONATE AND DRAMATIC LOVE STORIES

My wish list for next month's titles…

In stores from 17th January 2014:

☐ What a Rancher Wants – Sarah M. Anderson

& Back in Her Husband's Bed – Andrea Laurence

☐ Snowbound with a Billionaire – Jules Bennett

& Just One More Night – Fiona Brand

☐ Bound by a Child – Katherine Garbera

& Her Texan to Tame – Sara Orwig

2 stories in each book – only £5.49!

Available at WHSmith, Tesco, Asda, Eason, Amazon and Apple

Just can't wait?

Visit us Online

You can buy our books online a month before they hit the shops!